EYE OF THE
RAVEN

EYE OF THE RAVEN

The Whale Road Chronicles:

VII

TIM HODKINSON

HEAD
7ZEUS

An Aries Book

First published in the UK in 2024 by Head of Zeus,
part of Bloomsbury Publishing Plc

975312468

A catalogue record for this book is available from the British Library.

ISBN (PB): 9781801105453
ISBN (E): 9781801105439

Cover design: Simon Michele | Head of Zeus

Typeset by Siliconchips Services Ltd UK

Printed and bound in Great Britain by
CPI Group (UK) Ltd, Croydon CR0 4YY

Head of Zeus
First Floor East
5–8 Hardwick Street
London EC1R 4RG

WWW.HEADOFZEUS.COM

As always, to Trudy, Emily, Clara and Alice

Part One

...Like the howling of Irish wolves against the moon

William Shakespeare, *As You Like It*, Act 5, Scene 2

One

The water was black and smooth as glass. It was so flat it mirrored the night sky above; the reflections of the stars were so clear in the water that the Gael warrior could make out the constellations. Rónán amused himself by trying to make out the patterns the stars made by only looking at the water. It was a cold night and there was little to do, so anything to make the time pass was welcome. He made out the *Mathgamhain Mór* and the milky path of the *Síog na nAingeal*.

While he was looking down at the water he missed the eight figures that moved out of the trees on the lake shore about a hundred paces away and slipped into the water, barely causing a ripple on the surface.

Some sixth sense made Rónán look up again. He scanned the darkness of the woods on the shore, just in case someone – an attacker – lurked there. Unaware that the danger was already advancing towards him, silent and swift beneath the surface of the lake, he felt unconcerned. The *crannóg* he guarded was that of Cairpe MacCinaed, King of Deiscert Breg and one of the hardest rulers in all of Ireland. Part palace, part fortress and refuge in times of trouble, the man-made island was the safest place to be in the kingdom, if not the whole country. It was about one hundred paces across and built on stout pillars of oak, driven into the muddy bottom of the lough. The crannóg had been constructed on that base and now supported multiple buildings from the large, round king's house to more modest dwellings for the warriors who guarded the king and the slaves who served him. All of this was surrounded by a low palisade fence that ringed the crannóg almost at the waterline. The waters of the lake stretched all around, preventing anyone from charging the palisade.

Rónán, and the nine others unlucky enough to be on guard during the darkest hours of the night, patrolled the water's edge, just outside the fence. The crannóg was the home of a king but ten guards were enough. If someone did emerge from the woods, intent on attack, all they had to do was pull in the wicker bridge that stretched from the island to the shore leaving the only way over a swim which, for a war band armed and dressed for battle, was a very quick way to drown.

Besides, Rónán thought to himself, *those most likely to attack – the Gall, the hateful foreigners – were represented here tonight anyway. What was there to worry about?*

The daughter of Amlaibh, the *Gall* king of Limerick, was King Cairpe's guest on the crannóg tonight. The two kings were making an alliance and the marriage of Cairpe's son to Amlaibh's daughter would seal it.

Rónán spat into the dark waters of the lake. He did not approve of his king's dealings with the foreigners. They may have been settled here in Ireland for a hundred years but to him they would never be Irish. They were heathens for a start: pagans who worshipped the thunder and a one-eyed demon. Rónán crossed himself at the thought that his king, a man he admired so much, would have dealings with such people, damned to Hell as they were.

They are too strong at the moment, the king said. *Their armour too hard and their weapons could cut stone. So for now*

we will ally with the Gall. Pretend to be their friends and use
them so we overcome our own enemies. Then someday, when
we grow strong enough, we will turn their own long-bearded
axes on them, and drive the Gall from our land.

The pagan girl and her serving women now slept in the
women's house near the round house of King Cairpe. They had
all feasted and drunk to celebrate the upcoming marriage which
would happen after the festival of *Lughnasadh* and now everyone
except those – like Rónán – unlucky enough to be on guard that
night, snored in their beds. The heathen king had also sent some of
his own warriors with his daughter and it was a measure of how
much the two kings really trusted each other that three of
Amlaibh's warriors also sat awake at the door of the house the
women slept in, their spears and axes within easy reach.

A splash made Rónán look down. Ripples were disturbing
the black surface of the lake, causing the reflected sky to appear
distorted and wavy. He frowned, not sure what had caused the
disturbance. It could have been a fish. Then again, perhaps not.
He crouched down, trying to get a better look.

Something moved in the trees.

Rónán's warrior instincts were alert in an instant. He grasped
his spear and sprang back to his feet. Eyes narrowed, he scanned
the darkness between the trunks and bushes visible in the
starlight on the lough shore.

He caught his breath. A figure stepped out from behind the
stout trunk of an oak tree. Then he let go the breath he held.
This was no threat: no Gall warrior sneaking up on them in the
dark. Even at this distance he saw by the starlight that she was a
woman. She was dressed like any other woman of the Gaels in
a long dress with her cloak swept over one shoulder and pinned
there with a large, round brooch that sparkled in the meagre
light of the moon. Her long hair was tied behind her head in a

braid that curled around her left shoulder like a snake. In the starlight her pale skin looked white as a ghost.

Then a thrill of genuine fear coursed through Rónán's heart, mixing with the anticipation of battle. It was said that the *leannán sídhe*, the beautiful but deadly fairy woman who stole away handsome young men who took her fancy, walked these woods at night. Once under her power they wasted away as she used them until there was nothing left but hollow shells and they died. Rónán feared no man. He was ready to fight anyone in Ireland, but a supernatural creature was a different prospect altogether. Was that who this strange woman was?

Then she raised a bow and shot it at him.

The distance the arrow had to travel just gave Rónán enough time to start to move out of its way, so the arrow aimed for his throat instead struck him on the right shoulder. The young warrior gave a grunt, stumbling in a half circle from the impact. He opened his mouth to shout a warning to the others but at that moment hands reached up from the waters of the lake below him. They grabbed his ankles and pulled his feet from under him.

Rónán landed heavily on his back. The impact drove the breath from his lungs, turning his cry of alarm to just another grunt. Then there was a hand over his mouth and any chance of him raising the alarm were gone.

Wide-eyed, Rónán looked up and saw a face hovering above him against the night sky. It was smeared with some sort of black paint so as to be almost invisible against the dark sky above. The outline was strange, with what looked like pointed ears standing up on the top of whoever now pinned him down's head and for an instant he wondered if some creature – a wolf – had attacked him. Then he saw the whites of two eyes looking down at him. The eyes were cold, hard and utterly without pity.

He never saw the blade that opened his throat.

Two

Affreca Guthfrithsdóttir notched another arrow, then grabbed the hems of her skirt, lifted them as she ran as fast as she could towards the shore end of the wicker bridge that led to the crannóg. Her aim was now the opposite to what Rónán's would have been had he not now been dead. At the first sign of an attack the defenders of the crannóg would rush to pull in the bridge, cutting off the path to the fort on the man-made island. Affreca intended to stop them.

The other seven of the wolf pack company she was part of, their skins smeared with a concoction of grease and charcoal to hide them in the dark, had already swum out to the man-made island. The intent had been that they slid ashore without being detected while she provided cover with her bow from the shore. But one of the Irish warriors on guard had got too nosy and Affreca had been forced to intervene.

She reached the end of the bridge and began to advance along it. Affreca slowed her pace as her running made the light wooden bridge squeak and bounce, threatening to give away the fact someone was coming across it.

She was almost halfway across when she spotted a figure at the far end. Whether he was making for the bridge, had heard the rest of the úlfhéðnar coming ashore and was going to investigate or just happened to be there she had no idea. She stopped, raised her bow and shot him. Her arrow struck hard through the centre of his body, making him stumble sideways. He let out a gasp that seemed nerve-gratingly loud in the quiet of the night.

Affreca already had another arrow notched. She shot the man again, this time hitting him in the upper chest. She was less than fifty paces from him, and the powerful Finnish bow Affreca bore drove the arrow right through his body and out the other side. The man crashed backwards, landing on the flat of his back.

Affreca levelled a third arrow at the Irishman but he did not move. Deeming he was dead, Affreca lifted her skirts again and jogged the rest of the way to the island end of the bridge. Every step sent creaks and squeaks through the light wicker it was made of, shredding her nerves that the noises might alert other guards on the island.

Reaching the crannóg, Affreca crouched once more, looking left and right, surveying the darkened interior of the palisade. They had been watching from a hideout on the lake shore for most of the day and when night fell had counted the guards as best they could. As far as she could reckon there should be eight more of them.

She caught movement from the corner of her eye but when she looked around whoever it was had vanished and Affreca knew it was one of her fellow úlfhéðnar, trained to move through darkness as undetectable as ghosts and quiet as one of Freya's cats.

A moment later she was surrounded by her seven fellows. Five were Wolf Coats, úlfhéðnar, like her. They had fur cloaks around their shoulders made from the pelts of wolves, the creature's head forming their hoods so when pulled up they looked like beasts walking on their hind legs. They wore no armour. Tonight their stealth and the darkness were their mail.

They wore britches but were bare-chested, their torsos smeared with black grease to make them disappear into the night. Only the whites of their eyes were visible.

As they gathered around Affreca, water dribbled off their bodies from their swim under the surface from the shore to the edge of the crannóg. They were all big men, heavily muscled from days spent on the rowing benches of longships and constant training for battle. All, that was, except for their leader, Ulrich. While every bit as fit as the others, Ulrich was short and wiry. His brown hair receded from his forehead and, unlike just about every man north of the river Rhine (bar the Saxons), he grew no beard. Whether this was through choice or because he was unable to, no one had ever had the courage to ask.

Skarphedinn – Skar to his friends – Ulrich's right-hand man was recognisable in the darkness as Ulrich's opposite. The others may have been bulky but Skar was huge and towered over the others, tall and strong as the mighty ash tree that supported the realm of the world, *Yggdrasil*. Beside him was Starkad, his long blond hair and beard bound in tight braids. His keen eyes were watchful as ever, flicking back and forth through the night, on the watch for any hint of danger. The runes tattooed across Kari's shaved head and face like bird's footprints were obscured by the dark and the war paint. The last of the úlfhéðnar, Sigurd, looked as complacent as if he were on a boring afternoon walk.

Two more made up the company but they did not wear wolf pelts. They were respected members of the company but úlfhéðnar were warriors sacred to Odin and these two had different faiths. Wulfhelm was a Saxon and a Christian. His chest and face were smeared with the black concoction like the others. The last fellow had no need for it. His skin was black already, apart from the many scars that raked his body, remnants of the years he had spent as a slave and a ring fighter for King Harald Fairhair. His real name was unpronounceable to them, so the Wolf Coat company had named him Surt, after the great giant of fire who would burn the world at Ragnarök. He was not a Christian, but neither did he follow the *Aesir*. Affreca knew he followed the main Christian God, but not their Christ God. She did not understand the details but resolved it was probably something like the *Aesir-Vanir* war.

There should be one more here with us, Affreca thought to herself with a pang of rue. *Einar should be here.*

Ulrich shot a questioning glare at Affreca. She knew why he was annoyed: the plan had been that she waited on the shore until the úlfhéðnar had taken care of all the guards on the crannóg, then come across to play her part. Affreca pointed in the general direction of where Rónán's corpse lay. Then she pointed to her eyes with the forefingers of her right hand, then turned them towards Ulrich.

He spotted you so I dealt with him, she told him without words.

Ulrich made a face then nodded. Then he shot Affreca another questioning look. Affreca, still gripping her bow in her left hand, held up her right and flashed first five, then three fingers before his face, telling him how many guards she thought were left to deal with.

Ulrich nodded again then, using only silent gestures, ordered the others to spread out and find the warriors unlucky enough to have ended up on guard duty that night. One by one the úlfhéðnar flitted off into the dark until only Ulrich and Affreca remained.

Ulrich gave Affreca a final stern look and pointed at the ground.

Stay here, was the message.

Then he too was gone into the night.

Affreca was content to wait as the others went about their deadly work. There was little to give them away: a short cry of surprise, stifled within an instant as a hand clamped over the mouth it came from. A muffled cough that was the only sound possible from a slashed throat. There was nothing loud enough to waken the drunken sleepers inside the buildings. They slumbered on, content they were being guarded, unaware that those men who guarded them were being murdered one by one outside.

Affreca waited, bow ready, watchful for any threat, until all her companions returned. They gathered around her once more. Ulrich fixed her with his intense gaze and nodded. It was now her turn to play her part.

Affreca handed her bow to Ulrich and set off for the house where the unmarried women slept. It was a custom in the noble houses of Ireland that young lads and girls were kept apart at night, each having their own quarters in separate round houses.

The Wolf Coats had observed earlier that Olaf of Limerick, or *Amlaíb Cenncairech* as the Irish called him, had sent some warriors with his daughter. Ulrich guessed they would be keeping a close watch on the Norse princess. They would not be allowed into the women's house but they would no doubt be awake and watching the door. This would be the hardest challenge to overcome once the Irish guards were dealt with. That was where Affreca would come in.

Feeling naked without her bow, Affreca consoled herself by running her right hand over the hilt of the knife that was concealed under the sleeve of her dress. Its sheath was tied to her left forearm, the point of the blade towards her elbow to make it easy to draw. The others fanned out into the dark once more, disappearing like wraiths as she approached the door of the women's house.

At first she could see no one in the darkness of the portal, then movement and a quick gleam of metal caught her eye. She realised there was someone lurking in the shadows of the short passage that formed a sort of porch before the door. She continued to approach, walking like she was supposed to be there, just another Irish woman on her way to bed.

Three men emerged from the shadows of the entrance. Like the Wolf Coats they were much bigger than Affreca. They wore conical iron helmets, their eyes shielded behind visors and their noses protected by nasal guards. Their chests and arms were guarded by iron-ringed mail shirts over leather jerkins. One had a sword sheathed at his side and the other two hefted axes with long blades as if the metal wore a beard. These must be the Norsemen the úlfhéðnar had spotted earlier, the men sent by Olaf of Limerick to guard his daughter.

'Who are you?' the one with the sword said. He spoke in the Norse tongue. 'What do you want?'

'I'm going to bed,' Affreca replied in the tongue of the Gaels. She was the sister of the king of Dublin and had been born and raised there. She knew the language well.

As expected she saw frowns of irritation and incomprehension on the Norsemen's faces.

'I'm going to my bed,' she repeated, this time in Norse, though with what she hoped was a heavy Irish accent. 'Kindly step aside and let me in.'

The big man with the sword wrinkled his nose.

'How come you're so late?' he said. 'The other women went to bed ages ago.'

'I had tasks to do,' Affreca said. 'I was clearing up after the feast.'

'Don't the slaves do that?' the Norseman from Limerick said. He seemed unconvinced.

'Someone has to watch them,' Affreca said, 'to make sure they do the job right.'

The Norseman nodded acceptance then stepped close to Affreca.

'I'm going to have to search you though,' he said. 'Just in case you're carrying anything that might do harm to our king's daughter.'

He stepped close and began to run his hands over Affreca's torso. She looked up at the big man who now towered over her. If he searched her arms he would find the knife easily, though its short blade would be useless against his mail and helmet anyway.

He stopped. Affreca saw the look in the eyes behind his visor change.

'She's in good shape this one, lads. Not fat and soft like a lot of Irish noblewomen,' the Norseman said, his tone becoming threatening. 'You know what? It's a chilly night. Why don't you come in and keep the three of us warm, eh?'

The others grinned. The man with the sword did too, leering at Affreca he planted both hands on her breasts and squeezed hard.

Affreca tore the knife from its sheath and drove it upwards, stabbing the Norseman though his beard. The blade went up through his chin, crunched through the roof of his mouth and on into his skull. His eyes bulged for an instant and blood gushed from his nose. With his mouth pinned shut, however, he made no sound as he died.

Shielded from view by his bulk, his friends who stood behind him had no idea what had happened until Affreca withdrew her knife from his head. As it had been holding him up, the Norseman's corpse crashed to the ground like a stone.

His companions stared in astonishment. The one on the left recovered first and stepped towards Affreca, swinging his axe over his shoulder, beginning a mighty blow that if it landed would cut Affreca in two from the crown to the navel.

As Skar had taught her, Affreca stepped close to her attacker while the blade was still in the air. She rammed her left elbow into the inside of the man's extended left arm, pinning it in place so the blow stopped dead. Then with her right hand she drove the knife down, going behind the neck rim of his mail shirt, and the bone house of his ribs beneath, finding the slot at the base of his neck that allowed the blade to pierce straight to his heart.

Affreca felt the warmth of his blood gushing over her hand as the man gave a little grunt and toppled to the ground. The knife stuck in his chest, however, and the weight of his falling body wrenched it from her grasp.

Knowing she had no time to recover it, Affreca spun to see what the last guard was doing. He was already on her, axe raised and bringing it down. This time she had no time to move to counter the blow or get out of its way.

She flinched, squeezing her eyes shut and raising her hands in a gesture that had as much chance of warding off the blow as a mouse has when a cat pounces on it.

Nothing happened. Affreca opened her eyes and saw that now her attacker too was dead. The dark shapes of the other úlfhéðnar had swarmed from the dark, grabbed his axe and cut his throat.

For a moment they all stood in silence, their breathing heavy but quiet, listening intently, every nerve strained taut for any sign the noise of the brief struggle – slight though it was – had woken up the rest of the crannóg's dwellers.

When, after a few moments there were no shouts of dismay or raised voices of alarm, Ulrich looked at Affreca and cocked his head towards the entrance of the women's house.

She went in. It was dark inside. The red glow of the last embers of the fire in the middle of the floor barely reached beyond its hearthstones. She was aware, however, of the presence of many people. The air was filled with the sound of sleepers breathing, light snoring and the occasional fart. It smelled of woodsmoke, human bodies, the damp straw that covered the floor and the earthy aroma of the daub and wattle walls.

Moving her feet in a sweeping motion, with care and just off the ground, the skill Ulrich had taught her to move through darkness without tripping, Affreca made her way to the dying fire. There were women sleeping on the floor among the straw and she was eager not to stand on one of them, waking her and risking alerting everyone there to her presence.

After what seemed like ages spent creeping to the fireplace, Affreca eventually made it there. She crouched by the hearthstones, fumbling in the leather pouch at her waist until she found a tallow candle, which she took out and lit from the last embers of the fire.

Shielding the burning wick with her hand lest any sudden glare disturb any of the sleeping women, Affreca rose to her feet again and looked around in the ambient glow from the candle. A quick tally told her there were five women on the floor of the round room, all fast asleep. They lay nestled in the straw and were probably slaves or serving women. Around the walls were wooden compartments, just over the height of a man and open at the top, their entrances covered by drawn curtains. Affreca had been in enough noble houses in Ireland to know that inside these compartments were beds where the noblewomen slept, but in which one was the daughter of Olaf of Limerick?

There was nothing for it but to start going from one to the next around them all, drawing back the curtain and peering in to see who slept inside. Soon after she began her work a new dilemma struck Affreca. The first curtain she pulled back revealed an old, grey-haired woman, snoring in the wooden cot inside. Ragnhild, Olaf's daughter, was fifteen winters old, so this toothless old hag could not be her. The second compartment, however, contained a young blonde-haired girl about the right age. But was this her? Young women in their nightdresses, their hair undone, could all look remarkably similar.

Affreca spotted the gleam of gold around the sleeping young girl's throat as the light of the candle glinted across a cross she wore. This was not Ragnhild.

The next compartment contained a woman in her middle years so was not Ragnhild either. In the fourth bedstead was another young girl who looked about the right age. She was blonde-haired like the last one and lay on her side. With careful steps, Affreca entered the compartment. As the light of the candle got closer the girl gave a little moan. Frowning in her sleep she turned over onto her back.

Affreca spotted a little shelf on the wall above the bed that the girl had put her jewellery on. She placed the candle on it then crouched beside the bed to get a closer look at its occupant. Affreca brushed the girl's hair away from her throat and saw a *Mjǫllnir* amulet – the hammer of Thor – resting in the hollow of her neck. This must be Ragnhild.

At that moment the girl opened her eyes.

At the sight of Affreca leaning over her, Ragnhild's eyes widened. Her mouth dropped open to cry out in surprise as she began to sit up.

Affreca punched her, slamming her fist into the girl's chin just to the right of its point. Ragnhild's eyes rolled up into her head and she collapsed back into the straw of her bed. With a silent curse, Affreca realised she would now have to carry the girl out.

Making as little noise as was possible Affreca hoisted the unconscious Ragnhild over her shoulder. This was hard, given the manoeuvring she had to do in the cramped space within the sleeping compartment. Affreca then struggled to her feet again with the girl now draped over her right shoulder, arms and head hanging down her back. Affreca was not a tall woman and though she was strong, Ragnhild was not the lightest of girls. Affreca knew she had to get out of the building as fast as she could if she was not to drop the princess of Limerick.

Swaying under the weight on her shoulder, Affreca reached out to pick up her candle. As her fingers scrabbled for it they brushed against it and instead of picking it up she knocked it off the little shelf.

The candle toppled down into the straw of the bed. To Affreca's dismay the dry straw started to smoulder straight away. For a moment she stared in horror at the rising smoke and strengthening flame, trying to decide what she should do.

If she dropped the girl and tried to put out the fire out Ragnhild would possibly revive. The noise Affreca made would wake the others anyway. There was little choice but to get out as fast as she could.

Affreca turned and headed back in the direction of the door. Now there was little caution in her movements. She just needed to get out. When she was almost there her toe struck the soft flesh of a slave asleep on the floor and the woman cried out in shock.

Affreca stumbled sideways but regained her balance before she fell. There was nothing to do now but make for the door. Whether the slave saw her or not she did not know but when she heard the woman cry out 'Teine!' – the Gaelic word for fire – Affreca knew she had definitely spotted the growing blaze in Ragnhild's bed.

Affreca stumbled out through the door of the house. The other Wolf Coats stood waiting. Skar and Kari had picked up the big axes dropped by the now dead Norse guards.

'We need to go,' Affreca said to them, the need for silence now redundant. 'Now.'

The startled cries of women waking up to find the room they were in was on fire came from the doorway. Ulrich shot a reproachful look at Affreca. Affreca shrugged as best she could with the unconscious girl over her shoulder.

Sigurd gestured that Affreca should pass Ragnhild to him.

'I can carry her,' Affreca said, with reproach.

'I can carry her a lot more easily,' Sigurd said. 'I'm twice your size and we need to move fast. This isn't a contest. We need to get away.'

Affreca nodded and between them they manhandled Ragnhild from Affreca to Sigurd's shoulder. Affreca took her bow back from Ulrich. It felt good to have it back in her hands once more.

The sound of the women shouting was starting to be echoed from the king's house where the rest of his household slept, including the rest of Cairpe's warriors.

'Come on,' Ulrich said. 'We don't have much time.'

All their former stealth abandoned, they rushed across the crannóg to the end of the wicker bridge that led to the lake shore. At that point they had to stop to rearrange their company. There was only room on the narrow bridge for them to cross it in single file.

Sigurd, the Limerick princess over his shoulder, went first, then Wulfhelm the Saxon, then Surt. Affreca was about to go next when a shout made them all turn. An Irish warrior, still in his nightshirt, had dashed out of the king's house and stood just outside the door. His left arm was raised, counter to the spear cocked in his right hand, as he prepared to launch the weapon in their direction.

'Thanks for the warning, friend,' Kari said as he hurled the axe at the Irishman. It tumbled through the air, the long blade embedding itself in the left side of the Gael's chest, just below his raised arm, with a meaty thump. The man cried out and stumbled backwards. He managed to cast his spear but the weapon went over the Wolf Coats' heads. It landed in the lake with a splash.

Many more Irish warriors were now pouring out of the doorway of the king's house.

'Go,' Ulrich said. 'Run.'

Affreca followed the others down the bridge. Kari went after her, then Ulrich, Starkad and finally Skar.

The bridge, made of light wicker so it could be easily pulled in by one or two men in an emergency, bucked and bounced under the weight of their pounding feet. Affreca wondered if it would be able to take the weight of the whole company or would it break, sending them all tumbling into the cold, dark waters of the lake. The king's men would then pick them off with spears and slingshots while they tried to swim to the shore.

She had just made it to the other end when more loud shouting made her stop and turn around. Some of the king's warriors were already on the bridge behind them. Skar, who was about two-thirds of the way along it, turned around to face them.

He let out a roar that was frightening enough to make the first man halt, his two companions colliding with his back. The man raised his spear to strike at Skar but the huge Norseman was already bringing his axe down in a devastating blow that shattered the spear shaft and cleaved into the Irishman's left shoulder. With a cry of despair as much as pain, the warrior collapsed backwards, further entangling himself with his companion directly behind him.

The second warrior was stuck, unable to move as the weight of the dying man in front fell onto him. He could not even bring his sword up as Skar brought the axe down again, cleaving his unprotected head asunder.

The third warrior, however, had time to jump back out of the way. He had a spear which he then lunged with, just as Skar was withdrawing his axe from the second warrior's skull.

The point of the spear gouged into the heavy pack of muscle that surrounded Skar's shoulder. The big man let out a roar that was all anger rather than pain. He grabbed the spear shaft with his left hand and stepped back, the spearhead still embedded in his flesh, wrenching his attacker who still grasped the spear shaft forwards towards him. Skar swept his axe upwards, hitting the Irish warrior across the face with the back of its head. It was an awkward blow delivered at a difficult angle but nevertheless it split the man's upper lip and smashed two of his teeth. The Irishman let out a shout of pain. He let go of the spear and staggered backwards, both hands going to his injured face.

Affreca, standing on the lough shore, had been waiting for some space to open up between the two and now it had she loosed an arrow. It struck the Irishman firmly on the chest, sending him reeling back against the side of the bridge. Then he toppled over it and into the lake below.

The immediate danger lessened, Skar let out a gasp and stepped backwards, swaying a little as he tried to pull the spear from his shoulder. At the far end of the bridge, however, the rest of the king's warriors were gathering.

The first one stepped onto the bridge. Affreca shot him straight away. This made the rest pause for a moment but everyone could see that the Irish warriors outnumbered the Wolf Coats many times. If they all charged Affreca could only hope to take down two or three of them at most before she would be overrun with the others.

Surt and Starkad thumped back along the bridge to Skar. Surt grabbed Skar's axe while Starkad put his arm around the injured prowman and dragged him backwards towards the shore. With a snarl Surt hefted the axe and brought it down. The heavy blade smashed through the wicker of the bridge floor like it was made of bullrushes. Surt raised the axe and brought it down again, smashing another hole in the bridge.

Seeing what he was doing, the Irish warriors began to rush forward. Affreca brought one down with an arrow but a moment later they were almost halfway across. Surt dealt the bridge another blow, hurled the axe at the first Irishman coming down the bridge then turned to run back towards the shore.

Behind him there was a loud crack. The bridge floor lurched. Weakened by his blows, the bridge collapsed in the middle under the weight of the men charging over it, tipping the king's warriors on it into the lake water. Surt leapt for the shore as the bridge dropped from beneath his feet. Kari and Starkad reached out and caught his forearms, then hauled him the last of the distance to the shore.

There was no time to gather their breath. It would not be long before the Irishmen struggled ashore and resumed the chase. Ulrich's Wolf Coat company ran into the trees, seeking out the grove where they had earlier hidden horses so they could make a swift getaway.

Finding the steeds waiting patiently, they mounted. Sigurd threw the daughter of the king of Limerick over the saddle bow of one horse then climbed on behind her.

Then they did one of the things they did best, and disappeared into the darkness.

Three

'I'm getting too old for this,' Skar said.

His lips contorted into a grimace as Kari applied a handful of dried herbs to the wound in the big man's shoulder.

'By Thor's balls! That hurts more than the spear going in,' he said. He shot a bitter glance in Kari's direction. 'Can you not be a bit more gentle? You're being deliberately clumsy aren't you?'

'Remember all the pain you put us through rowing and running in battle practice?' Kari said, grinning. 'I have to get you back for all that somehow.'

Skar had removed the spearhead himself as soon as he mounted his horse. It was now later in the night. The Gaels had had to pause to fight the fire in the women' house before finding their own horses to pursue them and the Wolf Coat company with their head start had escaped with ease. Apart from their well-honed skills of evading capture, they were heading in the direction of the last place their pursuers would have expected someone who had kidnapped the daughter of the Norse king of Limerick to go to, which was to her father's fortress.

Now they felt safe enough to take a short break, rest the horses and tend to Skar's wound. They were dismounted in a small glen amid some woods that gave enough cover to light a small lamp and break out some skins of water and hunks of bread. Ragnhild, now awake, sat on the ground, sullen, her hands and ankles bound.

'My father is Olaf of Limerick,' she said, glowering around at them all. 'He'll carve the blood eagle in all of your backs for this.'

'Shouldn't we gag her?' Sigurd said. 'We don't want her shouting and giving away our position.'

'And we wouldn't have to listen to her gurning,' Starkad said.

Ragnhild became quiet.

'I really hope you're not getting too old,' Kari said to Skar. 'I don't know who else among us could stop a load of charging Irishmen with a just growl like you did back there. I swear sometimes the Volsung *aegishjalmur* sits on your forehead. You wear an invisible helmet that inspires awe and terror.'

'You're a bit of a terror yourself,' Skar said.

'Yes, but no one can make the enemy cringe like you do when you roar,' Kari said. 'Except for the lad—'

He stopped before he said the name, his eyes glancing in the direction of Ulrich, who sat a little apart from the others, outside the light of the lamp, brooding in the darkness.

'Aye,' Skar said, sending a look in the same direction. 'We could have done with him tonight. We made it but we were riding our luck. If we'd had one more man. Einar—'

'*Don't speak his name!*'

Ulrich's voice hissed from the dark. The wiry little Wolf Coat leader stalked into the glow of the lamp. His eyes blazed with a fury strong enough to make even Skar swallow hard.

'We don't talk about that traitor,' Ulrich said in a voice that was not much more than a growl. 'We don't speak his name.'

Skar and Kari both nodded. With one last reproachful look, Ulrich withdrew back into the shadows.

When Skar's wound was bound up they remounted and continued the ride through the night. The countryside was mostly deserted apart from horses, sheep and some of the strange small cows the Irish kept. Here and there they rode past a farmstead but as it was the dead of night, beyond a few barking dogs they showed no signs of life.

It was a good thing too, for Ragnhild, dangling over the front of Sigurd's horse, started her threats once more and continued with them as they rode. For such a young girl the filthiness of the language she used and the depravity of the revenges she promised that her father would visit upon the Wolf Coats for what they had done was impressive.

Affreca reflected on how similar she and Ragnhild were, and yet so different. She had been born daughter to the king of Dublin. Had Ulrich's band of vikings not landed in her father's hall, wrenching her life onto a different path, it could well be her whose destiny was governed by kings and jarls, married off to bind their deals, ending up kidnapped, tied up and hanging over the back of a horse when those deals went wrong.

They said that norns visited the birth of every child, supernatural women who granted the baby with gifts – skills and character traits – that would shape that child's destiny. Some norns were good, some intended evil. Watching Ragnhild hanging like a sack of grain over Sigurd's horse, jolting with every step it took, shouting impotent threats that depended on others to carry out, Affreca judged the ones who had visited her father Guthfrith's hall in Dublin on the night she was born had been better to her than to most noble girls.

After a long time an orange glow appeared on the horizon.

Affreca rubbed her eyes. She knew it was late but had not thought it was near dawn. Then she realised the light came from fires and not the sun. As they rode closer they saw the flames were blazing on an island in a wide lake, or *lough* as the Irish called them, their light flickering across the waters.

As they got closer they saw by the waning stars and the light of the flames that the lake was vast, almost as large as the huge one in the north they had raided an island on a few winters before, though while that one had been wide and broad like an inland sea, this one was long and narrow with multiple islands in it. It was on the largest that the fires were burning. There were several large buildings ablaze while the shadows of longships, their masts and dragon heads of war silhouetted against the flames, littered the shoreline.

'It looks like we were sent to a small feast while the main festival was happening here,' Ulrich said. 'Your father's stronghold is no more, Ragnhild.'

The king of Limerick's daughter had already realised this. From the first sight of the flames she had become very quiet, her threats and blustering dying out. Now that the source of the fires was clear she just stared at them from her awkward position draped over Sigurd's horse, her eyes empty with desolated hopes.

They made their way to the shore of the lake where another longship waited in the reeds. It was the *snekkja* that served the Wolf Coats on their voyages. Smaller than the average viking warship, it had a long, thin body like the snake it was named after which enabled its speed and manoeuvrability. A snekkja could cross an ocean fast or penetrate deep into a land by sailing up its rivers, which was how it had managed to get here in this wide lake.

The Wolf Coat company dismounted, tied their horses and then Affreca and Ulrich clambered on board. Sigurd manhandled Ragnhild onto the ship without too much ceremony. They offered to pull the injured Skar on board, but the big man just scowled and waved them away, before hauling himself onto the ship with some difficulty and evident agony from his wounded shoulder.

The wizened skipper of the snekkja, Roan the Frisian, with skin as dark and tough as old leather, sat on the deck near the steering oar, stroking Gandr the big grey ship's cat with one hand. Impassive as ever, Roan just nodded at the sight of the úlfhéðnar crew. If he was surprised, delighted or even angry to see them, it was impossible to tell.

The little man clambered to his feet and waved a hand at the rest of the crew who remained at the lakeside to shove them off. Kari, Starkad, Wulfhelm and Surt put their shoulders to the back of the ship, got it afloat then scrambled aboard themselves as the snekkja slid out into the dark waters.

They took seats on the rowing benches and soon the ship was gliding across the lake towards the island.

'Olaf of Dublin told us to meet him here once we'd taken the daughter of Olaf of Limerick,' Ulrich said, half to himself, half to Skar, who, with his injured shoulder, did not pull an oar. 'It looks like he's attacked without us!'

'The Dubliners arrived in force just after dark,' Roan said from the steering oar. 'They sailed up from the river *Sionainne*. It looked like old Olaf Scabby Head was having some sort of feast. They took him by surprise.'

'Do you know anything about this?' Ulrich said, turning his gaze on Affreca. 'What's that brother of yours up to?'

'I thought we were kidnapping Ragnhild to *prevent* a fight,' Affreca said with a shrug from the next rowing bench. 'I've no idea what's going on.'

Affreca frowned. Even though she was sister to Olaf of Dublin – Olaf the Red to most – he had not taken her into his confidence. They had never been close growing up. Few royal siblings in Ireland were. They tended to be reared apart in separate noble foster houses and while they may like and respect each other, it was understood by most that one day they may have to kill their siblings when their father's throne became empty. The ones who did not understand this were usually the first to die.

With the other Wolf Coats Affreca had sworn allegiance to Olaf when they sailed to Ireland from Francia earlier that year, but the young king of Dublin kept a wary eye on his sister, and Affreca felt he had never truly forgiven her for fleeing their father's household with Ulrich's band several winters before.

While she did not fear for her life, her heart was not easy as they rowed towards the burning island.

Four

The island was *Inis Cathaig*, set on the waters of the wide river Sionainne. Ever since the mighty Thorgestr, the first Norseman to conquer great swathes of Ireland, it had been home to the kings of Limerick. Thorgestr had built a fortress there ninety winters before and now it was the possession of Olaf, King of Limerick. Olaf was better known by the Irish nickname he bore – *Cenncairech*, Scabby Head – though few used that when he was close enough to hear.

There was a horseshoe-shaped bay on the shore of the island that made a natural harbour. It was choked with longships. Some were in bad shape, testament to the fighting that had occurred. They were sunk up to their prows, their decks ablaze or swamped, their broken masts tilted and their shattered hulls settled on the bottom of the shallows. Others were rammed onto the shore like arrows into flesh, their dragon-carved prows riding high in the air where they had been run aground to vomit screaming warriors onto the island.

There were dead men and drunken vikings everywhere. Most of the corpses were half dressed; some in nightshirts, many bare-chested. They wore helmets but no brynjas. They had shields but no fighting gloves. They had all the signs of men surprised while asleep in their beds who only had time to scramble for what was at hand to defend themselves against the impending death that was pounding its way onto the island from the ships rammed onto the shore.

Norsemen of Dublin, discernible by the emblem of a red stag painted on their shields, swaggered around, delighted to have won what looked like an easy victory. They laughed, sang and clapped each other on the back, congratulating each other for their prowess and bravery in what had, due to the huge advantage surprise had given them, clearly been not much more than a bout of murder. Olaf Scabby Head's ale store had been broken open and a party had begun among the raiders. Most of the armed, blood-splattered vikings were wandering around, gathering loot with one hand while grasping a frothing drinking horn in the other.

Those Limerick Norsemen who had survived the slaughter, either by surrendering or being overcome, now knelt in groups here and there, wrists and ankles bound, heads bowed lest they catch the eye of one of their drunken conquerors and attract derision or further violence, trying to ignore the cries of some of their womenfolk who were being pursued through the darkness or, once caught pawed and manhandled by the Dublin vikings.

'Get the ceremonial shields,' Ulrich ordered as the snekkja found a place to land.

The Wolf Coats kept a hoard of weapons and armour on the ship. They were warriors who were trained to fight in any type of country at any time of year, and different warfare meant they needed different war gear, each set specialised for whatever conditions they faced. Most of the gear was deadly but some was, like the shields Ulrich now referred to, just for show. They were old and battered. One good blow from an axe would have shattered their dried and split wood. They were not for defence, however. They had a red stag painted on them and their purpose that night was to signal to the drunken victorious vikings of Dublin who might wonder who the newcomers were that the Wolf Coats were on their side.

Ulrich, Affreca and the others made their way uphill towards the middle of the island. There was a stone building there that looked like a home for Christian wizards they called a "monastery". Beside it was a tall, round tower. There were fires lit inside the main building but it did not look like it was on fire. The roof was intact and the light was spilling out through open doors. From the number of men streaming in and out, carrying full horns of ale and armfuls of loot, this seemed to be the centre of celebrations.

Now on an island with nowhere to run to, they untied the ankles of the girl they had captured and she now walked beside them, looking on in dazed horror at the carnage around her.

'It's my father's house,' Ragnhild said. Her voice had lost all vehemence and was dull and listless. 'Thorgestr first took it from the Christians a hundred winters ago. Its stone walls were strong so it became his fortress.'

Inside the building was a scene indicative of a fallen enemy fortress now open to looting by its conquerors. Through a short stone porch was a large room where the Christians used to hold their rituals. It looked like every torch and lamp in Olaf Cenncairech's stores had been broken out and set alight. There was a fire blazing away in a hearth in the centre of the stone-flagged floor, which looked like it was now being kept going with shattered furniture from Olaf's home. The precious hoards of food and drink in the stores had been broken into. Several barrels of ale stood around the room, open for men to dip their horns in. Affreca saw one Dubliner with his head submerged in a barrel, his friends who stood beside him finding the whole thing hilarious. Warriors grabbed joints of salted meat and hunks of cheese from the larders as frightened slaves dashed this way and that, trying to fulfil the impossible demands of their new overlords. Men still in their war gear were laughing and feasting all around. The noise was incredible.

Ulrich looked around for a moment, then, spotting who he was looking for, led the others towards the far end of the room where stood the large stone table that the Christians had used for their blood-drinking ritual. A *vǫlva*, a woman with second sight, sat cross-legged on top of the stone table. She wore the traditional long blue-hooded robes of a seeress, and in one cat-skin-gloved hand she waved a metal wand in the form of a spinning distaff. She was chanting fortunes in a loud, wailing voice. Normally the prophecies of these women were treated with hushed respect, but this woman's predictions were drowned out by the intoxicated shouting, laughing and singing going on around her. Affreca could see, however, from the woman's rolling eyes and the long string of spittle that drooled from her lower lip that the vǫlva was too far gone into her prophetic trance to care if anyone listened or not.

On the floor before the stone table was a man who looked like he would have been happier to get as little attention as the prophetess. He was dressed in the robes of a Christian wizard – and an important one at that – and his arms and ankles were bound. His eyes were squeezed shut and face turned away as best he could to avoid a stream of hot urine that a burly viking who stood before him was directing at his head. From the sodden nature of his clothes and drenched face it looked like the man presently pissing on the monk was the latest of many.

Sitting a little way away – far enough to keep himself from getting drenched – was Olaf Kollisson, better known as "Olaf Scabby Head", the king of Limerick. He had at least had time to pull on his mail brynja but it had evidently not done him much good as his fortress island was lost to him. He was not bound, except perhaps by dejection. His bald head hung down. It was pitted all over by red lesions and pus-filled craters that spilled down around his eyes and covered the tops of his cheeks and points of his ears as well. It was this unfortunate skin condition that was the source of his nickname, Cenncairech.

At the sight of Olaf, Ragnhild rushed to her father before anyone could stop her. Olaf looked up as she threw her arms around him. He looked dazed and uncomprehending for a moment, then his face fell as his dejection deepened.

The man who was pissing on the monk finished and turned around, fixing his dress as he did so. This was not too difficult as like a lot of Norsemen in the east he wore the same sort of long skirt garment worn by the northern Gaels instead of britches.

He grinned at the sight of the newcomers, revealing a horizontal zigzag pattern filed into his front teeth.

'Sister!' he said to Affreca.

Five

Olaf Guthfrithsson, King of Dublin and brother of Affreca, thrust his shoulders back and spread his arms in greeting towards Ulrich and the others.

In contrast to the other Olaf, the king of Dublin had long, straight hair he wore in two braids down his back. It was a much darker colour than his sister's tawny hair and was matched by the red of his beard. It was not just because the shade of his hair, however, that he was known as *Óláfr rauði*: Olaf the Red. Red was a colour associated in Irish legends with death and violence and it was Olaf's foster father, one of the tribe of Gaels, who had first given the lad the nickname. Thor himself was also known to have red hair and Affreca saw that, as always, her brother wore his large amulet of Mjǫllnir, Thor's hammer, around his neck over his mail shirt.

'Ulrich!' Olaf said, grinning 'You're back. And it looks like you've been successful.'

'I thought, Lord Olaf,' Ulrich said, looking around at the chaos about them, 'that when you asked us to meet you here we were going to use the girl as leverage over her father so as to avoid a fight. It looks like you went ahead with the fight anyway.'

'You may have thought that, Ulrich,' Olaf the Red said, a

mischievous twinkle in his eye. 'But I don't think I ever *said* that was the plan.'

A look of consternation fell on Ulrich's face. For a moment Affreca's heart raced. She knew the little man's demeanour could switch from pleasant affability to murderous rage in an instant. If he attacked her brother now it would be disaster for all of them.

Ulrich, however, just shook his head.

'The games kings play,' he said. 'So what is this grand strategy that was so important we could not be told of?'

'The girl is still important. You didn't waste your time, don't worry about that,' Olaf said, puffing out his chest and hooking his thumbs into his belt. 'Soon I set sail to Britain. I'm marrying Eithne, daughter of King Constantine of the Scots. I don't want old Scabby Head here getting ideas about taking over Dublin while I'm gone and I needed to make sure he was in no position to. He's been up to all sorts of tricks. He made an alliance with Cairpe MacCinaed, the king of Deiscert Breg, which is one of the shitty little kingdoms of the Irish. Olaf's daughter here was part of the deal. And this Christian fellow here was meddling around too. It seems Olaf was thinking of forsaking our customs and the gods.'

Ulrich looked at the piss-soaked monk again. His eyes narrowed.

'I know this monk from somewhere,' Ulrich said, suspicion heavy in his voice.

Affreca looked at the monk. He was an old man, looking like he had lived perhaps fifty or more winters. His crown was shaved in the manner of Christian monks that was surrounded by a thick mop of white hair. Here and there a few curls still stuck out but most of it was plastered to his head and tinged yellow from piss. His face was a mask of utter misery. Despite all this, Affreca realised that she too knew who the man was.

'We met him in Jorvik,' she said. 'Brother, this man is a high priest of the Christians.'

'He is indeed,' Olaf said. 'This is Dub Inse, the bishop of Bangor. He was coming to officiate at the wedding of Scabby Head's daughter to the son of King Cairpe. It seems Olaf of Limerick also had decided to meet with the bishop to discuss religion.'

Ulrich spat in disgust.

'You should carve the blood eagle on both their backs,' he said.

'I should indeed,' Olaf the Red said. 'But to do that would provoke the rest of Ireland to rise up against me. Normally they fight each other but if they all got together to oppose me I would be in trouble. I don't want that while I am out of the country. I sail to Britain soon to marry the king of Scotland's daughter.'

Affreca frowned. Her brother was repeating himself. Was he very drunk?

'So what are you going to do?' Ulrich said, frowning. 'Let him go?'

'Yes,' Olaf the Red said.

He gestured to a warrior standing close by who bent down and cut the bonds that tied the monk's wrists and ankles. Bishop Dub Inse struggled to his feet; his face now wore an expression of disbelief.

'I think we've tortured you enough,' Olaf said to him in the Irish tongue. 'Off you go.'

The red-haired viking king waved his hand as if shooing away a naughty child.

Dub Inse did not wait to let the opportunity pass. Gathering up the hem of his soaking wet robe he scampered out of the door.

'I can't believe you just let him go!' Ulrich said. 'He understands our tongue. He's overheard what we were talking about. All these Christians talk you know.'

'Oh they talk all right,' Olaf the Red said, his amicable smile dropping a little to become a wolfish grin. 'That's what I'm counting on. They gossip inside their monks' houses like a group of old women. And each house talks to the next one. And that one in turn speaks to the next in a great spider's web that stretches over the world.'

'And in the centre of that web is Aethelstan,' Ulrich said. 'The man you are going to fight for the kingship of Jorvik.'

'Ulrich, my ambitions are greater than that,' Olaf said. 'Aethelstan calls himself Emperor of all Britain. If I defeat him in battle why should I stop at Jorvik?'

'And don't you think that this Dub Inse won't go running to Aethelstan to tell him you are sailing to Britain?' Ulrich said. 'He will be ready for us!'

'I don't think you were listening, Ulrich,' Olaf said. He was still wearing his supercilious smile and Affreca's previous concern began to grow again as Ulrich's face became paler. She could almost feel the anger starting to simmer within the Wolf Coat leader.

'I said I was sailing to Britain *to get married*,' Olaf said. 'And a king does not go to his wedding – especially if he marries the daughter of another king – alone.'

Ulrich grunted. His rising rage flipped in a moment to a broadening smile of begrudging admiration.

'Of course,' he said, nodding. 'A royal marriage is always about getting rid of a rival. Ostensibly by making him an ally and part of the family. But any king worth his salt knows if he has his rival in the heart of his realm, at his mercy, then he could just as well cut his rival's throat and keep his own daughter to use again for a different alliance. For that reason any king going to be married always travels with his war horde.'

'So if someone tells Aethelstan I have sailed for Britain and landed in the north with a horde of warriors?' Olaf raised an eyebrow.

'Aethelstan will say: *I've nothing to worry about*,' Ulrich said. '*My good friend Bishop Dub Inse tells me Olaf of Dublin is sailing to marry the king of Scotland's daughter.*'

'I will do that,' Olaf said. 'But then we march south straight away. We'll be in Jorvik before Aethelstan knows it. I have it on good authority that Aethelstan is too busy meddling in Francia to pay too much attention to what I'm up to.'

'"On good authority"?' Affreca said. 'You have reliable spies in Britain?'

'I have one,' Olaf said. 'I will tell you more later.'

'So the war for Britain is finally on?' Ulrich said. There was a gleam in his eye. 'Have you enough ships? Enough men?'

'I have over five and a half hundred ships,' Olaf said. 'And now I have... persuaded my scabby-headed friend here that his better option is to join us than mess around with the Gaels. With his fleet we will have nearly six hundred.'

'If your men haven't smashed half of my ships tonight that is,' Olaf of Limerick said. He jutted out his lower lip.

'He is joining us?' Now it was Ulrich's turn to raise his eyebrow.

'Well I'm certainly not leaving him behind where I can't keep an eye on him,' Olaf the Red said with a wink. 'We need all the men we can get if we are to go to war with Aethelstan. And just in case he forgets he is supposed to be on my side, his daughter Ragnhild will be held hostage in Dublin. If Scabby Head betrays me she dies.'

'Why did you not tell me about this?' Ulrich said. 'I swore an oath to you. Do you not trust me?'

'And you once swore an oath to Aethelstan too,' Olaf said. His smile had gone now.

'I fulfilled that oath,' Ulrich said, his voice descending to a low growl. 'I did what I swore I would do. As I always do.'

Despite the tension between the two men, Affreca could not help smirking. Ulrich fulfilled oaths, yes, but only in the way that suited him most and if it meant the ultimate betrayal of a man Ulrich had sworn the oath to, then so be it. The one he had sworn to Aethelstan was the latest in a long line of such promises.

'It was important that I surprise old Olaf Scabby Head here,' Olaf the Red said, his usual happy demeanour returning in a flash. He held up a forefinger. '*Let one know your secret, but never tell a second. If three know then a thousand will.* Isn't that what your Odin would say? I'm more of a Thor's man, myself.'

He touched the big hammer pendant at his throat.

'And you could not have trusted me with this knowledge either?' Affreca said. 'Your own sister? We are of one blood after all.'

Olaf chortled and put his arm around Affreca's shoulder.

'I've told you this before, sister,' he said. 'That is the problem. We both spring from the same infamous line of cut-throats, liars, rogues and maniacs: the sons and daughters of Ivar Ragnarsson. But do not take offence, Affreca. I have a vital task that I need you to fulfil for me. It is crucial to my future success.'

'If you don't trust me then why choose me for such a task?' Affreca said, wrinkling her nose a little.

'Because I need you to take a message to another branch of our wayward clan,' Olaf said. 'And I am told that that man is foolish enough to trust you.'

Six

Affreca stood on the rolling deck of the longship as it surged and fell on the endless waves. The dragon prow was set towards Britain, as if it was a messenger of her brother's intent towards that island.

The ship was in the lonely, desolate place on the open sea where the coast of Ireland had slipped below the horizon behind them and the coast of Britain was yet to rise from the sea before them. The crew were all busy with tasks and the skipper had asked Affreca to stand watch on the prow. The sea was empty as far as the eye could see, but lurking somewhere ahead was a *drengr*, an isolated rock that sat in the middle of the churning waves. It was infamous to travellers on this whale road, as it lurked in the middle of nowhere, ready to rip the hull from any unsuspecting ship that sailed over it.

Olaf of Dublin's plan was that Affreca should sail to Jorvik. There she was to meet an important man in the city who Olaf knew was willing to help prepare the way for his coming invasion. When her brother's army marched south he wanted to make sure the gates of Jorvik were thrown open to him rather than slammed in his face.

She had met this man before, indeed as her brother had said, like her and her brother, he was from a branch of the clans descended from the sons of Ragnar Loðbrók. She was reasonably certain where his loyalties lay but the task was still a risky one. She was travelling into the land ruled by Aethelstan, the king her brother was going to challenge for his kingdom, and the man she was sailing to meet was a Christian. Not just any Christian either. He was a Christian chief priest and such men saw Aethelstan as the champion of their god. They could be wily too, and adept at statecraft. Often their support lay in whichever direction the tides of war would bring most advantage to their own fortunes.

In a way Affreca was pleased her brother had entrusted this task to her, though he had added the usual barb that it was because he judged her crafty enough for the job. It would take considerable guile to ensure first that this man was on their side for sure before she revealed her brother's plan. Otherwise he could go running straight to Aethelstan.

Olaf did not fear battle with Aethelstan. It would come, there was no doubt in that. It *had* to come if the matter of who ruled these islands was to be settled. There was no peaceful process by which such matters could be worked out. None that really worked anyway. However, Olaf knew the further south he could travel before fighting Aethelstan, the more Olaf's army would grow, and the more men who flocked to his war banner, the greater his chances of winning would become. Affreca's brother's very presence with his own war horde would be a challenge to Aethelstan's claim to be 'Emperor of all Britain'. The Wessex king had trampled on many necks on his way to claim that title, leaving much resentment behind him, particularly in the north. Many men who had called themselves kings in the past now had to be content with the title of Jarl or Thane, and they had not relinquished their titles willingly. At the sight of Olaf and Constantine's army marching through Britain those men would seize the chance to regain their former status.

Something caught Affreca's eye in the water ahead. She narrowed her gaze against the wind and the sea spray, squinting to get a better look.

There it was, sure enough: the drengr.

It stood up from the sea that seethed around it, a tall piece of rock, black and slick, parts of it worn smooth by the endless waves that crashed against it but still rugged enough to rip the hull from any passing ship that did not spot it in time. The waves battered it in endless succession, throwing white foam high into the air as they smashed themselves against it but it did not move or fall. It had stood in that place since the dawn of the world and would still be there, no matter how much the ocean tried to wash it away, on the day of Ragnarök when the world itself would burn and fall into the sea.

Affreca held up her right arm, the signal agreed with the skipper who was watching her from his station manning the steering oar at the stern of the longship. She glanced around to check if he had seen her but the skipper was already turning his vessel to avoid the danger ahead. He nodded his appreciation to her for a task fulfilled.

It was not Roan who steered the ship. Affreca was travelling alone, the passenger on a merchant ship from Dublin that plied its trade back and forth between the two mighty islands. Olaf had judged it would raise too many suspicions at this time if she had sailed to Jorvik on a snekkja crewed by úlfhéðnar.

Their cargo was mostly slaves who, ill-clad for the weather on the open sea, huddled together for warmth, chained to the oar benches. Every one wore the hollow-eyed, hopeless expressions of the enthralled. The crew, a nasty bunch like most slave traders were, were nevertheless too scared of Affreca's brother to interfere with her, a single woman travelling alone, in any way. The worst she had to contend with from them were the resentful looks they cast at her, no doubt thinking what they could be doing to her if only she were not the sister of Olaf the Red.

So for most of the voyage she had been left alone with her thoughts. This was good, for Affreca had a lot to think about.

She watched the drengr as the ship slid past it, avoiding the danger it threatened, musing how drengr had another meaning in the Norse tongue. It was the ultimate compliment for a man. To be described as a drengr or to be *drengiligr*, was to say that a man stood for his principles and beliefs, he was like the rock in the sea, unmoved by the tides of opinion, challenges, fashion or kings. He stood alone, against a sea of enemies, and did not bow or bend to whatever they threw at him.

Einar was somewhere in Britain. He had betrayed the Wolf Coats crew and gone back to Aethelstan all because of some stupid idea he had got in his head about how the ideals Aethelstan represented were somehow admirable. It was so typical of Einar.

She spat over the edge of the ship, feeling her anger rise as she remembered levelling her bow at him as he left them. Then, for the first time in her life unable to let her arrow fly, she had lowered the bow and watched him sail away.

Ulrich had been furious. He had flown into an apoplectic rage at the news, a fury intense enough to have been a full *berserkergang*. Afterwards he had sulked for days, not speaking to anyone and brooding in his own dark thundercloud. The others – Skar, Sigurd, Kari and the rest had been more shocked that Einar would betray them than angry. He had been one of the crew. He had sworn the same oath of allegiance to Ulrich as the rest of them. They never thought in a thousand years he would do such a thing. Skar, she knew, believed Einar had done it in a moment of madness: the lad had made a stupid mistake and if he came back, and grovelled enough, Skar would probably forgive Einar. The others were the same but Ulrich was not, and Affreca knew that they all had too much respect – as well as fear – for the little man who was their leader to contradict his wishes.

Einar was in Britain, and he was in the service of Aethelstan, the king her brother and the Wolf Coats were going to war against. A time was coming when they would face each other across a battlefield. That fate was inevitable. She did not need a vǫlva to predict it. When it did, then perhaps there would be a second time when she would aim her bow at Einar.

This time, would she let the arrow fly?

She had brought this up with Ulrich just before she left Ireland, asking what she should do might she run into Einar while in Jorvik. The little man had curled his upper lip into a sneer, revealing clenched teeth beneath.

'Kill him,' he said, without hesitation.

Part Two

Norðimbraland er kallat fimmtungr Englands, ok er þat norðast, næst Skotlandi fyrir austan. Þat höfðu haft at fornu Danakonungar. Jórvík er þar höfuðstaðr.

Northumberland was reckoned a fifth part of England; it was the northernmost county, marching with Scotland on the eastern side of the island. Formerly the Danish kings had held it. Its chief town is York.

Egils Saga Skalla-Grímssonar, kafli 51

Seven

Jorvik, North Britain

Einar was right at the limit of his endurance. He clenched his teeth, willing himself to keep going.

The boredom was so severe it was almost painful.

The monk at the front of the church droned on, talking about something Einar could not understand. Einar frowned, thinking if he actually listened to the man it might help the time pass with less excruciating monotony.

At first he thought the monk was speaking in the Latin tongue, then he realised he was just using the strange affected tone used by Christian wizards when they chanted their spells or delivered their prophecies. The man was actually speaking in the Saxon tongue, something Einar was getting more accustomed to once more, now he had been in Britain for several months. Being back in Jorvik helped him in this, as many of the inhabitants were descendants of northmen like himself and spoke with a tongue that sounded as much Norse as Saxon.

Now he was paying attention, he began to comprehend that the monk, as was usual with those people, was moaning about the end of the world. Why Christians were so obsessed with the *Ragnarök* Einar did not know. It was not like there was anything anyone could do about it. The end would come at the time it was fated to happen. There was nothing that could be done about that. Fate had declared it. The world would be destroyed and that was that.

Einar leaned his elbows on his knees and blew out his cheeks, not realising how loud the noise he made was. Then he returned his attention to the runes he was scratching with the point of his seax knife into the wood of the uncomfortable seat he was forced to sit on. He knew runes well – the wise old woman who his mother had paid to nurse him as a child had taught them to him – but it was important to keep practising their carving. One slip in the etching of the stick-like letters could end up conveying a completely different message from the one intended.

The sound of a man clearing his throat in a pointed manner made Einar look around. Cynewulf, the East Saxon monk who King Aethelstan had appointed to guide and mentor Einar on the path to Christian faith, stood behind him. The older man's tonsured ring of tousled grey hair stood up all over the place as usual, while one of the bushy eyebrows that usually squirmed across his forehead like two fighting caterpillars was raised in questioning disapproval.

Einar shrugged, put his seax away and resumed pretending to listen to the monk at the front of the church. With a heavy sigh, Cynewulf shook his head and tapped the young Norseman on the shoulder. Einar looked around again to see Cynewulf hook his thumb in the direction of the church doors. Then the monk turned and headed for them.

Einar got up to follow him, relieved at being able to break the boredom of the church service but a little apprehensive of the angry reprimand that he had no doubt brother Cynewulf was about to deliver.

The monk did not wait long after they exited the church. He rounded on his younger charge the moment they were outside in the pleasant morning air.

'Really, Einar,' Cynewulf said, his tone reproachful. 'The king has charged me with making you a good Christian but how am I supposed to do that when you can't even sit through mass without destroying the seats?'

Einar lowered his head, unable to think of a response. He felt his face flush with shame. He was supposed to have been part of a religious service but instead he had been caught carving his name into the bench he sat on, like a bored child.

He flexed the remaining three fingers and thumb of his maimed right hand, balling them into what he could of a fist. It was a habit he had fallen into since returning to Britain. It helped him calm in the times when he felt the old rush of anger into his heart.

That's the Devil sends that, lad, Cynewulf had told him. *That's who old Woden is, really. His real name is Satan. It's him who's whispering in your ear and telling you to do evil. When you feel that, you must call on Jesus for help and he will send Satan running.*

'Do you have any idea what is at stake here, lad?' the monk said as he stomped off across the wooden planks that lined the street. 'The king has important plans for you, you know? He thinks you can be an example to your fellow Norsemen. You could be a Dane who can learn the ways of civilised folk. And he has tasked me with teaching you those ways. If you fail, I fail with you. And how can I even hope to succeed if you're not even listening to the sermon when you are in church?'

'Sorry,' Einar finally found some words. 'It's just that it's so...'

He trailed off, realising that to finish the sentence would make things worse.

Cynewulf stopped. He turned around to face Einar. Einar regarded the streak of white in the older man's grey beard that told of a scar beneath and the crooked bend of his broken nose.

Not for the first time Einar wondered how this monk – a man of peace – had come to have the face of a man of violence.

'Boring? Is that what you were going to say?' Cynewulf glared at the younger man, his own face darkening. 'Let me tell you, lad, you won't find Hell boring when you end up there, with the Devil and all his black angels tormenting you with red hot irons for the rest of eternity!'

He spun on his heel and strode off once more down the street, his heavy footsteps making the wooden boards rattle.

'Now come on,' Cynewulf said over his shoulder. 'The shire reeve wants to see you. He needs swordsmen.'

Einar's heart leapt. At last perhaps there was something to break his boredom.

Eight

Aethelstan, King of Wessex, Lord of all the *Aenglisc*, Emperor of all Britain, had admitted his surprise when Einar had returned alone to his capital at Wintanceaster. Aethelstan had commissioned Ulrich's *úlfhéðnar*, an infamous crew of vikings, which Einar had been a member of, with travelling to the war-torn lands of north-west Francia to recover a rare book of Christian lore. The main aim of the expedition, however, had actually been to ensure Vilhjálmr Langaspjót, Jarl of Rúðu (or William Long Sword, Count of Rouen as he was now more widely known) fought off a rebellion and remained in power. In return, William had promised his support for the return of Aethelstan's nephew, Louis, to the throne of France.

These had all been moves in Aethelstan's grand plan of statecraft, an impossibly complicated game than spanned most of the known world and had so many players Einar found it impossible to follow. The only thing he was sure of was that in it, Aethelstan was always several moves ahead of everyone else.

The king of Wessex had half expected Ulrich to betray his trust and disappear with the book, but when Einar had in turn betrayed his comrades and taken the book back to Wessex, it had proved an unexpected bonus for the king.

This tells me something about you Einar, lad, Aethelstan had said. *You are a man of your word. And that is something I value.*

Einar, still unsure if he had done the right thing at the time, had pointed out that by taking the book he had in fact broken his oath to Ulrich. Aethelstan had levelled the unsettling, probing gaze of his dark-brown eyes on Einar.

But you kept it to me, the king said. *And that is what I value.*

In the weeks that followed it became clear that Aethelstan had some purpose in mind for Einar, though what that was he did not share. He assigned Cynewulf as Einar's personal tutor in the ways of civilised Christianity and not long afterwards assigned a war band to Einar's command and sent him north to Jorvik.

Now, several more weeks into that assignment, Einar was still not sure what he was doing in the city. Like his God, Aethelstan worked in mysterious ways. The only vague command the king had given him was that Einar was there to 'help keep the King's Peace'.

For most of the preceding hundred years Jorvik had been the centre of a fierce, independent and very Norse kingdom. Aethelstan had taken advantage of the death of Sitric, King of Jorvik, to annex the realm into his own ever-expanding empire. That had been a few years ago now, but the city still had an air of one that was occupied by a foreign army. Saxon warriors, dressed for war, still guarded the gates, walls and important places in the city. The denizens of the city – who were mostly of Norse descent – went about their daily business under the Saxons' suspicious gazes, looks they returned with glances of resentment.

To his consternation Einar now found himself part of those occupying forces and the object of his fellow folk's hostility. He had lived in Jorvik previously but could not look up old friends or frequent his favourite taverns as the townspeople now looked on him as one of the Saxons who had stolen their city. To add to that, the Saxons Aethelstan had appointed him to lead regarded Einar as a Norseman, so treated him with as much suspicion as they did the locals.

The few weeks he had spent so far in the city had been lonely ones.

Thankfully what work they'd had proved easy enough. There appeared little appetite in the city at present for outright rebellion and Einar and his men had had little to do but strut around in their armour on patrol, harass locals and take their turns at guard duty.

Now, with the reeve's request for help, there was finally perhaps some excitement.

With Einar following like a scolded dog, Cynewulf the monk led the way along the network of *gatr*, the wooden walkways that criss-crossed the city, forming its streets. It was still early morning but the noise and stench were already close to overpowering. The streets thronged with people, their chattering and general racket filling the air. Smoke from cooking fires drifted on the soft breeze, catching the throat and mingling with the aroma of beer malting and the ever-present stench of piss.

The gatr were lined on both sides by long, narrow, thatch-covered buildings, some family homes, some the premises of merchants. All had their entrances at one end where their gables met the walkways. The merchants shouted to attract customers to the wares they had laid out on tables before their houses. Children ran to and fro amid the crowds clogging the walkways, some playing games of tag and some using their nimble fingers to snatch the purses of unwary passers-by.

Cynewulf did not have to tell Einar where they were heading. He could see the huge bulk of the minster, rising above all the other buildings ahead. It was taller and longer than everything around it and made of stone, rather than wood and wattle.

Instead of thatch its roof was covered with red tiles. It was so tall that looking up at it gave Einar a queasy feeling in his guts, especially the one tower that soared above the entrance, from which was often heard the strange metal clanging of Christian bells.

Like a fortress of Christ built to keep the heathen city dwellers out, the minster had a palisade around it, its ramparts and gates guarded by Saxon warriors. They recognised Einar and Cynewulf and let them in through the main gate.

Once inside Einar saw the front of the massive church was covered in a web of wooden struts and walkways: scaffolding for a crew of workmen who Aethelstan had sent north with Einar to work on the stone carvings on the outside of the minster. Einar could hear their hammers banging away. They were a strange bunch, the stone workers. Frankish craftsmen Aethelstan had brought to his realms so they could use their expertise to make his churches as magnificent as those in the Holy Roman Empire and beyond. They kept themselves to themselves and had their own secret ways. Einar was sure that, like him, Aethelstan had an ulterior motive for sending them to Jorvik.

Einar stroked his bare chin as he watched them, something that had become a habit since he had shaved off his beard, leaving only a long moustache, which was the style among the Saxons. He had been bearded since he was sixteen and the sensation of feeling the smooth skin of his face was still a novelty.

Standing just outside the wood scaffold was a tall, lean man in a leather jerkin. He was of middling years and going bald, something which he tried to conceal by tying his long, greying hair behind his head. His left ear was missing its lobe, his face bore several scars and he had two of his front teeth missing, which was all testament to the roughness of his job. Einar recognised him. It was Oswald the *Gerēfa*, the shire reeve, the man charged with enforcing the king's laws in this district.

The war band Aethelstan had assigned to Einar's command was garrisoned inside the minster in some outbuildings, and Einar knew that if the reeve had come there he must need help from Einar and his men. Oswald had his own band of men, and if necessary could conscript free men into a *posse comitatus* to hunt down outlaws. However, every now and again, especially in an occupied realm like Jorvik, a situation arose that required the extra support of a professional war band.

'Good morning, Oswald,' Einar greeted the reeve with a smile. 'I assume you are here to ask for the support of my men? What's the problem?'

The reeve sighed and glanced away, clearly unhappy that he was pushed to ask for help.

'I think we might have a problem with vikings,' he said.

Nine

Einar had been dreading this ever since he had arrived in Britain.

Ulrich and the other Wolf Coats he had broken from were headed for Ireland to join a viking army that Affreca's brother, Olaf the Red of Dublin, was gathering. That would mean raiding and they could very well end up attacking Britain. Also the rumours were that Olaf was planning to challenge Aethelstan's power. That would mean war.

Einar knew that finding himself on the opposite side of a battlefield from his former crew mates had been inevitable since the moment he decided to leave them. He had just hoped it would not come so quickly.

Even if whatever the reeve's viking problem was did not involve Ulrich and the others, Einar could be sure it could well mean violent confrontation with Norsemen like himself.

Einar took a deep breath, straightened his back and pushed his shoulders back. So be it. He had thrown his lot in with Aethelstan and this would be the first real test of his resolve.

'What can we do to help?' he said.

'There's been some trouble north of here: a couple of farmsteads near the coast were burned, their goods stolen,' Oswald the reeve said. 'Now a ship – a Norse one – has landed at Skarthi's Burh. I'm worried about its intentions.'

'Is it a dragon ship or a *knarr*?' Einar said. 'One is for war the other is for trading. The type of ship should give you a clue to what the crew intend.'

The reeve shook his head.

'You can't always tell by the type,' he said. 'The Danes sometimes come pretending to be peaceful traders. Then when you turn your back on them they raise heathen dragons on their prow and before you know it your mother's been raped and they're carrying your children off to the slave market in Dublin.'

He shot a sideways glance at Einar.

'As you would know,' he said.

Einar met the reeve's gaze with a cold eye but did not rise to the bait.

'The skipper of the ship, a man called Ljót, has already been causing trouble,' the reeve continued. Then he broke off, noticing a smile on Einar's face. 'You think this is funny?'

'I sympathise with the farmer, trust me,' Einar said. 'I'm just smiling at the name this viking calls himself. It's not by any chance Ljót *inn Blieka*? Ljót the Pale?'

'It is,' the reeve said, frowning. 'He's a notorious viking. One of those berserker maniacs. You know him?'

'If there ever was a Ljót the Pale he'd be about one hundred and ten winters old,' Einar said. '"Ljót the Pale" *is* like a nickname. Lone vikings use it: men who are either outlawed by their king or who are too much trouble for others to associate with. Or men who need to hide their identity while going viking: rich boys – sons of jarls and the like who want to misbehave without bringing a bad name to their family. So they call themselves "Ljót the Pale". It's a good sign for us. It usually means they can't get enough men to cause real problems, so they rely of the reputation of "Ljót" to scare folk into handing over their goods rather than fight for them. And it works. You've heard of him.'

The reeve frowned.

'Well he's been throwing his weight around, bullying the locals and extorting silver and goods by threats,' he said. 'I heard that up the coast this fellow challenged a farmer to a duel. The poor farmer wasn't a warrior. To fight a viking like Ljót would be suicide so he backed out. Ljót took the farmer's wife and all the silver he had as a forfeit. Now he's landed in Skarthi's Burh and I'd like to tell him to move on before he starts that nonsense in my shire.'

'Like I said,' Einar said, 'you shouldn't have too much bother from them. They tend to try to avoid trouble if they can. One ship of vikings can't afford to lose too many men fighting. Better to try intimidation and if that doesn't work move on to somewhere softer.'

'All the same.' The reeve's expression softened and he looked Einar in the eye again. 'I'd appreciate some support from the king's war band you lead. My men are fine for rounding up a few outlaws in the forest or grabbing a gang of thieves at the marketplace. A ship full of fully armed vikings though? And one led by a berserker? We wouldn't stand a chance. We have no mail, no helms and our weapons are mostly what they can bring from their farms or vegetable plots. I'm the only man with a sword.'

Einar nodded.

'Fair enough,' he said. 'This is the sort of thing the king sent us here for anyway. When do we leave?'

'Thank you.' The reeve looked relieved. 'As soon as possible. Meet you at the Mikel Gatr?'

'I'll get horses ready,' Cynewulf said.

'I'll go and get the lads,' Einar said.

They parted from the reeve and Einar headed towards a line of low thatched buildings that sat against the inside of the minster palisade. It was in one of those that his men were hosted. They would be done with morning training and more than likely taking it easy as he had been away and not there to find work to annoy them with.

He did not relish re-entering the company of the war band – the *dryht*. They were far from happy at being assigned to serve under Einar. Not only was he younger than most of them but he was also a foreigner and a heathen. There were times that he could almost taste their resentment in the air. They were not openly insolent. They carried out his orders and did their duty but it was neither with enthusiasm or goodwill. Nevertheless Einar could appreciate they were hardy warriors, proud Saxons who knew their trade – fighting – well. Perhaps one day he would win them over and gain their respect. Until then he would just have to learn how to deal with their disgruntled attitude.

He took a deep breath before entering the building. It was times like this he most missed his old crewmates, if not just that they spoke his own tongue. Those days were gone forever, however, and he had to get used to that. Ulrich would never forgive what Einar had done. He had put himself apart from them forever.

Still, he did not regret the choice he had made that day in Francia in the bloody aftermath of battle. He was only saddened by the consequences it had brought. It was Einar who had chosen to do the right thing; to fulfil the oath sworn to Aethelstan, even though it meant breaking with his fellows. All Ulrich had to offer was chaos and endless bloodshed in the discord sown by the old one-eyed god, Odin. At least Aethelstan stood for something. Order. Peace. Learning. He had a vision. He was building something special with his empire, and Einar knew he could play a part in that. Perhaps a large part. All he had to do was prove himself worthy to the king.

Einar pushed open the door and went into the hut, just in time to hear someone say: 'Look out, lads, here comes the Dane.'

It was one of the men – Garwulf, one of the few younger than Einar – who had given the warning. He had spoken in what he thought was a covert tone, but Einar shot him a glare and held it long enough for Garwulf to start to blush.

After a few moments Einar broke the look and surveyed the room where the warriors were lounging on their straw beds, sitting playing board games, or engaged in tasks like repairing clothes or whittling away at pieces of wood.

'Get your war gear, men, and meet me at the stables,' Einar said in a loud, commanding voice. 'We're going to hunt vikings.'

Ten

They rode south from Jorvik, following the path of the river that flowed through the city as it wound its way onwards towards the sea. Einar was at the head of his warriors, twelve men in all, riding in a column. The summer sunshine gleamed from their mail shirts and the polished iron of their helmets. It glittered across hundreds of red garnets and other semi-precious stones inlaid into their armour and weapons. Their dark green cloaks and the long plumes of horsehair trailed in the warm breeze as they trotted along. Big, round shields, painted with white dragons, the symbol of Wessex, were across their backs. Each man had two throwing spears holstered by his saddle, bore a heavy fighting spear in one hand and had a sword sheathed under his left arm.

Unlike his men, who wore Saxon-style helmets, Einar still wore his Norse-style visored helm, one more thing that made him stand out as different from them. However, he had spent a lot of time making sure it was comfortable and it fitted him well. It was battle-tried and he was confident in its protection, which was, after all, what the piece of armour was for.

Einar also had his *járngreipr*, his fighting glove, on. It was a special piece of war gear made for him by a smith so crafty Einar still suspected that perhaps the man had been a wizard. The glove was a modified battle gauntlet with two iron hooks and a leather strap added and it allowed him to grip a sword with all the steadfastness he had had before his right hand was maimed.

Einar could see the looks of awe on the faces of peasants and ordinary folk as they rode past and felt a surge of pride that – despite the fact that they resented him for it – he was the leader of such an impressive war band.

The reeve and his men added fifteen more to the company. Their dress and weaponry were much more humble. Some of them had the protection of leather jerkins while some had just their woollen shirts. Most had bows and knives while a couple were armed with spears but nothing to rival the Saxon warriors. Einar judged them a hardy enough bunch, though could also see from their pale faces and skittish glances the thought of perhaps having to face armed vikings was making them nervous.

Cynewulf rode with them too, which was curious as if there was one thing monks were usually very wary of, it was vikings. Yet here he was, trotting along as if eager for the confrontation. Yet again Einar wondered about this man's past.

The fields were thick with ripening barley and the warm summer sun blazed from a clear blue sky as it climbed overhead. The smell of sweet grass turning to hay mingled with the scent of wildflowers in the hedgerow they rode beside. Had it not been for the danger that lay ahead, the ride would have been most pleasant.

Einar mused how different the green, fertile countryside was to the rugged landscape of his homeland of Iceland. Life here would be comfortable. Every scrap of nourishment would not have to be wrenched from the hard, frozen soil. Somehow this thought sent a pang of homesickness through his heart, which puzzled him. It was now a few years since he had left Iceland yet it felt like a hundred. With a good wind and a fair sea you could sail there in a week yet somehow it seemed like it was further away now from him than if it had been on the moon.

Apart from his helmet, Einar was dressed the same as his Saxon warriors. King Aethelstan had given him a fine set of arms and armour before sending Einar north. He wore the same long cloak as the rest of his men and a bright, shining new *brynja*, or *byrn* as the Saxons referred to their coats of mail, encased his torso. He held a fighting spear in one hand with a new ash wood shaft and a shield painted with the same white dragon as the others was slung across his back.

If you're going to represent me in the north, Aethelstan had said, *we can't have you looking like a scruffy heathen.*

His mind went to the wolfskin cloak that he carried in one of the saddle bags, the symbol that he was an *úlfheðinn*, one of Odin's own wolf warriors. He was supposed to have burned it as a symbol of how he had left that life behind him. When the time had come, however, Einar could not bring himself to do it. It had been his proudest possession, for úlfhéðnar were not just any warriors. They were the best of the best, blessed by the one-eyed god himself with the special gift of divine rage. So Einar had hidden it.

He thought about how he now led a company of twelve men. It was a number sacred to Odin. Ulrich had striven constantly to have twelve in his úlfhéðnar crew, but it always proved elusive. Now here was Einar, in the service of a Christian king, leading twelve warriors in his own war band.

Movement overhead caught his eye and he saw two birds fly up from a nearby tree. Somehow he knew they were ravens even before he saw their black plumage and chisel-shaped beaks. Odin had two ravens – Huginn and Muminn – who he sent out every day to fly around the world. At evening they returned and reported what they had seen.

Were these his birds, sent here to witness deeds of valour and tell the All Father who deserved a seat on the mead benches of the Vallr Hall? If they were it meant there would be fighting for sure.

Einar realised Cynewulf was looking at him, one eyebrow raised.

'You're wondering if those are old Woden's birds, aren't you, lad?' the monk said. 'Remember what I told you: that's the Devil whispering in your ear. Don't listen to him.'

Einar pursed his lips and they rode on.

The brown-green meandering river broadened into a wide estuary, and the crowing of the ravens and tweeting of starlings was replaced by the squawking of terns and the cries of seagulls. The muddy waters of the estuary got ever wider until after midday the sea came into view.

As they approached the coast the water disappeared again behind a line of sand dunes that rose just before the beach. The backs of the dunes were covered in coarse grass and they undulated like waves, creating a series of humps and hollows. The furthest they could see was perhaps a hundred paces before a dune rose or a dip opened up.

Einar began to feel uneasy. Such terrain made it easy for an enemy to take you by surprise. The skin on the back of his neck began to crawl in a manner that had nothing to do with the sweat that was running down under his helmet.

Then a figure popped up from among the grass. Einar stiffened in the saddle, his knuckles whitening around the shaft of his spear.

Oswald the reeve, however, waved to the newcomer.

'Harald!' the reeve said. 'Are they still here?'

'Aye, I believe so, Oswald,' said Harald, a ragged-haired, scrawny man dressed in leather and wool like the rest of the reeve's men.

'You *believe* so?' Oswald said.

'I've been watching from the long grass up there like you told me,' Harald said with a shrug. 'I can't see what they're up to though. I didn't want to get too close. God knows what they'd have done to me if they saw me. The dunes hid them. I haven't seen their ship's mast move though and they did not leave by this path.'

The reeve let out a heavy sigh.

'There is one thing though,' Harald added quickly, eager to try to please the reeve. 'Four horsemen came this way. They rode down the path to the beach. Each of them had stuffed saddlebags. I could tell those bags were heavy because the horses were really sweating,'

'Who were they?' the reeve said.

'I've no idea,' Harald said. 'They had long cloaks on with the hoods up, which was odd on a lovely summer's day like this. Later they rode away again. When they rode away they had no saddle bags.'

'Do you think they were stolen by the vikings?' Oswald said.

'Don't know,' Harald said. 'But I'd say no. They didn't look too flustered when they were riding away. More likely they were trading with them.'

'What do you want to do?' Einar said to Oswald. 'If they are traders then we can't attack them just for being vikings.'

The reeve thought for a moment, sucking his teeth as he did so.

'All the same, I'd rather we got them to move on,' he said. 'You know what the Danes are like. You can't trust them. It's trading one day then raiding the next. Let's go and have a word with them.'

Einar nodded.

'Get ready, men,' he said over his shoulder.

With a murmur of pleased excitement Einar's war band dismounted and began readying their war gear.

'If I may make a suggestion,' Cynewulf the monk said.

Einar and the reeve turned to face him.

'Far be it for a man of peace like me to interfere in matters of war,' Cynewulf said, 'but when armed young men face off against each other matters tend to get heated very quickly. Perhaps the reeve and his men go forward first and ask politely if these vikings will be so kind as to move on? The war band can wait out of sight in case they are needed. No offence, Oswald, but your men may present less of a threat, and so be less provoking.'

'We're not afraid of Danes!' Garwulf, the young lad from Einar's *dryht* interjected, spittle flying through his clenched teeth. 'Why should we skulk in hiding like cowards?'

'For all we know this Ljót the Pale will just pack up and go when asked to,' Cynewulf said. 'And the best battles are the ones you win without a fight.'

'True,' Einar said, stroking his chin. 'He's only got one ship. He won't want to lose too many men.'

'Well if we can manage to get rid of them with no bloodshed then that would be the best outcome,' the reeve said, nodding. 'I'm not happy going with just my own men though. If the Danes might decide to cut up rough we could lose a few men before Einar's lot make it down there.'

'Einar and I shall go with you,' Cynewulf said.

'Very well,' Oswald said, though he did not look that convinced. 'Let's do what the monk suggests.'

With an exasperated gasp Garwulf shook his head.

'Listen for my signal, lads,' Einar said. 'And come running when you hear it. Don't worry. You still might get a fight. Be careful what you wish for, though. Fighting hardened vikings is a lot different to pushing peasants around.'

Einar, Cynewulf, the reeve and his men dismounted and set off down the little track that led into the sand dunes, leaving the heavily armed warriors to wait in reserve. As they walked Einar reached down and released the leather straps that held his sword in its sheath, just in case he needed to draw it quickly.

The trail twisted and turned through gullies that ran through the dunes. Beyond the top of one sand hill Einar caught sight of the top of a ship's mast, lying at a slight angle and knew they must be close to the shore. Round another bend they found the vikings.

In a natural bowl formed by a ring of dunes a party of nine men were gathered around a fire. Four lounged on the ground. Three of them were sitting on leather and wood sea chests working at repairing a fishing net. One was on his feet, searching for something inside a coarse wool sack. War gear – helmets, shields and spears – were scattered around the ground as well as various chests, boxes and clay jars.

A blackened cooking pot hung suspended from a tripod over the fire. A man with long blond hair sat on his haunches before the pot, stirring it with a long metal ladle.

Einar could tell even though the man was beneath him he was big. His shoulders were wide and his thighs long. The man's left eye was covered by an eye patch and Einar could not help noticing the number of the vikings – nine – was another number holy to Odin. He glanced skywards to see if the ravens still followed them.

It was said that Odin walked the world in disguise. Could this be the old one-eyed god himself, come to chide Einar for his betrayal of Ulrich?

Einar removed his helm and tucked it into the crook of his left arm. He could taste the salt in the air as the sea breeze tugged at his sweat-soaked hair. As they approached some of the vikings stirred. Two sat up. Three rose to their feet, watching Einar and the others approach with cool gazes. The big man squatting before the cooking pot took scant notice of them and continued stirring whatever was bubbling inside.

Einar and the reeve stopped before the fire. The reeve's men fanned out in a semicircle to either side. Einar glanced around. He saw their wide eyes, clenched teeth, pale faces and the white knuckles of their hands that gripped their spears and farm implements. He wished he had not listened to the monk and had brought his own warriors with them.

As if oblivious to the men who now confronted his crew, the big viking lifted the ladle from the pot and took a slurp from it. Smacking his lips he replaced the ladle and finally looked up. When he did it was with a gaze hard enough to make the reeve flinch.

'What's this?' the big man said in the Norse tongue. 'Some sort of farmers' outing? Has someone come to sell us their scarecrows?'

The other vikings laughed.

'I am the reeve of this shire,' Oswald said, his voice hoarse. 'What is your business here?'

The big Norseman raised his eyebrows and spread his hands wide.

'We are simple traders,' he said switching to Saxon with a heavy Norse accent. 'Trying to scratch out a living. Are you here to buy or sell?'

'Neither,' Oswald said. Einar could hear his voice hardening. 'We believe you are a crew of vikings who have been causing trouble up and down this coast for the last month or more.'

'Who? Us?' the Norseman said. He looked at his fellows who all chuckled. 'We're no trouble to anyone. Are we Bjarni?'

He winked at another Norseman who squatted beside him.

Despite the situation, Einar noticed the man's ostentatious hairstyle which was impressive enough to provoke a second look. The sides of his head were shaved and runes were tattooed in black across his scalp. A single strip of hair was left running over the top of his head to hang down into a ponytail behind his head.

'We're no trouble to anyone,' the man said, a vicious grin on his face.

'Are you Ljót the Pale?' Einar said in the Norse tongue.

The big Norseman's eyes, one good and one sightless, narrowed.

'Some call me that, yes,' he said. 'You speak our tongue, friend. Yet you wear the clothes of a Saxon. Like one of them your chin is as bare as a woman's. Are you some sort of frog, perhaps, that has legs and arms like an animal but lives in the water like a fish?'

His crewmates laughed.

'What's your real name?' Einar said. '*Ljót inn bleika* – Ljót the Pale – is a nickname berserkers use to protect their reputations when they do dishonourable work. Or to steal the reputations of others who have gone before.'

Ljót's nostrils flared.

'We are busy men and you're wasting our time,' he said, switching back to Saxon. 'Now are you here to trade with us or not? Last chance.'

'We're here to tell you that you're not welcome here,' Oswald said. 'Get back on your ship and move on.'

'And what if we tell you to fuck off?' Ljót said, fixing Oswald with his one good eye.

'Then we'll make you,' the reeve said.

Ljót and his crew mates guffawed. Bjarni spat into the sand.

'You and this bunch of peasants?' Ljót said, when his initial gale of mirth subsided a little. 'Really?'

All of the other vikings stood up. They put on the helmets and picked up weapons and shields. In moments they had changed from a ragtag band of sailors relaxing on the shore to warriors ready for a fight. In terms of numbers both sides were about equal, however the vikings with their iron helms and good war gear would make short work on the reeve's men with their leather jerkins and makeshift weapons.

'Now,' Ljót the Pale said. 'Why don't you just fuck off and you won't get hurt?'

'Well if you really want a fight…' Einar said. He turned his head and whistled through his teeth over his shoulder.

With a clinking of iron rings his war band came jogging down the track to line up alongside the reeve's men. Beside the ragtag band Oswald had gathered, Einar's dryht looked like true men of war as the sun glittered on their helms and mail shirts.

'It seems we have more warriors than you do,' Einar said, with a smile he hoped was as provoking as Ulrich's used to be. 'Now why don't you do what we ask? Get back on your ship and fuck off.'

To Einar's consternation, Ljót the Pale still smiled. Then he turned his head to the side and wolf-whistled in the same way Einar had.

All around the tops of the dunes above them figures stood up from the coarse grass. They wore visored helmets and had spears and shields. Einar's gut lurched as he realised they were more vikings. He had no time to count them but knew straight away they were outnumbered and surrounded.

'Shit!' the reeve said through his teeth. 'It's a trap!'

Eleven

Ljót the Pale rose to his feet.

Einar swallowed. He was a big man himself but the viking was huge. His chest was like the trunk of a mature ash tree, his shoulders were wider than Einar's and to Einar's further consternation he found himself having to tilt his head back to look up at the man.

Seeming to remember something, the viking glanced down, then in a swift movement of his left foot kicked a chest nearby shut. Einar just had time to glimpse a glimmer of silver inside before the lid closed with a rattle of metal.

Ljót looked up again. His face was split in a malevolent grin as he leered down at Einar with his one good eye.

'All right, all right!' the reeve said. Einar could hear the panicked edge in his voice. 'We'll leave.'

'I think it's too late for that,' Ljót said. 'You had your chance, but chose to try to be big men and try to push us around instead. I think it's time someone put you in your place.'

He hefted a war axe into a ready position, his fist gripping the long shaft about halfway down, the back of the head resting on his right shoulder. The rest of his viking crew readied their weapons too. As one, Einar's well-trained warriors raised their shields and formed a defensive line. The reeve's men were less composed. They looked around with wild eyes, some brandishing their weapons, some keeping them low as if already about to surrender.

Two lost their nerves completely and began sprinting back up the track, their feet sending little spurts of sand into the air behind them.

Ljót flicked his head in the direction of the running men. Two vikings on a dune top above cocked their spears then hurled them. Both men cried out in pain and surprise as the spears drove through their backs, impaling them back to front. They fell, face first, dying in the sand before they had even made it twenty paces.

'No one gets away alive,' Ljót shouted. 'They'll just bring more trouble for us. Now, lads, let's finish off the rest.'

Einar glanced around at his warriors. Their faces were pale but resolute. They would fight – they had no choice – but he knew, as would they, that the odds were very much against them. Perhaps they might be able to fight their way out but not without losing some of their number.

He cursed himself for letting himself be led into what was no so obviously a trap. Worse, he had led them into it too. From the cold resentment he saw in their eyes, he could tell his men cursed him for it as well. They had been ready to fight a fair battle, but now they were outnumbered and encircled.

'Well get on with it! Attack us, you cowards!' the reeve yelled. His voice cracked with strain. He was a brave man but Einar could see he was at his wits' end.

'As you wish,' Ljót said.

'Wait!' Einar said. He switched to Norse and the sound of their own tongue made the vikings hesitate. 'I have a proposition.'

All eyes fell on him.

'You called us big men, Ljót,' Einar said. 'But I hear you are a big man for *holmgangr*. You like to challenge weak men to duels, knowing they'll be too scared to fight you. When they forfeit you take their gold, their wives or daughters, whatever you can lift.'

Einar saw a hard gleam enter Ljót's one eye and knew his words had struck in the way he intended.

'What are you trying to say?' the big viking said, his voice becoming gravelly. 'It's not my fault that this country is filled with lily-livered Saxons and Danes who've lost their balls since settling here. If they can't stand up for themselves then why should we not prey on them?'

'Easy pickings, eh?' Einar said. 'You're quite the *drengr*.'

Ljót ground his teeth.

'How about you fight a real duel for once?' Einar said. 'How about you fight me? Let this be between you and I. I hereby challenge you, Ljót the Pale or whatever your real name is, to a holmgangr, a duel. This is a formal challenge according to the ancient rites and laws of our folk. My challenge is that you are a coward. My terms are that if I win, your men will let my men leave freely.'

'I will fight your duel, yes,' Ljót said, chuckling once more and shaking his head. 'But I do not speak for my men. We are a crew and they are their own men, not bound by the oaths of others. If we let you go you'll go scurrying off to King Aethelstan telling tales of vikings and before we know it a Saxon army will be onto us. You and I will fight, yes. Then – when you are dead – me and my crew will kill the rest of your men.'

Einar sighed. He had half expected this but it was still disappointing to hear. Pirates like Ljót could never be trusted.

'Where?' he said.

'Why not right here and right now?' Ljót said, his unpleasant grin returning. 'This space is about the right size and if you were thinking I was going to wait the usual seven days until the fight you're very wrong.'

He ordered a couple of his men to mark out an area beside their fire. Using some sticks of driftwood they drew a square shape in the sand, the sides roughly four paces by four. The corners they marked by driving spear shafts into the sand. This was the area dictated by ancient custom inside which the duel would be fought. If a fighter fled from it, or even set one foot outside the boundary, he would lose the contest straight away.

'What's going on?' Rothulf, one of Einar's Saxon warriors demanded, using his own language.

'This young fool has challenged that huge viking to a duel,' the reeve said, pointing at Einar. 'He's going to sacrifice himself so the rest of us can get away.'

'You understand the Norse tongue?' Einar said, raising his eyebrows.

'I need to.' The reeve nodded. 'I keep the King's Peace among Danes who have settled in this land.'

'So we can leave?' Rothulf said.

'Not yet,' the reeve said. 'The viking rat has no honour.'

'Never mind, lord. At least you tried.'

Einar was surprised to hear Garwulf say these words. He glanced around and saw the young Saxon warrior was looking at him with a renewed respect.

'Don't worry, lads,' Einar said. 'I know these sort of men. If their leader falls the fight will go out of the crew.'

'Then all you need to do is beat that big bastard,' Oswald said. The worried smile on his lips told Einar that the reeve was far from confident in Einar's ability to do that.

He turned around and began to ready himself for the fight.

Einar had been to the holmgang twice before – once against his own father. This did not make what he faced any easier now, however. As he regarded his big opponent at the far end of the duelling square he felt the same old knot of fear tighten in his guts and sensed the strange, detached feeling of disbelief that crept into his mind along with the thought that he could well be living out the last few moments of his life.

With a sharp intake of breath through his nose, Einar looked away from Ljót and began making his own preparations. He grabbed his sword with his fighting glove, sliding the metal hooks that replaced his bottom fingers around the hilt as he drew it from its sheath, then fastening the two leather thongs that secured the weapon in his grasp with his free hand. He shrugged his shield from his back and hefted it in his left hand, then rolled his head around, loosening the tension that gripped the muscles in his shoulders and neck. He danced a few steps from side to side, trying to get his leg muscles ready for the coming fight.

After that Einar closed his eyes for a moment. His heart was pounding like the drum of a Finnish wizard loaded on mushrooms. He needed to try to calm it, otherwise he would be too excited, rush into combat and probably get himself killed fast.

When it had settled a little, Einar opened his eyes and saw that Ljót was taking the opposite approach. He took great snorts of air in through his nose, his lips contorting in a gurn of rage, his eye getting ever wider and more glaring. He shouted and roared at the air and all those around him as he struck his own chest with the flat of the axe. As his rage grew to boiling point the big man's eye rolled around in its socket like it was loose. He twisted his head and bit down on the iron rim of his shield, heedless of the hard metal. Blood and frothing spittle dribbled down the front of his shield.

'He's mad,' Garwulf said in a hushed, awed tone.

'He's a berserker,' Einar said, looking around and seeing the rest of his men were equally taken aback by the big man's display of insane rage. The reeve's men looked terrified.

Ljót began swiping the air with his axe, the heavy blade making a swooping sound like the wings of a swan taking off.

It would not be long before Ljót was unable to contain his rage. An expectant hush fell on all those watching, broken only by the ranting of Ljót and the rustle of the wind blowing gently through the gorse and seagrass.

Einar closed his eyes again for a moment and bowed his head, intending to say a quick prayer.

To who?

He could not call on Odin now. He had been one of Odin's úlfhéðnar but Einar had turned his back on all that when he betrayed Ulrich. The old one-eyed god would just laugh if Einar called on him now. He had not prayed to Thor for years and the big red-bearded god would scoff if he came crawling for his help now.

He thought of the monk, Cynewulf, watching with his heavily lined face, seeming so concerned, and Aethelstan, the king he now served. They would expect Einar to call on their Christ for help. Einar's mother had been a follower of the Christ. Was this now the time he should too?

At that moment Ljót sprang forwards, bellowing like an angry bull. His feet churned the sand as he charged straight at Einar, axe raised. Startled from his brief reverie, Einar knew he had to meet the onslaught head on or risk being bowled over by the sheer power and weight of his attacker. He just had time to clench his jaw and power forwards himself, meeting the big viking shield to shield just into his own half of the duelling area.

The shields collided with a loud slap of linden wood on linden. Einar felt his teeth rattle as the impact rippled through his right shoulder. His momentum stopped Ljót's charge but sent Einar staggering backwards a few steps himself.

Ljót swung his axe and Einar blocked the blow with his

shield. The blade bit the wood and as Ljót wrenched it free Einar swung at him with his sword. The big man countered with his own shield and Einar's attack was deflected.

With another roar, Ljót unleashed a flurry of blows, chopping with his axe once, twice, three times in quick succession. The strikes were heavy and fast and it was all Einar could do to block them with his shield. Each hit forced him to take one more step backwards.

Einar felt a jolt of panic as he realised he must be near the edge of the duelling area. He struck back, putting his left shoulder behind his shield and swiping over the top of it in a blow aimed at cutting Ljót's head in two from his crown to his chin.

The viking swept his shield upwards. Einar's blade struck the metal rim of it instead of Ljót's skull. The force of the blow dissipated, Einar's sword skidded sideways along the rim then rattled harmlessly off the mail rings covering Ljót's brawny left shoulder.

Einar ducked to the left, swerving around the big man into the open space behind him. He was desperate to create some space between them while he tried to work out how best to deal with so large an opponent who was both fast and powerful. He turned around only to see to his dismay that Ljót had already whirled around too. They faced each other once more.

Einar's left foot hit something on the ground provoking a rattle of metal. He glanced down and saw he had kicked the chest Ljót had been so careful to close before the fight began. He just had time to see that several silver discs had fallen out of it when Ljót began shouting at him.

'I am gifted by Odin! I am one of his chosen holy berserkers!' Ljót screeched, spittle flying from his mouth. 'I have the strength of ten men. Your weapons won't even scratch me. Prepare to die!'

Ljót attacked with another overhead blow. Einar blocked it with his shield but this time the big man raised his left foot, planted it on Einar's shield and shoved. Einar went staggering backwards a few paces and Ljót leapt forwards, raining another strike down from above.

This time Einar did not have time to raise his shield. The world exploded into a blinding flash of light as Ljót's axe smashed into Einar's helmet. The clang of metal on metal rang in his ears then Einar felt the warm breeze on his face and a sudden sensation of lightness on his neck as the helmet shattered, then disintegrated into three pieces.

Though now completely disorientated, Einar had trained so long and hard under Skarphedinn and the other úlfhéðnar that his reactions in a fight were instinctive. Even as he stumbled backwards, the splinters of his helmet tumbling to the ground, he raised his shield. He was just in time to block a follow-on strike from Ljót.

His vision clearing, Einar took a more deliberate step back, so as to create a little more space between him and the big man so he could regain his composure more fully.

Ljót had different ideas.

'We finish this now!' he yelled and came barrelling forwards, leading with his shield. He made no attempt to strike with his axe but put everything in using his weight and size to overpower Einar. The shields clattered together once more and Ljót flexed his powerful thighs and shoulders, grunting as he shoved Einar with all his might.

Still half dazed, this time Einar did not have the time to move forwards himself to meet Ljót. He had no momentum of his own to counter the big man's charge and was sent sprawling, his legs collapsing under him as he thumped into the sand, landing flat on his back.

Ljót threw himself onto Einar like a mountain lion pouncing on a fallen deer. Einar, already winded from the fall, felt the rest of his breath being driven from his chest as the big man landed on top of him.

Einar went to raise his sword but found he could not move his right hand. Panic rushed into his heart as he realised he was trapped under his own shield, his right arm and shield pinned down behind it. Ljót lay on top of him, pressing down with his own shield so Einar was held fast beneath him.

Ljót's face was now just inches from Einar's. He could see the cold madness in the viking's one eye and smell the stench of onions and sour ale from his breath. Ljót grinned and a string of spittle dripped from between his teeth onto Einar's chin.

Einar saw the viking bring his axe up. Lying on top of him, Ljót had no room to swing it, so instead began pushing the blade down towards Einar's now unprotected face.

Einar let go of his shield handle – there was no need to grip it now – and managed to wrench his left hand free from under the shield rim. Reaching up he grabbed Ljót's right wrist in an attempt to stop the descent of the axe.

Ljót was immensely strong, however, and all Einar could manage was to slow the blade. The viking kept on forcing it downwards towards Einar's face. In moments the sharp iron of the axe filled Einar's vision and he knew he was a mere finger's breadth from death.

Then Einar felt a sensation he had not experienced for some time. A rush of cold ran through his guts at the same time as he experienced a feeling like iced water gushing down his spine. Then both turned to blazing fires that coursed through his body like the molten lava that erupted from the mountainsides in his homeland of Iceland.

Rage overcame him. Screaming every bit as loud as Ljót

had, Einar strained his head forwards, sinking his teeth into the big man's neck. He bit hard, unleashing a torrent of hot blood that gushed around his lips and chin. Einar felt a savage thirst overcome his senses as he tried to gulp down the copper-smelling liquid.

Ljót's deep bellowing turned to an alarmed scream. He wrenched himself away from Einar, struggling up to his feet and leaving his shield behind as his left hand went to the bleeding wound Einar had bitten into the side of his neck.

Einar rose after him, thrilled to see the look of dismay on the big man's face. They faced each other once more, readying to continue the fight. Einar had lost his helmet and his ears still rang from the blow but at least he had both sword and shield. Ljót had lost his shield but he still had his axe.

The rage that burned in Einar urged him to lay into the big man, cut him down and hack him to death. However, his training and the wild look in Ljót's eye told him the viking was still dangerous and he needed to be wary.

Einar raised his sword and lunged forward. He led with his shield, presenting a wide, flat surface to Ljót with intent. Ljót came back at him. With no shield of his own, like before Ljót raised his left foot, intending to plant it on Einar's shield and send him reeling backwards out of control. The move had worked before: why not now again?

This time Einar was ready. As the big man raised his leg Einar brought his sword down. The blade caught Ljót at the top of his right shin just below the knee, severing the bottom of the viking's leg in one chop. As his foot and shin dropped to the ground, Ljót overbalanced and toppled sideways. A bright red jet of blood spurted from his severed knee as he went, splattering the shields and faces of many of those watching.

Ljót let out a curse as he glared in disbelief at his ruined leg.

He began to struggle to get back up but straight away collapsed back onto his side again. His face was already turning a ghastly white as his life blood gushed from the stump of his severed leg into the sand.

'Now you really are pale, Ljót,' Einar said.

A gasp of dismay rose from the assembled vikings who still surrounded them. At the same time the reeve's and Einar's men all cheered.

'Get them, lads!' Ljót tried to shout from the ground. 'Avenge me! Kill them all.'

His voice was a ghost of its former self and already little more than a wheeze. Still, many of the surrounding vikings hoisted their weapons and shields. They did not advance, however.

Seeing this, Einar stepped out of the duelling pitch. He glared all around at them, wild-eyed, his face a bloodied mask of screaming rage.

'Come on, you bastards!' Einar guldered. 'Come and fight a real warrior if you dare. You followed a berserker but I am an úlfheðinn.'

An audible gasp came from the watching vikings. Einar could see the sudden apprehension in their eyes. They began to look at each other instead of him and the Saxons.

'Come and die,' he roared at them. 'Come down here and I'll kill every last one of you!'

They did not come. Instead, the surrounding vikings grabbed what they could and made for the beach where their ship lay. The ones closest grabbed their still-hot cooking pots and whatever else they could hold. Bjarni with the impressive hair grabbed Ljót's chest of rattling metal and dashed after the others. When any of the Norsemen came close by, Einar bared his teeth at them and made a feint as if to attack, sending them scuttling off to ensure a wider berth.

Emboldened by this, some of the reeve's men made as if to chase them.

'Let them go,' Oswald said. 'They've no stomach for a fight now. They'll go as we asked and leave us alone. There's no need for further bloodshed, on *either* side.'

Einar's men crowded around him. They were grinning and all held a new look of respect in their eyes. Some patted him on the back.

Cynewulf the monk looked more reproachful.

'Good work today, lad,' he said in a begrudging tone. 'But I think I have more work to do in driving that old devil Woden out of you.'

As the danger receded the rage drained from Einar, leaving cold exhaustion and nausea behind. He saw dark spots swim before his eyes and swayed a little. He sat down with a heavy thump on the sand. As he did so a faint chuckle reached his ears from nearby.

Turning, Einar saw Ljót was still alive, though only barely. He lay on his side. The sand around his butchered leg was clogged and clumped with his spilled blood. He was deathly white and his one eye seemed to stare at something that was an impossible distance away. He still grinned though. One of his hands was outstretched and he had grasped a handful of the silver discs that Einar had knocked out of the chest by accident during the fight.

'It seems,' the viking said, his voice rasping and weak, 'that my crew weren't much use without me to lead them. We did well, though, until today. We were a fearsome band. But now my luck has run out. Old Odin has lived up to one of his many names today: *Glapsviðr*. The swift deceiver. He granted me the gift of his divine rage, a blessing that granted us so much plunder, but it also brought you, an úlfheðinn, against me. What is your name?'

Einar hung his head. Cooling sweat was dribbling down into his eyes.

'I am Einar, son of Unn,' he said. Then added: 'She was my mother. I am also son of Thorfinn the Skull Cleaver.'

'Thorfinn the mighty Jarl of Orkney?' the dying viking croaked. 'It is no shame to be killed by the son of such a hero.'

Einar spat.

'He was no hero,' he said through gritted teeth.

Ljót gave his little chuckle, though it was little more than a hiss now.

'I heard he was killed by his son,' Ljót said. 'That must be you. So it is double the honour to die at the hands of both the son of Thorfinn *Hausakljúfr* and the man who killed him. Odin will have a bench reserved for me in his Valour Hall. Well, Einar Thorfinnsson. As you have killed me, and because you are blessed by the High One, I will tell you this: change your path.'

'What do you mean?' Einar said.

'I don't know why an úlfheðinn of Odin serves a Christian *hundasson* like Aethelstan,' Ljót said. 'But his days are numbered.'

'I've heard that many times before,' Einar said. 'But Aethelstan still reigns. What's your real name, Ljót the Pale? There's nothing to gain in hiding it now.'

'My name,' the viking said, 'is Magnus Kjartinsson. Maybe you've heard of me? If not you soon will. They will sing songs of my deeds.'

'Kjartinsson?' Einar said. 'Your father was an Irishman? What are you doing here?'

'I served Olaf of Dublin,' Ljót the Pale – or rather Magnus Kjartinsson – said. 'He is coming to bring an end to Aethelstan.'

'What?' Einar said, his voice becoming urgent. Then he stopped, seeing that the viking had spoken his last words.

Ljót, or Magnus, let out a last, long gasp. His head slumped to the sand and his eye stared blindly at the embers of the fire. As he died, his right hand relaxed its grip and the silver discs rattled from it onto the ground.

Curious, Einar leaned over and picked one of them up. Turning it over in his hand he saw that one side was flat and smooth, while the other was embossed with the image of a large cross. He frowned. The discs looked very like coins, but with only one side decorated. Looking down he saw the others that spilled from the dead viking's hand were all the same.

A shadow cast on him made Einar look up. The reeve, his forehead creased with a look of concern, was also looking at the discs.

'What do you make of this?' Einar said. 'An Irish viking with a chest full of half-made coins. What can it mean?'

'I don't know,' Oswald the reeve said. 'But I think the king should hear about this.'

Part Three

Æthelstan King,
*   Lord among Earls,*
*   Bracelet-bestower and*
*   Baron of Barons*

'The Battle of Brunanburh',
translation by Alfred Lord Tennyson

Twelve

Wintanceaster, Kingdom of Wessex

It took three days to ride to Wintanceaster. Einar, at the head of his troop of eleven warriors and with Cynewulf the monk in tow, rode south from Jorvik along the old Roman road. Though still more passable than most of the other main trackways, the thoroughfare was crumbling into the ditches at the edges. Stretches of it had been robbed of stones, leaving nothing but beaten, pitted earth while other parts had fallen into potholes deep enough to hold pools of water even though it was summer.

The countryside was a rich green, abundant with growth and fertility. Flowers bloomed in the hedges and along the roadside, golden barley ripened in the fields and the air was warm and pleasant. Not for the first time Einar found he could understand why so many of his fellow Norsemen, growing up like him in the harsh northern weather of Norway or Iceland, would find Britain such an attractive place to settle.

As they were on the business of the king, at night they stayed in the *burhs* that enmeshed the country. These were a web of forts, each one garrisoned with a band of warriors and within easy riding distance of the next. If vikings attacked or any other trouble arose, a fighting force could be gathered quickly to confront the threat.

Einar was pleased that his war band now treated him with respect. The cold looks and suspicious expressions were gone and they seemed more content now to be led by someone they still thought of as a Dane, though perhaps no longer as one of the enemy.

Wintanceaster, the capital city of Wessex, was almost on the coast of the southern sea. It was guarded by stout, Roman-built stone walls and formidable gates. Seeing the approaching war band, the Saxon warriors at the main gate stopped Einar and his men to check what their business was. The guards recognised Cynewulf and let them in.

'I will go to find where the king is,' Cynewulf said. 'It will save us all traipsing around the town in a band. You all find somewhere to wait near the gate and I'll return when I find out where he is.'

Einar looked around at the street they now stood in. Not far away was a long thatched building with a broom hanging above the door.

'I think that looks like a tavern, lads,' he said to his men. 'What do you say we wait there?'

'I'd say that's a great idea, lord,' Garwulf said, grinning.

Cynewulf sighed and rolled his eyes.

They left their horses in the stable beside the tavern, then set off to taste its ale while the scowling monk Cynewulf went off in search of where they might find King Aethelstan.

To their dismay, they did not have much time to savour their beer. Hardly started on their third drink, Cynewulf returned. Einar saw the serious expression on the monk's face as soon as he arrived at their table.

'The king wants to speak to you right away, Einar,' Cynewulf said. 'I'm to take you to meet him.'

'Enjoy the ale, lads,' Einar said, rising from the mead bench. He tossed a small leather pouch full of coins onto the table, which rattled as it struck the wood. 'Get yourselves a few more on me.'

The others cheered as Einar and Cynewulf went back out of the tavern.

'When I showed the king what we found with that viking,' Cynewulf said, 'he got quite excited – as excited as you ever see the Lord Aethelstan.'

They headed off down the street. Einar had been in Wintanceaster several times now but he was still astonished by the wealth and opulence of the city. It far exceeded Dublin, Jorvik or even Hedeby in terms of prosperity and sophistication. The arrow-straight streets were paved with stones rather than the wooden planking Einar had walked on in other cities. Each street intersected the others like a net so it was impossible to get lost. Channels ran alongside each street, both bringing fresh water into the town and carrying its filth away so the reek of Wintanceaster was much less pungent than other cities, though the summer heat and the pools where some of the water gathered still raised an unpleasant number of flies to annoy the denizens of the town.

Some of the buildings that rose along the street sides towered as high as three storeys; a few of them were built of stone, the work of the Romans who had founded the city. This was something which made Einar a little queasy as he looked up at their soaring heights, wondering how all that heavy stone stayed upright. He fought the compulsion to hurry past lest they topple over into the street. Nevertheless he appreciated the craft with which the town had been constructed and the efficiency with which it was run. All of this, to Einar, was down to the unique vision and skill of the king at its heart: Aethelstan.

The noise was just as great as Jorvik or Dublin, however. The clatter of horses hooves and the rumbling of cart wheels on the paving stones, the babble of a thousand conversations, the clang of church bells and the cries of merchants as they hawked gold and silverware, shoes, jerkins, vegetables and all sorts of tools and weapons from their stalls mingled into one chaotic cacophony.

All in all the city was a suitable residence for one of the richest and most powerful kings in the known world.

They continued on through the city until they came to a long, low building made of stone that Einar recognised from previous visits. The walls were old, perhaps built by the Romans, and rugged at the top as if they had once been much higher but they had fallen or had their stones robbed away from them. The roof was quite flat and covered by heavy thatch that was not the original covering, adding to the impression that the building had been repurposed. Einar had passed by this building twice before while in the city. On the first occasion he had seen thick smoke drifting from the roof and smelled the tang of hot metal, unmistakable to someone like him who had spent time working in a blacksmith's workshop. The impression that it was a forge was increased on the second occasion when he walked by and heard the distinct sound of metal being hammered. The odd thing was, however, that there was no smoke or smell of molten iron on the day of the hammering.

Whatever the purpose the place fulfilled, Einar had not been able to find out as every time he passed by it was heavily guarded. No less than twenty warriors, armed and ready for battle, surrounded the walls and blocked the doors. As soon as anyone walked too close or paid too much attention to the building the warriors sprung alert like guard dogs, glaring to deter any further incursion.

Einar's curiosity was piqued when Cynewulf strode towards this building. It seemed this was their destination.

As they got closer Einar saw that it was even more well protected than usual. A contingent of extra warriors, resplendent in shining mail and polished embossed helmets with plumes of horsehair or fur lounged around outside the large double doors of the low building. Their uniform red cloaks told Einar these were men of Aethelstan's personal dryht, the war band who protected the king. They looked relaxed now but Einar knew that every man was a well-trained killer. Even here in the heart of the main city of Wessex, their eyes flicked across everyone who passed by, assessing each one for any potential threat.

This meant the king was in this building, which made Einar even more curious. At the same time he felt his heart dip a little at the sight of the warriors. While it was their job to suspect everyone who tried to approach the king, this band of men had always shown particular animosity to him as a Norseman. Having just overcome the hostility of his own men, he did not relish renewed antagonism with Aethelstan's.

'Lads,' Cynewulf said, holding up his hand in greeting as they approached the doors.

The warriors knew the monk well and their leader greeted him with a smile.

'Still playing wet nurse to that Dane I see, Cynewulf,' he said, casting a derisive glance in Einar's direction.

Einar clenched his teeth and did his best to suppress the anger spurred by the man's casual prejudice.

'I've told you before,' Einar said, meeting the warrior's gaze with a glare of his own. 'I'm an Icelander, not a Dane.'

'Icelanders, Norwayans, Swedes, Geats,' the Saxon warrior said with a shrug. 'Whatever. You're all just Danes to me. Heathen pirates and vikings who want to steal our country.'

'The Lord loves all his children equally,' Cynewulf said with a placatory smile. 'Even the wayward ones. My task is to bring this one into His fold. Now the king wants to see him.'

The bodyguard straightened his back.

'Very well,' he said. 'But we need to search him for weapons.'

Cynewulf caught the spark of rage in Einar's eyes and held up his hands, palms towards the leader of the dryht.

'There will be no need for that, Ine,' he said. 'I can vouch for him. You've seen him many times and know he's not a threat to the king.'

The Saxon warrior looked at the monk for a long moment, then sighed and nodded.

'Very well,' he said. 'But it will be on your head if there is any trouble.'

He turned to Einar.

'The king has some purpose for you, Dane,' Ine continued, 'and while I do not question his judgement I can't for the life of me understand it. But his will must be followed.'

He stepped aside to let them get to the doors.

As Cynewulf led the way into the building Einar wondered yet again what sort of past this monk had lived through that hardened warriors showed him such trust and respect.

Inside it was dark and ill-lit. Einar squinted as his eyes became accustomed to the gloom. After a moment he spotted a group of figures at the far end of the long room they had entered. Einar had not seen most of them before; however, the man standing in the centre of them, conversing, he recognised straight away.

It was Aethelstan, King of Wessex and Mercia, King of all the Angles and the Saxons and Emperor of all Britain.

Thirteen

The inside of the building had the look of a workshop or craftsman's shed. As well as the glow of the fire, there were several lamps that allowed Einar to see long tables scattered with discarded tools and leather chests of various sizes all bound with iron. There were also stout barrels set on the floor.

Five men worked with hammers at one of the tables and the raised fire beside them filled with red-glowing embers strengthened Einar's suspicion that this was some sort of forge. On the other hand the fire merely smouldered. It would have blazed red hot if metal-working was going on. The way the men with the hammers worked was odd too. When Einar had worked in a smithy the objective had been to work as fast as possible, battering the hot metal into shape with a series of rapid blows before it cooled too much to be malleable. These men set something on the table before them, took careful aim, then struck it with a single, deliberate blow. Each strike filled the air with a ring of metal smacking metal, then the workman lifted something from where he had struck and set it aside.

Standing near them was Aethelstan. The king was dressed in everyday clothes, no gold or silver, though the wool and soft leather his garments were made from was of the finest quality. Even in the gloom Einar could see they were dyed vibrant colours, which showed how expensive they were. Around his shoulders he wore a red cloak like his bodyguards. Aethelstan was a little taller than Einar and still good-looking, though the lines on his face and the white strands that streaked the brown of his hair and long, Aenglisc-style moustache showed he was in the middle years of his life.

Two others stood beside him. Their muscled arms and the long leather aprons they wore suggested they were workmen, perhaps blacksmiths or butchers. As usual, Aethelstan was the focus of all attention. Einar had noticed that about the king. Whatever you thought of him, there was no doubt that he had a presence that commanded folk to listen to his words and follow his directions. The two men in the aprons stood, arms folded, attention fixed on Aethelstan as he talked, nodding their agreement every now and again. As Cynewulf and Einar approached the king broke off and turned to greet them.

'You asked me to bring Lord Einar here, lord?' the monk said with a bow of his head.

'Ah! Cynewulf,' Aethelstan said. 'How is the civilisation of our pagan friend here coming along?'

Cynewulf blew out his cheeks and made a pained expression.

'I'm doing my best, Lord King,' he said.

'Then I can ask no more of you than that,' Aethelstan said. 'A carpenter can only work with the wood he is given. I take it from your looks that Einar here is not the most avid of learners?'

'He does his best, lord,' the monk said. 'But he lacks attention and tends to get bored easily.'

He glanced sideways at Einar and heaved a heavy sigh.

'To be honest,' the monk went on, 'I'd have to admit I was probably the same at his age.'

'Weren't we all, Cynewulf?' the king said, nodding. Then he too turned his attention to Einar.

'I have great hopes for you, Einar lad,' Aethelstan said.

'I believe that you could serve as an example to my rebellious subjects in the north. You could show how a heathen follower of Woden can be civilised and become a good Christian. You could teach those who live under the Dane Law to stop looking overseas where their forefathers came from for their leadership and realise their home is now here in Britain, within my empire.'

'I will try not to let you down, Lord King,' Einar said, straight away. He was surprised by his own eagerness to please the king. The strange, compelling power of Aethelstan's presence was affecting him too.

'See that you don't,' the king said. 'One day I could let you rule a district in the north in my name. What better way to show my people there that you can be a Dane and a Christian? That there is room for all in my new Aengland? Would you want that? What would you say to maybe even sitting on the throne of Jorvik?'

Einar's eyes widened. Jorvik was an immensely wealthy trading city; that was why there was so much fighting over who ruled there. Its ruler would control that wealth, and be entitled to a portion of it himself. If he ruled Jorvik he could command an army. Perhaps he could even take back his birthright, his father's Jarldom of Orkney that had been stolen by Eirik 'Bloody Axe' Haraldsson.

What would Affreca think of that? Jorvik was her birthright just as Orkney was his. It was her ambition to rule there. Her brother wanted Jorvik too. When he had parted ways with the Wolf Coats he knew there would be no going back, no chance of reconciliation. If he took the throne of Jorvik then someday he could well have to fight both of them for it. It would be one more reason for Affreca to want to kill him.

Perhaps he and Affreca could form an alliance? They could

rule Jorvik together. The best way to do that – his heart began to beat faster – would be through a marriage agreement.

Was Aethelstan serious? Or was this just supposed to make him do Aethelstan's bidding? These sort of enticements were often thrown before men by kings so that those men would think they were pursuing their own goals rather than being led by the nose by the king.

'I won't do that before I'm sure you can be trusted, Einar,' Aethelstan said. 'I'm relying on Cynewulf here to judge that your heart has truly been opened to Christ. Then perhaps you will be ready for more responsibility.'

The king locked his gaze with Einar. As usual when this happened, Einar felt as if he were frozen in place, unable to tear his look away from Aethelstan's dark brown eyes, suffering the uncomfortable sensation like the king was looking straight into his heart.

'We shall see,' Aethelstan said after a moment. 'But that is for the future. Right now we have a mystery to solve. How you do that will demonstrate to me just how loyal you are. Also how resourceful.'

'What is it, lord?' Einar said. Already he felt a gnaw of unease in his guts.

'What do you know about coining?' Aethelstan said, sweeping his arm towards the table with the five men hammering at it.

Einar realised now what the purpose of the building was. It was a money workshop. One end of the table was piled with metal discs that glinted silver and bronze in the light from the fire and the lamps. The faces of the discs were smooth. Each worker took a blank disc, set it onto an iron mould. The workman then set another metal die on top. He then struck it a single blow with a heavy hammer. As he lifted the top off Einar saw that the metal disc was now stamped with a design. The workman lifted it from the mould and cast it onto a mound of other coins at the opposite end of the table. There, a couple of slave boys scooped them up and poured them into an open chest that sat on the floor.

This explained the armed guards who watched the building day and night. Coineries were important buildings. For kingdoms that used money, this was the source of all the wealth in the land.

Aethelstan lifted one of the coins and passed it to Einar. The metal was cold, which explained another thing: why smoke from the forge and the smell of hot metal only came from this place on certain days. They must have smelted the blank coins on certain days, then hammered the designs into them on the other days.

Einar turned the coin over in his hand. One side had a large cross stamped on it, the other the stylised portrait of a human head wearing some sort of helmet, which was supposed to be the king. Around the edges on both sides were the runes the Christians used, the only part of which Einar could read was those representing the king's name, *ATHELSTN*.

'Coins are power, Einar,' Aethelstan said. 'Every time anyone in the kingdom buys or sells anything they do it with the king's coins. They know it is the king who permits their business and on each coin they see the king's head. There is no doubt who rules the kingdom.'

'Like that Great Beast Cynewulf talks about,' Einar said. 'The one from your magic lore? No one can buy or sell without its mark? Its number is six hundred and sixty-six.'

Aethelstan glared at Einar in consternation for a moment, then looked sideways at Cynewulf.

'I see what you mean,' he said to the monk. 'He has a lot to learn yet.'

He turned his attention back to Einar.

'But understand this... Only the king must make the coins in his kingdom,' Aethelstan said. 'And he must keep an iron grip on their supply. Only the king's coins are accepted in the kingdom. If everyone started making their own then the king's become worthless. And the king's worth will diminish with the value of his coins. One king, one coinage. That is the way it works.'

Einar looked down at the coin again, considering how strange the craft of money really was. His mother, a Christian woman from Ireland, had once told him that the gods of the Norsemen only existed because people believed they existed. Nevertheless, she had allowed her son to be brought up in the faith and customs of the Aesir. She recognised that having a mother who was the former bed slave of the Jarl of Orkney would be enough to make Einar stand out as different – with all the unwanted attention that would bring – without adding a different religion as well.

Looking at the coin in his hand now, Einar thought how money was not that much different. It was a mixture of silver and other cheaper metals like tin. It was not actually worth the value men put in it. Unlike the long strip of pure silver wound around his own forearm. Norsemen like him paid for goods with real silver from bands like these. When they wanted to buy something they hacked off pieces of the band until it met the agreed weight the goods were worth. Their bands were real silver. Or gold, though that was usually in a purse or chest. Kings and jarls could get away with wearing gold arm rings, but in the sort of places Einar travelled to, walking around with one of those on was a quick way to lose an arm.

The value of these coins, however, lay in the faith men put in them, and therefore the king who made them. It was like witchcraft. Or mass delusion.

'Now take a look at this,' Aethelstan said. 'It's one of those you and Cynewulf brought with you.'

He flicked his thumb, sending another metal disc spinning through the air; Einar snatched it and looked at it as it nestled in his palm. It was one of the coins they had taken from Ljót the Pale. With a start Einar saw that while one side was smooth and blank, the cross stamped on the other was identical to one embossed on the coin with *ATHELSTN* on its reverse side.

'A task half done?' Einar said.

'You say those vikings had a chest of these?' Aethelstan said. Einar nodded.

'They took the rest with them, I'm afraid,' Einar said. 'We were outnumbered, lord. We were lucky to—'

The king held up his hand, the gesture enough to halt Einar talking.

'There is nothing to apologise for or explain,' he said. 'In fact I heard your actions saved the whole company. But if there are more of these then this is not good.'

'You think someone in the north is making their own coins?' Einar said.

'Coining used to be a free-for-all in this land,' Aethelstan said. 'Every bishop, thane or petty king in the land thought they could make their own. It was a disaster. There was no way to control the money in the kingdom. A loaf of bread in one shire might cost three times what it did in the next. I pulled everyone altogether at the Witan at Great Leigh. Since then there has been only one head on every coin the land: mine. Coins are only made in my coineries. I don't want things going back to the way they were.'

And if someone put their own head on those coins, Einar thought, *it would be a direct challenge to your power.*

'I want you to go back to the north and find out who is behind this,' Aethelstan said.

'Why me?' Einar said.

'My men are Saxons. The folk up there still treat them like an occupying army,' the king said. 'But you are a Norsemen like most of them – at least in traditions anyway. You speak the same tongue. You can move among them without suspicion.'

Einar winced at the thought that these were the very words Aethelstan had used when he had persuaded Ulrich to take the Wolf Coats to northern west Francia earlier that year. Was this all he really was to Aethelstan? Someone who could spy on his own folk?

'Why not ask Sweyn?' Einar said. 'He seems a decent, reliable fellow. And he is a Norseman just like me. Well, his father was, anyway. He was a nobleman of Northumbria too.'

'Unfortunately Sweyn is in Francia with most of my fleet,' Aethelstan said. 'Besides, there is a complicating factor which means he cannot do this task for me. Tell me: why do you think this building is so well guarded?'

'Because of all the coins in it,' Einar said.

'Partly, yes,' Aethelstan said. 'But there is something here even more valuable. I told you only the king can make the coins for his kingdom, but it would be impossible for me to make them all here in this one coinery. So there is one coin workshop in each borough of my realm. How do we ensure the coins made in those other places are authentic, though? How can the folk place their faith in them that they are my coins?'

Einar shrugged.

The king reached across the work bench and lifted one of the metal dies the coiners were using. He held it up so Einar could see the raised image on it of Aethelstan's head – the mirror of what it stamped into the coins it made.

'Each one of these dies was handmade by the most skilled of craftsmen,' Aethelstan said. 'It is almost impossible to replicate and each coin workshop in the kingdom has two of them. If a coin is made with one of these dies then you know it is authentic. However, if someone got their hands on one of these dies then they could make their own money. This is why coineries are so closely guarded. The only folk with access to the coin workshops are the highest in society. If you look at those one-sided coins you will note that the side with the cross was stamped with an official die. Which means those one-sided coins were either made in a royal workshop, or someone got access to one of the royal dies.'

'You suspect someone from the nobility?' Einar said.

Aethelstan shrugged. 'Such treachery would sadden my heart, but one thing I have learned in my years on the throne: greed can twist the whitest of hearts. If there is a traitor then I want you to find him for me.'

'Lord, there is something else,' Einar said. 'Perhaps more urgent than these half-baked coins. The viking I killed—'

'Ah yes, the notorious Ljót the Pale,' Aethelstan said. 'I was told about that. Good work.'

'He told me Olaf of Dublin is coming to Britain,' Einar went on. 'When I left Ulrich his crew were sailing to Ireland. The rumour was that Olaf was preparing for war, to take back Jorvik where his father once ruled. If he has crossed the sea now it can only mean his invasion has started.'

'Can it only mean that?' Aethelstan said. 'You forget, Einar, I have spies who watch my enemies. I have it on good authority – the word of Bishop Dub Inse of Bangor no less – that Olaf is travelling to Scotland to marry the daughter of the king of Alba. An alliance of two of my strongest enemies, true, but Olaf's intentions are dynastic, not belligerent.'

'All the same—' Einar said.

'Don't fret about this,' Aethelstan said, cutting him off with a wave of his hand as if trying to waft away a stink. 'I have set four doughty men as jarls to rule north of the Humber river. They are good men. One, Alfgeir, is of Danish heritage like you. They hold that land for me to provide a bulwark, a rampart against any invasion from Scotland. If Constantine makes any move south, Ingwar, Ethils, Alfgeir and Guthrek will fight him. They'll beat the Scots or at least slow them down enough to give me time to come north with the army of Wessex.'

Einar's mouth fell open a little. He recalled the board game he had once played against the king. Aethelstan had been many moves ahead of him at all times and beaten him easily. His statecraft was just the same.

'Einar, I hope someday you learn this for yourself,' the king said, 'but the life of any man who rules is made up of fighting one fire after another. Which one he chooses depends on how fiercely it is burning and how much harm it causes. Right now the situation in Francia is at a very delicate stage. Thanks to the work you did with Ulrich's crew, Count William of Rouen has pledged his support for my nephew Louis. Louis can now, with the support of my fleet of ships, take the throne of Francia but there are still some who oppose him. Right now that is the fire that I must concentrate on dealing with. However, these coins are also important. Someone is directly challenging my authority and I need to know who. Will you ride north and find out who is doing this?'

Einar thought for a moment, then realised Aethelstan was not really asking him. What the king wanted, the king got.

'The northern realms are a large place,' Einar said. He did not add that those former kingdoms between Jorvik and the border with the Scots also had a reputation as wild, lawless and dangerous. 'It's quite a lot for only twelve men.'

'The good news is that there are only two coineries,' the king said. 'Jorvik and Ad Gefrin. And to help you further all the most powerful men – the ones with access to the coin workshops – will be gathering at Ad Gefrin for the northern Witan.'

Einar frowned and looked at Cynewulf.

'The Witan is a gathering of wise and powerful men,' the monk explained. 'A moot. They meet several times throughout the year to settle disputes and decide on matters of statecraft. There are several throughout the country.'

'So it's like the *þing* in Iceland?' Einar said. 'If powerful men are involved then I will need more than my war band of twelve.'

'I'll make sure you get the help you need, don't worry,' Aethelstan said. 'Right now I need you to get back up north and start work.'

'All right,' Einar said.

'Excellent!' Aethelstan beamed from ear to ear. 'Though I think I would prefer it if I could get some sort of more binding assurance that you have at least moved a little way from your heathen beliefs. Have you been prime signed?'

'At least twice, Lord King,' Einar said, unable to suppress a smile. 'I believe my Christian name is "Peter".'

Christian kings were not supposed to take heathens into their armies. Yet some of the most fearsome warriors came from the pagan lands, so a system had arisen where heathens could enter service with a Christian army if he went through a ritual of being anointed and blessed by a priest. It was a cynical practice that Norsemen like Einar referred to as 'having a wash', but it saved face on both sides and worked out to the advantage of all.

'Yes, that's right,' Aethelstan said, the smile fading from his lips. 'It means little to you Danes, does it? I think this time we will need something more binding. Come with me to the minster.'

Fourteen

They left the coining workshop and Aethelstan's bodyguards accompanied them back across the town until they reached the open space in front of the old minster – or rather the cathedral – that dominated the buildings around it with its imposing bulk. There was a tower that housed bells, which was painted on the outside with strange Christian images of flying people with wings and humans being tortured. There was a mound to one side of the square where law cases were heard and decided. There was no court today so the crowd was not so thick there, and there was no need to shove their way through. At the sight of the king and his company of warriors the folk all stepped aside, bowing their heads in respect.

Once across the square the little company went through the large double doors that formed the entrance to the church. Inside, Einar felt straight away the strange sense of hush that permeated the air in these Christian temples. It was as if the residue of the combined prayers and reverence of countless people over many decades somehow gathered above and hung in the air. Einar remembered the same sort of atmosphere in the *hofs* of his homeland where the folk made sacrifice to the gods, except somehow the stone walls of the Christian churches seemed to enclose and intensify the feeling.

They strode to the far end of the church, where the stone

table the Christians used for their blood ritual stood. Aethelstan spoke to a monk there who hurried away, going to a door at the side wall of the church. The small entrance was barred by iron railings which the monk unlocked. Einar caught a glimpse of the shimmer of gold and silver in the room beyond as the monk went inside. He knew these Christian churches housed treasures of enormous value – that was why vikings loved to raid them – and wondered just what fabulous jewel-encrusted bauble the monk would emerge with. To his surprise, when the monk came back, he was carrying a spear. It had a long, heavy blade with two spiked wings protruding from it at the point where the head was fastened to the shaft. It looked a little old-fashioned, an impression bolstered by the discoloration of the weapon which was so dark it was almost brown.

The monk returned with careful steps, carrying the spear in both hands, his eyes wide and staring as if what he bore was as fragile and precious as a newborn baby. With trembling hands he laid it on the altar then withdrew, visibly relieved to no longer have the spear in his hands.

'This is the lance of Charlemagne,' Aethelstan said, his voice cracking a little.

Einar remembered Ulrich's contempt any time the name of Charlemagne was mentioned. He was the fanatic Christian king who had beheaded four and half thousand Saxons in one day because they refused to accept his lordship and his religion.

Einar glanced at Aethelstan, a little surprised at how he – the king of the West Saxons – could hold a relic associated with such a bloody tyrant in high regard. The Saxons of Britain had lived there perhaps four hundred winters now but they were still of one blood with those who had remained in their ancient homeland across the sea. They were still their kin. Their tongues were not that different. Could religion ever be more important than that?

'Charlemagne bore this lance into battle,' Aethelstan said. 'But he was not the first to do so. Constantine the Great, the first Christian Roman Emperor, carried it into the battle of the Milvian Bridge. *In Hoc Signo Vinces!*'

Einar gave the king a blank look.

'Before Constantine, Saint Maurice carried the lance,' Aethelstan said, 'and a line of Christian warriors that stretches right back to Saint Longinus.'

Seeing the look of incomprehension on Einar's face, Aethelstan glanced towards Cynewulf.

'Cynewulf really does have a lot to teach you,' the king said. 'Longinus, Einar, was the Roman soldier who was there when our Lord Jesus hung on the tree of pain, his side pierced by a spear. A spear that was most probably this very one I hold before you now!'

Einar really was confused now. It was Odin who hung from the tree, his side slashed with a spear. As the words of the High One himself taught:

'*I know I hung on that windy tree*
nine whole days and nights,
stabbed with a spear, offered to Odin,
myself to myself sacrificed'

Was Aethelstan confusing Odin with Jesus? Then again, Aethelstan had once told Ulrich he was a direct descendant of Woden, the name the Saxons used for Odin.

'I want you to swear an oath on the spear, Einar,' the king said, fixing Einar with his gaze. The look was challenging, confrontational. This was an order not a request. 'Swear that you will serve me faithfully. That you will reject the Devil and follow Christ.'

Einar reached out to touch the ancient old spear then stopped, his hand hovering in the air above it as if its metal blazed red hot. An oath was not something to be entered into lightly. It was the most binding, important thing a man could undertake in his lifetime. A man's word was his bond. At least any man who wanted to preserve any shred of honour that may remain in this blood-soaked world of backstabbers and murderers. To break an oath was the ultimate shame.

A lonely place in Hel's realm, the cold, dark kingdom that lay somewhere northwards and netherwards, was reserved for those who broke oaths. The valiant dead lived on in Odin's Valour Hall, the unworthy dead – the cowards, the shirkers and the oath breakers – ended up with Hel.

That aside, a person's worth, how he was regarded by others, his *drengskapr* – all depended on whether he kept his oaths or not.

A familiar feeling overcame Einar. It was a strange, dream-like sensation as if the world around him had slowed down, but he continued to think and move at his normal pace. He knew somehow that how he acted in the next few moments would be crucial. Every time he had felt like this in the past, however, his life had been in danger – in battle or under similar life-threatening assault where whatever movement he made next could either save him or be his last.

Somehow Einar knew that this was a similar situation. Whatever he did next would change things forever and it was this that inspired the same itchy-scalped sensation that usually overcame him as he charged into combat.

He had once sworn an oath of loyalty to Ulrich and the Wolf Coats. Had he forsaken that? He had left them, yes, but he had not broken any direct commands. He had not put himself in conflict with them. He had just walked away. But now a war was coming. Olaf of Dublin would attack Britain sooner or later. An oath of allegiance to Aethelstan would put him firmly on the opposite side to the Wolf Coats in the coming battle. What would happen then? Could he fight against his former shipmates? The thought both awed and terrified him.

I made my choice, Einar thought. *I chose to walk away because I believed what Aethelstan stood for was better than the chaos and endless bloodshed Odin stirred in the world.*

It was time to make the final commitment. Once he took this step there would be no going back.

Einar closed his eyes and took a deep breath. Then he grasped the blade of the ancient spear. To his half surprise the metal did not throb with energy. Instead it was cold and smooth beneath his right hand.

He started as an iron-like grasp seized his hand as it gripped the spear. Einar opened his eyes to see the king had laid his hand on his.

'Do you swear on all you hold dear and all that's holy to follow my commands?' Aethelstan said in a demanding tone as he glared into Einar's eyes, his face stern.

Einar blinked. Was there also a hint of triumph or uncertainty in the king's voice?

'I swear,' he said without hesitation. He felt as if the king were drawing the words from his mouth as a fisherman hauls a net full of catch into his boat.

'And do you swear that will you be true and faithful, love all which I love and shun all which I shun, according to the laws of God and the order of the world?' Aethelstan said. 'That you will guard my life as if it were your own?'

'I swear,' Einar said.

'And do you swear to reject Satan and all his works?' the king said.

'I swear,' Einar said.

'And the same for the demons Thunraer and Woden and all those devils who are their followers and put your trust in God the Almighty Father alone?'

'I do,' Einar said. He felt a strange chill in his guts at the names of Thunraer and Woden – Thor and Odin.

'And do you swear to be my shield and defend my life with your sword on the field of battle or wherever danger arises,' the king continued. 'And if I fall to seek revenge for me even unto your own death?'

Einar swallowed, uncomfortable both with the intensity of the king's words and the severity of the oath he was taking. It was too late to back out now, however.

'I swear,' he said.

'Good,' Aethelstan said. Einar felt the iron-like grip on his hand relax. 'Then enter my service as my oathsworn man. I swear to look after you and your loved ones. My advantage will be your advantage. My gains will be your gains.'

The king raised his hand and Einar let go of the spear. He suddenly felt dizzy and tired, as if he had been holding his breath all the while.

'Now ride back north,' Aethelstan said. 'And find out who is stealing my money. Whoever it is, you will be going against a powerful enemy. Good luck and may God go with you.'

Part Four

Come haste to the wedding ye friends and ye neighbours

Traditional Scots-Irish song

Fifteen

Scone, just outside Sankt John's Toun,
North-East Scotland

Skarphedinn – Skar to his friends – took a hefty swig from his drinking horn then let out a loud, appreciative sigh.

'This is more like it, eh Ulrich?' he said, elbowing his little, balding leader who sat on the bench beside him. 'Food. Drink. Lots of pretty girls. I do love a wedding!'

Ulrich scowled.

'I can't see this particular marriage lasting long,' he said. 'The husband already has two wives for a start and the bride looks like she was dragged here kicking and screaming.'

The two Wolf Coats sat at the end of one of many long tables set up on a meadow near a low ceremonial mound to celebrate the wedding of Olaf 'the Red' Guthfrithsson, King of Dublin to Eithne, daughter of Constantine, King of Alba. The tables thronged with nobles and important folk from the two kingdoms. They feasted on meat, vegetables and bread all washed down with a magnificent – in Skar's opinion – specially brewed bridal ale. It was high summer and a warm sun shone overhead, though they were still in the north-east of Scotland and two rain showers so far had sent the gathered assembly scurrying for shelter. However, when they passed, the rain had only enhanced the warm, pleasant air with the added aroma of the wet grass. The meadow was green turning to yellow. Wild flowers danced amid the grass, enriching the scene with both their colours and their scents. Not far away was a stone building, a Christian chapel, surrounded by many little round huts. A group of men hovered outside one of the huts on the edge of the meadow, watching the proceedings with eager, excited expressions. They were strange-looking fellows who had their heads shaved at the front all the way up to their crowns. Their eyes were painted with black all around and they all wore the same long, plain robes.

'I've never understood, Ulrich,' Skar said casting a glance in their direction, 'why monks in Ireland and Scotland look so different to monks in the south of Britain. And why do these ones live in those little huts that look like beehives?'

Ulrich shrugged and tutted.

'It's something to do with when their Christ died,' he said. 'As far as I understand it, the ones in the south think it was one day in spring; the Scots think it was a different day. So they shave their heads in a different way and live in beehives, just to make sure everyone knows they disagree. Idiots. Can you imagine what Odin would think if we got on like that? He would laugh. Their God probably does too, if he ever laughs at anything. Or even exists.'

The riot of colours that came from the flowers was echoed in the clothes the most important guests wore, their many colours proclaiming the wealth and social status of those in them. These folk sat at a long top table that was on slightly higher ground and set across the ends of all the other tables so that everyone could observe those who sat there. In the middle were the bride and groom – Olaf and his new bride Eithne. She wore a crown of fresh flowers and both were clad in the finest of wool garments. Olaf was wearing the formal dress of men in Ireland and Scotland of a rich, felted over-cloak pinned at the shoulder by ostentatious round brooches and short kirtles that left their shins bare.

'I don't see what's wrong with britches,' Ulrich said from the corner of his mouth. 'It's hard to tell the bride from the groom when they're both wearing skirts.'

Much to their annoyance, the rest of the Wolf Coat crew – Starkad, Kari, Sigurd, Wulfhelm the Saxon, Surt and Roan the skipper – were missing the feast. With the rest of Olaf's war horde they were with their ships several miles away on the coast. Only the nobility were invited to the wedding and King Constantine was far from happy with the idea of a whole viking army being there.

Ulrich and Skar, as leaders among the army, had been given seats at a table just adjacent to the top table. The other guests at their table stayed away from the wolfskin-clad warriors, keeping to their own conversations and seldom daring to meet the vikings' eyes.

Skar smirked as he regarded the rest of the most important wedding guests.

Constantine, King of Alba, and his wife sat next to the newlywed couple. The old king had long white hair and beard that cascaded around his shoulders and down his chest. What was visible of his cheeks was flushed red from the ale he had drunk but his eyes were sharp despite the sixty winters he had been on earth. It took a lot of craft and luck to survive that long on the throne and the way he glanced around him, always aware of what was going on, a half-smile on his lips, showed age had dulled none of his wits.

A Christian bishop, identifiable by the shepherd's crook that rested against his seat back, his large silver cross and his gold threaded robes, sat on the other side of Olaf and Eithne. His head was shaved in a different manner to the other watching monks and Skar judged that meant he was from the south of Britain perhaps. He looked uncomfortable with the revelry going on around him. The rest of the table was made up of Olaf Scabby Head of Limerick, two more Dublin noblemen as well as Scottish and Irish (who were basically the same people as far as Skar could discern) noblemen and women, along with a few others whose arms and faces were decorated all over with tattoos of stylised patterns and twisting beasts. They looked as happy at being at the wedding as the bishop was.

'Have you ever seen such a gathering of enemies?' Ulrich said. 'The only thing they have in common is their hatred of Aethelstan. Those Picts with the tattoos hate the Irish.'

He nodded towards Constantine.

'Or the Gaels as they call themselves,' he continued, 'because the Irish have stolen half of this country from them,' Ulrich continued. 'They hate us Norsemen because they are taking the other half. Olaf is the embodiment of both. They only swore loyalty to Constantine to avoid annihilation. Constantine says he'll unite Gaels and Picts but they all know it's just a matter of time before he wipes them out.'

Ulrich pointed at Olaf the Red.

'Constantine fought a battle against Olaf's father not far from here, maybe twenty winters ago,' Ulrich said. 'Olaf himself raided all up and down the west coast of Alba last summer. Now they're all one big happy family,' Ulrich said. 'Odin himself could not have come up with such mischief.'

'I can see now why they insisted everyone surrenders their weapons,' Skar said, glancing towards a large, well-guarded tent near the monks' huts where every wedding guest had been compelled to leave their swords, shields, helmets, knives and any other implements of harm they carried.

'We're taking quite a risk letting the Gaels take our weapons,' Skar said, an uneasy expression creeping onto his face. 'I hope Olaf knows what he's doing. The Scots and Irish are famous for turning weddings into massacres. I hope old Constantine isn't plotting something similar.'

'If he is we're all dead,' Ulrich said. 'Constantine's men are closest. I been watching. They surround this meadow. The rest of Olaf's war horde are back at the ships.'

'Well at least Olaf seems content enough with all this,' Skar said. The big, red-haired king of Dublin had a large ale horn in one hand and a chunk of venison in the other. Grease and ale foam flecked his ginger moustache and beard as he grinned like a ship's cat at the start of a voyage when it realises all the mice on board are now his. 'Look at him. He looks like Thor himself sitting up there. I suppose Thor had no problem feasting in the halls of his enemies.'

'Odin takes the noble who fall in battle,' Ulrich said. 'Thor owns the slaves. Olaf's a gambler. We saw that from his raid on Olaf Scabby Head. If that had gone wrong his whole plan would have collapsed. This wedding is another throw of the dice for him. If it pays off, he's one step closer to victory. If it goes wrong, he loses everything.'

'You think we're betting on the wrong horse in this fight?' Skar said. 'Maybe Einar was right? Aethelstan will be the victor in all of this.'

Ulrich scowled.

'I'd rather die on the wrong side than help that Christian tyrant win,' he said through gritted teeth. 'And I told you: we don't mention the traitor's name. He's dead to us.'

'He will be for real if Affreca bumps into him,' Skar said. 'How do you think she's getting on?'

'She's a capable woman,' Ulrich said. 'And she follows orders. Doesn't think too much about *why* she's been told to do something. She just gets on with it. Not like that other one, the traitor. I've no doubts she'll be successful.'

'That's quite a compliment, coming from you,' Skar said, hiding the mischievous smile on his lips by taking another drink of ale. 'Perhaps this wedding has put you in mind of a second wife for yourself?'

Ulrich glared at Skar, teeth bared.

'I had a wife,' he said, his voice a snarl. 'She's dead. I don't need another.'

Skar raised his eyebrows and sat back, deciding not to provoke his little leader any further. They had been friends for many years but Ulrich was a very volatile character. When he lost his temper he was truly frightening and Skar knew from experience just how far he could push him.

He looked away, his gaze travelling around the other assorted wedding guests. A band of about twenty men standing at the weapons tent caught his eye. From their britches and tunics, as well as the war gear, he could see they were Norsemen, and not the sort that had adopted the dress of the locals. They were arguing with Constantine's warriors, who barred the way to wedding feast.

Leaning forward, Skar closed his right hand over Ulrich's left wrist that rested on the table. Ulrich started and looked around at his prowman. Knowing he now had Ulrich's attention without drawing any to themselves, Skar nodded towards the newcomers. Ulrich squinted, trying to get a better view of who the Norsemen were.

'It looks like they aren't happy handing over their weapons,' Ulrich said. 'Which tells me they were neither invited here nor feel comfortable in this gathering.'

After a little more discussion the tallest of the Norsemen, the man who appeared to be their leader, shrugged and unslung his shield, which he then handed over to one of Constantine's warriors in an almost dismissive gesture. There was something in the movement that made both Ulrich and Skar sit up. The tall man then waved to the rest of his men and they began to disarm. Skar sucked a breath in through his teeth as he caught sight of the red axe painted on the face of each one of their shields. When they had disarmed everything else they took off their visored helmets and Skar saw a mane of black hair streaked with white tumble around the shoulders of the tall leader.

'Oh shit,' Skar said, in a low voice. 'It's him.'

As the tall Norseman began to lead his men through the tables in the meadow in the direction of the table with the nobles, Ulrich and Skar were able to get a better view of the black fur-trimmed cloak the newcomer wore and saw the piercing blue eyes that glowered at the revellers around him.

'It *is* him,' Ulrich said.

Eirik 'Bloody Axe' Haraldsson, former King of Norway and now usurper Jarl of Orkney, a man who for the most part of the last three winters had wanted Ulrich and his crew dead, had arrived.

Sixteen

'What's he doing here?' Skar said.

The big man grabbed his eating knife and the metal meat prong from the table. He looked around, seeking anything else available on the table that might be used as a weapon.

'Easy, Skar,' Ulrich said out of the corner of his mouth. 'Let's see what he's up to and while we do that try not to draw too much attention to ourselves.'

'If the rest of our crew were here we could take his twenty men,' Skar said. 'Easy.'

'What have I always taught you, Skar?' Ulrich said. 'Watch first. Observe the lie of the land and the situation. Then attack or run. Whatever's more wise.'

As Eirik, at the head of his band of men, got closer to the top table a hush fell over the revellers. The big man's presence seemed to suck the mirth from the air around him, leaving only brooding, sullen, threat in its wake.

Seeing Eirik approach, both kings, Olaf and Constantine, rose to their feet.

'Eirik son of King Harald Fairhair, if I'm not wrong?' Constantine said, speaking in the tongue of the Norse but with a heavy Scots or Irish accent, Skar could not tell which. 'Once King of Norway. Now Jarl of Orkney.'

'I am Eirik, yes,' Bloody Axe said. He replied in a heavily

accented tongue of the Gaels. 'But what do I see here, Constantine? Is this a wedding? Could my nearest neighbour be marrying off his daughter and I did not get an invitation?'

'Neighbours we may be, Eirik Haraldsson,' King Constantine said. 'But the earldom of Orkney and the kingdom of Alba have never been friends. Our warriors have clashed many times. Your predecessor, Jarl Thorfinn, stole Caithness from King Donal. It must be two years since you took Orkney from Jarl Thorfinn. We meet at last. What brings the former king of Norway to my realm?'

Eirik's customary scowl deepened at the sound of the word *former* as if he had been splashed with boiling water.

'I heard that Olaf of Dublin has sailed to Scotland with many ships and many men,' he said. 'And yet I saw no ships pass through the straits between Orkney and Caithness. Which means either he is not here, or took a less obvious route.'

'I am here all right, Eirik,' Olaf said. 'We sailed up the great loch through the middle of Scotland, dragging our ships overland where we had to.'

'Why the secrecy?' Eirik Bloody Axe said.

'There was nothing clandestine about it,' Olaf said. 'The seas south of Orkney are treacherous at this time of year. We took the safer route.'

'Really?' Eirik raised an eyebrow. 'Or did you just want to avoid my realm? I've heard it said that there is more to your voyage than just a wedding. When the royal houses of Dublin and Alba unite it creates a new power in the world. Other powerful men could see that as a threat.'

'Is that why you're here?' Constantine said. 'You think we're plotting against you?'

Eirik shook his head.

'You are of no concern to me,' he said. 'But if I were, say, King

Aethelstan of Wessex, the man who calls himself Emperor of all Britain, I might be worried.'

'What do you want, Eirik?' Constantine said, narrowing his eyes. 'I know you have a fleet of ships but do you think you can threaten our combined power?'

'I come in peace, Constantine,' Eirik said, holding up both hands.

'But you are accompanied by men of war,' the Scots king said, gesturing at the burly warriors who had lined up on either side of Eirik.

'These are my personal bodyguard,' he said.

'You think you need twenty guards here?' Constantine said, looking a little offended.

'Your reputation for guile is impressive, King Constantine,' Eirik said. 'So I prefer to take no chances. These twenty berserkers should be enough to keep me alive if necessary.'

Constantine smiled and sat back in his chair. He made a gesture to one of his stewards standing behind him. The man whistled through his teeth and all around the meadow many Gael warriors rose into view. They had been crouching in long grass, behind bushes or where ever they could find cover. Many had bows with arrows notched while some had slingshots.

Eirik and his men looked around, their surprise evident in the expressions on their faces. Olaf and his nobles looked almost as concerned and Skar could tell they too had not known about the lurking warriors.

'And these fifty warriors will shoot you and your men down like dogs if they make one wrong move,' Constantine said.

'Really, Constantine, there is no need for this,' Eirik said, spreading his arms wide. 'It is my belief that you are about to embark on a war to recover Jorvik. If so, I have something to offer you.'

'Didn't you also have something to offer Olaf of Limerick?' Olaf of Dublin said.

Olaf of Limerick bowed his head, his face flushing crimson.

Eirik cast a disparaging glance at his scab-crusted head.

'I did,' he said. 'But it seems I chose the wrong Olaf to make an alliance with.'

Olaf the Red sat down.

'All right, Eirik,' he said. 'The time is right to be open about this. Yes. We intend to march south. We will do battle with Aethelstan but Jorvik is only part of the prize. I intend to challenge Aethelstan for the whole island of Britain.'

Eirik raised both eyebrows. Many of those who sat at the tables in the meadow rose to their feet and cheered. Some beat the tables with their fists.

'I know you left Norway with many men and many ships,' Olaf said as the noise began to die down again. 'I would welcome a son of Harald Fairhair – the conqueror of all Norway – into our war horde.'

'I had something else in mind,' Eirik said. 'If you march south against Aethelstan, King Constantine will leave his kingdom of Alba unprotected from attack from the north.'

'Are you threatening me, Eirik?' Constantine said.

'Me? No?' Eirik's face took on an expression as if the very idea of such a thing hurt him to the core. 'But my realm in Orkney sits between Scotland and Norway. Hakon Aðalsteinsfóstri – Aethelstan's foster-son – rules there now. Aethelstan is strong. To wage war on him will take all your war horde, or at least most of its strength. If you march south to attack Aethelstan he is likely to call for help. Hakon will sweep down from the north. Your land will be unprotected. Unless someone comes between Hakon and Alba. I could offer that protection.'

'So the Serpent King continues his slippery crafts,' Ulrich said in a low voice.

Constantine nodded.

'Very well,' he said. 'As long as you stray no farther south than Caithness. I wouldn't like to think I'll march south with my army only for you to move in.'

'If I leave Orkney, Hakon will take it,' Eirik said. 'Or that cursed son of Thorfinn the Skull Cleaver. Don't worry, Constantine, I will keep to my own realm, and by doing that deter any thoughts Hakon might have of taking yours. If I don't move, he will not dare move. My fleet would take a terrible toll on his if he tried to sail past Orkney. If it becomes necessary even I can sail to Caithness – with your permission of course – and join with whatever forces you leave behind here to defend your realm, Constantine.'

Olaf leaned forwards, placing his elbows on his knees.

'And you would do this out of the goodness of your heart?' he said. 'I doubt that very much. What do you *want* Eirik?'

'I want to be rid of Aethelstan for a start,' Eirik said. 'For that we have common cause. With him out of the way, I can take back Norway and there will be no one to meddle in my affairs.'

'And?' Olaf said.

Eirik stood, scratching his beard for a moment, as if he were searching his mind and heart for another reason. The obvious pretence made Ulrich spit onto the ground.

'That sneaky bastard,' he said out of the corner of his mouth to Skar. 'He wants something and he knows fine rightly what it is.'

'When you have taken back the throne of Jorvik, Olaf,' Eirik said. 'You will need an under-king to rule Northumbria in your name. The current lord of Bebbanburh is a lapdog of Aethelstan. I doubt you would want him remaining in place.'

Olaf smiled.

'So now I understand,' he said. 'Northumbria is a wealthy realm. Certainly much more of one than the clump of bog-ridden islands you rule now. What if I say I want Bebbanburh for myself?'

'Then I would be happy to have Jorvik,' Eirik said.

Ulrich guffawed, though low enough not to draw attention to himself. Olaf chuckled to himself too.

'I admire your audacity, Eirik,' Olaf said. 'I must admit that.'

He looked at Constantine. The old Pict raised one eyebrow.

'We could do with him watching our back,' Constantine said. Olaf nodded.

'Then I am in agreement,' Constantine said. 'Come, sit. I will have room made for you at this table. Your men must leave and join the other warriors though.'

Eirik nodded and waved his berserkers away.

'Let's drink to new friends!' Olaf said. 'Our alliance gets bigger by the day. Victory will be ours!'

Servants began clearing a space at the top table as Eirik stood, a rare smile ghosting his lips.

'Quick. Let's get out of here. While they are all distracted,' Ulrich said from the side of his mouth. 'I don't want to be around when Olaf tries to introduce us to Eirik.'

He and Skar rose from the table and hurried off out of the meadow.

Part Five

For religion hides many mischiefs from suspicion.

Christopher Marlowe, *The Jew of Malta*

Seventeen

Jorvik

If the coin workshop in Wintanceaster had been well defended, the one in Jorvik was like a fortress. It stood beside *Konungsgarð*, Kings Gard, the tall tower that had been the home of the kings of Jorvik. It too was built of stone, a rare thing in Britain, which made Einar guess it must also stretch back to Roman times. What had been windows had been filled in with stones to stop anyone seeing inside. The flat roof had a palisade built around its edge. Smoke billowed from two chimneys and the smell of hot metal cut through the customary stench of the city: smoke from fires, the smell of beer malting and the ever-present reek of piss.

It was five days since Einar, Cynewulf and his war band had left Wintanceaster, riding north back along the route they had come by. A spell of bad weather had made the journey north longer than their trek south had been. Now, armed with a list of folk who are allowed into the royal coineries in the north, Einar was embarking on a round of questioning. Ulrich, he knew, would have spent time watching everyone with access before taking any action. Einar, however, felt he had little time to do that, and that the quickest way to flush out the culprit would be to start shoving his nose into their business and see how they reacted.

Einar, Cynewulf and the dryht were stopped by heavily armed warriors at the door of the coining workshop. After further discussions with the lead warrior guarding the door, he agreed to bring the chief of the coin workers out for Einar to talk to.

The man who came out of the workshop looked like Vollund the legendary smith himself. He was a huge man with a barrel of a chest and arms that bulged with muscles. He wore a leather apron, but underneath was stripped to the waist because of the heat of the forge, and his exposed flesh was streaked with soot and sweat. He looked glad of the chance to be out in the fresh air for a moment.

'How can I help you?' the coin master said.

Einar showed him the half-finished coin he had taken from the vikings.

'Did this come from here?' he said.

'Did you get this from the bishop?' the man said. 'Does the king need more?'

'Bishop Wulfstan?' Einar said. 'Did he ask for coins like this?'

'Aye,' the other man said. 'He requested a chest of them a week or so ago. He said the king wanted them and they had to only have one side stamped as Aethelstan wanted to test a new die of his head.'

Seeing the expression on Einar's face the coin master frowned.

'Is there something wrong?' he said.

'You didn't think that was strange?' Einar said. 'You didn't question him any further about it?'

'He's the bishop!' the coin master said. 'He's trusted by the king! He has his own key to the coinery. What is going on?'

'I'm starting to fear the king may have misplaced his trust,' Einar said. 'Did the bishop come here to pick the coins up himself?'

The coin master shook his head.

'He sent a messenger – a woman – to collect them,' he said. 'But she bore a letter with the bishop's seal. It could only have come from him.'

'A woman?' Einar said. 'What did she look like?'

'I didn't see her myself,' the coin master said. 'One of the guards dealt with her. I only heard him talking about her afterwards.'

Deciding he had learned all he needed to, Einar took his leave and went to rejoin his men at the gate, leaving the coin master, his face now wearing a mask of concern, to return to work.

'Well if I'd known about these coin workshops we could have come here last week,' Einar said to Cynewulf. 'I think we need to talk to the bishop. He looks like he might be involved in this.'

Cynewulf's eyebrows arched and his mouth fell open a little.

'Bishop Wulfstan is a lord of the church,' the monk said. 'He's trusted by the king. If you really mean to do this I would urge you approach the matter with delicacy.'

Einar pursed his lips as he thought for a moment.

'Very well,' he said. 'The rest of you men stay here at your billet. Cynewulf and I will talk to the bishop.'

Leaving the dryht behind, Einar and the monk crossed the city to the minster. At the gates of the great church they spoke to some monks, telling them they needed to see the bishop on the business of the king. The monks had gone off to relay the message.

After some time they returned, telling Einar that the bishop was in the minster and would see him there.

Einar and Cynewulf entered the cool gloom of the great church to find it appeared to be empty.

'I'm going to stay here if you don't mind,' Cynewulf said.

Einar nodded, understanding that the old monk was probably uncomfortable asking questions of so important a man of the church as a bishop. He then made his way down the great church to where the stone altar stood. He had just reached it when a monk stepped out from behind one of the very tall pillars that suspended the roof. He carried the crooked staff of a Christian bishop. The churchman was a little taller than Einar though his frame was a lot more slight. He was older too, though not so old as to be middle-aged. His long beard was braided beneath his chin and red, like the colour of his hair which was shaved on the top in the way of Christian monks of the southern British persuasion.

'I am Wulfstan, Bishop of Jorvik,' the monk said. 'I hear you wish to see me?'

'Yes, lord,' Einar said. He reached into a pouch at his waist and retrieved a rolled parchment, a letter that bore the king's seal, explaining the reason Aethelstan had sent Einar north.

'Surely you don't suspect *me* of this crime?' the bishop said. His face was livid and Einar could hear the indignation in his voice.

Bishop Wulfstan's raised voice still echoed around the stone vaulted ceiling above, mingling with the clack of the hammers the stonemasons were using on the exterior of the building.

'I'm not accusing you of anything, Lord Bishop,' Einar said, trying to remain as impassive as possible. 'I am just telling you of the situation.'

'If it wasn't for this letter from the king telling me you are working on his orders, I'd have you flogged for such insolence!' The bishop held up the rolled piece of parchment with the king's mark on it that Aethelstan had given Einar to show on whose behalf he was working.

'That's very Christian of you,' Einar said.

'Does the king think I'm involved in this?' The bishop's face took on a look of sudden concern. His eyes searched Einar's face as if desperate to see if any hint of the king's suspicions could be read from Einar's expression. 'He does, doesn't he? Aethelstan has never trusted me. It's because I'm half-Dane. He knows I want someone like me to rule here.'

'Someone *like* you, lord,' Einar said, 'or just you?'

'Don't be ridiculous!' Wulfstan's indignant expression got

even more acute. 'I am a bishop of the Church! I cannot take earthly power.'

'I do not know who the king believes is behind this,' Einar said. 'But he has sent me to find out.'

'I'm not the only one with access to the coinery in Jorvik,' the bishop said. 'Who else have you spoken to?'

'You're the first, lord,' Einar said.

Wulfstan spread his hands wide.

'And I am *not* supposed to think you are accusing me?' he said. 'We've met before, haven't we?'

Einar nodded.

'I thought you looked familiar, but I can't place you,' Wulfstan said.

'I was here before last winter, lord,' Einar said. He switched from the Saxon to the Norse tongue. 'I am Einar Unnsson, son of Thorfinn the Skull Cleaver. I was with Affreca Guthfrithsdóttir, who I believe is your cousin? I was a member of a crew of úlfhéðnar.'

The bishop's jaw fell open a little. Einar could see the confusion in his eyes, knowing that Wulfstan was trying to match the man who now stood before him with his memory of the wolfskin-clad viking he had met before. The bishop recovered himself fast though.

'Really?' he said with a smile. 'I would never have recognised you if you'd not told me that. You look quite the Saxon warlord now.'

Einar had to admit to himself that Wulfstan was right. His war gear was now almost indistinguishable from the rest of the dryht. Before he left Wintanceaster Aethelstan had presented him with a heavy red cloak of the finest wool, just like the ones his bodyguards wore. A magnificent new helmet, taken off when he entered the church as Cynewulf had instructed him to do, now sat in the crook of Einar's elbow. It was another gift from the king to replace his own Norse helm that had shattered in his fight with Ljót, or rather Magnus. It was decorated in the Saxon style, with a dragon protecting the wearer's nose, its wings spread over the brow guard, and it had cheek pieces that fastened under the chin with a leather strap. A long plume of horsehair hung down from the crown. Combined with his shaved chin and long moustache, he looked every bit a Saxon.

'Ah yes, I remember now,' Wulfstan said. 'The Lady Affreca was supposed to be married to King Hakon and take the throne of Jorvik. You all fled in the night and the marriage never happened. I imagine the king was not pleased, yet now you are here as his representative.'

'We left because we had business elsewhere,' Einar said. 'And because you told Affreca the truth about why Aethelstan wanted her to marry Hakon, causing her to go off the idea. I would imagine the king would not be pleased with that either. *If* he knew about it.'

'And does he?' the bishop said.

'Only if you told him,' Einar said.

Wulfstan held Einar's gaze in silence for a long moment.

'I merely told Affreca the truth. She is, after all, a cousin of mine,' he said at last. 'I'm descended on my mother's side from Ragnar Loðbrók. And it's because I am half-Dane that Aethelstan does not trust me. Half the folk in the kingdom of Jorvik and more than half of those who live north of the Humber are Norse through one or both their parents. Really, if he's serious about ruling all of Britain, Aethelstan is going to have to learn to trust folk like us. Just because our parents or grandparents grew up outside this land doesn't mean our loyalty lies outside it too.'

'Our folk have given the Saxons enough reasons to mistrust

us,' Einar said. 'We've been raiding them for most of the last two hundred years. And there are plenty of us who still would seek to challenge Aethelstan for this land. Olaf of Dublin, Affreca's brother, for example. Can you blame Aethelstan for his suspicion?'

'What do you know of Olaf of Dublin?' The bishop narrowed his eyes.

'I know he wants to reclaim the throne of Jorvik,' Einar said. 'And from your previous actions I know you are not as completely loyal to the king as you might say you are.'

'I went against the king's wishes because I wanted to avoid a war!' the bishop said in a thundering voice. 'There has been enough blood shed over this land. Dane and Saxon must live in peace. I am a man of God and that is what He would want. And His will comes before that of any king or jarl. *That* is something I would risk everything for. You are a northman, Einar. Yet here you are at the behest of Aethelstan, doing his bidding like a sheep. How did this come about?'

'The coin master tells me you ordered half-finished coins from his workshop,' Einar said. 'You gave them to a woman.'

The bishop hesitated for a moment. Then his lip curled in a sneer.

'I'd be very careful if I were you, Einar Unnsson, before I said another word,' he said. 'I am a very powerful man in this city. I am a bishop of the Church. If you want to challenge me you'll need a lot more than twelve men. I don't care how many letters you have from the king. You can't touch me. I am a wolf against whom Aethelstan has sent a lapdog. Why don't you run home to your master?'

Einar's mind raced. He had no doubt now this man was involved in the conspiracy, but realised the bishop was right. Aethelstan had sent him here to get results, but what could he do against a man as powerful as Wulfstan? The reeve would not arrest a bishop. These Christian churchmen were revered like *goðar* or *vǫlvar*, people whom the gods have touched. Everyone was scared of their power.

Bishop Wulfstan smirked and turned to go.

Einar set his helmet on the altar, laid his right hand on the bishop's shoulder and spun him back around to face him. Then he drove his left fist into Wulfstan's gut.

Wulfstan's eyes bulged and he doubled over. His face flushed purple. Einar grabbed him by the neck of his robe and hauled him back to his feet.

'I'm not here to fuck around,' Einar said. 'Now start talking. Who did you give those coins to? What are they for? Has this anything to do with Olaf the Red?'

'How dare you,' Wulfstan gasped, trying to recover his breath. 'I am a man of God—'

Still holding the churchman by the collar with his right fist, Einar cuffed him across the face with back of his left. Wulfstan's head rocked sideways, snot and blood spraying from his nose.

'You talk of God?' Einar said. His voice was rising in pitch and he could see a strange, red mist starting to encroach on his vision. He knew if he was not careful the Rage would take him. 'What would your God make of man who was a traitor to his king?'

'Traitor? Traitor to who? Aethelstan's God is one of empire and vengeance,' Wulfstan said through clenched teeth. His eyes were narrowed in pain but Einar felt a thrill to see there was now also fear in them. 'The Jesus I know is the shepherd of the folk. *Our* folk. He cares for the poor not for the kings.'

Einar raised his hand to punch him again.

'Let him go.'

A new voice made Einar look up over the shoulder of the bishop. At the far end of the church he saw a newcomer standing in the shadows near the back door. She wore a long, dark cloak with the hood down revealing her tawny hair that was braided and curled around her shoulders like a snake. She held a drawn bow in her hands, the notched arrow pointing at Einar.

It was Affreca.

Eighteen

Einar did not let the bishop go. Wulfstan was between him and the point of Affreca's arrow, a human shield that prevented her from getting a clear shot. If Einar let Wulfstan go he was a dead man for sure.

Over the bishop's shoulder he could see her, bow unwavering, one eye closed, the other staring down the shaft with cold, patient indifference as she waited for her moment to strike.

This was the last sight on earth for many men, Einar thought to himself.

Then Bishop Wulfstan cried out. He swung his crooked staff at Einar's head. Einar on instinct let go of the man and sprang back. The bishop stumbled away, half running, half staggering towards Affreca.

'Get out of the way!' she shouted, annoyance clear in her voice.

Einar, realising he was now exposed, grabbed his helmet and flung it at Affreca. She dodged it with ease and it bounced off a pillar then clattered across the stone flags on the floor.

Affreca swayed back into position. The bishop went into a crouch as he ran. Einar realised now there was nothing between him and her arrow. She was too close for him to be able to dodge her arrow once it was loosed. As soon as she let go of the bowstring he was a dead man. He and Affreca locked gazes for the final time.

Affreca hesitated for an instant.

'Come on men!' Cynewulf's voice came from the far end of the church. 'All of you charge! Einar, your commander, is in trouble. Grab that bishop!'

Einar dropped to the ground like a stone. Affreca shot her arrow. Einar heard the angry buzz as it shot through the air where his head had been an instant before. It passed by so closely he felt the air it disturbed part his hair. Then it passed on, smacking hard into the stone floor and shattering into splinters some distance away.

Einar did not know how the old monk had managed to get his war band here but he was very grateful. Crouching behind the altar, he shouted orders to his men.

'Look out for that bow, lads,' he said. 'She's deadly with it. Fan out so she has too many targets. Keep your shields up. Grab those bastards!'

There came the sound of scuffling feet, but to Einar's consternation it was not the clatter of the boots of a war band on the stones. No one shouted confirmation his orders had been heard. Then there was only a silence once more in the church.

Still crouching behind the altar, Einar spotted the face of Cynewulf as he peeked out from behind a pillar.

'Where are the men?' Einar said.

'Sorry, lord,' Cynewulf said. 'I was just pretending they were here. It worked though. Those other two must have believed me. They're gone.'

With utmost caution, Einar poked his head up above the altar, ready to duck back down at the first hint of danger. No arrow flew at him. Affreca and the bishop had indeed gone.

'Come on,' Einar said. 'We need to get after them.'

They ran to the door at the back of the church. It still lay open but there was no sign of Affreca or Wulfstan.

They raced outside. The sound of horses' hooves made Einar start. He looked around and saw Affreca and the bishop had jumped onto two waiting horses and were galloping towards the gate. Affreca swivelled in the saddle and aimed her bow again.

Einar shoved Cynewulf back inside then threw himself in after him, just as an arrow thudded into the wood of the door in the exact spot his heart had been a moment before. Cynewulf looked at the quivering shaft, an expression of disbelief on his face. Then a second arrow struck the door almost close enough to the first to split it asunder.

For a moment they lay, waiting, then Einar dragged himself to his feet. He went back to the door and peeked out, ready to pull his head back if he spotted danger. He just caught sight of the back end of Affreca's horse as it went out the gate.

Einar ran out of the church.

'More horses!' he shouted to one of the nearby monks. 'Where do you keep them?'

'There are none here, lord,' the monk said, his face pale and his eyes wide. 'We have no stables.'

'Where did the bishop and that woman get those horses from then?' Einar demanded.

'The woman rode in on one,' the monk said. 'The bishop brought the other one earlier this morning.'

Einar cursed. There was no way they could keep up on foot, even through the crowded streets of the city.

'You never thought to ask who she was?' Einar said.

'She said she and the bishop were working on the king's business,' the monk said.

'Aye,' Einar said. 'But which king?'

'What now?' Cynewulf said.

'We must tell King Aethelstan,' Einar said. 'Send word to the rest of the war band and tell them to join us here. For real this time.'

After that he and Cynewulf went to the writing room at the minster and drafted a letter outlining what had happened. Einar sealed it with wax in the way Aethelstan had taught him and then gave it to Dunstan, one of Einar's war band. The warrior was ordered to ride south to the king without stopping, except to change horses at fortified burhs.

Not long afterwards Oswald the reeve arrived, summoned by news that there was a commotion at the minster. Einar explained what had happened. Oswald was predictably astonished.

'I just saw the bishop and a woman,' he said, shaking his head. 'I was at the north gate of the city and they rode out. I'll gather my men and we can chase them.'

'No,' Einar said. 'If they've left the city then there's really no point in chasing them. Affreca got the same training that I did from the úlfhéðnar. One of the crafts we learned was how to disappear into the landscape when you think someone is chasing you. We've more chance of finding a ghost.'

The days passed as they awaited the return of Dunstan. Einar tried to find out more about what was going on from the monks in the minster but they remained taciturn, surly and did not like the implications his questions cast on their bishop.

Every time Einar went out of doors he felt his scalp crawl at the thought that perhaps Affreca had not left at all. Perhaps she had indeed doubled back and now waited in the shadows somewhere, arrow notched and bow drawn, waiting for him to pass by, the red cloak Aethelstan had given him marking him out as an even more obvious target.

Would she really shoot me? Einar wondered one of the times he crossed the open space before the minster, nerves stretched to breaking point as his ears strained for the tell-tale whistle of an approaching arrow. Ulrich would; he knew that. And Affreca was totally loyal to Ulrich.

But after all we've been through together? he thought. *And what we have between us?*

Einar frowned. What did they have between them, really? His cheeks reddened as he recalled his previous clumsy proposal of marriage to her. A proposal he had then tried to pass off as an offer to get her out of an uncomfortable situation. Her reaction had been telling though: a refusal. Worse, she had laughed at the idea. Was he just fooling himself? Was he living in a comfortable dream life, expecting some day he and Affreca would be married and together they would rule Orkney? Was this all just wishful thinking on his part? The thought made his heart feel cold.

At dawn on the fourth day a reply arrived from the king. It was not borne by Dunstan, who had been too exhausted to turn around and come straight back. Instead Aethelstan had sent one of his own riders, a man whose job it was to carry the king's orders up and down the length of Britain and was used to the exertion. With the network of burhs where they could change horses, these men could cover huge distances in a very short time, and this one had returned from Wintanceaster in half the time it had taken Dunstan to ride there. It was a system Aethelstan had learned from reading about the Romans.

The response from the king was written on parchment and sealed with his personal ring. Cynewulf read it for Einar, telling him that Aethelstan had heard from another source that Olaf of Dublin was in Alba and his intentions were more sinister than just marriage to the daughter of the king of Scots. Aethelstan had decided to move north with his army but it would take time to move them from Wessex. The king would arrange to send some military support but in the meantime the northern earls would have to do their best to discourage Olaf. Separate messengers had been sent ordering them to gather at Ad Gefrin and Einar was to accompany the messenger who had brought this letter there and help persuade them of the need to confront this danger.

'Well it seems the king has finally realised the danger from Dublin, like I've been telling him,' Einar said. 'Though he seems to have had to have someone else confirm it before he took action.'

'Listen to all news, but always verify from more than one source,' Cynewulf said. 'It's an old adage of statecraft.'

And so they rode north.

Nineteen

It took a further three days to reach Ad Gefrin. The fortified burhs with their garrisons of warriors they had been used to seeing every few miles were not evident, and with their absence disappeared one of the most obvious signs of the power of King Aethelstan.

The Saxons of Einar's war band joked about how they were riding beyond civilisation. Einar on the other hand found the land north of the Humber river was not the barbarous wilderness he had half expected it to be from the reputation it bore. In fact the countryside was beautiful. There were rugged mountains, and villages and settlements were much sparser than in the south but the fields were ripe with grain or rich green with grass. The climate was sunny and the wind did not cut the skin like it did in Iceland. There were full rivers rich with fish and the meadows were roamed by flocks of sheep, goats and herds of cattle.

The people they met too, were familiar to Einar. They looked like him and most of them spoke or understood the Norse tongue, which was not surprising as either one or both of most of their parents or grandparents were Danes or Norsemen who had settled in Britain. Einar could understand why they had come here. Compared to scratching a living from the ice-bound, shallow soils on the edges of the fjords of Norway, battered by winds and bound by frost, where every moment of life had to be fought for against the weather, the land or against enemies, this rich and bountiful land was positive luxury.

The many churches they passed showed what most of them had forsaken in return for this pleasant life: their gods. Perhaps this was actually the 'Heaven' the Christian God offered in return for following him? Not some far-off realm in the sky but an easy life in a fertile land.

When they camped at night, however, the howling of wolves reminded them that all was not the civilised, peaceful kingdom of Aethelstan's Wessex. As warriors of the king they were still in a potentially hostile land and they posted guards to keep watch through the darkness.

On the morning of the fourth day they rode into Ad Gefrin.

Cynewulf had described it as the 'villa' of the Earl of Northumbria, earl being the equivalent word for a jarl in the Saxon tongue. The jarl also had a mighty fortress on the coast but that was a resort in times of conflict. Ad Gefrin was his main, considerably more comfortable, residence for most of the year.

They approached it along a long, low-sided valley with a river meandering through it that reminded Einar of his home dale in Iceland. As they made their way along it the bubbling of the river began to mingle with another noise that Einar realised was the sound of many human voices. The riverbank was covered with scrubby bushes and low, wind-blasted trees so they could not see ahead, but after a while it cleared away and he could see the valley swept down towards a small plain on which sat a complex of buildings.

In the middle of the plain was a vast feasting hall, one of the biggest Einar had ever seen. It rose like a mountain ridge or a huge, crouching hog. Its roof, which from its apex ran almost to the ground on either side, was tiled with red clay tiles rather than the usual thatch. Smoke drifted from wind's eyes – holes to let the air in and smoke out – in both gable walls. Even from a distance Einar could see a metal weather vane was mounted on the centre of the roof, the sun glinting off its surface, which looked very like gold.

Even more impressive, the hall did not stand alone. A little to the west of it was another long hall, about two-thirds as long and half as tall.

There were numerous other huts, houses and wooden buildings around the big halls and on the far side of all of them there was what looked like a round palisaded area. Einar reasoned that this was possibly a fort or burh that could provide quick refuge from sudden attack.

The river looped around the whole compound and behind it rose and fell many barrows, the burial mounds that marked the final resting places of heroes and kings. Beyond them were a line of highs hills, their sides covered by heather, bracken and shale.

'It's like Odin's Valour Hall!' Einar said. 'This is one of the finest halls I've ever seen. It's finer than some of the halls of kings. And you say it belongs to a jarl?'

'A jarl who used to be a king,' Cynewulf said. 'Many of the rulers in the north were kings in their own right before Aethelstan subjugated them. Now they rule in his name as jarls. There is only one king.'

'And they accept that?' Einar said. 'A man who has been a king would find it hard to serve another.'

'Those who did not are no longer with us,' Cynewulf said, a bemused smile on his lips. 'They were replaced by someone who was prepared to accept the arrangement. That was the only choice King Aethelstan offered. The lords of the north hold the land for Aethelstan and stand as a wall against the Scots. That is what the king expects of them.'

Beside the buildings another temporary town had been pitched. The nearby meadow was covered by hundreds of leather and wool tents. Many people thronged around them, sitting at campfires outside or milling around, talking. The banners and pennants of noblemen fluttered in the air above. Lots more people gathered around the buildings. If was from them that the noise of voices arose. The size of the crowd was made more impressive given the largely deserted countryside they had ridden through to get here.

As they rode up to the settlement, Einar could see that the men and women gathered there were dressed in fine woollen garments and cloaks. Einar could tell these were not peasants. There were a lot of smiling faces and he was reminded of previous visits he had made when growing up to the *Alþingi* in Iceland, or even the Quarter Court where he had been judged and declared an outlaw from his homeland.

'What's going on?' he said to Cynewulf. 'They all can't have come here to see us.'

'It's the northern Witan meeting,' the monk said, shaking his head. 'All the most important men north of the Humber river gather here to discuss legal cases, matters of state and make judgements, agreements and strategies. It happens once a year in summer. We're just lucky it's happening now. Otherwise we'd have had to ride all over northern Britain to see the men we need to speak to.'

There were so many thronging there that no one paid much attention to Einar, Cynewulf and the other riders arriving among them. There was a big wooden pen set up for horses and they dismounted there, letting their tired mounts stray into the roped-off area to enjoy the luscious green grass.

Cynewulf appeared to know his way around and he led the small company towards the big palisaded area beyond the halls. As they got close, they passed a more sinister sight. A gallows had been erected near the gate to the palisade and fourteen corpses dangled from nooses hung from its crossbar. This was not unusual for a gathering like this, Einar knew. If this Witan was like an Icelandic þing, judgements on legal cases would be heard at it among other business. Those found guilty of more serious crimes who were not as lucky as him to be outlawed, would end up in the hands of the hangman.

One of the corpses twisting in the wind caught Einar's eye. The skin of the face was bloated and purple. The man's tongue, almost black, protruded from his mouth. His left eye was screwed shut, a permanent reminder of his last agony. A raven sat on his shoulder, picking at what was left of his right. It was none of this horror that had made Einar look again, however. It was the distinctive way the sides of his head were shaved, revealing stick-like runes tattooed on his scalp. A single strip of hair ran over the top of his head and hung down into a ponytail behind his head.

'Cynewulf,' he said. The monk stopped and turned around. 'Isn't this our friend Bjarni?'

The monk frowned, peering hard at the dead man.

'Yes. I do believe it is,' he said. 'And I think that one next to him is one of Ljót the Pale's crew too.'

'How did they end up here?' Einar said.

'I don't know,' Cynewulf said. 'But let's go and find out.'

Twenty

When they entered the gate of the palisade, Einar and the others of his dryht stopped and gazed around them in amazement. The construction was not a fortress at all. A circular ditch, filled with water, surrounded a double wall of wooden palisades which stood perhaps twice the height of a man. There were no fighting platforms or defensive ramparts on the inside of the palisades, however. Enclosed within the wooden walls was an area about one hundred and fifty paces across. On one side of it wooden terraces rose from ground level to the top of the palisade. This construction followed the walls to form a semicircle that covered almost two-thirds of the circle made by the palisade. It thronged with men dressed in their finest clothes – rich woollen cloaks and linen shirts – sitting in rows along it. Einar noticed that the wooden platform rose in steps, with each step forming a bench, then the step behind them was higher, so those seated on that one could see over the heads of the people sitting on the lower bench in front.

The rest of the circuit of the enclosure was flat. Five carved wooden high seats, the sort of thrones important men used as a symbol of their power, sat on the ground there, facing the ranks of men sat on the benches opposite.

Recalling his visit to the Alþing when he was young, Einar realised that this was like an artificial version of that place where the important men in Iceland gathered in a semi-circular formation of rocks on the *Þingvellir* plain, a natural enclosure and platform where folk could be seen and heard with ease. This whole enclosure had been constructed so that a very large number of people could gather round a few speakers on the floor. No one was too far away from the speakers so as not to be able to hear their words and everyone could see them.

Whoever had built this had been to the Alþing, Einar reasoned. Or else it was yet another clever idea that the Saxons had learned from the Romans.

'What are you all gawping at?' Cynewulf said. 'Have you never seen an amphitheatre before?'

'You've seen one of these before?' Einar said.

'There's a Roman one built of stone at Legacaestir,' the monk replied. 'The Mercian Witan meets there.'

'You know a lot for a monk,' Einar said.

'I am not just any monk,' Cynewulf said with a wink. 'I work for the king, remember?'

'Aethelstan does hold you in high regard,' Einar said. 'Which makes me think there is more to you than meets the eye. I don't think you were always a monk.'

Cynewulf scowled as if Einar's speculations annoyed him. Einar recalled Aethelstan's questions to Cynewulf about Einar's 'progress' or otherwise. Was part of the reason Cynewulf still accompanied them so that he could continue to observe and assess *him*, Einar, as well as update the king on the events in the north? And if that was the case, what was it exactly he was being assessed for?

'Men who poke their noses in where they aren't wanted should not complain if they get those noses punched,' Cynewulf said. 'Right now we have more important matters to address than the story of my life.'

They stood beside the seated section for a moment, observing what was going on. It soon became clear that a vigorous debate was in progress.

Four men (who Einar surmised to be the owners of the high seats) were on their feet before the thrones, pointing and shouting either at each other or at members of the audience. They were dressed in war gear though it was the kind meant more for display than battle. Their polished mail gleamed like silver and jewels glittered from their weapon hilts, sword belts and harnesses.

'Those are the four northern earls,' Cynewulf explained to Einar, speaking from the side of his mouth. 'These are rich lands, and Aethelstan allowing these men to rule them makes them wealthy beyond many others. It's worth the price of having hold the Scots, the Danes and the Northern Welsh in check.'

'Has someone not shown up?' Einar said, pointing out that there was one more magnificently carved high seat on the floor than there were earls to sit in them.

'When Aethelstan subjugated the north, ten winters ago,' Cynewulf said, 'there were five men who called themselves kings here. Two of them ruled what were the old kingdoms of Deira and Bernicia, with a high king – the *Jofri* – of Northumbria ruling over both of them from Bebbanburh. A fourth ruled Bretland where the Welsh are and the fifth, Jorvik. The king pushed the Welsh of Alt Clwyd further north then gave the kings the choice of being earls under him or death. Jorvik, however, was too troublesome and he found no one there he could trust, so he rules it directly. That empty chair is for the ruler of Jorvik. If Aethelstan were here himself he would sit in it. Perhaps one day someone will, if the king finds the right man to rule Jorvik in his name...'

The monk trailed off and Einar realised Cynewulf was looking at him, his right eyebrow raised.

'If Aethelstan believes we are about to be attacked then why is he not here?' one of the jarls was shouting.

He was a burly man wrapped in a brown bearskin cloak. The top of his head was bald and his broad beard, which was cut straight across so it resembled the blade of a shovel, was grey. These things along with the lines around his eyes told Einar that while clearly still fit and strong, he was not a young man. He wore mail that was unlike anything Einar had seen before. The rings looked thick as chains and the way it gathered around the jarl's neck and elbows reminded Einar more of the sort of heavy knitted woollen shirt his folk wore back in Iceland than a brynja.

'Surely he should have marched north with his army?' the bald man said. 'Or does he have more important things to do than defend his own kingdom? Meanwhile we must wait for the axe to fall on us.'

'I doubt an axe would do much damage to mail that thick,' Einar whispered to Cynewulf. 'What's he worried about?'

'That is Jarl Ingwar,' the monk said. 'He rules the west of the north, from the hills towards the sea between Britain and Ireland.'

'Bretland?' Einar said.

'In your tongue, yes,' Cynewulf said. 'We sometimes call it the land of the Cymbri. Most of his subjects are Welsh and just how far west his rule extends is debatable. There are a few Saxons and Angles but most of the others are Danes. With a folk like that to rule can you blame Ingwar for wearing mail so thick?'

'Aethelstan cares more about what is going on in Francia and Armorica,' the second earl who stood beside Ingwar said. 'Then when trouble comes who is expected to save his Aengland? Us! Alone!'

Their words provoked a storm of shouting and consternation from the ranks of men sat on the benches. Some rose to their feet and began shouting their disagreement; others began vigorous debates among themselves.

'That is Ingwar's brother Ethils,' Cynewulf said. 'He rules the lands to the south and west.'

Einar regarded the second earl who indeed had a familial resemblance to the bald Ingwar, sharing the same hawk-like nose and arched eyebrows. The norns who governed the fates of men had been more favourable to Ethils when it came to keeping his hair, though. His long brown locks were streaked with grey and white. Like his brother he was in the middle years of his life, and probably the later ones at that.

'Who are the other two?' Einar said. There was no need to whisper now the hubbub in the enclosure was so great.

One of the high seats was occupied by a young man with long black hair that was combed straight and then curled at the ends in a very deliberate manner. He wore a richly embroidered cloak and sat, his chin resting on his fist, his eyes cast down at the floor. His expression suggested he would rather be anywhere else than there.

'That is Alfgeir, Lord of Bebbanburh,' Cynewulf said. 'Jofri of Northumbria. Aethelstan put him here to replace the high king of Northumbria.'

'I thought Uhtred ruled Bebbanburh?' Einar said.

'You know of Uhtred?' Cynewulf said, eyebrows raised.

'Doesn't everyone?' Einar said. 'I met him in Wintanceaster last year.'

'Uhtred proclaims Bebbanburh is his birthright,' Cynewulf said. 'And perhaps one day he will attain it. However at this time Aethelstan put Alfgeir there to rule. He is the nephew of William, Count of Rouen. The one they call "Longsword".'

'Vilhjálmr Rúðu Jarl?' Einar said, with a little snort of half disbelief, half respect. No doubt this was all part of Aethelstan's statecraft and growing his constant web of alliances that stretched across the world.

'Which means he is half a Dane,' Cynewulf said. 'In as much as you can still call those Norsemen who settled in north-west Francia that. Aethelstan thought as such he might be more acceptable as a ruler to the Danes who have settled here.'

'He's Aethelstan's type of Dane though,' Einar said. 'Christian and allied to the Wessex court no doubt, not some berserker heathen from the northern realms.'

'He has not ruled for long,' Cynewulf said, ignoring Einar's cynicism except for a slightly reproachful glance. 'Aethelstan only put him in the high seat last year, which is probably why he's not saying much.'

'It looks like he's regretting taking that seat,' Einar said.

'The fourth earl is Guthrek. He rules the northern part of the realm, up to the border with Scotland. He's a hardy old Saxon whose folk have ruled here for centuries. This palace is his. Of all of these men he is the most reliable.'

'And clearly the most loyal,' Einar said. Jarl Guthrek was also in his middle years and wore a black cloak over his mail shirt. He was pointing at Ingwar as he shouted recriminations.

'Wait here a moment,' Cynewulf said to Einar. 'I'm going to talk to the *Thyle*.'

The monk hurried off in the direction of an officious-looking man who stood at the edge of the floor before the high seats. He wore long robes that were clearly ceremonial in nature, as well as a distinctive woollen hat. In his right hand he bore a long staff, which he was beating off the ground as he waved his left arm in the air and shouted in vain to try to bring some sort of order to the chaos that boiled around him. Seeing Cynewulf he stopped and the two exchanged words. The Thyle looked around at Einar, who thought he detected a distinct look of relief. He gestured that Einar should come and join them.

From his robes and staff Einar surmised this 'Thyle' was the Saxon equivalent of the Law Speaker whose job it was to run the Althing, try and keep order and make sure everyone's voice was heard, something he was struggling to do at that moment.

'You have come from the king?' the Thyle said to Einar.

'I have,' Einar said.

'Thank the Lord!' the Thyle said. 'Please speak to this mob before they all start fighting each other, never mind the Scots.'

The Thyle walked into the middle of the floor, placing himself deliberately between Jarl Guthrek and Jarl Ingwar. He waved his hands above his head, shouting for order. It took several moments but eventually the raised voices diminished and those on their feet sat down again. The Thyle waited until hush descended into complete, expectant silence, something which Einar, a trained *skald* himself, noted with respect. Here was someone who knew how to work an audience.

'My lords,' the Thyle said at last in a loud, booming voice, 'an envoy from King Aethelstan has arrived. Let us hear what the king's orders are.'

A murmur rumbled around the assembly as the Thyle beckoned to Einar. It died away as Einar walked out onto the floor, replaced by a silence so thick Einar could hear the rings in his mail shirt clinking with his every step. He turned and looked around, standing with the new Saxon helmet Aethelstan had given him tucked into the crook of his left elbow, surveying the ranks of faces before him. The weight of hundreds of eyes bore down on him, each one portraying the anticipation of the crowd.

For a moment Einar felt frozen, his throat tight, stopping any words escaping. How could he, a farm lad from Iceland, stand here before so many high lords and act like a representative of the king? Then he reasoned that he had been in similar situations many times before. He was a skald, a poet who had chanted before kings and jarls and had them all hanging on his every word. Was this really so different?

He glanced around over his shoulder at the empty chair of the ruler of Jorvik, then returned his gaze to the audience before him, took a deep breath and began to speak.

Twenty-One

'Lords, I bring news from King Aethelstan,' Einar said. 'Olaf of Dublin has sailed to Scotland with an army. The king requests you muster your war hordes.'

'And who are you that Aethelstan has sent to give us orders?' Ingwar said.

'I am Einar, son of Unn Kjartinsdóttir and Jarl Thorfinn, known as *Hausakljúfr*,' Einar said, doing his best to swell his chest as he spoke.

A murmur ran around the room.

'And how did a Dane, the son of the heathen Skull Cleaver of Orkney, come to be in the service of King Aethelstan?' Ethils said, eyes narrowed.

'Is that important?' Einar said.

'Do not worry,' Cynewulf said from the side of the floor. 'Einar is learning the ways of a good Christian. Under my personal instruction.'

'Well if you are his teacher, Cynewulf, then we all know he is in good hands,' Jarl Ethils said with a good-natured smile.

So even jarls respect this monk and his word is not questioned, Einar thought to himself.

'Olaf is in Scotland to get married to the daughter of Constantine of Alba,' Earl Ingwar said. 'We know that. The king need not worry.'

'He brought an army with him,' Einar said.

'Any king going into the realm of another king who didn't bring his army with him would be a fool,' Ingwar said.

'All the same,' Einar said, 'if Olaf and Constantine combine their forces they will represent a sizeable threat if they were to decide to march south.'

'And why would they do that?' Ethils said.

'Olaf's father was king of Jorvik until Aethelstan drove him out,' Einar replied. 'He still sees it as his birthright and could harbour ambitions to reclaim it.'

'Our father was a king,' Ingwar said, scowling. 'Until Aethelstan subjugated him. Neither my brother nor I have such ambitions. What makes you think Olaf does?

'All the king asks is that you northern earls gather your warriors and deploy them to the field,' Einar said. 'To discourage any foolish notions Olaf may have of straying south. If he sees you are ready for him he will think twice.'

'And what if Olaf has no such ambitions and he just goes back home to Dublin, leaving us standing waiting on an invasion that never comes?' Ethils said. 'Or worse, our presence provokes the Scots into a war they never intended. Putting an army in the field is expensive. Has the king any proof of Olaf's intentions?'

'I uncovered suspicious events in Jorvik which may be linked to Olaf's plans to retake the city,' Einar said. He gave a brief overview of what had happened in Jorvik.

'Coins you say?' For the first time the black-haired young man, Earl Alfgeir, appeared interested in the debate. Einar noticed he spoke the Saxon tongue with the same lilting accent that Jarl Vilhjálmr of Rúðu had spoken the Norse tongue.

'Yes,' Einar said. 'The crew of vikings ran off with them after I slew Ljót the Pale. I see you have taken care of the rest of Ljót the Pale's crew. I recognise at least one of them hanging outside.'

'When vikings plague our coast we must take quick action,' Earl Guthrek said, hooking his thumbs into his cloak. 'And thankfully Earl Alfgeir here did. They landed in his realm and he seized them. We're not barbarians though. We didn't just string them up. They had a fair trial here first.'

'That's just it,' Alfgeir said. 'None of you were at the trial, were you? I was. One of the charges against them was passing false coins. They gave them to a merchant they bought food off.'

'False coins?' Ingwar said, his face screwed up in confusion.

The young earl dug in his purse for a moment then pulled out a silver coin.

'Here's one,' he said, tossing it to Ingwar.

The bald man caught the coin and looked at it with interest. He turned it over in his hand and his expression darkened. Exchanging a look with his brother he tossed the coin to him. Ethils looked at it, nodded and passed it to Earl Guthrek. Guthrek examined the coin then took a sharp intake of breath. He reached out to Einar and passed the coin to him.

Einar looked at it. The face was stamped with the cross he had seen before. He turned it over and saw it was not blank as the others had been before. Instead it was stamped with the head of a king and there were runes around it, except they did not say the name of Aethelstan, they spelled out OLAFR REX.

'King Olaf?' Einar said, looking up at the earls.

'I think that makes Olaf's intentions very clear,' Guthrek said. His face was grim. 'We must do as the king asks.'

'Are we to fight alone?' Ingwar said.

'King Aethelstan is coming north with his own war horde to support you,' Einar said. 'He needs you to be ready in case Olaf attacks before he gets here.'

'And we are to fight him alone if that happens?' Alfgeir said. The young man looked concerned.

'The combined forces of we four should be equal to the Scots and Olaf of Dublin,' Guthrek said.

'What if Owain of Alt Clwyd joins in?' Ingwar said. 'Half of my and Ethils' subjects are Welsh. If Owain and the rest of the northern Welsh join Olaf and Constantine our subjects will be more likely to join them than fight for us.'

'We all knew what was expected of us when we took these earldoms,' Guthrek said. 'Even if we are outnumbered, it is our duty. We all swore oaths to defend this land against invasion from the Scots. It is the one obligation the king asks of us for our positions. Let there be no more talk. It is time for action.'

The others nodded.

'We will need some time though,' Ingwar said. 'Our lands are on the other side of the mountains. And we need to persuade the Welsh to fight with us.'

'I'm sure you can convince them,' Guthrek said with a shrug. 'Either that or coerce them. Whatever you do, we need every last man we can get in war gear and in the field. If Olaf and Constantine take one step over the border we must stop them dead in their tracks.'

Part Six

Óláfr Skotakonungr dró saman her mikinn ok fór síðan suðr á England, en er hann kom á Norðimbraland, fór hann allt herskildi.

Olaf king of Scots, drew together a mighty host, and marched upon England. When he came to Northumberland, he advanced with shield of war.

Egils Saga Skalla-Grímssonar, kafli 52

Twenty-Two

Southern Scotland

'Is Olaf going to make us to walk all the way to Jorvik?' Skar said.

'He seems to have forgotten vikings are supposed to sail in ships,' Kari said. 'Not hike into battle.'

'Olaf is doing the right thing,' Ulrich, who was walking a little way ahead, said over his shoulder. 'Aethelstan has a huge fleet of ships. Even with the ship horde we came from Dublin with he will outnumber us. The Scots fleet is little more than a bunch of rowing boats. Aethelstan's fleet could stop this whole adventure dead in its tracks before we even reach the Saxon coast. We're better walking.'

'I thought Aethelstan's ships were busy with his meddling in Francia?' Sigurd said.

'Ships move fast,' Ulrich said. 'Aethelstan can move his from Francia to the North Sea very quickly if he has to.'

They were trudging up a low hillside in the south of the land of the Scots in the midst of a vast horde of warriors. Olaf of Dublin's army, combined with the men Limerick's Olaf Scabby Head had sent and the war horde of Constantine of the Scots, had spent the last week crossing the country from Constantine's capital in Sankt John's Toun in the north to here, the very southern extremity of the kingdom of Alba. Almost everyone walked, their belongings and their war gear on their backs, their helmets, if they had one, dangling by their chin straps from their spears. Slaves and boys struggled under the weight of long poles set across their shoulders from which heavy shirts of iron mail, the poles threaded through their sleeves, dangled.

'I don't see why we can't all ride?' Surt grumbled, sending a longing, jealous look towards Olaf, the Scots king and the other nobles who trotted at the front of the army on the backs of ponies. 'I'm not as young as you pups. These old bones of mine ache in this terrible damp weather.'

'There aren't enough horses in this whole country to carry us all,' Ulrich said. 'So we walk.'

There were some other horses but they hauled carts with shields, weapons and the other provisions required by an army on the march.

'What age are you, anyway, Surt?' Starkad said.

They all knew Surt had come from the hot, burning lands to the south of the great middle sea. To him all weather in the northern realms was damp and terrible. The hard life Surt had lived, however, had also made him very fit and strong, and his dark skin made it hard for the rest of them to judge his age. Yes, he had some grey hairs but apart from that there was little to give a clue how old he really was.

'Let's see now,' Surt said, pursing his lips. 'Many years ago I was enslaved, then brought to these benighted, freezing northern lands. I spent many years as a ring fighter for King Harald of Norway, and after his death, his son Eirik Bloody Axe. After that I joined this crew which I've been with for the last three winters. If I add all that up it comes to…'

The others looked at him with expectant eyes.

'A lot,' Surt said with a shrug and a grin.

The countryside they passed through was rugged and could have been easily stripped bare of what little crops and livestock it supported by the passing army. King Constantine, mindful of the damage that could cause to his kingdom and his own standing, made sure plenty of supplies were provided from his own, his noblemen's and their people's stores. As long as everyone was sharing the burden, no one could complain.

The weather was damp – a typical Scottish summer, Skar said – and often they trudged through rain and mud, but spirits were high. For enemies who had been at each other's throats for a century or more, the Scots and the Norse got on very well. Where they could make themselves understood to each other they found they shared a similar, very black sense of humour. At night, when the army camped, they shared tales and chanted poetry around the fires as barrels of ale brewed by the Picts and flavoured with heather were tapped.

'Someday, when things return to how they were before, we'll have to kill some of these men,' Skar had said in a wistful tone one evening. 'That will almost be a shame.'

As they travelled, their numbers swelled as more and more Scots warriors flocked to join their king's army.

The further south they went the more the countryside around them transformed from high, heather-clad mountains that rose beside deep lakes – or *lochs* – that brimmed with fish to more gentle rolling hills. In this territory their ranks began to be swollen also by Welsh warriors from Alt Clwyd and elsewhere across *Yr Hen Ogledd* – the Old North, the last of the free kingdoms of the Britons – who came to add to the strength of the force against Aethelstan.

It was about midday on the eighth day of the march. Skar squinted at the horizon.

'Is that a wall?' he said, shielding his eyes from the sun with the palm of his right hand.

'If it is, I've heard of this,' Kari said. 'The Romans built a great wall across Britain that stretches east to west, from one sea to the other.'

The others looked. It was not a wall, however. It was a grass-covered ridge that spanned the whole horizon, from a wooded area to the east to a hill that rose before it in the west. It was higher than a man and there was a ditch before it. Whatever it was, it had the look of some sort of ancient defensive structure.

'It's a kind of rampart,' Sigurd said.

'What is that?' Ulrich said to a nearby Scotsman. The man made a face showing he did not understand. A nearby Pict did respond though.

'Some say it was built by the Romans,' the man with the tattooed face said. 'One of their emperors, Antoninus, ordered it built to keep the Caledonians out. They were scared of our forefathers and it was to keep us out. But the Saxons called it Grim's Dyke.'

'Grim's?' Ulrich said. 'That's one of the names of Odin. I wouldn't be surprised if this was not something he raised with his magic in days of old. This is a good omen. We walk in the steps of the All Father himself.'

As they got closer, they saw there was a single rider mounted on a pale horse on top of the ridge, outlined against the blue of the summer sky.

'What about that?' Skar said. 'Is that a good sign, do you think, Ulrich?'

'Whoever it is can't be a threat,' Ulrich said. 'Olaf will have scouts riding ahead of the army checking for ambushes and enemies.'

'I hope so. You said Olaf yourself is a gambler,' Skar said. 'Let's hope he's not gambling with sensible war craft.'

The lone rider turned their horse and began to gallop towards the approaching horde. As they approached the wind pushed the long hood the rider wore back and they saw her pale white skin and the long braided rope of tawny hair that ran down her back.

'It's Affreca!' Skar said. 'She made it! Good girl.'

Ulrich looked sideways at his big prowman.

'*Good girl?*' he said, a bemused smile on his lips. 'I dare you to say that to her.'

They watched as Affreca approached her brother Olaf and Constantine. They exchanged words but were too far away for Ulrich and the others to hear. After a time Olaf turned in his saddle and pointed in the direction of the Wolf Coats. Affreca nodded and rode over to join them.

'Success?' Ulrich said as she swung herself out of the saddle and jumped down beside them.

'Olaf's plan worked,' she said, smiling. 'The bishop of Jorvik gave us the half-finished coins from the coinery there. We paid a viking to bring them north. They were stamped with the head of Olaf and we've been distributing them all across the north through Ljót's vikings, merchants and the like. The folk here will think Olaf is already king before he even has to strike a single blow.'

'And Aethelstan still suspects nothing?' Ulrich said, clenching his fist. 'This is excellent.'

Affreca made a face.

'Not completely,' she said. 'He ordered a monk and a company of warriors north to poke their noses into what was happening. But Aethelstan has other spies in Jorvik too.'

'The Christian churchmen all work for him,' Ulrich said, turning his head to spit. 'They can't be trusted. Constantine has brought lots of them on this march. I pray to Odin it's not a mistake. I'm surprised this bishop of Jorvik is going against Aethelstan. Are you sure *he* can be trusted?'

'He's a Ragnarsson on his mother's side,' Affreca said, grinning. 'Which makes him a cousin of Olaf and I.'

'The crafty bastard!' Skar said, shaking his head.

'Aethelstan once told me Odin's blood flowed in his veins,' Ulrich said. 'When I hear things like this I start to believe it.'

'The net was closing in on the bishop and I had to get him out of Jorvik,' Affreca said. 'Aethelstan will now be alerted to our plans. I told Olaf that we need to move fast and take Jorvik before Aethelstan has time to muster his army and move north to stop us.'

Ulrich nodded.

'What of Einar?' Skar said. 'Did you see any signs of him on your travels?'

Affreca scowled.

'I saw him in Jorvik,' she said. 'I almost shot him.'

'Almost?' Ulrich said.

'He was lucky,' she said. 'He's strutting around in Saxon armour, looking more like a Saxon every day. I thought he *was* a Saxon warlord until I saw his face. Then I had to run or I'd have been caught myself.'

'But you would have killed him had you'd known it was him, I'm sure,' Ulrich said.

'Of course,' Affreca said.

She looked away, movement from the head of the army catching her eye.

Olaf rode into the ditch ahead, then drove his horse hard, making it run up onto the turf rampart. Once on the top he stopped and wheeled his mount around. It reared up on its back legs then settled back down again.

'He's such a show-off,' Affreca said, shaking her head.

Olaf waited as the warriors of the army gathered around the bottom of the rampart. Soon they were a great thronging mass, all vying to get close enough to hear what the king of Dublin was about to say. Ulrich and the others shoved their way through the crowd until they were nearly at the front. The heat and the pressure from so many standing together was oppressive and it was a relief when Olaf held his spear above his head as a signal for quiet. A scrawny-looking Scottish monk clambered up and stood beside Olaf's horse. Ulrich and the others recognised the man who often translated the Norse tongue for King Constantine and his nobles. The monk looked pale and nervous.

All voices died away until all that could be heard was the buffeting of the gentle wind in the warm air. Olaf waited a few more moments, then began to speak.

'Men, I stand on Grim's Dyke,' Olaf shouted. The crowd beneath him was so large there was no way those at the back would be able to hear him so he paused, allowing some of those below to relay what he said to those behind him.

The monk repeated the words in the tongue of the Scots for the benefit of Constantine's warriors.

'Interesting he changed the name of the wall of Antoninus,' Affreca, who understood the Gaelic tongue the Scots spoke, said in a quiet voice.

'This is the work of Odin himself,' Olaf continued. 'This marks the boundary between Constantine's kingdom and that of Aethelstan. South of this rampart is Aengland, a kingdom which is ours for the taking. Ulfr, bring me my war shield.'

'I've always wondered where this strange journey would take me,' Wulfhelm the Saxon said to the others in the Wolf Coat crew. 'But I never imagined being part of an army invading my own land.'

As the Scots monk translated Olaf's words, Ulfr, a big Irish warrior who served Olaf as his *merkismaðr*, his standard bearer, scrambled up the embankment carrying a large leather bag with him. When he reached the king, Olaf unslung the brightly painted, light, ceremonial shield that he had over his shoulder and passed it to his flag bearer. Ulfr unlaced the leather bag and pulled a more utilitarian shield from it. It was made of thick wooden boards and bound with iron and leather. Its sole decoration was the red stag, the symbol of Dublin, painted on its face.

Olaf grasped the shield. He brandished it and his spear in the air. The warriors gathered below all cheered, the Norse Irish ones among them making the most noise.

'Once over this rampart take what you want, burn what you don't,' Olaf shouted. 'We will bring havoc and hell to this land until its people bend their knees to us and acknowledge us as their overlords. We will take back what belonged to our forefathers. We will take revenge for the thousand indignities Aethelstan has forced upon us. From now until victory our swords will not sleep in our hands and we will not stop fighting until the blood on our swords is the blood of a king!'

Deafening, bloodthirsty cheers erupted from the army. They shook their weapons and hammered spears against shields.

'Brothers, we go to war!' Olaf screamed.

He wheeled his horse and rode off, disappearing from view down the far side of the dyke. Roaring with grim excitement, the army surged forward, scaling the rampart and crossing the top, tramping down the other side and into Aengland.

Twenty-Three

Caer Ham, Northumbria

Einar peered towards the horizon, shading his eyes from the glare of the warm sun with his hand. The enemy was approaching – the scouts had told them that – but so far there was no sight of them. Ominous columns of smoke rose from several points in the distance, however.

He stood on a hilltop, surrounded by the armies of two of the Earls of the North, Alfgeir and Guthrek. The banners of Saint Cuthbert, Saint Oswald and Bebbanburh snapped in the wind above their heads. The smell of leather and polished metal from the war gear worn by all those around Einar mingled with the earthy aroma of crushed grass, trampled under the feet of hundreds of warriors. Little midges buzzed around, causing some to spit in irritation as they caught on beards and lips.

The hoarse caws of crows and ravens made Einar look up. Above their heads many of the ominous black birds wheeled and swooped in an ever greater flock.

'It's like they know there will be carnage,' he said, mostly to himself.

'The wolves will be in the trees too,' Earl Guthrek said. 'When they see men marching to battle they all know a feast of carrion will soon he laid out for them.'

It was almost a week since the Witan. The Earls Ingwar and Ethils had departed to gather their forces, agreeing to return with their armies and converge on Caer Ham, a settlement Guthrek said was bound to be on Olaf's route south. Guthrek and Alfgeir gathered their own war hordes; though with their lands being closer this had not taken as long.

Two days later word came that Olaf of Dublin and Constantine of Scotland were advancing south with their army, pillaging and ravaging the countryside as they went. Any remaining doubts that Olaf was not in Scotland just to get married had been swept away by fire, destruction and slaughter. Tales began to arrive at Ad Gefrin of massacres and cruel acts of wrecking and robbery. These were soon followed by streams of people fleeing south ahead of the oncoming army. They carried with them all they could save of their lives and belongings, their expressions empty from the horrors they had seen, their manners jumpy from living through terror.

After another two days passed without any sign of the return of the western earls, Guthrek had decided they could not risk waiting any longer. He moved his army to Caer Ham, a day's march north-west of Ad Gefrin. Late in the same day Alfgeir had also brought his forces from Bebbanburh and the armies set up camp to wait for the approaching invaders.

Now, the next morning, they all stood on the top of a small, rounded hill that lay before a little meadow in the bend of the river. The men were ready for war. Mail and helmets polished, blades sharpened, shields painted. The earls stood on the summit of hill, in the centre of the army. Their most trusted men of their personal dryht, stood around them, a bulwark and bodyguard. Surrounding them were the lesser nobles, thanes, the *Geoguth* and the *Duguth* and their own war bands. Then there were the ordinary folk, the *Fyrd*, levied from the farms and villages of the realm, armed with ancient weapons handed down from generations past or the farm tools from their barns.

'What makes you so sure Olaf will come here?' Einar asked, surveying the surrounding landscape with its low, rolling hills and the wide meandering river.

'It's a natural crossroads,' Guthrek had replied. 'Any army moving south this side of the mountains has to come this way. It's the only place the river is fordable for enough of its length to allow a chieftain to get most of his men across without the risk of leaving half on the other bank at the mercy of attack. One old Roman road runs west from here and the main one goes south. Ingwar and Ethils will bring their men east across it and meet us here. There have been many battles here. Since our folk came here from across the sea the Welsh, the Scots and now the Danes have tried to drive us back into that sea many times. And every time we have ended up fighting them here.'

Guthrek had sent scouts north and west and they had reported back that Olaf was indeed on his way and the other earls were also coming from the west.

'What if Ingwar and Ethils don't arrive before Olaf?' Alfgeir said. The young man's face was gaunt. His eyes roamed the horizon as he spoke.

'My scouts tell me that our forces, Alfgeir, are about equal to Olaf's without the other two,' Guthrek said. 'We can beat them without the others. If they do arrive in time we'll outnumber them and victory will be even more assured.'

'All the same,' Alfgeir said. 'We should wait for the others so we outnumber the enemy, yes? The time for heroic stands is when you really have no other choice.'

Earl Guthrek tutted.

'You are the nephew of Vilhjálmr of Rúðu?' Einar said. 'Your homeland is beautiful.'

'I sometimes wish I was back there,' the young earl said absently, as he looked at the rough countryside around them.

'I was in Rúðu with your uncle last winter,' Einar said. 'He was outnumbered five to one. He still charged out of the city and won the battle. It was a victory that will live in memory forever.'

The young earl scowled at Einar. Guthrek pursed his lips in appreciation.

'It's good to have the king's man stand with us,' Earl Guthrek said. 'And good to know you are not scared to make a stand.'

He glanced sideways at Alfgeir, who did not miss the slight.

'I am not scared, if that is what you are saying,' Alfgeir said through gritted teeth. 'What I suggested was sound war craft. You don't throw away the lives of yourself and your men without need.'

'There are times when there is only one option and that is to fight,' Guthrek said. 'We have arrived at one of those times now. Foreigners invade our land. Our home. You would not understand this. You have only been earl here for a year or so. This land is not in your blood. But the king gave you this realm for a reason. To hold it for him. Not just him but for his folk who live here. My men are hardened for war. Every one of them will fight to the death to defend our home.'

Looking around, Einar saw what he meant. The warriors who stood around Guthrek were grim-faced, hard men with scarred faces and eyes that glared challenge. They were killers every one of them. He had little doubt if they were put to the test then they would fight to the last man to defend their lord, their families and their land.

Alfgeir's war band were a little different. Every one of them looked just as dangerous as Guthrek's did; however, the looks and sideways glances they shot in their earl's direction made Einar think they had their own doubts about their lord. The feeling was no doubt mutual. If Alfgeir had only been in this land for a year or so, then he would not have had time to build up the same unflinching loyalty in his men that Guthrek had. Guthrek's warriors probably were the sons of men who had served his father before him. Their ties to each other and the land probably went back generations. Alfgeir was not scared, he just did not share Guthrek's confidence that if it came to it, his men would fight to the death to protect him, or if he fell, battle to the end to get revenge.

Einar looked at his own war band, the hardy Saxons who until very recently had borne no respect for him. He had won some of their respect but would they fight for him now?

The realisation made Einar himself feel a surge of nerves. This was not his first battle. Knowing the odds he had been feeling confident until then, almost excited. If the western earls arrived in time they would outnumber the enemy but if there were cracks in their alliance then everything could fall apart.

The sound of horns blowing came from the distance. Einar strained his eyes toward the horizon once more. Out of the shimmering haze he saw men emerge. An army marched towards the river.

'They're coming,' Guthrek said.

'Lord, look!' Guthrek's standard bearer was pointing to the west.

Looking around with the others, Einar saw a second army was marching from that direction as well. Green and white banners fluttered over them.

'It's Ingwar and Ethils,' Alfgeir said, smiling for the first time that day. 'They are just in time.'

'Come,' Earl Guthrek said. 'Let us march down and meet them in the meadow. Then we shall confront the invaders together. We will slaughter them as they cross the river.'

Twenty-Four

'Do you think that's a good idea?' Einar said, his previous misgivings veering towards panic for a moment. 'We'd be giving up the high ground.'

Even as he spoke, however, Guthrek was waving to his signallers who began blowing horns. The whole party began to march forwards, tramping down the slope towards the meadow below.

'What do we do, lord?' Garwulf said.

Einar turned and saw his men were looking at him. He could tell from their expressions they shared his doubts about the wisdom of this move. He opened his mouth to speak but stopped himself. What was the right thing to do? His men needed clear direction. If he wavered they would follow him. They were only a small part of a much larger force but if they did not follow everyone else would it encourage others to do the same? The whole army could fall apart. The battle would be lost before it started.

He wished Cynewulf was there. The monk, strangely wise in the crafts of war and state, would know what to do but he was in the rear of the army with the rest of the churchmen, praying for victory.

'Come on,' Einar said. Resolving that there was in fact little choice. 'This is the homeland of these men around us. We can be sure they'll know what's best. They'll know the best place to fight the enemy.'

The others nodded and to Einar's relief there was no sign of scepticism on their faces. They joined the others in tramping down the hillside towards the meadow below. All around them horns blew and the air was filled with the rattling of spear shafts on shields and the clinking of iron mail rings.

When they reached the bottom of the hill the army began to fan out across the meadow.

'Form the shield wall,' Guthrek shouted. His signallers blasted their horns and with a resounding clack of wood on wood the front rank of the war horde joined their shields together, each warrior's shield overlapping that of the man to his left's to form one, continuous line of defence.

They all let out a mighty shout of defiance, directed at the Scots, Norse Irish and Picts who gathered on the opposite bank of the river. They too fanned out. Einar could see the banner of Olaf – the red stag – flying over the men in the centre of the enemy line. They were Norsemen; he could see that from their mail brynjas, their visored helmets and their round shields which, at the sight of the Saxon army doing so, also locked into a shield wall to mirror it. On either side of the Norsemen were the Scots and Picts. They were much less orderly. Some had shields, some just little round bucklers, some had only sticks to defend themselves with. Their ranks bristled with spear shafts. Einar noticed that while nearly all the kerns who made up the army of the Gaels wore the skirt-like garment that left the bottom half of their legs bare, by no means did all the Norse wear breeches and many also wore the same skirts.

He wondered if Ulrich and the others were among the warriors thronging the far riverbank. Was Affreca notching an arrow right then, scanning his own ranks for targets. She would try to kill the leaders. It was what Ulrich had taught them: *Kill the kings, the jarls, the hirdmen and the ordinary peasants won't know what to do. They'll soon break and run.* Today, Einar was one of those leaders.

While he felt the now familiar prickling sensation of being vulnerable to Affreca's unerring aim, Einar otherwise felt quite confident. This looked to be nowhere near as harrowing or dangerous as some of the previous battles he had been in. There was always real danger in a war, but unlike at Viken where he had been shoved into the front ranks, Gandvik where he had defended a decrepit old fort, desperately outnumbered, or even at Rúðu when they had risked a potentially suicidal charge to take the enemy by surprise, today he stood beside the earls, surrounded by their most daunting fighters, at the heart of an army that would outnumber the enemy. The only thing that really worried Einar was how he would react if he found himself shield to shield with one of the Wolf Coats. They would not hesitate to attack, and aim to kill. Could he do the same?

Einar glanced to the west. The armies of Ingwar and Ethils still approached. They were much closer now. Amid the clouds of dust kicked up by their boots Einar saw their banners and ranks of shields and knew that Guthrek was right. Once the earls joined forces they would easily outnumber the opposition. The thought made him even calmer and he could see from the expressions on those around him that they too now had little doubt about the outcome of this fight. It would be victory.

'Wait,' Garwulf, the young lad by Einar's side said. 'I think they're on the wrong side of the river.'

A murmur went through the gathered warriors as others noticed the same thing. Einar felt his guts lurch as he realised that the war hordes of the brother earls were indeed on the other side of the river, the one which the army of Olaf and Constantine was arrayed on.

'What are those fools doing?' Guthrek said. 'Do they think they can steal the glory of victory by attacking alone?'

'They're not going to attack them,' Alfgeir said, his voice was tinged with despair. 'They're going to join them.'

Shouts of anger and disbelief rose from the surrounding warriors as everyone realised what was happening. Einar stared, longing to see something that told him his eyes were deceiving him. His last hope of that vanished as the warriors of Ingwar and Ethils began to line up alongside the Norsemen and the Scots on the other side.

'Those treacherous bastards!' Guthrek shouted. 'They're betraying the king. They're betraying us!'

'That's the banner of Owain of Alt Clwyd,' Alfgeir pointed at a standard portraying a green lion on a white background that fluttered amid the other banners of the brother earls and their noblemen. They've joined forces with the Welsh.'

'So now we fight Scots, Irish and Welsh,' Garwulf said out of the corner of his mouth with black humour that provoked smiles around him even in that desperate moment. 'Is there anyone left on these islands *not* about to attack us?'

Horns sounded on the far side of the river, as did a steady thump of spear shafts on shields. In time to the beating spears, the enemy on the other side of the river began to advance.

'We should leave while we still can,' Alfgeir said. His voice was rising in pitch.

'You would run away?' Guthrek shouted. 'What sort of a coward are you?'

'I mean withdraw,' Alfgeir said. 'It is the prudent move. We can retreat south and wait for Aethelstan to bring the main force north. We're outnumbered now.'

'We can still hold them,' Guthrek said. His eyes glared with the intensity of burning coals from the shadows beneath his helmet. 'We can give them a bloody nose, *then* we can retreat with honour. If we retreat at all!'

'Lord Guthrek,' Alfgeir said. 'Why should we all die for nothing? Our warriors can swell the ranks of the king and ensure final victory. They can't do that if they are all dead!'

Einar was about to say *a corpse on his pyre is no use to anyone* but remembered just in time that this was a saying of Odin's and the Christians around him would not appreciate that.

'And when we turn our backs on our enemies and run away,' Guthrek said in a growl, 'do you think they will just stand there and let us go? If I die on a battlefield I have no desire that when my corpse is delivered to my wife she sees all the wounds are in my back. You will stand here with us, Alfgeir, and if you take one step backwards I will kill you myself!'

Both earls glared at each other, chests heaving with emotion.

'Lords, with respect, we have other folk to fight today,' Einar said. 'And the time to run is over anyway.'

With a final snort of derision, Guthrek tore his gaze away from Alfgeir.

It was time to make final preparations. Einar drew his sword and slid it into the prongs at the bottom of the fighting glove on his right hand. Then with his free hand he laced the leather thongs around the hilt to hold it in place. He shrugged his shield off his shoulder and held it ready.

The enemy army was halfway across the river. Einar could see that for a long stretch the water was very shallow, probably made even shallower by it being the latter half of the summer. The warriors splashing across it were barely getting their feet wet. They were still in reasonable order, holding a straight enough line, but their front ranks were becoming ragged on the east flank as Scottish warriors began to push forwards, moving ahead of Olaf's ordered shield wall, eager to get the battle started.

'Stand firm, men,' Guthrek said in a commanding tone to all who stood around him. 'The Scots will fly at us like mindless furies. We know what they are like. All we need do is keep calm heads and hold the shield wall. Soon their anger and their breath will be spent and it will be easy to kill them.'

Einar's memory shot back to the screaming, charging mass of Scotsmen who had poured down the hill at him and the others when they raided Cathair Aile. It had been a terrifying sight but Guthrek was right. If they could hold the initial surge aimed at punching holes in the shield wall, they could stop their attack. Then there would just be the Welsh, Norsemen and the warriors of Ingwar and Ethils to deal with.

'Ready!' Guthrek shouted.

Einar felt all those around him tense, steeling themselves for the first onslaught. The shield wall at the front clicked as it clamped together even tighter. Everyone seemed to hold their breath.

Then the army advancing towards them stopped. A burly Norseman shoved his way through the front rank to stand before all the rest. He was broad-shouldered, his mail shirt was magnificent, polished to shine like silver and reaching almost to his knees. His helmet was decorated with beasts, dragons and other monsters, that curled around his eyes and crossed his crown. From beneath the helmet visor tumbled a long red beard, which was braided. Likewise his hair, the same fiery colour, tumbled down his back in three braids. In his left hand he grasped his shield, painted with the red stag of Dublin. In the other big fist he clenched a spear.

Einar recognised him. It was Olaf the Red Guthfrithsson, King of Dublin.

Olaf cocked his arm back, crouched, then hurled the spear into the air, sending it hurtling high over the heads of the warriors of Guthrek and Alfgeir. It was not a mistake. It was the custom to start a war, going back to when the world was young.

'Odin owns you all!' Olaf screamed at the top of his lungs. 'You are my sacrifice to him.'

Twenty-Five

With a deafening roar, the army of Olaf launched its attack. Scottish warriors, unburdened by the weight of mail shirts or heavy shields, came pounding across the last of the river, sending sprays of water in all directions. Behind them the Norsemen in their helmets and brynjas advanced in a steady line, their shields locked together like a moving palisade fence. A great dark wave rose from behind them as the Welsh archers loosed their bows; other Scots and Norsemen at the rear launched spears.

As the first Scots rammed into the Saxon shield wall, Einar felt the impact as it rippled from the front rank back through the ranks of men pressed together before him. He rocked back and forward on his feet along with those around him.

The wave of missiles arrived at almost the same moment.

'Shields up!' Guthrek shouted as every man behind the shield wall in the front rank raised their shields above their heads. A manic battering began as the arrows and spears pelted down onto the wood of the shield faces. Einar felt his shield bounce and buck as arrows hammered into it. A spear thumped into the shield of a warrior not far to his left. The weight of it made the shield unmanageable and the man lowered it so he could break the shaft with his sword. Almost immediately an arrow struck him in his now uncovered face. Einar felt the warrior's warm blood splatter across his left cheek as the warrior dropped to the ground. The crush of bodies was so great there was nothing Einar could do to get to the fallen man and those around where he had dropped risked being shoved over themselves in the crush of bodies around them. There was no choice but to leave him to his fate. Einar consoled his conscience with the thought that the lack of sound from the warrior meant he was probably already dead.

The deadly hail of arrows and spears abated. Einar and the others lowered their shields. Scots warriors, their faces twisted with hatred, battered the shield wall in the front ranks. They stabbed spears over the top of the Saxon shields and through any gaps they spotted. They hurled their shoulders against the shield faces or slashed and swiped with swords, axes or knives. Here and there they managed to cause injury but they were attacking individually, so lacked the concentrated weight and impact to breach the Saxon defensive formation.

The men behind the shields remained calm, then when the opportunity came, struck out. Their swords and spears soon began taking a heavy toll on the unprotected Scots warriors. Bodies began to pile up before the shield wall.

'My father told me this is how the Scots fight,' Garwulf, who was in the crush of men to Einar's right, shouted to the others around him. 'They care more about winning glory for themselves than sharing in victory. Thank God Almighty for Scots' pride.'

'Let them waste their lives in a vain pursuit of fame,' Guthrek shouted above the clamour.

Behind the Scots the Norsemen continued their relentless, disciplined march. Soon they would meet the Saxon shield wall.

Something moving very fast pinged off Einar's helmet. It made a clang, hitting him hard enough to make his head rock back and forth. Looking at the enemy, he saw Scots with slingshots hurling stones in his direction. The smooth pebbles – still wet from the riverbed the Scotsmen had picked them from as they walked across – began to clatter and clang off the helmets and shields of the Saxon warriors around Einar. Einar lowered his head a little as another stone bounced off his helmet. He was sure the head guard would save him from fatal injury, but if one of the pebbles hit him on the exposed part of his face beneath his visor it would mean a broken jaw or smashed teeth.

As if to confirm his concerns, one of the warriors on his right cried out in pain, the sound competing with the sharp crack of bone. A stone had struck Garwulf on the knuckles of his right hand. Despite the heavy gauntlet he wore his hand was smashed and he dropped his sword, unable to grasp it any longer.

'Get out of here,' Einar shouted to him. 'There's no point in you being here if you can't hold a weapon.'

Garwulf nodded. With a sheepish look at the others, he began pushing his way back through the throng of warriors towards the rear of the army where the monks could provide medical help.

Then the Norsemen arrived to add to the so-far ineffective Scots assault. With a loud slap of wood on wood, the shield faces of the advancing Dubliners crashed into those of the Saxon shield wall. Einar once more felt the thump of the impact as it rippled through the mass of tightly packed bodies.

The battle then descended into an exhausting shoving match. The Norsemen tried to drive the Saxons back, the Welsh and Scots lending their weight from behind. Einar and the others behind their own front rank did the same, planting their feet as wide as they could and lending their shoulders to the effort.

Here and there one of the front rank fell, stabbed through a chink in the shield wall or losing his footing and slipping into oblivion beneath the hordes of trampling boots. Every time this happened he was replaced fast before the enemy could exploit any break in the defences.

Stones and arrows continued to rain down on Einar and

those around him, each shower taking its grim toll. The Saxons replied with their own spears and arrows, shot from the ranks behind the earls. Einar and the others around him cheered when they saw them cause harm.

The battle dragged on, now little more than an angry pushing match, though one in which the penalty for losing your footing was death. No side was advancing more than a few steps, which were inexorably lost again within moments as the mass of bodies staggered back the other way. Einar knew it would keep on like this until one side tired more than the other, though neither wanted to be that one as to turn your back on the enemy to retreat would be fatal. It would stay this way for a long time, unless someone tried a risky move to break the stalemate.

Then he caught sight of movement behind the front rank of the enemy shield line. It was like a flow of people exchanging places. For a moment he assumed they were rearranging their ranks, bringing fresh warriors from the rear to the front to increase pressure on the Saxons. Then he spotted what looked very like a wolf's head. Not just any wolf's head either. The black pelt of a wolf's head drawn up like a hood over the iron helm of a very tall, broad-shouldered Norse warrior.

It was Skar. In an instant Einar knew what was coming.

'*Svinfylking! Svinfylking!*' he shouted a warning to those around him. Seeing the blank looks on their faces added. 'The boar's snout. They're forming the swine array, the formation to breach a shield wall!'

Horns blasted among Olaf's army. A section of the front rank split and pulled back to the right and left in one rapid movement like an opening gate. It was obvious this was a planned, rehearsed move. Behind them was a formation of men arrayed in a triangle, its point aimed straight at Earls Guthrek and Alfgeir's shield wall. At the head of it was Skar, a towering figure with shield in one hand and battle axe in the other, his wolfskin cloak pulled up over his helmet so the pointed ears stood up. Einar knew the other Wolf Coats would be in the formation too but there were all sorts of big men as well, some wrapped in bearskins, some stripped to the waist, gnawing at the rims of their shields as battle rage took over their minds, drowning all reasonable thoughts or mercy.

One moment the men in the earls' shield wall had been shoving with all their might against an enemy who was pushing back just as hard, then the next they were simply gone. The pressure disappeared. Four men in the centre, unable to stop themselves, stumbled forwards, breaking the shield wall up where they were.

Before they could recover the men in the viking svinfylking came screaming forwards. Skar went straight for the stumbling men. He smashed one aside with his shield and chopped a second down with his axe as he shoved his way into the gap they had left in the earls' shield wall. Then he was through and the others were pouring in after him, the weight of their numbers pushed open the gap wider still. They hacked and slashed, kicked and bit on either side, rending the shield wall asunder in moments as the men who made it turned in on themselves to face this new threat now beside them in among their own men.

Chaos and panic spread through the ranks of the earls' men. What had been two masses of warriors pushing against each other dissolved into countless hand-to-hand battles. The Scots, recovered from the exertions of their initial charge, poured through the gaps in the now ragged shield wall, tearing it further to pieces until all that remained was a churning mass of men trying to murder each other.

One thing Einar was sure of was that if they did not restore some sort of ordered formation very soon the battle would be lost. They needed to create some space between them and the enemy to do that.

'Pull back!' Back!' he shouted to his own men, but their backs were pressed against Guthrek's men and there was nowhere for them to go.

'We need space!' Einar yelled at the earl, who was glaring at the turmoil before him as if personally offended by it.

'You!' Guthrek screamed. Einar looked and saw the earl was levelling his sword at someone in the tangled crowd before him. 'Traitor!'

Einar followed the direction of Guthrek's sword tip and saw, scrambling over the corpses of men who moments before had formed their shield wall, Earl Ingwar. He had a conical helmet which hid his bald head but Einar could see the bottom half of his face with his broad, square-cut beard and his torso was wrapped in the same thick coat of mail, which in places had such excess it hung in rolls. His great wide-bladed sword was streaked with blood. The earl was clearly not one to leave the fighting up to his men.

Despite the appalling noise of the battle going on around them, Ingwar heard Guthrek's shout. Grinning, Ingwar began loping towards him, cutting down anyone who was in his way. Just before he reached him, one of Guthrek's bodyguard stepped in front of his earl. The Saxon drove his spear into Ingwar's guts but it stopped dead, the blade unable to penetrate the thick mail. Ingwar swiped down with his sword, shattering the Saxon's spear shaft. Then he wrenched it back up, slashing the man's throat open and unleashing a torrent of blood.

'You betrayed us all,' Earl Guthrek roared. 'You betrayed our king. Stand back, men. I will fight this coward alone.'

Einar saw that most of the rest of the earl's personal dryht were too busy fighting for their own lives to be able to help their earl anyway. He could, though. He was close enough and began shoving others out of the way to get closer.

As his bodyguard collapsed to the ground, Guthrek charged at Ingwar. He swung his sword, its bejewelled hilt flashing in the sun. It caught Ingwar across the chest in a blow that should have sliced him asunder from his right shoulder to his left waist. Yet again, however, Ingwar's mail thwarted the attack. The sword blade could not sever the thick mail rings. Instead the blow just sent Ingwar staggering backwards a few paces.

Einar now understood why Ingwar bore no shield. His mail was so good he did not need one. The brynja he wore must have been the work of a highly skilled master craftsman.

Still grinning like a madman, Ingwar recovered and strode forwards. He stabbed at Guthrek who tried to leap back out of the way. Guthrek collided with the man behind him, however, and Ingwar's blade went right through Guthrek's thigh. The earl collapsed onto his backside.

Einar scrambled the last few paces to get to the fallen Guthrek. Ingwar was already raising his sword for the killer blow. With a desperate lunge, Einar drove his sword into Ingwar's exposed side. Einar was at full stretch, trying to throw all his weight behind the blade. The point dug deep into the mail but to Einar's dismay the rings still held. His blade bowed, then with a rattle of metal on metal the sword twisted in his grip. The leather thongs holding the hilt in place within his fighting glove popped open and the sword fell from his grasp as Einar stumbled off balance.

Ingwar, his grin now a rictus of annoyance, struck at Einar instead of Guthrek. Einar was sprawling sideways and had no chance to move out of the way. The world exploded into a thousand spinning lights as the blade struck him across the side of the helmet. Already falling, the impact sent him reeling faster and Einar went face first into the ground.

Twenty-Six

The noise of the battle abated to a muffled, distant rumble. All around him was darkness. Was he dead?

Then someone stood on him and the world came roaring back. The stench of trampled grass, blood and shit filled his nose. A forest of legs surrounded him as men stumbled back and forth around and over him. He was not dead. For some reason Ingwar had not finished him off but if he lay there much longer he would be trampled to a mush beneath the boots of those around him.

Then he felt a hand reach down and grab him under the arm. A moment later he was being hauled to his feet. Still dazed, he found himself looking into the dark eyes of a young man. Then he realised it was Earl Alfgeir.

'The battle is lost,' Alfgeir said. 'Perhaps you'll finally listen to me. We must go now or we'll all die.'

'Earl Guthrek…' Einar said, looking around him at the carnage that was ensuing.

'Ingwar killed him,' Alfgeir said. 'Then Guthrek's bodyguards rushed forward and swept him away.'

'Is Ingwar dead too?' Einar said. His head felt like it was full of wool. It was hard to think.

'I don't know,' Alfgeir said. 'But if we don't go we will be.'

'My men,' Einar said. 'I can't leave without them.'

'Half are dead,' Alfgeir said. 'A big viking clad in wolfskin killed two of them. The rest are lost in this confusion. Come on. This is the last chance you'll get to live.'

Einar felt his heart sink. He had led those young men here and now some of them had lost their lives. It had been his choice to follow Guthrek down the hill.

The young earl guided Einar for a few paces until he felt more steady on his feet. Einar's mind began to return to him and he realised he had no sword. He looked around but there was no sign of it. It had either been kicked away in the throng or someone else had taken it. One of Alfgeir's men rushed forward, and the young earl passed Einar over to him.

'Signal retreat,' Alfgeir shouted. 'We must get out of here. It's up to every man to look to his own safety now.'

The others from Alfgeir's bodyguard closed around Einar and Alfgeir. One of them began blasting a series of notes on a horn that rose above the sound of battle, telling all who could to withdraw. Then they began to force their way through the battle throng, hacking down enemies and shoving aside those from their own side who were in their way. By the time they reached the bottom of the hill they were free of most of the battle crush and began to jog.

The fog in Einar's head began to clear, leaving a sharp pain behind that spiked with every step. However he felt enough like himself that he shrugged off the helping arms of Alfgeir's dryht and ran, unaided up to the summit of the hill. There they paused for a moment and looked back.

From the summit of the little hill they could see the slaughter unfolding in the meadow below. Men struggled hand to hand in mortal duels amid piles of corpses. Severed limbs and hacked carcasses lay all around like the meadow was the workshop of some monstrous butcher. Einar was not sure if it was due to the blow he had taken to the head, but it looked as though the water of the river flowing downstream was tinted red.

Some pockets of order had formed where groups of warriors had banded together to form little shield walls or squares. Perhaps those men would be able to fight their way out but they were desperately outnumbered. Einar could see the horde of warriors still thronging the far bank of the river and knew that even if the remainder of the earls' army on this bank managed to kill all those they currently fought, there were plenty more to take their place.

Amid the throng the banner of Saint Oswald still waved, which meant Guthrek's standard bearer at least was still alive. The standard bearer stood amid a formation of warriors who were probably the last of Guthrek's dryht.

'They will fight on to their death,' Alfgeir said, noticing the flag as well. 'They won't heed the signal to retreat.'

'Brave men,' Einar said. 'But such a waste of life.'

'You are like me – brought up overseas with Danish ways,' Alfgeir said with a half grin. 'This is the way of these Saxons. Each warrior swears an oath to defend his lord with his life, and if his lord falls in battle to not leave the field until he has gained revenge or is dead himself. It is their duty.'

'Not all men fulfil their duty,' Einar said, remembering with a chill the oath Aethelstan had induced him to swear. He realised he was now under the same obligation if the king fell in battle. The next time they fought Olaf, Aethelstan would be in field too. If he fell, what would Einar do then?

'We could have defended this hilltop,' Einar said, looking around with rueful eyes.

'It's unfortunate that the mistake of one man can lead to the deaths of many,' Alfgeir said. 'Now we must go if we don't want to make similar mistakes.'

They ran down the other side of the hill into a temporary camp set up by the army before marching into battle. The horses the nobles of the army had ridden here on were tethered, attended by servants and slaves. Carts and chests of war gear, food and other supplies waited for owners who would never return. A large number of monks and churchmen were there, some praying but most attending to the wounds of those warriors injured in the battle who had managed to struggle back to receive attention.

As Alfgeir, Einar and his warriors trotted into the camp, all eyes turned to the little group of bloodied, battered warriors, their mail streaked with gore, their faces plastered with sweat and dirt. The expressions on the faces of the churchmen and wounded fell at the sight of the earl. If Alfgeir was retreating from the battle it could only mean one thing.

'Lord, what news from the fight?' a monk asked. Einar saw he bore the staff of one of their chiefs, perhaps a bishop.

'The battle is lost,' Alfgeir said. He spoke in a loud voice, ensuring as many as possible heard him. 'Those of you who can, should leave. There is little time before Olaf and his army will come over that hill.'

Groans of dismay ran around the gathered men.

'We had begun to suspect as much, lord,' the lead monk said, 'from the reports of the wounded coming back for treatment.'

The young Saxon, Garwulf, was sitting nearby. Cynewulf squatted beside him, binding a splint to the back of the lad's injured hand. Both looked up and saw Einar.

'You survived, lord?' Garwulf said. 'Sorry your fancy cloak didn't.'

Einar lifted the edge of the red cloak Aethelstan had given him and saw it was filthy and torn.

The sound of approaching hoofbeats made them all turn. Three horsemen were riding from the south. They were going hard. As they rode up to the encampment Einar saw they wore mail that was holed in places; it was smeared and dirty. Their faces were covered in sweat and dirt. Their eyes were hollow and there were looks of concern on their faces. If they had not been riding from the opposite direction they had all the look of warriors who had been in the battle.

'Where is the earl?' the lead rider said.

'Earl Guthrek has fallen in battle,' Alfgeir said. 'I am Alfgeir, Jofri of all Northumbria. You can speak to me as you would speak to him.'

'Lord, I bring grave news,' the rider said. 'Ad Gefrin was attacked this morning. Raiders came and with the army gone they overran us in no time. Those who could escaped. Those who could not were killed or enslaved. Ad Gefrin is in flames.'

'Who did this?' Alfgeir said.

'Norsemen, lord,' the rider said.

Alfgeir sighed.

'Well I have news for you too,' he said. 'You have ridden in the wrong direction if you look for safety. This battle is lost.'

'Ingwar and Ethils will have told Olaf that Guthrek and your war horde was gathering here to confront him,' Einar said to Alfgeir. 'He will have sent raiders on horseback to take Ad Gefrin while it was unguarded. He has both captured it and cut off any retreat for us to run there for refuge.'

'We're between the hammer and the anvil,' Alfgeir said.

'Ingwar and Ethils' realms are to the west. Olaf's army to the north and south,' Einar said. 'It doesn't leave us a lot of choice.'

'We head east, towards the coast,' Alfgeir said. 'It may be a blessing. There is a large port there. We can get ships and sail down the coast to my fortress at Bebbanburh. It's impregnable. We should be safe there.'

Or trapped there, Einar thought to himself but said nothing.

'Whoever can ride, grab a horse,' Alfgeir ordered. 'The rest, God be with you.'

Einar looked around. Many of the wounded looked like they had been carried here. They were sprawled around the ground, some missing limbs, some near death. Even those who were not, looked too injured to walk never mind ride.

'Some of the monks will stay with them,' the bishop said.

'What about the rest of the lads, lord?' Garwulf looked at Einar. His expression was expectant.

Einar bit his lip. If some of his men were still alive then he could not leave them behind. It was bad enough he had left them behind on the battlefield. He had led them here so he should make sure they got away.

He felt a hard shove on his left shoulder. It was strong enough to send Einar reeling sideways. He was still staggering, trying to recover his balance as he heard an angry buzz whiz past him, followed by a soft thump. Garwulf cried out. His shout turned to a cough as he fell backwards, an arrow embedded in the centre of his chest.

Einar stared, shocked, at the young warrior who hit the ground flat on his back. The arrow had gone right through his heart. His mouth was open as if to speak but his eyes were already fixed and staring at something very far away in the sky.

Cynewulf was standing half crouched, arms outstretched, above him. It was he who had shoved Einar to the side and out of the arrow's path. The monk was looking back towards the hilltop behind them, as yet unaware of the consequences of what he had just done.

'Archer!' Cynewulf cried, pointing up at a lone figure who was on the hilltop, outlined against the sky. She – Einar was sure it was a she – had a bow in one hand and was pulling another arrow from her arrow bag.

'After them!' Alfgeir shouted to his men. They turned, shields raised, and with an angry shout began dashing back up the hill. Einar grabbed a shield from one of the wounded nearby and rushed after them. The archer on the hilltop loosed off a couple more arrows as they charged. The first, unable to find a target behind the lead warrior's large round shield, thudded into its surface. The second one skidded off the helmet of a warrior coming behind.

When they were about halfway up the hill the figure on the summit turned, her long black cloak swirling around her, and disappeared from sight down the far side. Einar and the others scrambled on until they reached the top but the archer was gone when they got there.

What looked like a large contingent of Olaf's army was coming up the other side.

'Our men have been totally overrun,' Alfgeir said. 'We really *must* flee now.'

Einar could see there was little hope. The vikings, Scots and Welsh were swarming everywhere. What few pockets of Saxons still stood were surrounded and it would only be a matter of time before they were defeated. The battle had been lost so fast it was hard to comprehend.

His head was beginning to hurt with a stabbing, intense pain but the strange dreamy feeling that had got in the way of his thoughts had now cleared like a morning fog from the river. He took a deep breath, feeling the resolve returning to his heart. Garwulf was dead and his other men may or may not be. He could stay and die like Guthrek's men did but that would be a waste. This was a war. There would be other battles to come and a dead man would be no use in them.

'*A corpse on his pyre is no use to anyone,*' Einar said, this time aloud. 'You're right. We must go. They may have won the battle, but we can still stop them getting their hands on you, Lord Alfgeir. You are still Lord of Bebbanburh and Jofri of the North. While you live, Olaf cannot claim to have taken all of Northumbria.'

They all turned and ran back down the slope. Heedless to the cries of some of the wounded, every man grabbed what horses they could. Einar took a black and white pony and Cynewulf leapt onto a brown horse beside it. His face was grave but if he was troubled by causing the death of Garwulf through his saving of Einar he did not show it.

The company kicked their heels and the horses set off, galloping to the east along the bank of the wide, twisting river. As they left the encampment, Einar glanced over his shoulder and saw hordes of Norsemen and Scots pouring over the top of the hill and down towards the encampment. He could only hope they would be merciful to the wounded and the Christian Scots would stop the Norsemen murdering the monks who had stayed behind. However, as he heard the first screams rising above the pounding of his horse's hooves on the turf, he knew that hope was a most forlorn one.

They rode on, pushing the horses as fast as they could. The people at the encampment who could get away had scattered in all directions, and now less than thirty remained in the company who rode around Alfgeir.

They galloped along a narrow track beside the river as that weaved its way through woods. The countryside around them was green and verdant. The river carved along the base of a valley between low hills where the earth was so thin purple rocks, like the bones of the land, were visible in places. Sheep dotted the fields but apart from the occasional isolated farmstead, there was little sign of people. Birds sang from the bushes and trees. As they rode through this peaceful, beautiful landscape it was hard to believe that only a short distance behind them was a scene of horrific slaughter.

Einar felt bone-tired and a sharp pain shot through his head with every footfall of his horse. He was grateful when, after a while, the trees thinned out a little and the company began to slow their flat-out gallop, aware of the toll it was taking on the horses.

'Let them drink,' Alfgeir said, holding his hand up to signal they should stop.

They halted and let the horses take water from the river. Some of the riders, Einar included, jumped off their mounts and sucked down gulps of the cool, clear water too. Einar pulled off his helmet and plunged his head in, hoping the shock of the cold water might dispel the pain a little.

'Let's have a look at you, lad,' Cynewulf said, dismounting himself.

The monk tilted Einar's head back and looked into his eyes in a way that reminded Einar of how his mother had used to examine vegetables she was buying, as if checking for damage or bruising. Cynewulf pulled Einar's left lower eyelid down, peering down his nose at the pink flesh and the bottom of Einar's eye. Then he let it go, sat back and patted Einar on the shoulder.

'You'll live,' Cynewulf said. 'You've had a couple of decent bangs to the head in the last week or so but the pain will leave you soon and you'll be right as rain. Sometime in the future you'll find it hard to remember folk's names and start calling everyone "lad" or "son" instead. It happens to most old warriors. Right, lad?'

He winked.

Einar smiled.

'You were once a warrior, weren't you?' he said. 'Before you were a monk.'

'I was,' Cynewulf said. His jaw became set and he looked away at the trees. 'A fearsome one at that. I fought for the king's father and for the king too. But now I fight God's fight. I win souls instead of taking lives. I will tell you this, though, lad: if I'd had a sword in my hand today, by God I would have cut a bloody swathe through those bastards!'

He stopped and looked down, aware of the fire that had entered his voice.

'Silence,' one of Alfgeir's warriors said.

They all looked at him and saw he was crouching, both hands flat to the ground.

'Someone's coming,' he said.

They all froze, ears straining. Einar placed his hand on the turf of the riverbank and felt the slight vibrations through the soft soil. Then, through the bubbling of the water and the warbling of the birdsong, he caught the unmistakable sound of thrumming horse hooves.

'They're coming after us,' Cynewulf said.

'We could set a trap for them,' Einar said. 'In these trees they'll probably ride right into it.'

'There could be a hundred of them,' Cynewulf said, shaking his head. 'The safest thing is to get going again.'

Without need for further instruction, they all clambered back into their saddles, pulled their reluctant horses away from their drinking and set off once more.

Soon they were back up to speed and galloping along the riverside once more. The river itself was wide and getting wider as they rode, a sure sign to Einar that they were getting closer to wherever it finally opened itself into the sea.

As they came to the end of a very long bend in the river Einar glanced back. He could see movement – flashes of horsemen between the trees and bushes – coming after them. Their numbers were hidden by the green foliage and they were still some way away but there was no doubt they were following them.

They rode on, the vegetation getting sparser and the river ever wider. Glancing back again Einar got a better look at the company pursuing them. Like those around Einar, they rode in a column because of the narrow track beside the river. There was no time to count, but Einar could see by the length of the column of horsemen chasing them that their numbers were substantial. The would outnumber Alfgeir's company so Cynewulf had made the right call.

All they had to do now was get away.

As they galloped on, the river became less twisting, and the countryside around them flattened out, all more signs that they were getting nearer the sea. The horses were covered in sweat and Einar could tell his could not keep up the pace they were going at much longer. He glanced over his shoulder again and saw their pursuers had edged closer. Then they rode into another little wood and he lost sight of them again.

'You say we can find ships at the coast,' Einar called to Alfgeir. 'Are you sure about that?'

'This river ends in a fishing port,' the earl said. 'There are always boats there.'

'Will there be enough to fit all of us?' Einar said.

'Let's just hope the locals aren't all out fishing,' Cynewulf said. 'And if they aren't, they don't object too much to our taking their boats.'

Einar glanced over his shoulder, catching another glimpse of their pursuers through the trees. If there were ships waiting there, it would be a close-run thing for their company to board and launch the ships before Olaf's men caught up with them. Then, if there were enough ships for them too, would they continue the chase by sea?

'Look! I told you there would be ships,' Alfgeir said. He was grinning and pointing above the trees ahead where several masts were visible, rising over the treetops.

They galloped through the final clump of trees and halted, dead. Horses skidded on the turf, some colliding with those in front. Three men fell off, one landing with a large splash in the river. Usually this would have caused much hilarity among the company. Instead, all eyes stared in disbelief at the fleet of ships that thronged the mouth of the river ahead as it finally sprawled wide into an estuary.

The ships had just arrived by the look of it as some had their sails still unfurled. The sails were large and square. The hulls of the ships were sleek, their sides lined by many brightly painted shields, set to protect the ranks of rowers on the benches behind them. The prows of the ships bore the images of fantastic carved beasts – dragons, *jǫtunar* and other monsters – carved in wood and painted to make them look even more fearsome. A horde of men had already disembarked and were setting up a camp on the waterside. They were warriors in brynjas and even at a distance their visored helmets were visible.

'Those aren't fishing boats,' Cynewulf said. 'They're viking ships. This must be Olaf's fleet.'

The sound of hooves approaching behind them got ever louder.

'We're trapped,' Alfgeir said.

Twenty-Seven

Einar narrowed his eyes, peering at the banners that flapped in the wind above the tents of the viking encampment ahead. There was a wolf's head on a yellow background but beside it fluttered two standards in the shape of dragons, their long tails waving in the wind making it look like the tails of the creatures.

'I might be wrong,' he said. 'And I don't understand how this could be, but is that the dragon of Wessex flying down there? Those warriors are definitely vikings, but why would they fly Aethelstan's standard if they are men of Olaf?'

'Perhaps some of your Dane relatives have come from Francia to help you, lord?' Cynewulf said to Alfgeir.

'None that I was expecting,' the earl said, 'but let's go and find out. It's either that or wait here to be attacked from behind.'

They set off again, though now at a more restrained pace. Whether the camp ahead held friends or foes, galloping straight into it was the fastest way to get on the wrong side of them. At the same time they're were all painfully aware that with every passing moment the riders chasing them were getting closer.

Like any force arriving in a new area, warriors in mail, helmets and shields guarded the perimeter of the camp while the rest went about erecting tents, lighting fires and otherwise establishing their bridgehead. At the sight of the approaching horsemen the guards sprung to their feet, swords drawn. Einar had no sword to threaten with, but those who had kept their swords sheathed and spears in holsters to show they meant no harm.

'I am Earl Alfgeir, Jofri of Northumbria,' Alfgeir said as they stopped before the warriors guarding the waterside track.

Einar saw the vikings look at each other, puzzled, and say some words between them.

'Speak in the tongue of your fathers,' Einar said to Alfgeir in Norse. 'They don't understand you when you talk with the Saxon tongue.'

The earl repeated what he had just said, this time in the *Dansk* tongue.

One of the vikings gave a brood smile.

'Do you know a man called Einar Thorfinnsson?' he said.

Startled and confused, Earl Alfgeir turned and pointed to Einar, who was just as surprised to hear this.

'That's him,' he said.

'Excellent!' the viking said. 'Then we'd better take you to our *höfðingjar*, the man who leads us. Dismount, please.'

'There are men following us,' Einar said. 'They mean us harm.'

He pointed to the track behind them. Just at that moment the pursuing riders burst through the trees they had come through earlier. Now Einar could see some wore visored helmets, some did not and many were bare-legged due to the Irish skirts they wore: a mixture of Norse and Scots. They were Olaf's men for definite.

At the sight of the viking encampment they too hesitated. Einar took this as a good sign. As the whole company emerged from the trees he judged there were perhaps forty or fifty of them. It was obvious without needing to count them that the vikings from the ships outnumbered Olaf's riders several times.

The horsemen saw this too. This, combined with the banners

of Wessex made up their minds. They wheeled their horses and rode back into the trees, heading back the way they had come.

Einar felt most of the tension drain from his spine. This confirmed to him that these vikings in this camp were not allied to Olaf.

'It looks like your friends have left you,' the viking guard said. 'Come with us. We will take you to Thorolf. Just Jarl Alfgeir and Einar though. Can't be too careful. Also if there is a Cynewulf?'

The company dismounted then Einar, Alfgeir and Cynewulf followed the viking guard into the camp. They passed many tents where men were settling in, lighting fires and starting to prepare food. All around was the sound of Einar's native tongue. He saw faces he recognised – not literally, but familiar in their shape, the tint of their eyes, the colours of their hair. The way they laughed or the tone they shouted at each other was also comforting, as were the fashions of their clothes, their hairstyles and the way they wore their beards. He felt a sudden sense of awkwardness at his own naked chin and Saxon war gear.

In the centre of the camp a large leather tent was set up. The banners flew around it, mounted on tall poles. A big fire blazed before the tents and two men sat on folding chairs before it, drinking horns in their hands. Both were on the young side of their prime of life. One was handsome, with long, straight blond hair and beard and blue eyes. He was laughing about something as Einar and the others approached. The man who sat beside him looked similar in features, but his brow was heavier and he had a pondering, serious expression on his face. His hair was black but thinning on top and his hairline had already receded far towards his crown. In that respect he reminded Einar a little of Ulrich. Both were burly, well-conditioned fighters, though that evening they wore comfortable furs and robes rather than brynjas and boots. They looked wealthy men, and must have been to command such a company. His tiredness and the pain in his head told Einar not to care, though he could not stop a sudden pang of self-consciousness at his ripped cloak, battered helmet and mail streaked with dirt and blood.

'What have we here, Gorm?' the blond-haired viking said, seeing the company approaching.

'It seems, Lord Thorolf, that it will not take much effort to find the men we were sent to help,' Gorm, the viking who had led them there said. 'In fact they have come to us.'

He swept a hand towards Einar and the others and stepped aside.

'I am Alfgeir,' the earl said. 'Jofri of Northumbria. This is Cynewulf, personal cleric to King Aethelstan and Einar—'

He stopped, a look of confusion on his face.

'Who would you say you were, Einar?' Alfgeir said. 'Warrior of Aethelstan?'

'I'm Einar Thorfinnsson,' Einar said.

'Aethelstan told us about you, Einar,' the blond-haired viking said. 'You're an Icelander?'

'I am,' Einar said. 'My mother was Unn Kjartinsdóttir of Midfjord. She married Harp the *Goði*.'

'Then you are most welcome!' the blond man said, a broad, infectious grin splitting his face, showing a line of perfectly straight, very white teeth. 'Get this man a drink! I am Thorolf Grimsson of Borg. This is my brother Egil. We're fellow Icelander sausage-munchers like yourself. Did you play *knattleikr* for Midfjord?'

'I did,' Einar said, as he regarded the brothers and mused how they were like day and night. Thorolf was light-haired and skinned, and infectious camaraderie seemed to exude from him like sweat. His brother Egil, on the other hand, glowered from under beetling eyebrows, his presence like a threatening storm on the horizon.

He had not met these men before but he had heard of them. Their homestead at Borg was far north of where he grew up. Despite this, the reputation of their father, Grim, was fearsome. Grim – or *Skallagrim*, baldy grim, as he was also called, though not to his face – was said to be a berserker and as he got older and more irascible folk tried to avoid his farm lest he caused them trouble. Thorolf was equally well known across the land. When he was young he had been captain of his district knattleikr team, great at wrestling and other sports. Unlike his father, everyone liked Thorolf. Tales of his overseas adventures had been told around the firesides of Iceland. His brother, the dark-haired, rather ill-favoured Egil was the opposite. What Einar had heard of him ranged from his being surly to downright dangerous.

Slaves filled horns of ale and passed them around until everyone had a drink.

'Your very good health,' Thorolf said, tilting his horn to everyone in turn then quaffing about half of the contents with one swig. His brother tipped his horn towards Einar, ignored the others and finished the horn's contents in one glug.

'We come from a battle not far from here,' Alfgeir said. 'Olaf of Dublin and Constantine of Scotland have invaded this realm. We stood against them but I and Earl Guthrek were defeated. We were betrayed. Our own fellows turned against us.'

Einar heard Alfgeir's voice crack and saw he swallowed hard. The day had been long, exhausting and daunting for all of them but he was not surprised the young jarl was taking it to heart.

'But regardless…' The earl recovered himself, throwing his shoulders back and straightening up. 'There is a large hostile force not far from here. They know you are here and they know you are on Aethelstan's side. Perhaps we should all avail of your ships and sail for my fortress at Bebbanburh?'

Thorolf turned down the corners of his mouth.

'So you are the lord of Bebbanburh?' he said. 'An impressive stronghold. But I thought it was Uhtred's?'

'So do a lot of folk, for some reason,' Alfgeir said with a sigh. 'I was appointed lord of Bebbanburh and Jofri of Northumbria last year by the king. I did not grow up here so I do not know the stories of who owns what or who took what from whom. What I do know is we will be safe there.'

'We will be safe here,' Egil said. His voice was gruff. 'At least for the night.'

'My brother is right,' Thorolf said. 'Olaf will come for us in the morning maybe, but not tonight. His men have already fought one battle today. Marching them down the river to fight another is a sure way to lose if not the second battle then at least a lot of warriors.'

'We've three hundred men here,' Egil said. 'It's enough to put them off until tomorrow or perhaps for a few days. And we've only just landed and planted our banners. To turn and flee now would make us look like cowards.'

'Besides,' Thorolf said, 'if I know Olaf he'll already be halfway through his first barrel of ale by now, celebrating his victory. He'll not want to be bothered coming here to deal with us tonight. So relax, sit with us and have a drink. You all look like you could do with one.'

'Well, that is true,' Einar said.

It was obvious that the viking leaders would not be persuaded. Slaves brought more folding leather chairs and he, Alfgeir and Cynewulf flopped into them, taking long, grateful draughts from their drinking horns.

'So what are a pair of heathen Icelanders doing fighting for the Christian king of Wessex?' Einar asked. 'I'd be much less surprised if you were on Olaf's side.'

'I could say the same about you, Einar,' Thorolf said. 'Though I have to say you look more like a Saxon in that cloak and helmet. But our family has never seen eye to eye with the kings of Norway.'

'What Icelander does?' Einar said. 'Our fathers and grandfathers not wanting to be ruled by Harald Fairhair is the reason most of us ended up in Iceland.'

This was not the reason his mother had come to Iceland – she had been on the run from his father who wanted her dead – but it applied to most of his friends and neighbours.

'Our family tends to take things further than most,' Thorolf said. Egil grunted a little laugh. 'Our forefathers had a personal feud with Harald. It's a tit-for-tat bloodbath that has cost the lives of many. We have carried on that tradition with his son Eirik. We had a falling-out with Bloody Axe and that witch of a wife he has – they tried to kill my brother. So we took to wandering the eastern way. We were raiding in Flanders and Saxony and heard Aethelstan was in need of warriors.'

'Eirik no longer rules in Norway,' Einar said. 'You must know that.'

'Yes,' Thorolf said. 'Ousted by Hakon though unfortunately not dead and still causing trouble. Hakon is still a Haraldsson, but he was lucky enough not to be brought up by the old bastard. Instead he was fostered by Aethelstan here in Britain. We thought, well war is always an opportunity for booty and our enemy's enemy should be our friend and all that.'

Einar recognised their type: young men with ships and warriors out to make a name for themselves. They fought for whoever would pay them for whatever cause was needed.

'Aethelstan is short of warriors right now,' Thorolf went on.

'We showed up at just the right time, with ships and a sizeable fighting force ready for battle. He contracted us to come north and back you up while he gathers his own forces from their farms and estates and moves them north. So here we are. And not a moment too late.'

'Don't worry, cleric,' Egil said, glowering at Cynewulf. 'We've all had a good wash. Each one of us has been prime signed so you needn't worry about heathens fighting in the army of your Christ.'

'The army we fight is no different,' Cynewulf said, holding Egil's intimidating glare without flinching. 'Christian Welshmen, heretic Scots and heathen Irish Norsemen. But with Aethelstan to lead us I know God will be on our side.'

'So let us drink to heathen Christians and Saxon Norsemen,' Thorolf said, holding his horn high in the air. 'And all the silver and gold we can get our hands on.'

Twenty-Eight

After a drinking session with the viking chiefs, Einar and the others, exhausted and full of ale, had ended up falling asleep either where they sat or rolled up in fur blankets on the ground. As predicted by Egil and Thorolf they had remained unmolested by Olaf's warriors during the night. The next morning Egil and Thorolf had insisted Einar take them back west to get a look at Olaf's army.

When they got to the battlefield at Caer Ham there were only bodies to be found. They lay in heaps, pale and naked, stripped of anything that could possibly be of value and left to rot. A cloud of crows pecked and picked on the dead flesh while wolves, crept in from the hills beyond, tugged and tore at limbs and torsos. The place stank already and the sun had hardly risen over the horizon.

'The bed of heroes,' Egil said, a grim smile on his face. 'Such is what Valhalla is.'

Einar looked at the surly Icelander, eyebrows raised. For such a taciturn dark cloud of a man he had a surprisingly poetic turn of phrase at times.

They tracked Olaf's army south-east. They were not hard to follow. The swathe of flattened grass showed their progress, as did the burned-out and looted farmsteads and villages they went past from the battlefield to Ad Gefrin. When Einar and the others got there they found the palace ablaze and Olaf and Constantine's army helping themselves to its stores and ale.

The viking chiefs had not needed to get any closer. It was plain to them that even with three hundred men Olaf outnumbered them with ease. Any attack on him except a hit-and-run raid would be futile. They turned their horses and rode back to their ships.

The two forces shadowed each other for almost a week like two wrestlers, each wary and ready to fend off the other's attack, while waiting for the right moment to launch their own. Olaf knew they were there, and posted companies of warriors on his flanks to deter any surprise assaults and Thorolf and Egil's force never strayed too far from the shore in case they needed to flee to their ships. All the while the Norse, Scots and Welsh continued to harry the countryside. Everything that could be taken was taken. Anything that could not was burned. Anyone who tried to stop them was killed.

Olaf appeared reluctant to attack Thorolf and Egil's force, however. He outnumbered the hired vikings many to one but a fight would mean casualties on both sides, and Thorolf reckoned that Olaf was saving all his men for the coming confrontation with Aethelstan. The presence of Thorolf's men at least meant that the invasion horde did not ravage the towns and villages along the coast as well.

Finally Thorolf announced they were to sail south. Embarking onto his fleet of longships, they put out to sea and set sail. Alfgeir wanted to head for Bebbanburh but Thorolf, as captain of the fleet, overruled him, saying that they were under orders to meet Aethelstan who should by now have brought his army north.

They sailed until they reached a wide estuary that Einar recognised, having sailed in and out of it several times. The river that opened to it led to Jorvik. With the rest of the vikings settled on their ships, Einar, Thorolf, Egil, Cynewulf and Alfgeir took horses and rode inland towards the city.

Aethelstan had indeed arrived. It would have been easy to mistake the encampment on the meadow outside Jorvik for some sort of fair or summer festival, except that there was a war on and the purpose of the gathering was much more serious.

Hundreds of tents thronged the meadow. The banners of earls, ealdormen, thanes and other nobles of Aethelstan's Aengland fluttered in the warm air. The smoke from many campfires mingled into one cloud that smeared the sky above grey. Warriors sharpened swords, repaired shields, polished armour or practised movements and formations. The aroma of woodsmoke and food cooking mingled with the of smell of piss and shit from the toilet trenches dug near the edge of the encampment. This merged with the stench of the nearby city so Einar and the others smelled the camp before they rode over the nearby hill and it came into view.

'Aethelstan is wise not to spend too much time in the city,' Cynewulf said as they paused for a moment on the brow of the hill. 'The way things are he might get a knife in the back walking through the streets.'

'The king has brought quite an army,' Einar said, surveying the multitude of tents and warriors. 'But do you think it's enough?'

Egil pursed his lips.

'Not from what we saw,' he said. 'Even with our three hundred as well.'

From their vantage point Einar could see that some sort of gathering was happening in the centre of the camp, where it looked like there was a low mound ringed by many men.

'It looks like the king has called a meeting of the Witan here,' Cynewulf said. 'Come on. We need to be part of that.'

They rode on down the hill into the camp. Four men were no threat to a whole army and it was camped in what was, after all, supposed to be friendly territory. There were always plenty of folk coming and going and no one questioned Einar and the others.

The crowds got thicker as they made their way towards the centre of the camp. Everyone was gathered around the mound in the middle. As Einar and the others pushed their way through they saw the king stood upon the mound along with seven other men. A ring of warriors in armour, helmets and shields faced the surrounding crowd, making sure no one could encroach. Among them Einar spotted the red cloaks of Aethelstan's personal bodyguard and in the middle of them their leader, Ine.

The king stood on the mound. Today he was dressed as a war leader in full battle harness, though instead of the *Cynehelm* – the battle helmet that denoted kingship – he wore the circular gold crown with the upward-pointing spikes Aethelstan had taken to wearing instead. Cynewulf had told Einar that this was what Charlemagne had worn, and he had worn it because it was what the last of the Roman Emperors had also worn, and Aethelstan preferred to look like a Christian emperor than an old heathen warlord.

There were seven men on the mound alongside him. Five of them, like the king, were dressed for battle, their mail polished so it glittered; their sword pommels, scabbards and harnesses studded with garnets and gold, winked red and flashed yellow as the sunlight danced across them. Around their shoulders they wore the finest of woollen cloaks that were pinned at their shoulders, denoting their wealth. They too did not wear helmets but instead had the conical yellow hats of ealdormen, the second rank of society below the king. Einar could see banners displaying the dragon of Wessex, the golden cross of Mercia and the knives of the East Saxons and surmised that three of the men in war gear were the ealdormen of those realms. There was also a very tall, broad-shouldered man with long blond hair and beard that reminded Einar of Thorolf, and a Saxon with a hard, scarred face and watchful green eyes.

The other two men on the mound wore the robes of important Christian churchmen. Einar recognised one of them, a clean-shaven young man who bore the shepherd's crook of a bishop. This was Aethelwold, Bishop of Wintanceaster who Einar had previously met before the journey to Francia which had led to his breaking company with Ulrich's Wolf Coats.

'We must bring Olaf to battle as soon as we can,' one of the ealdormen, a stout fellow with a white beard, said. 'Every day we hear more news of his atrocities. If we don't stop them there will be nothing left of Northumbria.'

'That's Beohtric, Ealdorman of Mercia,' Cynewulf said to Einar. 'And that tall blond man is Thorketil, Jarl of the Five Dane Boroughs. It's a good sign he is here. Most would expect that lot to side with Olaf.'

'I hope he really is here to support Aethelstan,' Einar said. 'Given what Ingwar and his brother did I'd say the king needs to be careful who he chooses to trust. Who is the other Ealdorman? The one with the green eyes?'

'That's Singrin,' Cynewulf said. 'Lord of the tribe of Wiccii.'

'The Scots, Welsh and Irish Danes are like a plague of locusts devastating the land,' Bishop Aethelwold said. 'The blood of innocents cries out for justice.'

Those watching nodded, cried 'Aye' and otherwise showed their agreement.

Einar and the others shoved their way through the throng to the edge of the mound. Ine and Aethelstan's bodyguards spotted them and barred the way.

'Well look who it is,' Ine said, glaring at Einar. 'The Dane himself. And he's brought another two with him.'

Egil bared his teeth at the Saxon.

'This is not the time, Ine,' Cynewulf said. 'We've come from the north. We need to talk to the king.'

Any further discussion was cut short by Aethelstan catching sight of Cynewulf and those with him.

'Let those men up,' the king said.

A sour expression on his face, Ine stepped aside and Einar and the others scrambled up onto the mound.

'Lord Alfgeir, Thorolf,' the king said. 'What news do you bring from the north? Is it true we are betrayed by Ingwar and Ethils?'

Alfgeir outlined the experiences of the past week and delivered his assessment of the situation.

When he finished the crowd of nobles and warriors was even more discomfited. Men muttered to each other with folded arms, shook their heads or otherwise showed their displeasure at the sorry state of affairs that were occurring.

'This is grave news indeed,' Aethelstan said. 'We are here with the army now to support you in regaining your losses.'

Beohtric, the Ealdorman of Mercia, raised a forefinger at Alfgeir.

'Lord Alfgeir was appointed Jofri of Northumbria to stop this very situation happening,' he said. This was met by many angry cries of agreement around the mound. 'Is there to be no penalty for such drastic failure?'

'Aye!' another of the ealdormen said. 'Alfgeir is to blame for this. He should lose his seat!'

Aethelstan sighed and rolled his eyes.

'Who's that?' Einar whispered to Cynewulf.

'Odda of Wessex,' the monk said from the corner of his mouth.

'Lord Odda, we were all taken by surprise by Olaf's invasion,' the king said. 'If we had not got a second warning about Olaf we would all still be in the south, preparing to sail to Francia. I don't see Alfgeir as being especially to blame.'

Einar frowned, a memory surfacing in his mind. What did Aethelstan mean by a *second* warning? Had the king someone else in the north he had not told Einar about?

'Perhaps, Lord Aethelstan,' the Ealdorman of Mercia said. 'If we had a Saxon as Jofri of Northumbria instead of a half-Dane, he would have made a more steadfast defence.'

'Guthrek did not flee the battlefield,' Ealdorman Odda said.

'And Guthrek is dead,' Alfgeir said. His cheeks were flushed and his voice raised.

'Perhaps I should take the Danish warriors of the Five Boroughs home again?' Jarl Thorketil said. He spoke in the Saxon tongue but with a lilting accent similar to Einar's. 'If you only want Saxons to fight beside you…'

'Calm down, all of you!' Aethelstan said in a thundering voice. 'Do you forget that the enemy is out there and not among us!?'

He pointed to the north as silence descended around him.

'I will hear no more talk of Angles, Saxons, Jutes, Danes and the rest,' the king said, glaring around him. 'I don't care if your forefathers rowed across the northern sea with Hengist and Horsa four centuries ago or arrived in a longship twenty years ago. All of our ancestors were once foreign here. But if you were born in this land, love God, swear loyalty to me and fight by my side then you are all Aenglisc men in my eyes. This land is ours and we will fight to defend it. If we fall to fighting among ourselves then we may as well hand this country over to Olaf now.'

The ealdormen blushed. Odda found the sight of the earth before them suddenly fascinating.

'Lord Alfgeir will remain lord of Bebbanburh,' Aethelstan said. 'Yes, he failed in defending the north but Ingwar and Ethils betrayed us all. We will give Alfgeir a chance to atone for himself when we march north to stop Olaf. I'm sure Lord Alfgeir will not let us down again when we meet the Scots and Danes in battle.'

Alfgeir nodded, though Einar thought there was a hint of disappointment in his expression. The others all nodded as well.

'There's one problem with that,' Egil said. All eyes turned to look at the surly Norseman with receding hair. 'You'll lose.'

Angry shouts arose from all around.

'What my brother means to say,' Thorolf said, waving his hands in a conciliatory gesture, 'is that Olaf's army outnumbers yours. The Welsh of Alt Clwyd have joined him, as well as the armies of Ingwar and Ethils.'

'How do we know this isn't just some sort of Danish trickery?' Ealdorman Beohtric said. 'A strategy to stop us fighting until it's too late to stop Olaf?'

'It's true I'm afraid, my lords,' Cynewulf said. 'And Olaf's army grows by the day. Folk from all across the north think he has as good as won and is king already. This is a mighty force gathered here but we need a much bigger one if we are to defeat Olaf.'

An uncomfortable silence descended. For some moments all that could be heard was the buffeting of the wind and the whip and crack of the banners above.

'If that is the case, Lord King,' Ealdorman Odda said, 'we will need to raise the whole Fyrd of Britain. Every town, village and farm will need to send its men and that will take time. Something we don't have a lot of!'

'And it will also take you to do it, lord,' Beohtric said. 'Men will listen if it's the king himself who asks them to fight.'

'I did not come here just to turn and flee again like a frightened dog!' Aethelstan said.

'If you want to win then you must do this, lord,' Cynewulf said.

'And meanwhile Olaf goes on pillaging the realm?' Bishop Aethelwold said. 'By the time we return with a bigger force will there be anything left worth saving?'

Aethelstan sighed and looked at the heavens above for a moment.

'Perhaps there is a way,' he said. He looked at Einar. 'Remember you challenged that viking to a duel?'

'Ljót the Pale?' Einar said, frowning. 'Of course.'

'Well kings can do that too,' Aethelstan said. 'You and our Danish friends here will go back north. Tell Olaf that I will meet him in battle at an appointed, marked field, one week from now. Where is he now?'

'Ad Gefrin, lord,' Cynewulf said.

'Good,' Aethelstan said. 'Tell him the field will be... where?' He looked at those around him.

'I need somewhere about halfway from there to here,' he said.

'The heath at Vincaester would be a good spot,' the Earl of Mercia said, stroking his beard. 'It's wide enough and mostly level. There's a bit of a slope but if we got there first we could make sure we take whatever advantage there is to be had.'

'Near the Brunan Burh?' Aethelstan said.

'Just north of there,' Beohtric said, nodding.

'All right, tell him we will meet him there,' the king said to Einar. 'Once a king offers another battle then it's considered shame to carry on harrying a land.'

'Do you think a pagan Dane like Olaf will honour such a custom?' Ealdorman Odda said.

'Even if he doesn't,' Aethelstan said, 'moving his army all the way there will keep Olaf busy for a few days at least. In the meantime I shall go south and gather the whole army of Aengland.'

Murmurs of assent rose from all around.

'We will be back,' Aethelstan said. 'But in the meanwhile I am depending on you men. Hold Olaf, Einar. Make him think I am already there. Make sure he is where I want him when I get back. I'm counting on you.'

Part Seven

Hvat es yðr, hrafnar?   *Hvaðan eruð ér komnir*
með dreyrgu nefi   *at degi ǫndverðum?*
Hold loðir yðr í klóum;   *hræs þefr gengr ór munni;*
nær hygg ek yðr í nótt bjoggu,   *því es vissuð nái liggja.*

What is the matter with you, ravens? From where have you come with gory beaks at break of day? Flesh hangs from your claws; the stench of carrion comes from your mouths; I think you lodged last night near where you knew corpses were lying.

'Hrafnsmál' – 'Raven Song',
ninth-century Old Norse poem

Twenty-Nine

Flames licked the stones of the church tower. Black smoke belched from the windows and boiled up into the sky where it darkened the summer sun. Norsemen and Scots ran this way and that through the chaos, pursuing screaming women or shoving now-enslaved peasants into line. Others loaded whatever valuables they could find – silver platters, jewellery, old weapons – in leather bags, sacks or anything that was available to take them away as loot.

The now burning monastery had been founded there by Saint Finan nearly three centuries ago and over that span of time the little village had grown up around it, from a few huts of locals servicing the monks' needs to a whole community that existed in its own right.

It had taken less than a morning for Olaf's warriors to destroy it, strip it of its valuables, kill anyone who resisted and enslave anyone who did not run away. By sundown all that would be left were ash and smouldering ruins.

'I'll say one thing for these Christian monks, Ulrich,' Skar said, leaning back on his chair legs and placing his boots on the wooden table. 'They always have really fine stores of wine.'

He held up a bejewelled cup he had taken from the stone altar at the top of the church. It was the sort used by Christians in their rituals. Now it brimmed with ruby red liquid. A barrel of the wine, robbed from the cellars of the monastery, sat on the table as well, its top removed so Ulrich, Skar, Surt and Wulfhelm the Saxon could dip their cups in for refills. They had carried the table out into the graveyard that surrounded the blazing church and sat down to drink amid the smoke, the screaming and the chaos.

'Do you think we're getting old, Skar?' Ulrich said, squinting a little as the smoke made his eyes smart. He was hunched over his cup, looking around as three warriors chased a terrified young woman past the church. 'There was a time when I'd have been running after that girl like those lads, or filling my bag with as much loot as I could stuff in it. Now I'm happy to sit here and enjoy a really good cup of wine.'

'Perhaps,' Skar said. 'Though I would prefer to say mature, rather than old. The way these wines get better the older they get. Besides, we're plundering a village or town a day. Sometimes two. If we took part in all of them we'd have no strength left.'

'What's your excuse?' Ulrich said to Wulfhelm. 'You're still a young slip of a lad.'

A troubled look passed over the Saxon's face. He sighed.

'These are my people,' he said. 'This was once my land. This all... pains me.'

He took a long, deep draught from the wine cup he held.

Ulrich nodded and pursed his lips.

'I hope you're not thinking of turning on us,' he said. 'We don't need any more traitors.'

There was a dangerous gleam in the little man's eye that Wulfhelm did not miss.

'Don't worry,' he said. 'I will keep my oath to you. Besides, while Aethelstan rules in this land I cannot call it my own. I was sworn to Edwin, his half-brother, who tried to usurp him. Aethelstan will never trust me fully.'

'There are plenty of other Saxons joining Olaf,' Skar said. 'It's not just the Welsh and Scots now, nor is it just Ingwar and Ethils' men. Every day more of the folk from Northumbria come to Olaf's banner. They see the size of his army and reckon he has as good as won already.'

'It's not just that,' Wulfhelm said. 'There were many men unhappy with Aethelstan's great plan of a united Aengland. There were men who ruled here who bore the title king until Aethelstan came along.'

'What about you?' Ulrich said to Surt. 'You have no connection to this land. Don't you want to grab yourself some loot, or maybe some Saxon women?'

'No.' An expression of distaste crossed the black-skinned man's face. 'I'm a warrior. I'm not a barbarian. And these Scots…'

Surt shook his head.

'I feel like they have never seen a man with dark skin before,' he said. 'They are always touching me, rubbing my skin to see if the colour will come off.'

'I would say yes, you're the first black man they've seen in their lives,' Skar said. 'And they are *very* pale themselves.'

'A fine bunch of vikings we are,' Ulrich said with a grunt. He took another swig of wine.

'Ulrich!'

The sound of his name being called made the little viking turn. A gust of wind cleared a hole in the billowing smoke, revealing Kari standing by the churchyard wall.

'You'd better come and see this,' he said.

'What is it?' Ulrich said, noting the serious expression on the tattooed face of the big viking.

'Just come,' Kari said. He turned and jogged off. Ulrich and Wulfhelm set down their wine cups, got up and went to follow him. Skar sighed and followed them, though he brought his cup with him, which he stopped to refill from the barrel before doing the same.

Kari led them over the trackway that ran through the devastated settlement to the other side of it where a sharp, green slope led down to a meadow. Olaf's army had set up camp there and a temporary city of tents filled the lea.

'Where are we going?' Ulrich said. 'This had better be important, Kari.'

'It's Einar,' Kari said.

'What?!' Ulrich stopped dead.

'A rider came a short time ago,' Kari said. 'He was one of Constantine's Scottish scouts, those scrawny lot who ride like they are part horse. He came to the camp with a message for Olaf, saying Einar Thorfinnsson, Emissary of King Aethelstan, requested a meeting.'

'Where?' Ulrich said.

'There's a circle of standing stones south of here,' Kari said. 'They've requested a meeting there. Olaf and Constantine have left to meet them there.'

'Are they fools?' Ulrich said. 'It could be a trap.'

'They've taken about a hundred men,' Kari said. 'And scouts ride ahead.'

Ulrich pursed his lips.

'What does that bastard think he's doing?' he said. 'He has some balls just riding here knowing we are in Olaf's army. Does he think we'll do nothing?'

'Same old Einar,' Skar said.

'Don't start getting sentimental about him, Skar,' Ulrich said with a snarl. 'If Einar's here I want him dead. Where's Affreca?'

'She's already gone,' Kari said. 'She rode with her brother.'

'Well let's hope she leaves some of him for us,' Ulrich said, a wicked grin on his face. 'Let's go.'

The five of them grabbed horses and galloped off to the south. There were others, curious as to what was going on, making their way, so they joined an ever-growing river of horsemen riding along a little track along the floor of a dale. It was not long before they came to the end of the dale, which rose up to a low, flat-topped hill where even from a distance a ring of grey standing stones could be seen. A small crowd was gathered there as well.

When they arrived at the top of the hill they found that inside the ring of stones also stood a circle of armed vikings and Scotsmen, the personal bodyguards of King Olaf and King Constantine, a force of around forty men. Ulrich spotted Affreca standing near one of the stones. Her bow was still in its leather bag and slung over her shoulder.

'What's going on?' Ulrich said.

Affreca nodded towards the middle of the circle. Standing in a line were Einar, two large Norsemen and a monk who none of them had seen before. Olaf and Constantine stood opposite them. Just behind them stood Earls Ingwar and Ethils. A Welsh warrior stood beside them and beside him stood Olaf of Limerick, his bald head pitted and pocked with leaking scabs.

'Why is that bastard still alive!?' Ulrich hissed through his teeth. 'Why is your bow still in its bag?'

Affreca pointed to the Scottish Christian bishops and Olaf's personal *Galdramaðr*, the man who carried out the rituals expected by the gods, who also stood in the circle.

'This hilltop has been designated a holy area so negotiations can take place here,' Affreca said. 'The Christian wizards and the Galdramaðr blessed it for that purpose just before you arrived.'

'So anyone who spills blood here will be hanged,' Skar said. 'It's the law, Ulrich.'

'Don't tell me about the law,' Ulrich said. His voice rose in pitch as if his throat was constricted.

'Skar's right though,' Affreca said. 'My brother has given orders to his bodyguards that anyone who tries to harm any of Aethelstan's party will pay with their lives. Unless Olaf himself orders that they are to be harmed.'

'Since when did you follow his orders?' Ulrich said, his lip curling in a sceptical sneer. 'You are sworn to me, remember? Just as Einar was.'

'Let's hear what they have to say at least,' Affreca said. 'You're the one who always says: *Watch first. Learn what you can. Then attack.* That's what Olaf is doing. Isn't that what you say Odin teaches?'

Ulrich narrowed his eyes.

'I hope you're not going soft,' he said.

'I'm not,' Affreca said, her voice cold. 'In the past two weeks I've come very close to killing him.'

Einar stood between the two burly vikings who both still wore their helmets. A scrawny-looking old monk stood at the end of the row. Einar's hands were clasped before him and his now battered Saxon helmet rested in the crook of his right arm. He no longer wore the magnificent red cloak Aethelstan had given him and his chin was now stubbled from not shaving but his long moustache was still prominent.

'It looks like he's dressing up as a Saxon,' Skar said.

'Yes,' Affreca said. 'A Saxon I'm pretty sure I shot at twice. Odin must still watch over him or he'd be dead. Einar's luck hasn't deserted him; I can tell you that.'

'He always was a lucky lad,' Skar said. 'That was one of

the reasons he was great to have as part of the crew. His luck rubbed off on all of us.'

Ulrich was about to speak when Olaf said in a loud voice: 'So has Aethelstan sent you to deliver his surrender?'

A hush fell on the gathering. The only sound was the soft buffeting of the wind.

Einar smiled.

'No,' he said. 'The king asks you to leave his kingdom. For King Constantine to go back over the border to his own realm in Scotland. For you to take your ships and return to Ireland. In return he will send you much compensation. Gold and silver.'

A ripple of laughter ran around the circle, led by Olaf.

'Danegeld?' the king of Dublin said, grinning. 'Does Aethelstan think this is just some viking raid? Some hit-and-run attack that can be paid off? No.'

His face became serious.

'I am here to retake the throne of Jorvik which Aethelstan stole from by family,' Olaf said. 'I am here to free Britain from the tyranny of Aethelstan. King Constantine of Scotland, King Owain of Alt Clwyd, the Saxon earls Ingwar, Ethils and all the others who join our army every day, join our ranks for the same reason: to fight for their freedom. If Aethelstan thinks he can simply pay us silver and we will give all that up then he's a bigger fool than I already thought he was.'

Einar took a deep breath.

'In that case,' he said, 'the king makes you this offer: he will meet you in battle. This battle will decide the throne of Britain once and for all. The folk of this land have endured generations of war. Aethelstan will not put another generation through another prolonged war. Whoever wins this battle wins the throne. A field will be marked out at Vincaester and Aethelstan's army will meet yours there. The fight will be in one week from now.'

Einar glanced at Cynewulf to check he had said everything in exactly the way the king had instructed him to. The monk nodded, a look of satisfaction and approval on his face that made Einar feel pleased with himself.

'Have you seen my army?' Olaf said. 'Aethelstan must know how large it is and it grows by the day. His own folk are deserting him.'

'He knows all this,' Einar said. 'Nevertheless, he will meet you in battle, one week from now, at Vincaester. The winner will take the throne of all Britain.'

'So there's some fight left in him, eh?' the king of Dublin said. 'That is good. I'd hate to have won all of Britain without meeting Aethelstan in battle at least once and had the pleasure of beating him. And you must be the vikings we chased around Northumbria for a week. Who are you two?'

Olaf gestured to the burly Norsemen who stood either side of Einar.

'I am Thorolf Grimsson and this is my brother Egil,' said the taller viking, whose blond hair and beard tumbled from beneath his helmet all around his shoulders and chest.

'Shouldn't you be fighting for me?' Olaf said. 'I see that hammer around your throat. What cause do you have to fight for a Christian king like Aethelstan?'

'The oldest and most pure cause in the world,' Thorolf said, his face split in a grin. 'Gold.'

'You know what this means?' Earl Ingwar said.

'Aye! I know what it means all right,' Ulrich, unable to contain himself any more, shoved his way into the ring. Olaf saw him and waved at his bodyguards to let him through.

At the sight of the little Wolf Coat, Einar lifted his chin. The two men glared at each other, unflinching for a long moment. Ulrich's right hand twitched above the hilt of the dagger sheathed at his waist. Seeing the movement, Einar dropped his own right hand to hover over the hilt of his seax. Skar fancied he could almost see lightning dancing in the air between the two. Everyone within the circle of stones could sense the tension.

'This man is an oathbreaker,' Ulrich said at last. He spoke in a low, gravelling voice that suggested he was only just managing to keep a lid on his wrath. 'A traitor. He is *níð. Ergi.* An *eingangr.* He deserves the place that has been set aside for him in the lowest, coldest, darkest, most lonely part of Hel's kingdom. A place he will not have to wait long to take, for I swear I will send him there.'

'Your revenge will have to wait for the moment, Ulrich,' Olaf said. 'These men are under my protection as emissaries of King Aethelstan. To kill them would bring shame on me and as future king of Britain I have a reputation to consider. You were saying? About what vikings fighting for Aethelstan means?'

'It means, Lord King,' Ulrich said, still glaring at Einar. 'That Aethelstan is bringing men from overseas to swell his army. We won't just be fighting the Fyrd of Aengland. He knows you outnumber him and he is doing his best to fix that.'

'Aethelstan has big treasure chests and a web of influence all over Europe,' Ingwar said. His face had fallen into a frown of concern. 'If we give him time he could outnumber us before we know it.'

'Still,' Olaf said. 'A week though? We can allow him that, I think. He won't be able to bring too many warriors from overseas in that time. I prefer to fight Aethelstan for Britain. It will be cleaner this way. This way when I win no one will be able to dispute my right to the throne. The gods—'

He broke off and glanced at King Constantine.

'—God will have shown his favour by allowing me to win,' Olaf continued.

'And to not meet Aethelstan's challenge would make you look like a coward in the eyes of the folk of Britain,' Constantine spoke for the first time. 'And who would want a coward for a king? Better to meet him in battle and sort it all out once and for all.'

Olaf nodded his assent.

'But, Lord King, you know what this also means, though?' Olaf Scabby Head said. He wore a look of concern. 'It's a binding agreement. Neither side can plunder or harry the land once the challenge has been accepted until the battle.'

'Don't worry, Olaf,' Olaf of Dublin said. 'I will accept Aethelstan's challenge. All you have to do is wait one week. Then we will annihilate Aethelstan and his army. When he and all these men are dead, then you will have the whole of Britain to plunder at your leisure. I will have the throne and Ulrich here, will have his revenge on Einar Thorfinnsson.'

Thirty

They mounted and rode south. As they galloped away from the stone circle Einar felt the same uncomfortable itching sensation in his back, knowing Affreca was behind him somewhere with her bow. Would Olaf's forbidding harm to Aethelstan's emissaries be enough to stop her shooting him? When they were still alive when they reached a river ford well out of arrow shot he surmised that it must be the case.

'Now we just need to make sure we get to Vin Heath before Olaf does,' Cynewulf said as they splashed through the shallows of the river crossing and galloped off up the far bank.

They then headed west until they met Deira Street, the old Roman road that ran from Jorvik to Edin Burh. Once on the main thoroughfare they rode hard, heading south and taking advantage of the long days of late summer to keep going until it was almost pitch dark. They camped by the road for the short night then were up again as the sky lightened, heralding the return of the sun. After a quick breakfast they mounted their horses who were tired as they were, and set off again.

Midway through the day they arrived at Vincaester, the little town beside the road, near the ruins of an old fort built by the Romans.

North of the settlement was a very large heath. A river ran down one side of it and the other was lined by thick woodland.

'There it is,' Cynewulf said, pointing to the heath. 'We'd better get to work.'

Thorolf and Egil's three hundred vikings were there already. The vikings had been collecting hazel wood and from the stack waiting at the edge of the moor Einar judged there would be little harvest of nuts when the leaves fell from the trees this year, which would only be in a few short weeks. He also wondered how many of the men around him would live to see that day. The time and place of the battle were now set; there was still much to do before it happened.

Aethelstan had also sent a company of ten monks to Vin Heath. These men consulted books on the correct size a battlefield should be made, then adjusted it to allow for the estimated size of Olaf and Aethelstan's respective armies. The monks drew pictures on parchment and used various arts to work out where the edges of the battlefield should lie on the heath.

Einar watched them, not for the first time musing that this was the real strength of Aethelstan, or what he liked to called 'civilisation'. Even a battle, that most visceral, fatal and primitive contest of men, was here controlled by a system and a process.

Under the monks' direction, the warriors divided into groups of two, each group taking a hammer and a bundle of hazel sticks, and began to mark out the field of conflict. Just as Ljót the Pale had marked out the area that he and Einar had fought their duel on, so they marked a rectangular boundary between the river on one side and the woods on the other. However, this area would be used for a duel between armies, and the death of many, many more than just one man would decide the outcome.

Einar took a bundle of sticks with the others. He had the misfortune of ending up with Egil Grimsson as his partner. As they walked along, Einar planting a stick every ten or so paces into the soft earth, and Egil hammering them in, the surly viking did not say a word, despite several attempts by Einar to start a conversation. Soon Einar's mind began to wander.

'So this is the battlefield on which the future of the Saxons' Aengland will be decided,' he said, half to himself as much as to Egil. 'Yet most of the people here are Norsemen like us.'

Egil just grunted.

Einar pushed another stick into the soft ground, wondering as he did so how many men would die in the length of ground between this one and the last one they had planted.

A raven landed just nearby him. It hopped across the heather before him, as if leading him towards where the next hazel stick should be set.

Einar made a little laugh.

'Are you showing me the way?' he said. 'Of course you are. I'm laying out the table for your feast, aren't I? Soon you and your family, Lord Raven, will have more food than any of you can eat. A real glut.'

He looked up and saw more ravens circling overhead.

'It's like they know there will be a battle,' Einar said to Egil, feeling a strange sensation pass down his spine. 'Somehow they can tell that soon there will be mounds of corpses here for them to feast on.'

'*What is the matter with you, ravens?*' Egil said. He spoke in the rhythmic chant of a poet.

'*From where have you come with gory beaks at dawn?*
Flesh hangs from your claws; the stench of carrion comes
from your mouths;
I think you lodged last night near where you knew corpses
were lying.'

Einar turned down the corner of his mouth.

'You know the *Hrafnsmál*?' he said. 'You are a skald then?'

This was something he had not expected. The Hrafnsmál was an ancient poem. It was regarded as difficult to recite and so was known only to a few skalds who saw it as a test of skill. The last person he had expected to hear the lines from was the balding, taciturn viking who stood nearby.

'I am,' Egil said. 'And I've heard you are one yourself, Einar Thorfinnsson. But perhaps it's not so much that these birds know there will be a fight, more that they have been sent.'

'What do you mean?' Einar said, straightening up.

'It is said,' Egil said, 'that every morning Odin sends his two ravens, Huginn and Muminn, out into the world. They go to see what is happening, to witness the deeds of heroes and the crimes of traitors. At the end of the day they go back to Old One Eye and tell him everything. A battle this size? You know Odin will be watching. He will have sent his birds here. And who says they won't tip their friends off? Come and wet your beaks, lads. Come on, Old Blacky Tell your wife Sable Back the banquet is prepared. There will be blood and flesh enough for all over us here before the week is out.'

'You're a follower of the All Father, then?' Einar said, holding a hazel rod as Egil raised his hammer.

'Of course,' Egil said. 'Aren't you? Or did you take that washing Aethelstan insists on all us heathens taking before we can fight for him seriously?'

Einar sighed and looked at the raven again.

'I don't know,' he said. 'Sometimes when I look around at what happens in the world – the madness and randomness of it all, the cruelty, the treachery, the... injustice – it makes it hard to believe that there are gods running things.'

Egil gave a little chortle. It was the first time Einar had seen any sign of real mirth in the man.

'It's funny you should say that,' Egil said. 'When *I* look at all those things I find it hard to believe an untrustworthy, selfish, crazy one like old Odin *isn't* in charge.'

This time Einar laughed, but there was a hard, bitter edge to it.

'I mean, to take your earlier observation,' Egil said. 'This battle is about who will rule the Angle and Saxon lands, yet the battlefield is defended by three hundred Norsemen. Why do you think that is?'

Einar shrugged as he placed another hazel rod into the ground and held it for Egil to hammer in.

'Aethelstan needs every man from his kingdom he can get for his army,' Egil said. 'Olaf thinks Aethelstan waits for him here so we are here to hold it. Sooner or later, though, Olaf will come trundling down that road from the north. He will undoubtedly get here before Aethelstan does. If he thinks Aethelstan isn't here he might claim he has won already, and many of the folk of Britain would agree. Or he might risk an attack before the appointed time, and grab victory.'

'There's only three hundred of us,' Einar said. 'That would be a risk worth taking...'

'Indeed it is,' Egil said. 'And they say Olaf is a gambler. Which makes it very likely. However, if he does take that risk then Aethelstan has much less at stake if this field is defended not by his own oathsworn Saxons but by paid warriors from overseas. We are hired swords, lad. We're expendable.'

'Speak for yourself,' Einar said. 'I'm one of Aethelstan's oathsworn men.'

'But he's put you here just like me,' Egil said.

Einar sighed. Yet again Aethelstan had every possible move calculated, every eventuality covered.

'If Odin really has stirred up this war and then put us right in the middle of it,' Einar said, 'then what does that tell us about the nature of the All Father?'

'He's giving us a chance to prove our worth,' Egil said, fixing Einar with both eyes. 'If you want to sit in his Valour Hall someday, you won't do that by spending your life sitting by the hearth.'

'You don't think we're on the wrong side for Odin to watch us?' Einar said. 'Aethelstan is a Christian.'

'Do you think he cares whose side a great warrior fights on?' Egil said. 'In the end they will all fight in the same army: the *Einherjar* who will march into battle on the final day of this world. Besides, they say that Odin's blood flows in Aethelstan.'

They went back to work. When they had finished and the battlefield was laid out, Thorolf ordered his men to move their tents onto it and began to set up a *tjaldborg*, a defensive camp.

'The town looks like it would provide more comfortable lodgings,' the leader of Aethelstan's monks said, looking at the sturdy buildings with no doubt comfortable beds and well-stocked store rooms.

'We need to hold the field for Aethelstan,' Thorolf said.

They moved the tents but there were so few of them Einar reckoned that 'holding the field' was quite an exaggeration. They were on part of it, that was true, but most of the area remained open heath.

Alfgeir and his men arrived the next morning. Many of his war band who had survived the previous battle had scattered as they fled the disaster at Caer Ham. In the days following they had regrouped, travelled south and sought their lord until they had come together once more outside Jorvik.

Einar and the Grimsson brothers gathered to meet them as the jarl swung himself down from his horse.

'So now there are four hundred of us,' Thorolf said.

'Olaf has thousands,' Alfgeir said, looking with apprehension at the small cluster of tents pitched on the battlefield.

Alfgeir did not just bring warriors, however. The first of Aethelstan's supplies for his army came with them: waggons, carts and pack horses laden with sheaves of spears, other weapons, whetstones, leather jerkins, smithy charcoal, tools and lots of other gear needed by an army going to war.

'Any decent food?' Egil said. 'Or better still, wine?'

Alfgeir shook his head. 'I'm afraid not. Just this and more tents than any of us need. I have my own supply of wine of course.'

'There'll be no ale or wine until the main army arrives,' Thorolf said. 'I don't want Olaf arriving here finding us all passed out and taking the field unopposed.'

'There's also a lot of silver,' Alfgeir said.

'I'm glad to hear that,' Egil said. 'We will need to be paid some time.'

'Not with this you won't,' Alfgeir said. 'It's the fake coins with Olaf's head on them. Aethelstan doesn't want them in circulation and has ordered all found to be sent here. He'll melt them down and recast them once they're all gathered in.'

'What's that about tents?' Einar said.

'Aethelstan sent most of the army's tents with me,' Alfgeir said. 'There's enough of them to house us and Olaf's men.'

'Get the men,' Thorolf said, becoming excited. 'Tell them to unload those tents and bring them onto the field.'

One of his men jogged off to carry out his order.

'What good are empty tents?' Alfgeir said.

'Perhaps a lot,' Thorolf said. 'Come with me.'

He began striding off towards the heath where the battlefield was marked.

Thirty-One

The late summer sun peered over the low hills on the horizon when Olaf's scouts arrived. Word spread quickly through the camp and Einar found himself woken by the chattering and shouts outside his tent.

He groaned in protest. Exhausted, he had been sunk deep in a dreamless sleep. The ground of the heath was covered in heather, making it softer than any bed he had ever slept in and there was no one else in the tent with him to snore, fart, roll over into him, mutter in their sleep or otherwise disturb his rest. He was not privileged. There were now so many tents pitched on the battlefield that everyone got one all to themselves.

Einar heard the name of Olaf and 'the Scots' being mentioned by those outside and knew he had to get up.

Scrambling out of his leather sleeping bag he dragged on his britches and boots and fastened on his belt which now just bore his seax, his only remaining weapon since losing his sword in the battle at Caer Ham. Patting down his tousled hair, he unlatched the door of his tent and stepped out.

It was a beautiful morning. The sun was breaking over the horizon and the world was coming to life. Birds tweeted from the grass and heather around him as they swooped across the clear blue sky.

Thorolf was striding along the line of tents, shouting orders to his men who, like Einar, were coming out of their own tents.

'Come on, lads,' the big, blond viking said. 'Everyone up. You know what to do. I want this place looking like there isn't room to slide a blade between the tents.'

'Do you think they'll fall for it?' Einar said as he joined Thorolf.

'They'd better,' the viking leader said. 'Or we might be in trouble.'

They had spent the previous evening rearranging the campsite. They had dismantled the original round tent fort that huddled in the south-west corner of the field and stretched them out in a long line straight across the field from the river to the woods at the point where it was narrowest. The thirty or so tents were strung out, with large gaps between them. The company then set about unpacking the baggage train Alfgeir had brought with him and carrying all the tents to the battlefield. They first set to work erecting the biggest tents – the tall, wide ones meant for noblemen, for communal eating and meeting spaces in poor weather or for stores – in the gaps in the line of their own tents. Then they set up more of the largest tents in a line behind, careful to place each one so it blocked any potential view on down the field. A third line of tents was set up beyond.

It was when the third rank of tents was being erected that Einar noticed that although the monks had gone to great pains to try to find a piece of ground wide enough and flat enough that neither side could claim unfair advantage, there was a slight slope from the middle down to the southern end of the heath. This meant that anyone approaching from the north would not be able to see past the first few rows of tents.

Then Thorolf and Alfgeir's men erected tall standard poles, and hoisted the banners of Wessex, Northumbria and the

Grimsson brothers' own. Any other flags they had were also raised, whether on poles, sticks or spears, anything to give the impression of a forest of standards.

Then the company had gone to work building numerous campfires at random points all over the field from the tents to the far southern end. These had sticks set in them, then they were doused in oil and covered as best they could in case it rained during the night.

Now Einar and Thorolf watched as the ten Scots horsemen who were Olaf's scouts galloped off the Roman road, crossed the river at the ford then onto the north end of the hazel-rod-marked field from the north. There they halted.

They were still some distance away but Einar could make out the bare shanks of their legs and the patterned woollen garments they wore pinned over one shoulder that could serve as a rain cloak and a sleeping bag. They had spears in one hand, the reins of their hardy, swift ponies in the other. They were peering up at the encampment, several shading their eyes with their palms for a better look.

'Look busy,' Thorolf said to those around him. 'And be as noisy as you can, remember? We need to sound like four thousand men, not four hundred.'

All of the company began milling around, working their way in and out of around the tents. Behind the lines of tents men with blazing torches were dashing around the multiple campfires, setting fire to the oil and wood in them. Soon grey smoke was rising from multiple places behind the tents, as if thousands, not hundreds of men had crawled out of bed and were preparing to make their first meal of the day. Some of the vikings sang, some laughed, some beat pots as if cooking, some shouted at each other, anything to swell the noise among the tents.

Earl Alfgeir came jogging over. His clothes were crumpled

and his usual careful hairstyle a mess. It was clear he too had just crawled out of his tent.

'What's going on?' he said, then seeing the horsemen at the bottom of the slope added: 'Ah. Olaf's men are here. Do you think we will fool them?'

'This slope should stop them being able to see beyond the first few ranks of tents,' Thorolf said. 'Hopefully we give them the impression that most of Aethelstan's army is up here already.'

The Scottish scouts watched the campsite for a little more time, then kicked their heels into their horses' flanks and spurred them up the slope.

'Shit,' Alfgeir said. 'They want a closer look.'

'Calm down please, Lord Alfgeir,' Thorolf said. 'I would want one myself.'

They pushed their way through the edges of the tents so they stood before them. Thorolf put his fingers in his mouth and let out a loud wolf whistle. It was still echoing across the field when twenty armed warriors, the men who had been on watch through the night, guarding the camp from any surprise attacks, came running out to line up beside their höfðingjar.

'Just in case,' Thorolf said to Alfgeir, turning his head to wink at Einar.

The Scots riders came up the slope. The vikings around Thorolf raised their shields.

The lead scout, who had a bald pate but a long braid of dark hair down his back, reined his horse to a halt. The others did the same, though their horses were so lively, despite no doubt having already had a long ride, continued to prance and wheel.

The lead scout said something in the tongue of the Gaels.

'Speak in the Saxon tongue,' Thorolf said, pretending to be a man of Wessex. 'Or we will not understand you. I'm sorry but this camp is full. There is no room for anyone else.'

'We are outriders of King Constantine of Scotland,' the lead scout said, switching to the Saxon tongue as he struggled to keep his horse facing Thorolf and the others. 'Is this Aethelstan's war horde? Are you ready to do battle?'

'We are indeed his army,' Thorolf said. 'Here to await battle at the appointed time.'

Einar could see the scout's eyes dart back and forth along the rows of tents, trying to reckon their number. He could almost see the thoughts flashing through the man's mind as he counted the row of tents he could see and multiplied it by ten for every man sleeping in each tent, then again by countless rows stretching behind out of sight to the end of the field. Some of the men behind them stood up on their stirrups, trying to get a better view.

'Lads?' Thorolf said to his warriors around him. They clapped their shields together into a shield wall and levelled their spears over the shield rims, creating a sharp hedge no sane horse would try to ride into.

'How about you lot fuck off now?' Thorolf said.

The lead scout spat, though his spittle fell short of even the nearest shield, then he wheeled his horse and started riding away back down the slope. His companions kicked their heels and galloped off after him.

When they had left the battlefield and crossed the river back to the Roman road, Einar heaved a sigh of relief.

'It worked,' he said, grinning at Thorolf. 'They must think Aethelstan's whole army is camped here!'

'With any luck,' Thorolf said. 'Time will tell though. Let's hope Aethelstan really does arrive here with the rest of the army before Olaf decides he wants a better look at just how many men we have.'

Thirty-Two

It was the next day when Olaf, Constantine and their armies arrived. Einar and the others could see the huge cloud of dust they kicked up as they moved south along the old Roman road long before they came into view. Then as the day went on, a column of warriors, horses and carts came in view, marching down the road from the north. They looked like a vast, dark snake, slithering across the land, its tail lost from view in the far distance.

'It's like *Jörmungandr* himself has come,' Egil said as he watched the approaching army from their camp at the top of the slope. 'And you know what that means?'

Einar, who along with Cynewulf and Thorolf stood beside him, nodded. Many of the men from their camp had also come out to get a better view of the arrival of the enemy.

'Ragnarök,' he said. 'The great battle at the end of the world.'

Jörmungandr, or the *Miðgarðsormr*, was one of Loki's monstrous children, a huge worm. Odin had thrown him into the sea where he had grown so vast he could wrap himself around the world so he bit his own tail. On the final day he would rise from the waves, spraying venom all around.

Thorolf touched the hammer amulet that hung from a leather thong around his throat.

'Thor will kill the serpent at Ragnarök,' he said. 'Just as we will kill this one.'

'Thor will kill the Miðgarðsormr,' Einar said. 'But he'll die himself before he walks nine steps away.'

Cynewulf gave a loud tut.

'This is all heathen nonsense!' he said. 'I know you vikings don't really take prime signing seriously, but Einar I'm disappointed in you. Remember Aethelstan has important plans for you.'

When they reached the ford in the river, Olaf's army turned and began filing across onto the heath.

For long moments all of those at the top of the slope held their breaths, waiting to see if the Norse, Scots and Welsh warriors would continue their advance up towards them. It soon became clear, however, that the scouts had delivered their message as the warriors began to spread out on the heath beyond the north end of the marked-out battlefield.

As the first arrivals began setting up a camp the rest of the army kept on coming down the road. Now with a turn in the column, they looked even more like the Midgard Serpent, except he was spewing warriors from his head instead of poison.

Einar and the others were about to turn and go back into their own camp when a group of horsemen emerged from the main body of the enemy army and began riding up the slope. As they got closer Einar could make out a burly merkismaðr, the standard bearer, who rode in front, bearing a tall pole from which flew the banner of Olaf the Red. Olaf rode just behind him, as did Earls Ingwar and Ethils, along with twenty Norsemen and another twenty Scots. It was with a little relief Einar saw that neither Ulrich or any of the other Wolf Coats were coming.

Thorolf did his wolf whistle and this time a line of archers, with bows drawn and arrows notched, rose from the heath, around thirty paces from the edge of the camp of the Wessex advance guard. After the approach of the scouts they had all agreed it would be best to deter anyone else from the enemy side getting too close.

As they neared the archers, Olaf and the others slowed their horses to a halt.

'Is this the way to welcome the new king of Britain?' Olaf said in a loud voice. As usual, his red beard was cracked open in a wide grin.

'Has King Constantine gone home already?' Thorolf said. 'I don't see him with you.'

'The king of Scotland is old; he travels in a cart so it will be some time before he gets here,' Olaf said. 'My scouts told us Aethelstan's army had already arrived. My congratulations for beating us to get here.'

'It won't be the only time we beat you here this week,' Thorolf said, matching the king of Dublin's grin.

Olaf gave a little chuckle.

'You see, that's why you should be fighting for me,' he said. 'You can banter like a Norseman. A Saxon would be all bluster and grim threats. I've been asking about you and your brother. It seems you have quite a reputation for a couple of Icelander sausage-munchers. You sure you won't consider switching sides? You say you fight for gold but I will have all the gold and silver in Britain when I defeat Aethelstan. You will have nothing but your graves to lie in.'

All the mirth faded from Olaf's eyes and grin as he spoke the last words.

'I did say we fight for gold and silver,' Thorolf said. 'But there is something else I didn't mention. My family has long feuded with that of Harald Fairhair and I hear you have made a pact with Eirik Bloody Axe. Eirik wants Egil and me dead. So you see we must pass on your offer.'

'So be it,' Olaf said. 'I won't ask again. But I thought I should come and give my regards to the man who will become my predecessor on the throne of Britain. I wish to speak to Aethelstan.'

Einar, Egil and Cynewulf all glanced at Thorolf.

'I'm afraid that is not possible right now,' Thorolf said.

'What do you mean?' Earl Ethils said, his eyes narrowing. 'Why not?'

'The king is staying in that town just to the south,' Thorolf said. 'There is a church there, and a town is a more fitting accommodation for a king than a campsite, wouldn't you say? I take it you are putting your tent up to the north, Olaf?'

'Ha. Ha. Ha,' the king of Dublin said. He spoke each word without actual laughter, making each one laden with threat. 'I grow tired of your humour. When Aethelstan returns to your camp tell him I will to speak with him. If he wants to discuss his surrender he knows where he can find me.'

He turned his horse and set off back down the slope. The others with him did the same.

When they were sure Olaf and his company were far enough away the archers relaxed their bows.

Einar blew his cheeks out.

'Good thinking,' he said to Olaf. 'But what if he comes back?'

'We could be sunk,' Thorolf said. 'It's only two days now until the appointed time for the battle and I doubt we will keep getting away with this until then. Let's hope Aethelstan isn't too far away or we could all be dead before he gets here.'

Thirty-Three

Einar did not sleep that night. As Olaf rode away the thought occurred to him that the enemy had now tried directly riding up to the camp two times. If Olaf decided to send more scouts to probe the true strength of Aethelstan's army they would not come in the same way. They would come in the dark, with stealth. And he knew the exact company who would be best for that task.

He alerted Olaf and Egil of the danger, urging them to set extra watchmen at the perimeter and beyond it, including in the woods that lined one side of the camp, reasoning that if he was going to sneak into the camp that would be the route he would take. Then he thought how Ulrich would do what was very least expected, so requested the viking brothers place guards along the side of the camp along the river as well.

On hearing that there were úlfhéðnar in the enemy forces, Thorolf and Egil did not hesitate to follow Einar's requests.

Meanwhile, throughout the day, warriors began arriving at the camp to swell the forces of Aethelstan. They were Saxon nobles from realms not far to the south or others who the king had dispatched ahead of the rest of the army – or so Einar and the others hoped. The empty tents began to fill with real warriors which was very welcome. They were very welcome, however, they were war bands of only thirty or forty men. The numbers in the camp were growing, but the size of Olaf's army was still overwhelming.

Along with the gathering men the hordes of crows, magpies and other carrion birds continued to grow as well, as they waited for the feast to come. The tents of the campsite became splattered white with bird shit. The woods began to be haunted by ever more numbers of wolves.

When darkness fell Einar had retired to his tent but sleep would not come and it was not the occasional howl of a wolf that kept him awake. He had crawled into his sleeping bag still wearing his brynja, which in itself caused enough discomfort to make sleep difficult. Even though he knew that Ulrich and the others would have no way of telling which tent he was in, every footstep outside, every snap of a broken twig had him reaching for his seax and wishing that he had a more substantial weapon to protect himself with.

As the night wore on he could stand it no more and got up. Outside his tent he was relieved to find that it was not pitch dark. There was a bright crescent moon in the sky, some stars peered down but the darkness was also dispelled by multiple braziers and fires that blazed across the campsite, both to keep those on watch duty warm and to provide light so they could see if anyone was creeping up in the dark. Given that was the very thing Einar was worried about, he felt some solace to see the flickering flames.

He walked around the perimeter of the campsite, peering out into the darkness beyond, eyes alert for any hint of movement. As he moved around the camp he talked to warriors on guard, asking how things were going, had they noticed anything out of the ordinary and otherwise passing the time. No one had seen anything unusual, beyond the sight at the far end of the sloped battlefield, where the embers of countless campfires dotted the darkness like orange stars in a night sky reflected in a lake. It was a fascinating but daunting sight, driving home the huge size of Olaf's army.

Einar was about to return to his bed when something caught his ear. It was not loud by any means. It was like a little soft cough. Most would have thought it was maybe the wind, or perhaps a deer, and indeed the men on watch did not bat an eyelid. Einar, on the other hand, froze. He know exactly what the sound meant. A man had just died.

'Alarm! Sound the alarm!' he shouted, snatching the horn from a nearby watchman and blasting several notes on it. At his lead other warning horns around the camp began to sound. Einar drew his seax. With only a small blade to protect him he felt almost naked. Looking around, desperate, he spotted a shield resting against a tent not far away. He grabbed it and held it before him, wishing it was much larger.

Peeking over the shield rim he scanned the edge of the trees, looking for any sign of movement, his thighs tense at all times, ready to leap left or right. If one of Affreca's arrows came whizzing out of the dark he would have almost no time to dodge it.

Around him the camp erupted into chaos. Horns were blowing all around. The warriors scrambled from their tents, grabbing weapons and shields and making ready for whatever attack was coming.

'What's going on?' Egil Grimsson said as he jogged over to Einar. He was bare-chested and wore only britches, though he had a sword in one hand.

'There's someone in the trees,' Einar said. 'Just outside the camp. They've killed one of the sentries.'

'How do you know?' Egil said.

'I heard it,' Einar said. 'Most probably a knife to the throat.

Someone is creeping through the dark out there in the trees. They came upon a watchman but weren't able to get close enough to him to kill him in complete silence. He maybe had a torch or something or was standing in a shaft of light from the camp.'

Einar could almost picture what had happened in his mind.

'So they hurled a knife or throwing axe,' he said. 'It would have hit the watchman in the throat. The attacker will have been running forward at the same time. The victim will just have time to make a little sound before his killer will have reached him, clamped a hand over his mouth and finished him off.'

'You sound like you've done that yourself,' Egil said, looking sideways at Einar.

'The man who taught me how to do it is out there in those trees, I believe,' Einar said,

Thorolf arrived, demanding to know what was going on.

'More light,' Thorolf shouted to his men around him. 'Arm yourselves. I want as many men as we can spare in those trees. Find those intruders.'

'We'll lose more men if you send them in there,' Einar said.

'And we'll lose more men if we let those bastards sneak into the camp in the dark,' Thorolf said. 'Come on. Let's flush them out.'

Einar knew they had little choice. Despite his dread of the darkness and what lurked among the tress he gripped his seax, hefted his shield and set off with the others to search the woods. They moved into the woods in strength, perhaps a hundred men or more, all armed and with enough forces to flood the woods with light like it was daytime. They prodded the undergrowth with spears, looked in bushes and hollows, searched behind tree trunks and looked up into the trees all along the side of the camp to a distance of three hundred paces.

The whole time Einar's skin crawled and his nerves felt so tight they might snap. In every shadow he imagined a killer lurking, ready to spring out and murder him. Every step he took he anticipated one of Affreca's arrows would come streaking out of the dark to impale him.

After some time, however, nothing had happened to him and they found no one hiding in the woods. They did, however, find a murdered watchman, a knife in his throat, exactly as Einar had suspected.

'Well, someone was here,' Thorolf said as his men gathered up the dead viking. 'If it was your friends then they've decided getting away undetected – and with their lives – was more important than spying on us or whatever it was they came for. Let's get back to the camp. It's only one more day until the time of the battle. Aethelstan better arrive tomorrow with his army or we'll be like a dog who thinks he can fight a bear.'

They returned to the camp, but Einar did not sleep. He stayed up, returning to his former activity of touring the perimeter of the camp and checking with the men on watch. Ulrich and the others may have gone, but they might come back.

At dawn, dog-tired and with eyes that felt like they were full of hot sand, he finally had to give in. Comforting himself that there was no longer any darkness for the úlfhéðnar to creep about in undetected, Einar got into his sleeping bag and was asleep before he knew it.

The noise of the campsite meant he did not sleep too long, though the sun was high in the sky when he did wake.

Leaving his tent, he noticed straight away how the atmosphere had changed. The camp was abuzz with activity. The happy-go-lucky air of Egil and Thorolf's vikings had gone. There was palpable tension in the air and it was not just because of the attack on the camp the previous night.

There was now only one day until the appointed time of battle. Warriors were beginning preparations for it in the quiet, serious manner in which men whose job was fighting went about such work. Each one knew that in the coming fight his life could depend on how well his armour had been prepared, how solid the binding of his shield was and how sharp he could make the blade of his sword. Some practised manoeuvres and formations in groups. Others rehearsed strikes and parries alone.

Still the king had not arrived with the rest of his army. Other warriors from the south in advance of the rest had arrived though while Einar had slept and with them they had brought more of Aethelstan's baggage waggon. Einar joined Thorolf, Egil and others in helping them unpack the supplies. The newcomers had also brought the news that the king had been delayed. Gathering an army that size and moving it right across the country took time but he was on his way and making his way north.

'Well he'd better arrive in time for the battle tomorrow,' Egil said as they lifted sheaves of spears and bags of arrows off a cart loaded with weapons. 'Or else we'll have more swords and spears than we have men to use them.'

'I could do with some of this war gear,' Einar said. 'I lost my sword at Caer Ham. All I've got is this seax.'

He patted the hilt of the sheathed knife.

'Well you'll need more than that tomorrow,' Thorolf, who was on top of the cart, passing the bundles of weapons down to the others, said. 'You may as well stand in front of Olaf with your dick in your hand. Take your pick of these. As Egil said: there's more than enough for us all with more to spare. I'm taking a few spare spears myself.'

He stopped, something among the cache around him catching his eye.

'Here,' he said, stooping to pick up a weapon and tossing it to Einar. 'A big lad like you should be able to handle that.'

Einar caught it in both hands, dipping slightly as the weight of the weapon took him a little by surprise. It was a vicious-looking implement, like a fighting spear but not like any one Einar had seen before. It had a short, thick shaft more like a fence post than a spear. If Einar had planted the butt of it in the ground he could have grasped the top of it about the height of his chest. The blade was a wicked-looking thing, the shape of a feather and about two-thirds as long as the shaft. It ended in a ring of four spikes where it met the shaft.

'What is *this*?' Einar said, turning the weapon over in his hands.

'It's called a *bryntroll*. A mail troll,' Thorolf said. 'See the way the blade is tapered to a point, the waves in it, its strength. It's specialised for ripping and tearing brynjas, parting the rings of mail shirts and otherwise causing all sorts of mischief. If that doesn't work you can smash him round the head with the spiked bit.'

Einar thought of his sword sliding across Ingwar's thick coat of mail.

'I'll take it,' he said.

By the time they finished the unloading, all the storage tents were packed with equipment, supplies and food. There was so much some had to be stacked out in the open.

'Now all we need is someone to use it,' Thorolf said, his face grim.

Their apprehension was in part allayed as Saxon warriors kept on arriving at the camp throughout the course of the day, increasing their numbers until what had been an advance guard could start to be reckoned at least a small army. Aethelstan himself still did not arrive though, and Olaf's force still outnumbered them three, perhaps four to one.

More and more of the silver coins with Olaf's head of them kept on arriving as well. Aethelstan had proclaimed across the country that wherever they were found they were to be sent here. He seemed to fear the effect they may have on the people if allowed to circulate. They came in ones or twos, or bags and purses and a group of monks emptied them into chests kept in a brown tent near the centre of the camp. Soon there was a small fortune gathered there and warriors joined the monks to guard it.

Later in the day, when the king had still not arrived, Thorolf, Egil, Cynewulf and Alfgeir met in Thorolf's large tent to discuss tactics and strategies for what they should do if Olaf attacked early. They agreed plans for each possibility they could think of. There was no consensus though, even between the brothers, on what they should do if the king did not arrive with the main army by the appointed time for the battle. Cynewulf was adamant that they should stand and fight until the king arrived.

'King Aethelstan *will* be here,' the monk urged. 'We must hold the field until he gets here. That is what we were ordered to do. It is our duty.'

'We'll all die,' Alfgeir said. 'And what would that achieve?'

Einar glanced at the young earl, noting the stubble on his unshaven face, the red rims around his eyes and the ruffled appearance of his usually well brushed hair. Over the last week the normally well-groomed and dressed young man had become ever more dishevelled.

'*A corpse is no use to anyone,*' Egil said, quoting the words of Odin.

'Those are the Devil's words!' Cynewulf said through clenched teeth. 'And do you think the king will pay you if you run away and don't fulfil the task he hired you for?'

'No one said we would run away,' Thorolf said, his voice dropping to a low growl. 'But if the situation is hopeless we must withdraw. What use is silver if you're too dead to spend it?'

The old monk gave a sigh of exasperation and rolled his eyes. The big viking Thorolf remained impassive.

Unresolved, they went about the rest of the day making final preparations. Egil spent some time giving Einar a lesson in how to use the mail troll, how to thrust so the long blade caught in the enemy's mail shirt, then how to twist it so as to burst the metal rings and gut your opponent. As Thorolf had said, the heavy shaft with the spikes around the top could also be used as a brutal club. As the weapon was wielded in both hands, Einar did not even need his fighting glove to use it.

When evening fell they partook in quiet, sombre meals. Thorolf had forbidden any wine or more than one horn of ale. Everyone needed to stay alert in case there was an early attack, and facing Olaf's forces in the morning would be difficult enough without a hangover as well. Einar did however spot a slave carrying a wine flagon to Alfgeir's tent.

A solemn, serious mood pervaded the camp as the warriors contemplated the daunting prospect of what lay ahead in the morning. Einar also detected an air of disbelief that the king had not yet arrived. All the Saxons Einar talked to still believed Aethelstan would come, perhaps in the middle of the night, or maybe with the dawn but he *would* be there. From the light in their eyes Einar could see the faith they had in their king and knew that if the rest of the land shared in it then Aethelstan would indeed be able to raise a large enough army to defeat Olaf. Whether he would be able to do it in time was another question.

With everyone else, Einar passed another sleepless night. Thorolf was determined there would be no repetition of the previous night's sneak attack and posted sentries with lighted torches deep into the woods and along the river, no man less than ten paces from the next and each one relieved at regular intervals.

Everyone was fully armed and ready for battle in case Olaf decided on an early assault. They snatched sleep where they could but the overwhelming sensations of anticipation and apprehension for what was to come made more than a few short moments of rest impossible.

Still, throughout the night the Saxons and Cynewulf insisted Aethelstan would come. When the sky began to be streaked with the grey of dawn, however, Einar could almost taste the sense of disbelief and disappointment in the air when they remained the only forces in the camp at the top of the slope.

As the sun rose the distant sound of horns blowing in the camp of Olaf and Constantine drifted through the air. The force of Aengland buckled their helmets, tightened the straps of their brynjas, hoisted their shields and gathered before their camp at the top of the slope. The air of anticipation that had been building all night had grown to an intimidating fever pitch as every warrior looked to their leaders for orders as to what to do now. Would they stand and fight, and most probably die, or would they retreat? And if that was the option what would be the consequences? They would live to fight another day, yes, but would they also lose the war and the realm be given to Olaf?

Einar found Thorolf, Egil, Alfgeir and Cynewulf standing before all the others. For once Thorolf was not grinning. His handsome face was set in a grim expression. Cynewulf looked wild-eyed as if at his wits' end, as if the realisation that his king had not in fact arrived in time as he had believed he would had thrown the monk into confusion. Alfgeir looked wretched, his face wearing an expression of misery that Einar had no doubt was exacerbated by the contents of the wine flagon the young earl had most likely finished the night before. As he watched, Einar saw Alfgeir was swaying a little and wondered if in fact he was still drunk. Egil was the exception. He looked positively excited.

Whether or not these men knew hundreds of eyes were boring into their backs in expectation, they did not show it. Instead they were watching as in the distance, beyond the hazel poles that marked the far end of the battlefield, Olaf's army began filing out from their own campsite to begin forming battle lines. The one, huge snake it had been on arrival now separated into countless little serpents which marched out to form into ranks and companies. The morning sun glittered on their helmets and mail and gleamed off countless blades like sparkles on the surface of a lake. Einar did not have to look around at the men he stood among to know Olaf's numbers were overwhelming.

Still no one spoke.

'Well?' Einar broke the silence. 'Aethelstan has not come. What do we do?'

Thorolf opened his mouth to speak. All eyes fixed on him. He hesitated.

Cynewulf gave a cough.

'I did not think it would come to this,' he said. His voice was low and gravelling. 'The king warned me it might, but I did not believe him. However King Aethelstan had prepared for this situation. He told me that if it came to this we are empowered to make Olaf an offer of gold in exchange for peace.'

'What?!' Alfgeir said. His voice was slurred and Einar could see his teeth were stained from wine. 'Why in God's name didn't you say something before now? We've all been standing here shitting ourselves thinking we're about to die when there was no need for any of it! I should have you flogged, you wretched idiot.'

'The earl has clearly disregarded my order on drinking,' Thorolf said. 'But he has a point: why didn't you say something before now, you crazy old monk?'

'I did not think the Lord God would allow this to happen,' Cynewulf said. 'But it has. This was to be strictly a last resort in the event of this happening, so we should now go and talk to Olaf. I will put the king's offer to him.'

'He didn't take it before,' Einar said. 'Why would Olaf accept Danegeld now?'

'He did not hear the details of the offer,' Cynewulf said. 'It is… substantial. When Olaf hears if Aethelstan believes it might give Olaf reason to consider it.'

'Well let's go and make Olaf this offer,' Alfgeir said, pointing at the enemy army. 'As an earl I can speak on the king's behalf.'

One of his eyes was half closed and he swayed back and forth on his feet.

'I think the earl has had too much wine to enter into negotiations,' Egil said. 'I think someone else should take responsibility.'

'I'll do it,' Einar said. The words were out of his mouth before he had time to think.

'Well, what are we waiting for?' Thorolf said. 'Let's get down there before it's too late.'

Thirty-Four

'So here we are talking again,' Olaf said. 'If this goes on much more we'll become too good friends to kill each other in battle.'

He was sitting on a folding chair that had been set up for him by some slaves. King Constantine sat in another beside him. The brother earls Ingwar and Ethils stood nearby, as did all the major war leaders and captains of the enemy army, gathered not in standing stones this time but just a natural circle they had formed around Einar and the others.

'It won't,' Earl Ingwar said. 'We go into battle this morning.'

Einar, Thorolf, Egil and Cynewulf had told Alfgeir to stay behind. They said he was needed to take charge of the war horde in case they did not make it back from talking to Olaf. It was really because he was too drunk to be trusted. The coming negotiations could be delicate, like a game of *hnaftafl*. The last thing they needed was Alfgeir, his wits befuddled by wine, blurting out some information Olaf was not supposed to know, like how many men they really had in their camp.

Then they had mounted horses and trotted down the slope straight towards the front ranks of the opposing army. They knew they had to hurry but at the same time did not want to provoke a violent response from warriors ready for battle, so for the last part they had reduced their mounts to a sedate walk.

There were some uncomfortable moments as Einar and the others found themselves staring straight at hundreds of raised spears, the pointed ends all aiming in their direction, as Olaf's warriors eyed them with suspicion.

They announced that Aethelstan had a message for Olaf and Constantine and some warriors had hurried back through the ranks to seek orders. They had returned a short while later and Einar and the others were stripped of all weapons then led on foot into the heart of the war horde, where Olaf and all his leaders awaited them.

'Well? What has Aethelstan got to say for himself?' Olaf said. 'I see he was too cowardly to come himself.'

'King Aethelstan is ready for battle,' Einar said. 'And he has a mighty host gathered. But the king is a man of peace, like his God. The thought of the shedding of so much blood as now looks likely because of a quarrel between two men appals him.'

He glanced at Cynewulf to check he had got the words of the king that the monk had recited to him on the ride down correct. Cynewulf nodded.

Einar's eyes also flicked right towards where Ulrich, Skar, Affreca and the others from his former Wolf Coat crew stood among the other warriors of Olaf. He tried to ignore the hatred, betrayal and disappointment in their eyes.

'King Aethelstan entreats that Olaf go home to Ireland and King Constantine retire to his realm of Scotland,' Einar said in a voice loud enough that all could hear.

Growls of anger and disapproval murmured through the crowd around them.

'And as a friendly gift,' Einar said, raising his voice further to make sure everyone who could would hear, 'King Aethelstan offers to give one shilling of silver from every plough through all his realm as a token that they should become friends.'

There were some sharp intakes of breath. The previous angry mutterings stopped.

'That's a lot of silver,' King Constantine said. He glanced sideways at Olaf. 'An awful lot.'

Olaf scratched his beard but did not speak.

'We could take that and return to Ireland with honour,' Olaf of Limerick said. 'Olaf, think about this. In Ireland that offer is wealth unimaginable. When the world knows Aethelstan was willing to offer that, all will know how much he feared you. It would be no shame to take it.'

Excited conversations broke out all around. Einar of a sudden recognised just how clever – or crafty – Aethelstan was. All around there were warriors of Olaf and Constantine thinking exactly how much this offer actually meant to them. Some might take it, leaching support from their leader; others might not, which would sow dissent and discord among their ranks.

Olaf saw this too.

He rose to his feet, glaring around him at his counsellors, and leaders of his army.

'Enough chatter!' he said in a loud, commanding tone. 'Whatever you have to say, say it to me.'

The gathered nobles fell into a chastised silence.

'It's a trick,' Ingwar said. 'Lord Olaf, you cannot trust Aethelstan or any of the Witan. I know these folk. They're like a nest of vipers. Does Aethelstan think us a backward hill folk who when shown some wealth our eyes go glassy? It's not an honourable offer. It's an insult.'

And, as a traitor, you need Olaf to win now, or you're a dead man, Einar thought to himself, looking at the angry expression on Ingwar's face but perceiving the desperation beneath.

'It's not a paltry sum, Olaf,' Olaf of Limerick said. 'The pair of us could win all of Ireland with that amount. We could build a whole fleet of ships and fill them with vikings. We could rule every island from Norway to Hispania!'

'It's not a paltry sum, no,' King Constantine said. 'But Aethelstan could afford more…'

The previous muttering among the gathered nobles resumed, despite Olaf's disapproval.

'King Constantine,' Olaf turned to the white-haired old man. 'You have fought Aethelstan before. What is your counsel?'

The old king of Alba steepled his fingers and sat for a moment, thinking. Then he took a deep breath in and out through his nose.

'I have fought Aethelstan, yes. The mistake he made was to leave me strong enough that I now can fight him again. For him to make this offer means he must be desperate. But we should not let him off. We should put more pressure on him. Aethelstan has very deep pockets. He can afford to offer us more.'

Those watching shouted their assent. Einar could see Olaf was not happy with the way things were going.

'We came here to conquer but now when the king of Aengland flashes some silver at us your thirst for battle disappears?' Olaf said.

'There is more than one way to humiliate an enemy than to beat him in battle,' Olaf of Limerick said. 'If he pays you to leave him alone there is no doubt who the victor is.'

'We can get Aethelstan to pay more,' Constantine said. 'We should bleed him and his kingdom dry. We should leave him with nothing so he is weak. He won't have enough gold or silver to threaten us again.'

Olaf of Dublin thought for a moment. He looked at the ground, stroking his beard. Then he looked up again.

'Go back to Aethelstan,' he said to Einar. 'Tell him we will not accept this offer.'

Einar's heart sank. Did this mean the battle would now go ahead?

'However,' Olaf said, 'if Aethelstan wishes to make us an increased offer – one that shows more respect to me and King Constantine – we will consider that.'

'What do you think?' Constantine said to Einar. 'Can you do that?'

'Yes... I... uh...' Einar looked at Cynewulf for help.

'We can have you an answer in three days,' the monk said.

'*Three days?!*' Olaf said, frowning.

'The gold and silver the king offers must come from the people, the folk of the realm,' Cynewulf said. 'If he is to offer more the king must get approval of the Witan, the council who rule in his name.'

'And they are slow to make decisions?' Olaf said. 'Surely they can decide in less than three days?'

'Yes, Lord Olaf,' Cynewulf said. 'But the Witan are comprised of the old, the wise and the powerful of the realm. Such men send warriors to war but they do not fight themselves. They are gathered at Jorvik. It will take a day to get there. Another day to discuss the offer and a day for us to bring their response back.'

Olaf thought or another moment.

'Very well. Go,' he said at last. 'But tell Aethelstan he has three days. No more. Otherwise we fight this battle whether he is ready or not.'

Thirty-Five

Olaf of Dublin sat on a folding camp chair in his tent, gazing down at a small pile of sticks on the floor. Like most of the tents of the noblemen, Olaf's was the size of a small house and made from the hides of many oxen. Several lamps on stands were lit to dispel the darkness and the cloying smell of their burning whale oil filled the air.

Olaf sat bent forward at the waist, elbows on his knees. A half-drunk cup of wine sat on the arm of his chair. The floor around him was covered in straw and a rug had been put down on top of that. Another lamp was set on the rug so the witch could see what she was doing.

The vǫlva wore the long blue dress of a seeress. Even though inside a tent, she kept her hood up, no doubt, Olaf surmised, because it added to the air of mystery around her. She was crouched on her knees, one cat-skin-glove-clad hand still extended and open before her from when she had thrown the sticks to the ground. Each stick had a rune carved on it, and the way they fell would give indication of the future.

Olaf had been careful not to bring his own witch with him on this expedition. He needed the support of the Scots and Welsh and as Christians they were squeamish of what they called heathen practices. However he had been delighted to find there were many settlers and children of settlers in the north of Britain who still adhered to the customs of their Norse forefathers.

Olaf was not a superstitious man. He preferred to rely on the strength of his sword arm and the counsel of his own wits than gods and norns. However he was also not one who sought the counsel of others often, so in uncertain times he saw no harm in consulting with spirits. If he learned nothing then nothing was lost. If he did learn something, then that was an advantage. Either way there was no harm in it.

The witch had wandered into the camp offering to tell fortunes. She had been making a small fortune from the Norsemen of Olaf's army. Some were nervous of what lay ahead and wanted to know what their future might hold. One of Constantine's clerics had seen her, however, and had insisted on her being thrown out of the camp before she brought the wrath of his God down on them. Olaf had told Constantine he would see to it, then asked her to come and cast the runes for him in private.

'What do you see?' Olaf said.

'I see blood, lord,' the old woman said in her croaking, high-pitched voice. 'Oceans of blood. Kings will clash on the gory field of slaughter. Many men will die. This land will be ravaged by war.'

'Perhaps you might tell me something I don't know?' Olaf said, a half-bemused, half-impatient look on his face. 'I'm leading an invasion of Britain, after all.'

The witch shot a sharp, reproachful look at Olaf, then realised she was working for a king and changed it to a more respectful one.

'The black-plumed fowl, that darkened raven, gathers to watch the battle,' the vǫlva said, turning her attention back to the rune-carved twigs. 'They know they will divide the carrion with the horn-beaked and hazel-feathered eagle, the greedy war-hawk and that grey beast, the wolf of the forest. All will feast on the flesh of the dead. There will not have been a slaughter like it since the Saxons and the Angles crossed the sea to come to this land.'

'Good. But am I going to win?' Olaf said. His voice had an edge of impatience.

'The fog is thick,' the witch said. 'I see a snake, a gigantic worm, perhaps a dragon crawling through the bodies, stealing gold from corpses, Saxon and Dane alike.'

Olaf glanced at the little green bottle that sat on the ground beside the vǫlva. It contained the potion that these women drank to enable them to see their visions of the future. It was a secret concoction of herbs and mushrooms. Sometimes, if they drank too much of it, the visions became too wild and strange to make any sense. He wondered if perhaps this woman had drunk a little too much tonight.

'Lord Olaf.' A new voice made Olaf and the witch look up. Ulfr, his standard bearer and the lead of Olaf's bodyguards, stood at the entrance of the tent. 'There are two men here to see you. I said you were busy but they insist I ask you.'

'Who are they?' Olaf said, frowning.

'One is the bishop who visited you in Dublin,' the big Irishman said. 'Wulfstan of Jorvik. The other is...'

He trailed off as if unable to believe his own words.

'The other says he is Eirik Haraldsson, Jarl of Orkney,' he recovered and said. 'Son of Harald Fairhair of Norway.'

Olaf rose to his feet.

'On your way,' he said to the witch.

'But what about your future, lord?' she said, a look of confusion and a little hurt on her face.

'I'll learn more about that from these men than from your blethering,' Olaf said. 'Now get out of here.'

He flicked a silver coin at her. There was no need to tempt the spirits too much.

The woman caught it. Realising how much it was worth she let out a squeal of delight and rushed out of the tent, not even bothering to pick up her magic sticks.

Ulfr ushered Wulfstan and Eirik into the tent. From their dress no one who did not know them would have guessed they were a bishop and a jarl, indeed, a former king no less. They wore simple hooded riding cloaks along with leather britches and riding boots. They did not look like peasants, but at the same time would not have been distinguishable from any other freeman dressed for travelling the roads.

'Get some more chairs and more cups, Ulfr,' Olaf said. 'Then leave us.'

The big man fetched two more folding seats. Eirik sat down but the bishop remained on his feet. He handed the cups to Olaf then went out the tent flap. Olaf refilled his own wine cup from a jug that sat beside his chair, then filled one each for the others.

'So this is unexpected,' Olaf said, sitting down himself. 'Aren't you supposed to be in Orkney, Eirik? Guarding my back from Hakon?'

'We wanted to speak to you personally, King Olaf,' Wulfstan said. 'Away from the eyes and ears of… others. Especially now your success so far bodes well for your overall success in this venture.'

'We?' Olaf said, raising an eyebrow. He looked at Eirik who, as usual sat in taciturn silence, a brooding presence that seemed to suck all the mirth from any room he entered.

'The Jarl Eirik and I,' Wulfstan said. 'Just the two of us.'

'I take it from your humble attire this is some sort of clandestine mission?' Olaf said.

'We travelled here in ordinary clothes because, yes, we did not want others recognising us,' Wulfstan said. 'Especially our Scottish friends.'

He tipped Olaf a knowing look.

'Jarl Eirik has a proposal for you,' Wulfstan went on. 'I think you should listen to what he has to say.'

'Eirik is a son of the famous Harald Fairhair first king of all Norway,' Olaf said, raising his cup to toast the glowering giant. 'And was a king himself. I always have time to listen to the words of great men.'

Eirik's face moved into a half-smile.

'That is not your reputation, King Olaf, but I am grateful. However, I sense a guarded attitude from you,' Bishop Wulfstan said. 'Perhaps I should leave you two alone so you both feel more free to speak openly?'

Turning down the corners of his mouth, Eirik nodded.

'Perhaps that would be better,' Olaf said.

Wulfstan nodded and hurried out of the tent.

When he was gone, Eirik leaned forward in his seat.

'Olaf,' he said, ignoring the look of slight displeasure on the red-haired king of Dublin's face that he had not used his title. 'When we last met we were in the heart of Constantine's realm, surrounded by his warriors and folk. It was not the time or place to discuss the matters that I feel we need to. There were too many prying eyes and ears – Scottish ones – around there.'

'There are no less around us now in this camp,' Olaf said.

'One Scotsman in particular is not with us in this tent, however,' Eirik said. He locked eyes with Olaf. 'Constantine.'

'Go on,' Olaf said.

'I made a deal that I would guard your rear against an

attack from Hakon in good faith,' Eirik said. 'But a time will come when this war is over. The way it's going you will win it. Aethelstan will be defeated or sent packing and you will rule southern Britain, or at least Northumbria and Jorvik, as well as Dublin. Hakon will no longer be an issue.'

Olaf nodded.

'What is it, Eirik?' he said. 'Is Bebbanburh not enough for you now?'

'By no means, Olaf,' Eirik said. 'But if it all works out, you will rule the south of Britain from Jorvik or even Aethelstan's home in Wintanceaster. I will be in Bebbanburh.'

Eirik paused. He looked down at his wine cup and ran a finger around its rim.

'And Constantine will be at both our backs,' he concluded.

He looked up and met Olaf's gaze again.

'I appreciate he is your ally now,' Eirik said, 'but he was also once Aethelstan's ally.'

'He fought Aethelstan before as well,' Olaf said.

'I think that is my point,' Eirik said. 'Constantine is the ally of whoever he thinks he will gain most advantage from and their enemy when he thinks he'll get more from that. For all we know he might make a deal with Hakon someday. Their realms are side by side across the sea. They don't call him *the wily old Scot* for nothing.'

'What king isn't at least a little like that, Eirik?' Olaf said.

'Indeed,' Eirik said. 'Odin teaches men of power that they must be so. But you and I know that because of the customs in which we were brought up. We are both what Aethelstan would call Danes. Constantine is Scots. And what if, once you've won this war for him, he decides he would rather rule all of Britain alone? Do you really want to have a potential rival lurking at your back?'

Olaf thought for a moment. He took a sip of his wine.

'Caithness was once part of my realm of Orkney,' Eirik said. 'But Constantine took it. Your own father fought battles against him twice. He cannot be trusted.'

'So what are you suggesting?' Olaf said.

'I propose that once you are king of Britain we rearrange things a little,' Eirik said. 'Between us we get rid of Constantine. That way your realm and mine will run together with no strangers in between. Hakon will also think twice about crossing the North Sea.'

'And your earldom would stretch from Orkney to Northumbria,' Olaf said. 'That's about half the island of Britain.'

'It is a realm that is largely empty of people,' Eirik said. 'Most of it is mountains and bogs. Wealth comes from taxes and you need people to pay them. Don't worry, Olaf, I am not trying to rival you. I have sons who could rule Scotland. Or you could yourself. I don't mind.'

'I doubt you are so selfless, Eirik,' Olaf said. 'If you are, then you are not your father's son.'

'I will be a great help to you, Olaf,' Eirik said. 'You know you can trust me. We are both baked in similar bowls. We are both sons of kings, born to rule. We have the same faith and the same customs.'

'And what of this bishop?' Olaf said. 'Where does he come into this? Isn't he a Christian? Isn't he a prince of that faith in fact?'

Eirik made one of his very rare chuckles.

'Bishop Wulfstan is a crafty one,' he said. 'Yes, he loves his Christ, but he says he loves his folk as well and would do anything to protect them. By his folk he means *our folk*, the Danes and sons of Danes who settled in Britain. He sees an alliance between us as a way to ensure his people's future. No doubt he thinks he will convert us to the customs of his Jesus after that but he does not realise who he is dealing with in that respect. I think I have the measure of him. He wants people to think he is a servant of the people. That he is the shepherd of the Danes in Britain. But what he really wants is to hold onto his power and the wealth it brings. With him on our side we can be sure of the support of the Danes in Britain who now worship Christ, and there are a lot more of them than you perhaps realise.'

Olaf sat back and took a long, deep breath through his nose.

'It's a tempting offer,' he said after a moment.

'You know it makes sense,' Eirik said.

'However, you and I hardly know each other,' Olaf said. 'I know of your reputation of course. How can I be sure I can trust you?'

'You can't,' Eirik said. 'But I'm willing to do whatever it takes to convince you that you can.'

'Really?' Olaf raised an eyebrow.

'Absolutely,' Eirik said. 'Name your price.'

'Well, these sorts of alliances are usually sealed with a marriage,' Olaf said.

'Go on,' Eirik said.

Olaf thought he detected slight discomfort in Eirik's voice.

'I think I would be more content to trust you if you and I were related,' Olaf said. 'If someone of my blood was joined to you.'

'You mean you want to have someone in my household you *do* trust who can serve as your eyes and ears?' Eirik said. 'It's a reasonable ask. Who have you in mind?'

Olaf thought for a moment.

'What about my sister?' he said. 'I tried to marry her to your predecessor as Jarl of Orkney and that did not work out. This way I could kill two birds with the same stone.'

For a most unusual second time in the same night, Eirik chuckled. Though the sound was more ironic than cheerful.

'The lovely Affreca, Guthfrith's daughter? That would hardly be a chore,' he said. 'I don't know what my current wife will say about it, but I accept.'

Olaf reached out his wine cup out and Eirik clinked his own against it.

'Good,' Olaf said. 'Then we have an agreement.'

'We do,' Eirik said. 'There is just one more thing.'

Now it was Olaf who chuckled.

'What?' he said. 'You don't have enough already?'

'If Affreca is here,' Eirik said, 'then there will also be a company of úlfhéðnar led by Ulrich Rognisson. These men are very dangerous. They used to be my bodyguards but we... had a disagreement. I would not feel safe knowing these men still live.'

Olaf made a face.

'They are useful,' he said. 'And I may need their special skills in the next few days. After that, once I've won this war, things will be different. In peacetime such men tend to become a problem, I grant you. So I will see what I can do to get rid of them for you when the time is right.'

Thirty-Six

Einar and Cynewulf rode south. Einar's heart churned with mixed emotions as they galloped along the Roman road. He felt guilt at leaving the advance guard behind, facing the uncertainty of whether or not Olaf would lose patience and attack. At the same time he felt relief from the constant strain of waiting for that. Recognising that relief only made his guilt worse that others continued to endure the threat and danger while he got some respite.

Unlike the unreality of the peaceful countryside they had fled through after the fight at Caer Ham, it was clear that southern Northumbria was a land preparing for war. Every village or farmstead was building defences, digging ditches, barricading entrances or packing carts with the intent to flee. Einar and Cynewulf rode past many companies of ordinary folk – peasants, slaves, women and children – trudging southwards laden with whatever parts of their lives they could carry with them, away from the looming threat in the north. A heartening number of fighting men were riding and marching in the opposite direction to join the advance guard at Vincaester. The more the day wore on, the more of these companies of warriors they passed.

Finding the king's location was just a matter of asking these men where they had last heard where Aethelstan was. The further south they rode, the more they reported he was at a place called Concaester. Cynewulf knew the place well. It was just off the main road they were travelling on and not that far.

The sun was past its highest point when Einar and Cynewulf arrived at Concaester. It was not a town, as Einar had expected, but a large, widespread mound of stone rubble – the stubs of walls and floors of buildings, the remnants Einar surmised of a Roman settlement given the place's name.

There was a large wooden church and another building beside it that looked like a second church, which was strange. Gathered next to them were multiple smaller buildings, as well as cultivated plots and penned animals. As they rode closer Einar saw many monks working in the fields around the buildings and surmised Concaester was a monastery.

A contingent of warriors stood outside the second church. Among them were a company in bright mail and red cloaks. It was Ine and the rest of the king's personal bodyguard, which confirmed Einar and Cynewulf were in the right place.

'I'm glad the king is close,' Einar said. 'But I would have hoped to have seen more warriors.'

They both looked around seeing no sign of an army in any of the surrounding fields.

This time there were no sarcastic comments nor hostility from Ine. At the sight of Einar and Cynewulf approaching his face fell into a deadly serious expression.

'I know what this must mean,' the Saxon *hirdman* said. 'You've had to make the king's offer of Danegeld to Olaf?'

'We had no choice,' Cynewulf said with a sigh. 'Otherwise Olaf would have started the battle. We would not have prevailed with the size of the force there and the conditions were that whoever won would take the throne of Aengland.'

He shrugged.

'The king is in the shrine,' Ine said. 'He left orders not to be disturbed, except if it was of the utmost urgency. This is.'

Ine led the way to the doors of the building. They were made of thick, heavy wood and just as elaborately carved as those of a great lord or jarl, except that these had images embossed on them of Christ, his arms outstretched, as well as the winged men that Christians were so keen on.

'This is the shrine of Saint Cuthbert,' Cynewulf said in a hushed voice.

Einar had heard of this man. He was a Christian holy man the Saxons held in almost as high a regard as Christ himself. What a 'shrine' was he did not know, but he could guess it was some sort of church.

'Lord Einar! Is that you?'

A voice made them all turn. Einar saw a little man hurrying towards them. He wore the outfit of a monk but his head was not shaved in their strange manner. Instead he wore his long white-streaked black hair combed back so it fell around his shoulders. Unlike the usually clean-shaven brethren, this man wore a little pointed beard on his chin. Neither did he have the normal pale appearance common in monks who spent too long indoors. Instead his skin was sallow, like one who spent time outside or who had been born in the hot climates far to the south.

'Israel the Scholar!' Einar said. 'You really do get around. So this is where the king sent you off to?'

'Yes,' the little man said. 'I've been here since you saved me from those dreadful vikings in Francia. That book we brought back is vital to the work of the monks here. I can't thank you enough.'

'It wasn't all down to me,' Einar said. 'There was a whole crew of us.'

'Yes, but you left the others to return me and the book to Aethelstan,' Israel said. 'If your friends had had their way I'd be a hostage of Olaf now. Or tortured and killed more likely. You did not have to do that but you chose to. You did the right thing and for that I cannot thank you enough.'

Einar felt his cheeks blushing crimson.

'So the book we found was of some use then?' he said, keen to divert Israel from his gushing gratitude. 'I'm glad.'

'The monks here are translating the gospels they brought from Lindisfarne into the Saxon tongue,' Israel said. 'I'm working alongside them. That book was the vital link between the original texts and Latin.'

'And they are treating you well?' Einar said. 'They don't mind that you're…'

Not a Christian but a Jew, was what he was about to say but the pained, pleading expression on Israel's face told Einar that the monks did not know this, and if they did, they probably would mind, so he stopped himself.

'… a bit of a bore when it comes to these old parchments?' Einar finished with instead.

'Not at all, lord,' Israel said, his expression changing to one of relief.

'Well this is all very well—' Ine began to say.

Israel held up both hands and began to back away.

'Ah! I'm sure you have much more important work to be getting on with, what with the invasion and the war and all that,' he said, 'I just wanted to say my thanks again.'

Einar nodded and the little man hurried off in the direction of one of the outbuildings that surrounded this 'shrine'. Israel had not gone far when he stopped and turned around again.

'Lord Einar,' he said, then hesitated, as if unsure of whether or not he should proceed.

'Yes?' Einar said.

'I really do mean it,' Israel said. 'You bringing that book back – and me along with it – was crucial to the work of the monks here, and to Aethelstan's grand plan. The people of his realm will be able to read God's own words in their own tongue.'

'There's no need to go on about it, Israel,' Einar said, his face now deep red.

'I only say this in case you are regretting your decision,' Israel said.

'And why would I do that?' Einar said, frowning.

'You and I are outsiders here,' the little scholar said. 'Aethelstan has his uses for us but to the Saxon people we are, and will always be, outsiders. Foreigners. We will never quite fit in. I understand this. You chose to forsake your own folk and friends for a higher cause. It is a noble thing to do.'

Einar was left speechless as Israel turned and hurried away once more, this time actually leaving. Ine, Cynewulf and Einar then went inside the shrine.

When they entered, Einar felt the familiar sense of peaceful hush that pervaded these places. The aroma of beeswax candles mingled with exotic spices. There was a company – a choir as Cynewulf called them – of monks singing in tones which were so beautiful it made Einar's head swim a little. The interior of the building looked like a normal church, with tall, arched windows, rows of benches and the stone table for carrying out the Christian rituals at the front. The table was laden with wealth: a huge silver plate, goblets that looked like they were made of pure gold and a tall cross that was sheathed in silver and studded with red and green gemstones. The walls were decorated with more Christian paintings and more crosses, all sheathed in silver or gold. From the amount of wealth on display, Einar surmised that a shrine must be some kind of very rich church.

The one incongruous thing was a long, battered old box or chest that sat on another table before the ritual one. It lay flat and Einar could see it was about the length an average man was tall. Its width was about the distance between an average man's shoulders. The purpose of the box then became clear to him.

'Is that a coffin?' he said out of the corner of his mouth to Cynewulf. 'Is this someone's funeral?'

The monk looked scandalised. If they had not been in such a holy place Einar was convinced Cynewulf would have struck him in reprimand.

'This is the coffin of Saint Cuthbert himself!' he said in a hoarse whisper.

'You mean he's *in there*?' Einar said, his face screwing up in disgust. 'Hasn't he been dead for nearly three hundred winters?'

Cynewulf rolled his eyes.

Ine made a small, respectful cough and for the first time they noticed that two figures were kneeling before the coffin, heads bowed, hands clasped in the position of Christian prayer. At the sound of Ine's polite interruption they both stood up and turned. One was a whey-faced man who wore the robes of a Christian bishop. The other was King Aethelstan.

'Einar! Cynewulf!' the king said. 'You gave Olaf my offer? I take it that's why you are here?'

All three of them bowed as Aethelstan strode down the church to meet them.

'Yes, Lord King,' Cynewulf said. 'Olaf was about to begin the battle. My hand was forced. Einar delivered your offer to Olaf.'

'Einar?' Aethelstan looked taken aback. 'Where was Earl Alfgeir? He's the highest ranking noble there. Why did he not do this?'

'He was... unable to, Lord King,' Einar said. Aethelstan's

expression and tone of voice warned him the young earl would be in trouble if he revealed the real reason.

'He was drunk, lord,' Cynewulf said. 'The earl is not dealing with the situation very well.'

The king sighed.

'So what did Olaf say?' he said.

'After some debate,' the monk said, 'Olaf says that if your offer was higher he might consider it.'

The bishop, who now also stood beside them, gave a little gasp.

'Is there no end to the greed of the pagans!' he said.

'Was there much debate among Olaf's army?' Aethelstan said.

'Yes, lord,' Cynewulf said, a slight grin touching his lips. 'Once gold and silver were mentioned they started arguing among themselves.'

'Good,' Aethelstan said. Einar knew for sure then that part of the king's plan in making this offer was to try to sow dissent among his enemies. 'Very well. I will send him a higher offer if that is what he wants.'

'Lord King, I must protest!' the bishop said. 'This community moved here from the holy island at Lindisfarne because of the predations of the heathen Danes. They brought the relics of the blessed Saint Cuthbert and the precious gospels here for safekeeping. There were plenty of stones available but they built this church and shrine of wood, as a symbol that they did not mean to stay here forever. We always meant to return the relics to the Holy Island when the Danes were defeated and it was safe once more. That was fifty-three years ago! We are still here and the Danes still ravage the land.'

'I am aware of the regrettable situation of this monastery, Bishop Wigred,' the king said. 'But this offer I will make is intended to buy peace, and what gold or silver is too high a price for that?'

'It is because of this misguided practice of paying these devils off that we are still here, lord,' the bishop said. His eyes were wide and staring, and spittle was beginning to spray from his ample, red lips. 'It does not work. They are not men of honour. They just take it and then come back for more. The only thing these barbarians understand is cold, hard steel. We must fight them and we must kill them all. Only then will we bring peace.'

Aethelstan smiled.

'Pay attention, Einar,' he said, pointing to the bishop. 'That is the fever of true Christian faith. Bishop, I request you join my army and come north with us. If it comes to a fight, with you haranguing them into battle our warriors will be whipped into such a frenzy nothing will stand in their way.'

'A frenzy a berserker would be proud of,' Einar said, unable to stop the words before they were out of his mouth.

'A berserker for Christ,' Aethelstan said, his tone was admonishing. 'Cynewulf, I see Einar's education is not yet complete.'

'Not yet, lord,' the monk said, head bowed.

'Well you must persevere with it. I have big plans for young Einar here, remember?' Aethelstan said. 'Plans which may be even more pertinent if Earl Alfgeir continues to be unreliable.'

He placed a hand on Einar's shoulder. Einar felt his chest swell and his back straighten.

'But only when you judge him to be worthy,' the king continued. 'I rode ahead of the main army to pray here for help from the saint in our current struggle. The rest are following up the road and when they get here we will be strong enough to face Olaf if we have to. In the meantime you can take this further offer back to Olaf…'

Thirty-Seven

For the third time Einar and Cynewulf stood before Olaf, Constantine, the leaders of their army and their councillors. It was the next afternoon and they had returned to the invader's camp with Aethelstan's renewed offer.

The arrival of Einar and Cynewulf had created the same amount of excitement and as many as could manage to press themselves into the crowd within hearing distance ringed the circle of their nobles. As before, Olaf and Constantine sat in folding chairs with their nobles behind them. Einar and the monk stood before them.

'You got back early,' Olaf said. 'You said you needed three days.'

'We rode fast,' Einar said. 'Such a matter is too important for sleep.'

'And what has Aethelstan to say for himself?' Olaf said.

'The king is willing to make a further offer,' Einar said. He spoke in a loud voice to make sure as many as possible heard him. 'He does this out of generosity and because he loves peace, not because of weakness or fear of you.'

A ripple of laughter went around the gathered crowd. Olaf chortled.

'The king offers all he did before,' Einar said. 'But on top of that—'

Einar raised his voice even louder.

'For distribution among King Olaf's warriors, a silver shilling to every freeborn man.'

An audible gasp ran around the assembled crowd.

'And a silver mark to every man who leads a company of twelve men or more,' Einar said.

The crowd broke into an excited babble.

'And—' Einar had to raise his voice even higher so as to be heard over the hubbub. 'And a gold mark to every lead warrior in the king's guard, as well as five gold marks to every man who holds the equivalent rank to an earl.'

The listening warriors burst out into cheering. Men grinned and slapped each other on the shoulders.

Constantine smiled and leaned over to pat Olaf the Red on the back.

'You've won, lad,' the king of the Scots said. 'You've done it.'

'Have I?' Olaf said, glowering around him with a dark look. 'I came here to be king of Britain, remember?'

'You've as good as beaten Aethelstan in battle,' Constantine said. 'To make such an offer is utter humiliation for him. The world will know the great Aethelstan is just a painted warrior. No real threat. You've beaten Aethelstan, you've hardly lost a man of your army and into the bargain you've made them all rich! They'll love you for that. And if you take that away from them they won't like it.'

'I'm still a king,' Olaf said. 'It's my job to make decisions people don't like.'

'And you are stronger than ever,' Constantine said. 'You've brought Aethelstan to his knees without a fight. He's a nothing now. You have him exactly where you want him. If he'll make an offer like that, it shows he'll do anything to avoid a battle with you.'

Olaf stroked his beard, his previous dark look fading.

'You really think so?' he said, raising one eyebrow. 'Anything?'

'Anything!' Constantine said.

'Then I may as well get what I came for then,' Olaf said.

He rose to his feet, waving his arms for quiet. The noise around him subsided to an expectant hush.

'Tell King Aethelstan I will accept his offer,' he said.

Cheering broke out again. Olaf raised his hand for quiet again.

'*If*,' he said, shouting to be heard over the din. It dropped once more as rapidly as it had begun. '*If* the king is also prepared to grant me the kingdom of Northumbria, and all of the tributes and taxes belonging to that land.'

The cheers turned to gasps, then more enthusiastic cheers. If was clear Olaf's warriors were impressed by the audacity of their leader. All eyes turned to Einar once more.

'We will take this response back to King Aethelstan,' Einar said when the noise had died down enough for him to be heard. 'We will need three days again to get you the answer.'

Earl Ingwar gave a loud tut.

'This is a trick,' he said, glaring at Einar. 'Aethelstan is playing games with us.'

'You were back in two last time,' Olaf said.

'This is a larger question,' Cynewulf said. 'There already is an Earl of Northumbria. He will have to be removed. The Witan must—'

'That is Aethelstan's problem, not mine,' Olaf said, cutting the monk off.

Ingwar's face was dark with anger.

'King Olaf, this is trickery!' he said. 'I know Aethelstan. You cannot trust him. What if he's just buying time with all these offers he never intends to keep? How do we know he's even at that camp or in the town or wherever he's supposed to be? Sure they *say* he's there but we've never seen him. For all we know he's still in Wintanceaster and only half his army is up there.'

Einar tried his best to remain as impassive as possible.

'Let me and my men attack them,' Ethils said. 'Right now. We'll find out for sure.'

Olaf took a deep breath. He looked at the ground for a long moment.

'I will give you until sunset today,' he said to Einar and Cynewulf.

Both opened their mouths to speak but Olaf held up his right hand.

'No more words,' he said. 'All you need to do is ride up the slope to that camp or else to that town just beyond to the south – wherever he is – to speak to King Aethelstan. *He* needs to decide the answer, not this Witan. Is he really king or is this land actually ruled by a council of old men?'

'Very well,' Einar said, taking a deep breath. 'But King Aethelstan requests that this time rather than I and Cynewulf returning to you, you send your own messengers to him, so that they can hear his response from his own lips and know it came from him.'

'Very well,' Olaf said. 'Expect them when the sun goes down.'

The crowd began to disperse, many of the warriors already talking about what they would do with the silver and gold that was coming their way. Einar and Cynewulf returned to their horses and rode back up the slope.

Olaf, however, sat down again, stroking his beard and looking at the ground. Deep in thought, he appeared oblivious to all that was going on around him, including the brother earls Ingwar and Ethils, who still hovered near him.

'I still say this is trickery, Lord Olaf,' Ingwar said after a few moments.

'Perhaps,' Olaf said. 'But if this trick results in me becoming king of Northumbria, then all the better.'

'But what if it doesn't?' Ethils said. 'What if this is all just craft aimed at making us lose our advantage?'

Olaf was quiet for another moment. Then he said: 'You know my father always said, if you want something done right, you must do it yourself. And that in war you should plan for every eventuality. Go and get me Ulrich Rognisson.'

'The Wolf Coat?' Earl Ingwar said.

'Yes,' Olaf said. 'He and his men know some very special crafts. They can get me in and out of that camp up there without being noticed.'

'They tried a few nights ago and it didn't work,' Ethils said.

'What do you mean by "work"?' Olaf said. 'They may not have got right into the camp, but they got very close and got away again without being caught. Ingwar, I want you and Ethils to act as my emissaries and ride to Aethelstan's camp later to hear whatever his answer is. If all goes well then he will agree and that will be the happy outcome covered. Meanwhile I will go up there in secret with Ulrich. I think it's time I took a look to see what really is going on up there for myself. Depending what I find, we may yet unleash the more bloody outcome.'

Thirty-Eight

Einar could tell something had happened in his absence as soon as he arrived back at the camp. He could feel the excitement in the air. Warriors exchanged lively chatter and everyone except those ordered to guard the perimeter of the camp appeared to be hurrying towards the middle. Einar joined the throng and as he did so heard the same words all from those around him: *Aethelstan is here*.

He breathed a sigh of relief. As they had ridden back up the slope he and Cynewulf had expressed their fears that Aethelstan may still have been at the shrine of Saint Cuthbert, or had waited for the rest of the army to arrive and would have been hard pressed to get to him and back before sunset.

Einar, with Cynewulf in tow, pushed his way to the front of the crowd. Seeing Thorolf and Egil he joined them. There was no sign of Earl Alfgeir anywhere. In the middle of the crowd the king stood outside a large tent above which the dragon standard of Wessex had been raised. There was a cart nearby as well that looked like it had carried the tent. The king was surrounded by noblemen, warriors and ordinary folk alike, all grinning like children, as he acknowledged their cheers and shouts of goodwill.

Spotting Einar in the crowd he gestured that he should

approach. Ine and his other bodyguards grabbed Einar and hauled him out of the crush of bodies.

'What did Olaf say?' Aethelstan said.

Einar told him.

Aethelstan's eyes widened.

'Despite my generosity Olaf still wants more?' the king said. 'Did you tell him my conditions?'

'Yes, Lord King,' Einar said. 'He is sending his messengers here at the end of the day to hear your answer. We could not delay him any longer.'

Aethelstan nodded.

'Perhaps when he sees your strength, Lord King,' Cynewulf said, 'Olaf will be more likely to accept your already generous offers you make in the name of peace.'

'I'm glad you're here, Lord King, but where is the rest of the army?' Einar said. 'Our numbers have grown here but we're still not enough to match Olaf.'

'The rest of the army are on their way, don't worry,' Aethelstan said. 'We will match Olaf's numbers have no fear. I felt with us so close I had to come here to be among my valiant warriors, the men who have held this field for me throughout this week.'

Aethelstan scrambled up onto the back of a nearby cart so as many people as possible could see him. He stood for a moment, looking around him as silence descended on the crowd that thronged around the cart. When he judged it was quiet enough, he began to speak.

'Men, you have held this field for more than a week now,' Aethelstan said. 'With the knowledge that at any time Olaf could have attacked in strength. He did not, but that is down to you. You held your nerve. He thought my whole army awaited here and held off. It was your bravery that bought me the time

I needed to gather the army of all of Aengland and I thank you for it.'

'Never mind thanks, what about some silver?' Thorolf, smiling, said out of the corner of his mouth.

'Now I want to tell you that your wait is over,' the king said. 'There is an army coming up that road—'

He raised his left arm and pointed to the south.

'When it gets here you will no longer stand alone,' Aethelstan said. 'We will have enough warriors to face down Olaf and Constantine's challenge. We will send them home to think twice before they enter our realm again.'

Raucous cheers broke out around the camp.

'So the king is perhaps prepared to fight after all,' Thorolf said.

His brother Egil grunted.

'It's all goat shit,' he said. 'Where has all this talk about fighting come from all of a sudden? For most of the last week Aethelstan has been offering Olaf the sun, moon and stars to avoid battle.'

'We will find out at sundown,' Cynewulf said.

Thirty-Nine

'Someday you will have to come up with a new plan for getting into enemy camps,' Skar said. 'Sooner or later this "just walk in" tactic won't be a success. I just hope it's not today.'

'It's always worked so far,' Ulrich said. 'I don't see why it won't today. Armies are on guard for whole companies coming their way. Three men are no threat to three thousand. This tactic has certainly been more successful over the years than sneaking in in the dark like we tried the other night.'

They were trekking across the heathland, giving the camp of the Aenglisc a wide berth to the east of them. Ulrich and Skar had left their wolfskin cloaks behind in their tents. They had taken more mundane weapons and helmets from their war gear chests and now looked just like any other workaday Norse warrior. One difference was the large white crosses painted on the round shields slung over their backs. It was a detail they had spotted during the previous night raid on the enemy camp. They already knew there were Norsemen hired to fight among Aethelstan's army and they intended to pass themselves off as two of them. The painted cross was, Ulrich hoped, another convincing piece of the disguise.

King Olaf hiked along a little behind them. He too had left his fine clothes and weapons behind but was dressed a little differently to the others. He wore a long, hooded cloak, he had a wide-brimmed, felt hat on his head and his plaited red beard was tucked inside a plain linen jerkin to make it less conspicuous. Over his shoulder he bore a triangular leather bag.

Now you look less like Thor and more like Odin, Ulrich had commented when they had first donned their disguises.

'I hope you know what you're doing, Ulrich,' the king of Dublin said as they trekked across the heath, leaping from peat hag to peat hag and skirting around heather clumps. 'I feel half naked without a brynja on. And this harp is a delicate, expensive instrument you know. It not the sort of thing you drag across a bog.'

He patted the bag slung over his right shoulder.

'They're all vital pieces of your disguise, Lord King,' Ulrich said.

'Aethelstan will have watchmen posted,' Olaf said. 'Won't they see us coming?'

'We're well on the other side of the woods,' Ulrich said, gesturing to the dense trees far to their left which obscured any sight of the camps that lay on the moor on the other side. 'If anyone challenges us we shall say we were sent out here on patrol from their camp in case Olaf tries something from beyond the trees.'

'Which is something you might bear in mind if this war ever gets started,' Skar said. 'This would be a great route for a surprise attack.'

'Perhaps I should have you lads as my war councillors as well as Constantine, those earls and the Welsh princes,' Olaf said. 'Maybe we'd have had this whole island conquered by now.'

'Perhaps,' Ulrich said. 'But statecraft bores me. I would be no use trying to keep such a diverse army together. Scots, Welsh and Norse should fight each other, not together. I speak my mind too much. Sooner or later I'd offend someone and your whole alliance would fall apart. Besides we're just here for whatever plunder we can get. I'm happy with that.'

'Like true vikings, eh?' Olaf said. 'And when this is all over you will sail off with all that loot, no doubt.'

'Aye,' Skar said. 'In this world of war and ruin there is always work for the likes of us.'

'You nearly lead twelve men, Ulrich,' Olaf said. 'If you'd had three more in your crew you'd have qualified for Aethelstan's offer of a silver mark on top of whatever plunder you've taken so far.'

'There once were twelve of us,' Ulrich said. 'And there will be again. It is Odin's sacred number. Nine plus three. And if that bastard Einar had not betrayed us I would have been even closer to achieving it.'

'If you get me in and out of this camp I'll tell them you were part of my personal guard,' Olaf said. 'Then he'll have to give you a gold mark. What about that, eh?'

'Very generous of you, Lord King,' Ulrich said.

'It's the least I can do,' Olaf said. 'Especially as I will be diminishing your crew even more.'

'What do you mean?' Ulrich said.

'My sister, Affreca,' Olaf said. 'I have an important plan for her. Or rather she plays an important part in my plans. I can't let her sail off with the rest of you. I'm going to be marrying her off to seal an alliance.'

Skar frowned and exchanged a glance with Ulrich. Ulrich shook his head.

'Your sister is a strong-willed woman, Lord King,' Ulrich said. 'She's escaped from more than one marriage proposal in the past.'

'Don't I know?' Olaf said. 'One of them I arranged. She was supposed to marry Thorfinn the Skull Cleaver of Orkney, remember?'

Ulrich did not reply.

'Don't think I don't know you helped her escape either,' Olaf said. 'That's one of the reasons you *aren't* part of my war council. But she won't get out of that alliance this time, I promise you. She'll do what's she's told this time.'

'Thorfinn is dead, lord,' Skar said. 'Killed by his son, Einar, the very lad who left our crew. How can the alliance go ahead?'

'Look never mind that now,' Olaf said. 'We can discuss everything when all is settled with Aethelstan. And the midges are feasting on me. When are we getting off this fucking bog?'

'As soon as we are far enough south of Aethelstan's camp to look like we are not approaching from your camp,' Ulrich said.

'A day as hot and sticky as this is not one for hiking,' Olaf said, wiping sweat from his brow.

'A storm is coming,' Ulrich said, looking to the sky. 'You can smell the water in the air.'

They trudged on crossing the heath further until they were far beyond the trees, then they began to cut east. After some time they came in sight of Aethelstan's camp once more, which was now to the north of them. They could also see the little settlement to the south and the Roman road which snaked north. Columns of men, horses and carts – warriors and supplies for Aethelstan's army – were making their way along the road in groups that stretched off into the distance.

'It looks like Aethelstan's army is still arriving!' Olaf said. There was an edge of anger in his voice. 'I really need to see their strength at the camp now.'

They crossed the last of the heathland to the river. After finding a place to cross, they made their way to the Roman road and joined the others moving north towards the camp where Aethelstan's army was gathering. As they passed the settlement they saw that there were many warriors there and a ditch had been dug around it with a palisade of sharpened stakes behind it. The banners of noblemen fluttered above some of the houses.

'What do you think?' Ulrich said. 'Is Aethelstan at the town or the camp?'

'The accommodation here looks more comfortable than a tent,' Olaf said. 'Certainly the one I've been sleeping in for a week. If I were Aethelstan I'd rather stay here.'

'Wait here,' Ulrich said.

Skar and Olaf sat down beside the road on an old stone Roman mile marker while Ulrich sauntered across the road and over to the settlement. They watched as he conversed with some Saxon warriors who guarded the bridge over the ditch, seemingly oblivious to the fact that all three of them were one slip-up or one recognising glance away from a swift death.

'He really has balls of iron, doesn't he,' Olaf said. 'I'm glad you lot are on my side.'

After a while Ulrich came wandering back, walking like he had all the time and little care in the world.

'He's at the camp,' Ulrich said as he rejoined Skar and Olaf. 'I told those Saxons we were more hired Norsemen newly employed in the south and we are here to join our fellows. One of the Saxons told me the rest of the Danes are at the camp. A second one said he hoped the king knew what he was doing hiring Danes given that he was sleeping among them.'

Olaf gave a little chuckle.

'Let's go to the camp, then,' he said. 'I suppose this is where I should put my hood up in case anyone happens to recognise me.'

'No,' Ulrich said. 'What's more suspicious that a man going about with his hood up on a sunny day in late summer? Let me take a look at you.'

He produced a length of cloth which he wound around Olaf's head so it covered his eyes.

'I'm here to try to find out more about Aethelstan's army, remember?' Olaf said. 'How do I do that if I can't see?'

'Hold on,' Ulrich said, fiddling with the cloth around the king of Dublin's eyes. 'Any better?'

'Ah!' Olaf said. 'I can now.'

'It's special cloth with a very open weave,' Ulrich said. 'From this side it looks like you shouldn't be able see a thing but you should be able to make out plenty. So if we do run into anyone who might know you, the cloth will also mask the most memorable part of your face, the eyes. We will lead you into the camp so you can have a good look around.'

'Right,' Olaf said.

'You are a wandering blind harper, remember?' Ulrich said. 'You are seeking some coins from the nobles in return for a few songs. Skalds and poets are always trying to make money off an army. They flock after one like flies to shit. When men are sitting around campfires contemplating coming death they need something to distract them and cheer them up. Songs of heroes and monsters. Often noblemen pay for poets to entertain their men, just to distract them and stop them falling out among each other or deserting.'

They followed the road, now going north, exchanging pleasantries with others travelling in the same direction.

When they reached the camp they joined the column of men filing off the road and into the rear of the site. The cordon of warriors who ringed the camp was broken here to let the newcomers arrive. They walked in, without so much as a challenge from the defenders; Ulrich could not help smirking at both Skar and Olaf. Before long they were well inside the circular defences, surrounded by countless tents. Their nostrils were filled with the smell of woodsmoke from fires, the aroma of grass trampled under the feet of hundreds of men and the ever-present stench of the latrine pits dug just outside the perimeter. There were warriors, their servants and their foot soldiers everywhere, preparing weapons, making food or just lounging around outside their tents.

'They've a good lot of men here,' Olaf said in a quiet voice as he looked around from behind the thin cloth. 'But not as many as us. I'm starting to believe Ingwar and Ethils were right. Aethelstan's main force is not here yet.'

'Let's see what we can find out, eh?' Ulrich said. 'The nobles' tents will be in the centre of the camp so we should go there.'

Holding Olaf by the arm Ulrich steered the 'blind' man towards the centre of the camp.

'We're nearly there,' Ulrich said. 'There's a few really big tents, the dragon of Wessex flies above them. Aethelstan knows Skar and me so we can't go with you from here. You will have to go on alone. Go up to the tent doorways and announce yourself. Say what you are here for.'

Olaf nodded.

'If you do find Aethelstan, what will you do?' Skar said. There was a hint of concern in his voice. 'If you do something rash this won't be an easy position to escape from. We are right at the heart of our enemy's camp. I doubt any of us will get away.'

'Don't fret,' Olaf said, a smile crossing his lips. 'If I meet Aethelstan I will sing him a song and take some coins from him. Then when we meet again I will take great pleasure in telling him about how I was right under his nose and he did not even know. Besides, if he's going to accept my demand to rule Northumbria then I would be stupid to risk that.'

The king of Dublin, in his guise as a harper, wandered off towards the first of the large tents. Ulrich and Skar stood, pretending to be deep in conversation though keeping a covert watch on Olaf's movements from the corner of their eye.

After a short while Olaf came back. He was smiling.

'Lads, I've had good luck already,' he said.

'Did you find Aethelstan?' Skar said. They spoke in quiet, conspiratorial tones.

'Not yet,' Olaf said, 'but mark that brown tent well.'

He gestured towards a smaller tent that sat alongside the big one with the dragon of Wessex flying above it.

'I went in there,' Olaf said, 'announcing that I was here to entertain the nobles. There weren't any in there but there were a bunch of warriors in red cloaks and four or five clerics. They nearly pissed themselves when they saw me but then realised I was "blind" and couldn't see what they were doing. I could of course.'

'What were they at?' Ulrich said.

'They were counting coins,' Olaf said. 'There were chests of silver all over the place in there. I can't be sure but it looks like they've been gathering up all the silver coins with my name on them we've been passing out. That tent is a treasure house. When we win this battle we'll need to be sure we get here fast to take it.'

Ulrich nodded.

'Good start,' he said. 'Now get going again. We cannot wait too long, remember? We have to get back to our own camp without being noticed as well.'

'Don't worry,' Olaf said. 'It won't take me long to learn enough that we can win any coming battle outright.'

Forty

Einar found himself at a bit of a loss. Now they had fulfilled their task of delivering messages between the kings there was little to do but wait. Aethelstan had gone to his tent to discuss matters with his nobles and those of the Witan who had arrived at the site as well as Thorolf and Egil. Einar assumed they were considering Olaf's demand to rule Northumbria. Cynewulf had gone to pray with other churchmen and Einar was left alone.

He went to his tent and tried to get some sleep but the noise outside made that impossible. He checked his war gear which passed some more time but when he was done he again found himself bored. Failing to come up with any other plan he decided to walk around the camp to see if there was anything happening.

As he neared the middle of the camp he spotted a familiar figure weaving his way through the crowd towards him. It was Earl Alfgeir, the lord of Bebbanburh. The young man was in a worse state than the last time Einar had seen him. He swayed as he walked. His haggard cheeks were covered in stubble, there were dark rings under his eyes and his hair was tousled. His once fine clothes bore stains down the front.

As he was approaching, Alfgeir stumbled and fell forwards. Einar caught him, saving the young lord from going face first into the muck.

Alfgeir struggled to his feet, sending a blast of wine-soaked breath into Einar's face.

'Thank you,' he said in a slurred voice. Then his eyes seemed to focus and recognition dawned in them. 'Ah. It's you. Aethelstan's other tame Dane. We are quite the pair.'

'Aren't you from Armorica in Francia, Lord Alfgeir?' Einar said.

'I was born there, yes, but like you my father spoke the Dansk tongue,' Alfgeir said. 'He was a viking adventurer who went there in search of land, gold and adventure. What he found were beautiful women and a warm, sun-soaked climate. Not like the godforsaken rock I live on now. A godforsaken rock I am expected to fight and die for, it seems.'

He grunted.

'I come from the king,' he said, his lip curling. 'He summoned me to his tent. Like a lapdog. I was told I was to give an account of my actions. Why you, a Dane, gave Aethelstan's offer to Olaf and not I, the most senior nobleman here. Why I was not here to greet the king on his arrival.'

Einar could see the resentment and accusation in the other man's eye and it fired anger within himself.

'Did you tell him it was because you were too drunk?' he said, looking Alfgeir straight in the eyes.

'Can I help it if the only thing that helps the misery of my situation is a little wine?' the earl said. 'When I took Aethelstan's offer to become lord of Bebbanburh I did not realise it meant I would be expected to fight and die to defend a rock in the sea and a land that is mostly heath and bog. To rule a people who hate me. The Angles and Saxons because they think me a Dane. The Danish settlers because they think I've betrayed our Danish heritage and customs.'

'But you took the taxes, the revenues, the tributes that come with ruling Northumbria all the same,' Einar said.

The earl sneered.

'So you regret taking Aethelstan's offer to rule here?' Einar said.

'Regret it?' Alfgeir shook his head. 'I had little choice. I'm the second son, you see. My big brother inherited the land and the fortress in Armorica. Two very important things if you want to live there. It's a beautiful place but the Welsh who live there hate our kind every bit as much as the Welsh who live here hate the Saxons. They call it Brittany, you know that? Little Britain beyond the sea. Aethelstan had some deal with my brother. He wanted him to support the Count of Rouen in his struggles, because that would gain support for getting Aethelstan's nephew onto the throne of Francia. So Aethelstan can rule there as well, through his relatives, just as he now rules Norway through Hakon his foster son. And Aethelstan is a very persuasive man. He could trade snow to the Finns, as my father used to say.'

'It takes a special sort of person to rule,' Einar said.

'I'm starting to wonder if I am that sort of person,' Alfgeir said. 'All I've ever wanted to do was grow grapes and make wine. I can do that in Rouen, you know.'

Einar's thoughts flew to his own father, to Eirik Bloody Axe, Aethelstan himself and Hakon. Then he thought of the offer Aethelstan had made him. Could he rank among them? Could he be every bit as ruthless? As crafty?

'Why do you fight for Aethelstan, Einar?' Alfgeir said. All of a sudden it seemed as though the wine fumes in his head had all evaporated. He looked at Einar with clear, questioning eyes. 'I heard your fellows fight on the other side. For Olaf.'

Einar took a deep breath.

'I suppose I thought Aethelstan stands for something... better,' he said. 'His kingdom is a light of learning and justice in a world of darkness and barbarity. I believed that.'

'Aethelstan weaves a magic on men,' Alfgeir said. 'When he speaks they hear him telling them he will give them everything they wish for, as long as they follow him. They say he is a very holy man, but who does that remind you of?'

'He has promised me the throne of Jorvik if I meet his standards,' Einar said.

'So he's made you an offer similar to the one he made me,' Alfgeir said. 'He wants a Dane to rule a land full of half-Danes. To fool them so they don't realise they're really being ruled by Aethelstan.'

'I don't see it like that,' Einar said. His anger was beginning to return.

'Well let me give you this advice,' Alfgeir said. He planted a forefinger on Einar's chest. 'Make sure you meet the standards he sets. I have fallen short. He made that very clear to me. Now if I don't redeem myself through blood I will be cast out, penniless, homeless, perhaps even thrown into prison. I'm to get one last chance. I am to lead my warriors against Olaf in the battle. From the front. We must triumph or fall. And we will have the "honour" of leading the way. We will be the very spear point of the army.'

'So Aethelstan offers you death or glory,' Einar said.

'Indeed,' Alfgeir said, a bitter smile creasing his lips. 'Death or glory. There will be no in between.'

Einar laid a hand on the young earl's shoulder.

'If it's any consolation,' he said, 'at the moment it looks like the battle might not happen. Olaf wants your realm in exchange for peace. And it seems Aethelstan is prepared to offer anything for that.'

Alfgeir snorted again.

'Olaf can have the shithole and good luck to him,' he said. 'Good luck, Einar. And remember: never let the great Aethelstan down. His displeasure is harsh.'

He patted Einar on the chest and stumbled off.

Einar stood for a moment, wondering about what Alfgeir had said. If Aethelstan really was going to give in to Olaf's demands then why was he telling Earl Alfgeir to prepare to fight for Northumbria? Then he recalled the words of the bishop at Saint Cuthbert's shrine. When vikings were paid Danegeld they always came back for more. Aethelstan could pay Olaf off now but sooner or later he would be back. Perhaps Aethelstan's army was not as strong as he said it was. Was this whole venture just Aethelstan buying time so he could build his strength and be sure of beating Olaf sometime in the future?

He shook his head. He would never be able to fathom the minds of kings and jarls. Perhaps he was a fool to dream of ruling Jorvik or even Orkney. He began to walk again.

Then he stopped. Dead.

At first he could not believe his eyes. Nearby, in the direction Alfgeir had stumbled over from, was the large tent of the king with the dragon of Wessex fluttering over it. Ine and the rest of the king's personal warriors stood outside the door on guard. Many other nobles, warriors, clerics and slaves moved around outside. Standing about twenty paces from the door of the king's tent were two Norsemen. One was short and wiry and his companion was a giant of a man, tall as a ship's mast. Both had shields slung over their shoulders painted with the white cross of Aethelstan's hired warriors. They wore visored helmets, but there was something in the way the two held themselves, the shape of them and the way their heads moved as they chatted to each other – like they did not have a care in the world – that was very familiar to Einar.

If it were not impossible, he would have thought the two were Ulrich and Skar.

Then the short one turned around so he was looking in Einar's direction and he no longer had any doubt. The visor of his helmet covered the top half of his face, but it *was* Ulrich. There was no doubt.

In the same moment Ulrich recognised Einar as well. He stiffened. Skar noticed and looked where Ulrich was looking, then he too saw Einar.

Einar's mouth dropped open but no sound came out. His hand dropped to the hilt of his seax. Ulrich's went to the hilt of the sword sheathed at his waist. Skar laid a hand on Ulrich's shoulder as if to stop him going any further.

Einar's guts churned. One shout. One *word* of warning was all it would take from him, and Ulrich and Skar would be dead men.

He could not believe such audacity, not even from Ulrich. They were right at the heart of Aethelstan's camp, surrounded by hundreds, perhaps thousands of his warriors. They had no hope of escape. Yet Einar found himself unable to say anything.

Ulrich locked eyes with Einar. He glared at him. Einar felt like the little man was almost willing him – *daring* him – to do something about them being here.

A memory stirred in Einar's mind. The night he became one of Ulrich's úlfhéðnar. Of Ulrich, skin painted black, framed against burning torches before an arch made from a strip of turf cut from the ground. He remembered the words that were said on that night: to follow the will of Odin, to obey the ancient viking laws, and above all else to be part of the wolf pack and support the others, especially if they were in danger. They were wolves among men, outcasts and outsiders. They had to protect each other because no one else would.

Einar kept his mouth shut.

Then another figure came out of the king's tent. He was wrapped in a cloak and was putting a harp into a leather bag but making hard work of it because, as the band of cloth around his eyes told Einar, he was blind. There was something familiar about this man too, though this time Einar could not place who he was.

The blind harper joined Ulrich and Skar. He turned around and suddenly Einar realised he was looking around.

You're not blind at all! Einar thought.

The three exchanged a few words then Ulrich cast one more look at Einar. Einar could almost taste the contempt in it. Then they hurried off. In moments they had disappeared from view among the myriad tents and milling people of the campsite.

What had he done? He could have got rid of Ulrich once and for all right there and not had to spend the rest of his life looking over his shoulder, wondering if the little Wolf Coat was there. But then Skar would have shared Ulrich's fate and the big man had always been good to him.

Then sudden panic gripped Einar. Who was the third man and what had he been doing in the king's tent? Had the harper perhaps murdered Aethelstan and now he, Einar, had allowed him and the others to get away?

That did not seem likely. Aethelstan was not alone in his tent and the harper was just one man against many. Even if he had managed to kill the king the others would have overpowered him and there had been no outcry. The king's bodyguards still stood in their position outside the tent.

He resolved to look for himself. With his heart still feeling like it was somewhere in the back of his throat, Einar approached the door of the tent. Ine nodded to him and let him go through.

The first thing he heard was laughter. His panic began to calm. The interior of the tent was lit by oil lamps that stood on tall metal stands. The king sat, unharmed and smiling in a folding camp chair in the centre of the floor, which was spread with fresh straw and fur skins. His lords and men of the Witan,

Bishop Wigred, as well as Thorolf and Egil, all surrounded him on other chairs. They had goblets of wine and all looked to be in an excellent mood.

'Einar!' Aethelstan said as he caught sight of him. 'You just missed some excellent entertainment.'

'A blind beggar came to the tent,' Singrin, Ealdorman of the Wiccii, said. 'A wandering *scoff*. A skald as you Danes call them. He said he was going from tent to tent singing and for a few coins he could entertain us.'

The nobles seemed to find this hilarious.

'Poor man,' another member of the Witan said. 'He had no idea he was singing for the king!'

I wouldn't count on that, Einar thought.

'Nor that he left here a rich man,' Bishop Wigred said. 'The "pennies" we gave were silver marks.'

'He was good though,' the king said, still smiling. 'As we've little to do but wait for Olaf's messengers to arrive, he did help pass the time. I hear you're a bit of a poet yourself, Einar. Perhaps you could entertain us for a little while too?'

'Who told you that, lord?' Einar said, a fixed smile on his lips.

'Egil here,' the king said.

'Did he?' Einar said. 'Did he also tell you he is a skald himself?'

'He neglected to mention that,' Aethelstan said, sending a look of mock reproach in Egil's direction.

'I will chant and play for you if he does too,' Einar said.

All eyes turned to Egil who stood, scowling, arms folded over his chest. The surly viking nodded and rolled his eyes.

Einar realised there was now nothing he could do about Ulrich and the others. What was he going to say? *Lord King, your enemies were here right in your tent and I let them get away?*

'I will get my harp,' he said, and left the tent again.

Forty-One

Einar fetched his harp and played for Aethelstan and the nobles. Then Egil took over and chanted more poetry.

Einar found himself both surprised and a little jealous at how good the other Icelander was. His kennings were subtle, his turn of phrase both striking and witty. His voice was clear and the fingers with which he plucked the strings of his harp were dextrous and a sharp contrast to the deliberate, backwards, somewhat plodding manner Einar was forced to play in since losing one of his little fingers. Egil held his audience rapt, their attention fixed on him as if he had cast a spell on them.

All the while Einar kept on wondering what it was that Ulrich and Skar had been up to. The inescapable conclusion was that they were surveying the strength of Aethelstan's forces. Did that mean an attack was imminent? If that was the case then he would have no choice but to raise the alarm, which would put him in the very position he was trying to avoid: explaining why he had let Ulrich and Skar go.

As these thoughts tormented Einar, Egil continued to chant and every time the tent door opened it showed the shadows outside were lengthening as the sun sank towards the horizon. Despite this, the clammy warmth that had lingered in the air all the day only got more intense, with still no sign of the storm it threatened.

Then horns began to blare out warnings.

Was this the attack? Einar tensed.

Ine put his head in through the tent flap.

'Riders are coming from Olaf's camp, lord,' he said.

In a moment everyone in the tent were on their feet and filing out of the tent. Outside everyone was hurrying towards the perimeter of the camp. Men rushed to grab weapons in case this was the long-awaited attack.

When they reached the perimeter ditch, however, they saw there were only six horsemen approaching. They could only be Olaf's messengers.

As they galloped closer, Einar saw that they were the Earls Ingwar and Ethils, accompanied by two Norsemen and two Scots. One of the Scotsmen looked like the first of Constantine's scouts who had ridden up to the camp what seemed like an age ago but had only been a week. The Norsemen he did not recognise but surmised they must be Olaf's men.

They approached the edge of the defensive ditch and halted. The opposite, interior side was now lined with a shield wall of warriors.

'We have come to hear Aethelstan's response to Olaf's demand,' Ingwar shouted. 'If he is even here.'

'I am here,' the king said in a loud voice, stepping up to behind the first rank of shield men. 'Why would you doubt me, Earl Ingwar?'

Ingwar's face paled at the sight of Aethelstan. His brother Ethils looked more irritated than annoyed to see the king.

'Aethelstan,' Ethils said. 'So you *are* here after all.'

'You're surprised?' Aethelstan said. 'I find it amusing that a traitor like you would accuse me of cowardice.'

'A traitor to who?' Ingwar said. His face and bald head were now flushed deep crimson. 'A tyrant who wants to rule all the world?'

'Your father swore fealty to me,' Aethelstan said. '*You* swore fealty to me. You ruled in my name. You betrayed me and all these men who stand beside me now.'

'Our father was a king!' Ethils said. 'Who you made treaties with as an equal. Did you not betray him when you took his title and reduced him to just your subject? How do you think that made him feel? He died a broken man.'

'Enough of this talk,' Ingwar said. 'We are here for the answer to King Olaf's demands. What do you have to say for yourself?'

'I have a new offer for Olaf,' Aethelstan said. He looked to his left and right, as if keen to ensure everyone was listening.

Ethils and Ingwar smirked at each other.

'I'd have thought you had little left to give, Aethelstan,' Ingwar said. 'Olaf has stripped you so bare. But let's hear it. What are you now prepared to offer Olaf to avoid meeting him in battle?'

'Nothing,' Aethelstan said.

A gasp rose from the assembled warriors.

'Except that I will allow Olaf to live,' Aethelstan said. 'He and his men can leave this country *if* he makes restitution for all the goods and property they have stolen here and pay weregild for the men they have killed. If he really wants to rule on this island I will allow him to be king of Scotland. But only as my vassal. He will rule in my name. He will have to deal with his father-in-law, the current king of Scots first, of course, but that will be his problem. I have fought Constantine enough now. He can no longer be allowed to rule. Now go back to your master and tell him all of that.'

After a moment of stunned silence, the gathered Saxon

warriors broke into a cheer every bit as raucous as they had been earlier.

Realising any further words of their own would be drowned in the din, Ingwar, Ethils and the others turned their horses and rode away, sour expressions on their faces. Those in the camp jeered them as they went.

Egil turned to Einar. To Einar's surprise the usually surly viking was grinning.

'It looks like this war is on after all,' he said.

A terrible thought came to Einar. Olaf would attack now; there was no doubt. If Olaf sent another night attack like before and this time the Wolf Coats were successful in getting into the camp, they would know exactly where Aethelstan's tent was.

The king began pushing his way back into the camp. As he went all those around him clapped him on the back, grinning their approval.

Einar shoved his way through the throng, hauling indignant people out of his way until he reached the king.

'Einar!' the king said. There was excitement in his eyes that Einar had not seen before. 'Thanks for the part you played in relaying those messages to Olaf. I am sorry you did not know the whole plan but it may not have worked if more than a few did.'

'So it *was* all a ploy?' Einar said. 'A trick to delay Olaf long enough for the army to get here?'

'After a few days we realised a week would not be enough time to raise the whole army of Aengland. So we had to come up with a way of stalling Olaf without making it look like we were not ready,' Aethelstan said. 'If he'd known he would have attacked early. We would have lost the battle and I would have lost the throne. And you played a vital role in all this. I am in your debt.'

'If that is the case, Lord King, will you do me this favour?' Einar said.

'Of course,' Aethelstan said, becoming serious. 'What do you want?'

'Do not stay in the camp tonight, lord,' Einar said.

'What?' Aethelstan looked puzzled. 'I want to stay with my warriors.'

'But the rest of the army is not yet here,' Einar said.

'They will be here by morning,' the king said.

'Lord, I saw a pair of ravens flying over your tent,' Einar said. 'It is a bad omen.'

'I put no store in pagan superstitions, Einar,' Aethelstan said, frowning. 'And neither should you.'

'Lord, the camp has been attacked in the night during the week,' Einar said. 'It is not as easily defended as the town which has a rampart. I was one of Ulrich's Wolf Coats, remember? They have the skills and crafts to get into the camp in the dark. If they do, who knows what mischief they could work?'

Aethelstan thought for a moment.

'Very well,' he said. 'Perhaps you're right. I don't want the men thinking I'm scared to face the same dangers as them, though.'

'Leave after dark, Lord King,' Einar said. 'Go quietly. It is the sensible thing to do. You know it.'

'I will think about it,' Aethelstan said. 'The rest of the army will be here by first light. Tomorrow we fight Olaf.'

Forty-Two

Affreca sat in her brother's tent. The interior was gloomy, lit only by a couple of oil lamps on stands. There was no one else there and not for the first time she wondered why her brother had summoned her there.

After some time she was just about to get up and leave when she heard familiar voices outside. Moments later Ulrich and Skar came through the flap of the tent entrance. 'What a bunch of tossers!' Ulrich said, grinning. 'We walked right into their camp. Olaf was *inside* Aethelstan's tent. Then we walked back out. And they did nothing!'

Affreca could tell both were giddy with the euphoria that often comes after missing death by the breadth of a hair.

'Well we couldn't have done it alone,' Skar said.

'What do you mean?' Ulrich said.

'Einar let us go,' Skar said. 'He could have stopped us but he didn't.'

'Like I said,' Ulrich said, his upper lip curling. 'They did nothing. Einar didn't have the guts to try and stop us. I'm glad we are rid of him.'

'He just saved our lives, Ulrich,' Skar said, becoming very serious. 'I think you should recognise that.'

'You saw Einar?' Affreca said.

Skar related what had happened.

'Well, he must have some loyalty left,' Affreca said.

'Aye,' Skar said. 'He was always a good lad, Ulrich. You once considered him as a successor to yourself.'

'That was before he betrayed us,' Ulrich said.

'Well, considering what happened today,' Skar said, 'perhaps you should—'

'Should what?' Ulrich cut him off. 'Forgive him? Welcome him back with open arms like a good Christian would? He's on the enemy side in a war, in case you've forgotten.'

'Wars end, Ulrich,' Affreca said. 'And when they do there is always a settlement.'

Ulrich sighed and looked up into the darkness gathered in the roof of the tent.

'What are you doing here anyway?' he said.

'Don't try and change the subject,' Affreca said. 'But my brother asked me to come and see him here when he got back. Where is he anyway?'

'He was just behind us,' Ulrich said. 'He said he had to go and fetch someone but he should be here any moment.'

'There is that *other* matter we should talk to Affreca about,' Skar said, flicking his eyes in her direction.

'Your brother intends to marry you off,' Ulrich said.

'What?!' Affreca said, her jaw dropping open. 'To who?'

'To a most worthy man, Affreca.'

The sound of Olaf's voice made them all spin around to see the king of Dublin, now out of his disguise as the blind harper, standing in the tent entrance.

'I don't recall asking you to play matchmaker, Ulrich,' he said, glowering in the direction of the little Wolf Coat. 'There is no need anyway. It's all arranged already.'

'I don't remember you asking *me* about this?' Affreca said. There were spots of red on her usually snow white cheeks. 'Who is it this time? The last time you tried this you wanted me to marry Thorfinn Skull Cleaver!'

'And you disobeyed me in that,' Olaf said.

'Disobeyed *you*?' Affreca said. 'You're my brother, Olaf. Not my father.'

'I am head of the family now our father is gone,' Olaf said, his face flushed red and anger making him raise his voice. Then he sighed, as if forcing himself to calm down again. 'Hear me out, sister. I have not changed my aim of creating a strong alliance with Orkney. You turned down the opportunity to marry Thorfinn so I now offer an even better prospect. A former king no less.'

'No!' Affreca said, her jaw wide open. 'Not Eirik Bloody Axe?!'

'Right first time!' Olaf said, pointing his forefinger at her and grinning. 'A son of Harald Fairhair, and Jarl of Orkney. Who could be better?'

'His current wife will kill him,' Ulrich said with a scoff. 'Have you ever met Gunnhild? Not a very forgiving woman. Do you know she's a witch? If she doesn't kill Eirik she'll kill Affreca. No. I can't allow this.'

'For a start, Ulrich, no one is asking you,' Olaf said, his grin fading to a threatening grimace. 'For another thing, Eirik himself seems most keen on the idea. He's even looking forward to it.'

'But why?' Affreca said. The expression on her face was a combination of despair and confusion. 'What good is an alliance with Orkney to you?'

'We're all Aethelstan's enemies,' Olaf said. 'But apart from that, I believe I heard you say just before I came in that after a war there is always a settlement? It looks like this one will end with me ruling Jorvik. I don't trust Constantine. We've fought each other much longer than we've been allies. If I'm in Northumbria with Aethelstan still to the south of me I don't want to be worrying about Constantine to the north. However, with Eirik on my side we can deal with Constantine together, and with you in Eirik's household, I can make sure he is staying in line too.'

The sound of raised voices outside the tent interrupted the conversation. A moment later the flap of the tent entrance was thrown back and the brother earls Ingwar and Ethils strode in.

'Lord Olaf, I bring grave news,' Ingwar said. 'It is as I suspected. There are tricksters in the enemy camp. Those we have been dealing with were just playing us along.'

'You got Aethelstan's response?' Olaf said.

'We got it right from the king's mouth,' Ethils said.

'And?' Olaf said. 'What is his new offer?'

'His new offer is *nothing*, lord,' Ingwar said. Then he repeated Aethelstan's words.

A stunned silence clogged the air of the tent for several moments. Olaf's face darkened. Ulrich let out a low whistle.

'Such guile is worthy of Odin himself,' he said.

'That bastard!' Olaf roared, loud enough to make Earl Ethils flinch. 'How dare he?'

'We cannot let him get away with this,' Ethils said. 'He must be punished.'

'Oh, he will be,' Olaf said, his eyes widening. 'We go to war. I will ready the army. We will attack.'

'Lord,' Ethils said. 'It will take time to assemble the army for battle. Half of the useless bastards were already counting the silver they thought they were getting from Aethelstan in their heads and got drunk.'

'Don't fret,' Olaf said. 'When fully arrayed we've more than enough men to sweep them off the field. I saw that for myself. They will be ready by morning. Then we attack.'

'My men are ready now, Lord King,' Ingwar said. 'I've always suspected something like this was going on and kept the men prepared for battle. Let us attack tonight.'

'In the dark?' Olaf said.

'Yes,' Ingwar said. 'I still believe most of Aethelstan's army is still to arrive. We can wipe out those in that camp now before the rest of their men arrive and claim victory.'

'Perhaps you're right,' Olaf said. 'There are a lot of them already there though.'

'We will take them by surprise,' Ethils said.

'Better than that,' Olaf said. 'Ulrich here knows exactly where Aethelstan's tent is. If you take them by surprise we could catch him asleep in it. Ulrich, I might have need of your special skills again.'

'The fastest way to kill an enemy is to cut off his head,' Ingwar said with a vicious grin.

'All right,' Olaf said. 'Do it.'

Part Eight

Ne wearð wæl mare
on þis eiglande   *æfre gieta*
folces gefylled   *beforan þissum*
sweordes ecgum,   *þæs þe us secgað bec,*
ealde uðwitan,   *siþþan eastan hider*

Engle and Seaxe   *up becoman,*
ofer brad brimu   *Brytene sohtan,*
wlance wigsmiþas

Never was there more carnage,
Folk felled by the sword's edge,
On this island before this –
This the books and elder scholars say –
Since hither from the east
Angles and Saxons, proud war-smiths
sailed over the broad seas seeking Britain

      'The Battle of Brunanburh' – Old English poem from
The Anglo-Saxon Chronicle (translated by Tim Hodkinson)

Forty-Three

It was another night with little sleep for Einar. When he first went to his tent he had no problem dropping off. It was as if the arrival of the king and the excitement of the previous day had left him drained and it was not long before he sunk deep into a heavy sleep.

Then a dream of Ulrich with a blood-splattered knife in each hand standing over the butchered corpse of Aethelstan wrenched him from his slumber. He tried to get back to sleep, but thoughts of the coming battle just disturbed his mind further.

This would not be his first, but it may well be the biggest battle he had ever fought in. Almost every man of fighting age on the island of Britain would be in this fight. The sides were evenly matched. No one was assured victory. He needed rest. A good night's sleep. Like a cat chasing its own tail, frustration made sleep even more difficult to return to.

It was also uncomfortably warm. The storm that had threatened all day still had not arrived and the air was close and still as death. Sweat broke out all over Einar and sat on his skin, refusing to melt into an air already pregnant with coming rain.

Through all that the nagging anxiety that Ulrich and the others were creeping through the dark again, this time knowing exactly where to strike, continued to vex him.

Foolish is the man who lies awake at night, worrying about his troubles. In the morning he finds his troubles are still there, only now he is tired as well.

These words of Odin kept surfacing in Einar's mind, as if the old one-eyed god was scolding him. Ulrich and the others, if they were not indeed sneaking through the night, would have no problem sleeping; he had no doubt about that.

Eventually, with a heavy sigh, Einar gave up on slumber and scrambled out of his tent. Perhaps if he went to the king's tent and all was quiet there it would put his mind at ease and he could finally go back to sleep.

The first thing he noticed was how busy the campsite was. It was the dead of night, almost the blue hour by his reckoning, but warriors were hurrying around. Some were already in full war gear while others were preparing theirs. From the predominance of Norwegian visored helmets and round shields painted with white crosses among them, Einar judged them to be mostly Thorolf and Egil's Norsemen. Many torches and braziers blazed, fighting back the darkness to well beyond the boundaries of the camp.

Einar spotted Thorolf himself standing near the perimeter ditch. Like his men, he was ready for war.

'What's going on?' Einar said as he joined the big Norseman. Thorolf just pointed down the slope.

Einar narrowed his eyes, peering down into the dark. He saw shielded helmets.

'There's someone out there,' he said.

'King Aethelstan ordered Alfgeir to lead his warriors out into the heath as an advance guard,' Thorolf said. 'In case Olaf tried an attack during the night.'

So this was Alfgeir's last chance to redeem himself, Einar thought.

'He just sent a messenger back to us,' Thorolf went on. 'They think someone is moving onto the battlefield from the far end. We're getting ready to move the men out and go down there for a closer look.'

'I'll go with you,' Einar said.

'You'd better get your war gear on first,' Thorolf said with a grin. 'Unless you're planning to confront the enemy in your night clothes.'

Einar jogged back to his tent. Passing the big tent with the flag of Wessex above it on the way, he saw to his relief that all seemed quiet and normal there. Warriors stood guard at the entrance, which was another good sign.

Back at his own tent, he scrambled into his brynja, slung his shield over his shoulder and plonked his helmet on his head. As he did so, his eye fell on a scrap of fur that was hanging halfway out of his travelling satchel. It was his wolf skin cloak, the garment that showed he had once been an úlfheðinn.

Einar thought for a moment. Then he pulled it out and put it on. Then he grabbed the heavy mail troll and left the tent, jogging back to where he had left Thorolf. By the time he returned, Egil had joined his brother, as had many of their warriors. All were dressed for battle. There was a calm expectancy among them as they waited for Thorolf's orders.

As if the sky was aware of what was going on below it, far in the distance a rumble of thunder echoed.

'Thor rides his chariot tonight,' Egil said. 'I hope we give him some entertainment.'

Thorolf signalled to an archer who held an arrow over a burning brazier. The arrow was wound in cloth that must have been soaked in oil and sprang into flame in an instant. The archer notched the arrow, drew his bow then loosed it, sending the burning arrow high into the night air. Hundreds of eyes watched as it arched through the dark. It reached its apex about two hundred paces away from the camp where its light gleamed across the armour and weapons of Alfgeir and his men. It travelled on, falling now. It went perhaps another two hundred paces before thudding into the ground, still alight. The light of its flames flickered on metal at the edge of the darkness beyond. A figure ran forward and stamped out the flaming arrow but it was too late. It had already shown the men in the camp what they needed to know.

'They're down there all right,' Egil said.

'Let's go,' Thorolf said. 'Where's Thorfinn the Mighty?'

A limbering giant of a man came forward. In one hand he bore a standard pole with Thorolf's battle flag on it, a black raven on a white background. It was not unlike the mythical raven banner Einar had once been part of a quest for. The pole it flew from was twice the height of a man but Thorfinn the Mighty grasped it in one hand like it was a wooden spoon.

Einar made a little ironic laugh.

'You don't like my banner?' Thorolf said.

'I do,' Einar said. 'I was just thinking, however, that I've spent most of the last year learning to be a good Christian for Aethelstan, and it led me here, fighting under the raven banner again.'

'The norns' humour can be dark,' Egil said.

'Lead us out, Thorfinn,' Thorolf said.

'We're going down there?' Einar said. 'Wouldn't it be better to defend the camp? There's a ditch built for that.'

'Chances are this is just a raid,' Thorolf said. 'And we can't fight in here. There is no room. There's tents, campfires, horses, carts. Too much to get in the way. Better to get out there and stop them in their tracks.'

Another rumble of thunder echoed in the distant sky. Then, led by the mighty Thorfinn, the vikings filed out of the camp and down the slope until they drew alongside Alfgeir's men. As his eyes grew accustomed to the dark, Einar could see they were already arrayed in a shield wall, facing down the slope. There were not enough of them, however, to stretch right across the field so they were staying towards the river side.

Thorolf brought his men alongside them, spreading out in a line from the middle of the field to the woods on the opposite side.

Looking ahead, Einar could see movement in the dark. Here and there moonlight or distant flames in the camp gleamed across helmets, spear points or swords. It was impossible to tell how many there were.

Then a flash of lightning split the night. For an instant the blinding white light showed the two opposing forces to each other. A little way down the slope were two companies of men. They were fully armed and bore shields and spears. Above one company flew the banner of Earl Ingwar and above the other was the banner of Ethils.

'It's the Earls of Bretland,' Egil said as darkness fell again.

Then a mighty blast of thunder ripped the sky, so loud it made everyone flinch. Another flicker of lightning crackled as rain began to gush from the heavens, coming down in torrents as if they had all walked under a waterfall.

'Now Thor's pissing on us,' Egil said. 'It's his way of telling us to get on with it.'

Horns began blasting from down the slope. The enemy charged and the battle began.

Forty-Four

From the scattered flashes of light on metal, Einar had guessed that the enemy were few and scattered. The lightning revealed that they were in fact tightly packed and there were in fact many more of them than in Thorolf and Egil's war band. However they were mostly lightly armed and the glints of light he had spotted were from the few scattered among them with helmets and mail shirts.

With a roar that drowned even the thunder, the vikings linked shields and charged down the slope. Ingwar's company charged to meet them. Ethils' war band did the same but Alfgeir's stood in position, forming a shield wall to resist the attack.

'Svinfylking!' Thorolf shouted.

His signallers took over and began relaying the order through a series of horn blasts. As they ran, the Norsemen formed into a wedge, biggest men to the front, the rest falling into ever wider ranks behind them. Thorfinn the Mighty bore Thorolf's banner in the centre and Thorolf, Egil and Einar ran in front of him.

Light flared overhead as archers back in the camp began launching flaming arrows into the sky. They were not trying to hit the enemy but cast light for the fighters to battle by.

Einar felt a thrill of exhilaration as they charged forwards. All doubts, tiredness, concerns and fears were gone. He was surrounded by his own folk who were not just any Norsemen but hardened vikings who he no doubt could cause fearsome damage to the enemy. He had no idea who they rushed to fight but he longed to get to grips with them. His clenched teeth itched and he felt a fire ignite somewhere deep within his heart.

With a crash like a huge sack of loose metal being dropped onto rocks the vikings powered into Ingwar's company. Einar felt the shock of the impact as it rippled through the packed ranks of men. Their advance checked, then surged forward again as the point of the wedge formation split the front rank of the enemy and drove deep into the heart of their formation. Men screamed, weapons clashed and the thunder crashed overhead. Lightning flashed and rain lashed down.

Ingwar's company was almost split in two. The vikings hacked and stabbed to the left and right, forcing themselves deeper into the formation. Einar could make out Ingwar's banner retreating as the earl pulled himself back from the encroaching danger.

Einar was shouting, like those around him, but he did not know who to or what the words were. Then several warriors to his right stumbled and fell over. Whether they were knocked down or missed their footing in the dark it was impossible to tell. Welsh warriors came piling through the gap they left in the viking formation and Einar found himself with nothing between him and them.

Grasping his mail troll in both hands he drove it at the first attacker. The Welshman countered with his shield but the long, thick blade of Einar's weapon punched through its wood. Einar pulled it upwards and the serrated blade ripped the hole in the shield wider. Then he twisted it and the shield shattered into two pieces.

The Welshman hacked at Einar with a long-bladed knife but Einar turned away from him and the knife clattered into the shield still slung over Einar's back. At the same time Einar raised his right leg and kicked into the shield of the second enemy coming his way, sending the man staggering away again.

Einar spun back to the first man. He was too close for Einar to wield the mail troll like a spear so he swung it like an axe. The weighted blade with the spikes around its base smashed into the Welshman's face and he collapsed as though the blow had shattered every bone in his body.

Recovering his balance, the second man came forward again. He was about to attack with his spear while covering himself with his shield when Einar rammed his mail troll straight through the man's shield and into his guts behind. The stout, feather-shaped blade, made for piercing chain mail, punched through the wooden shield like it was made of straw. Einar wrenched back his weapon and the enemy sank to the ground.

The vikings closed the gap in their ranks and Einar stepped back. He realised he was panting from the sudden exertion. The strange, detached voice that sometimes came to him in these situations told him there were two dead men beside him. Two men he had killed. They were probably someone's sons, someone's fathers or brothers. There were people who would miss them and grieve when they did not return from this war. Einar felt nothing but excitement. They were the enemy. They had come up against him and he had stopped them. They had tried to kill him and failed.

The Welshmen and Angles of Ingwar's company recovered from the initial shock of the vikings' charge. There were many dead men of the enemy around their feet, but the vikings' advance was halted, their wedge formation lodged halfway inside Ingwar's company like an arrow head sunk in a man's chest.

The men along the edges of the svinfylking had their shields locked together as the Welshmen vented their fury on them, trying to batter a way through. Einar and Egil stood in the rank behind the right edge, using their long weapons – Egil's battle spear and Einar's mail troll – to poke and stab at the enemy over the shoulders of the men before them.

The sound of horns blowing an alarm made Einar turn around.

'Einar! Egil! Come with me,' Thorolf shouted above the cacophony of battle. 'They're trying to surround us.'

A flash of lightning allowed Einar to see enemy warriors had broken from their main company and were dashing along the viking lines to outflank them. If that happened Einar and the others would be stuck, surrounded by the enemy, unable to retreat or advance, unable to do anything but fight until they were exhausted, or had lost too many men for effective defence. Then they would be finished.

Einar, Egil and others from the inner ranks of the formation dashed to the back to join the line that formed the sides, extending it so the arrow head was now hollow, but too long for Ingwar's men to effectively surround it.

The mail troll needed both hands to wield. So to stand in the shield wall Einar had to sling the weapon over his shoulder by its long leather strap so he could use his shield. Einar drew his sword; a workaday weapon taken from the supply train. It was little more than a sharpened iron bar and nowhere near as fearsome as the mail troll but it was effective enough to batter any of the enemy that attacked him until they either retreated or fell.

All the while it was getting easier to see what was going on. The dawn was approaching and despite the heavy clouds that still masked the sky ambient light was growing all around. Archers at the camp still shot blazing arrows overhead which added to the light. The thunder was receding into the distance too, the rain slackened to a drizzle as the storm moved on across the sky.

'Thor's got bored of us now,' Egil shouted to Einar. 'He's gone on to find something more entertaining elsewhere.'

A great shout that sounded like triumph mixed with dismay rose from behind the enemy company attacking Thorolf's vikings. There was a Welshman attacking Einar at that moment. He thrust his spear over the top of Einar's shield, the tip aimed at Einar's face. Einar ducked his head sideways and the spear blade skittered along the side of his helmet. Einar struck with his sword, bringing it down in a cleaving blow to the Welshman's left shoulder. The now-blunted edge of the cheap sword did not manage to slice through the leather jerkin the Welshman wore. The weight of the blow, however, was still heavy enough to smash the man's collarbone. Einar heard it snap. The warrior dropped his spear and stumbled away, his shoulder collapsed with his left arm dangling at an unnatural angle.

With the immediate danger gone, Einar looked across the battlefield. In the growing grey pre-dawn light he could make out the mass of men fighting, and flying over them was the banner of Alfgeir, flapping in the breeze on its high standard pole.

The banner was moving and it was moving away. It was moving sideways across the slope at an ever more rapid pace.

'They're running away!' Einar shouted. He turned to Egil who was finishing off an enemy on the other side of their shield wall. 'Alfgeir is leaving the battlefield!'

Egil looked around and Einar saw the grim look that crossed his face.

'This is bad for us,' he said. 'We're already outnumbered as it is. If Ethils' company joins with Ingwar's we'll be surrounded for sure.'

Forty-Five

'I need to warn Thorolf,' Egil said. He nodded to Einar and tapped the man on his right on the shoulder. 'Fill in for me.'

Einar felt a surge of anxiety within his guts as Egil stepped back from the shield wall. Einar took a step left and the man on Egil's right took one left as they both tried to cover the gap Egil had left along with their own positions.

Their enemy spotted the potential weak spot and threw themselves at it with renewed vigour. Einar and the viking to his right had to fight hard to stop them breaking the shield wall. They did not have to struggle long though. Egil returned with orders from Thorolf that they were to withdraw, make a half-turn and put their backs to the woods that lined that side of the battlefield.

'The trees are tightly packed,' Egil said. 'They'll protect our backs.'

Alfgeir's banner had disappeared from sight now and along with it any sign of his war band.

'The coward has saved his own skin,' Egil said. 'He's run for the Roman road. Ethils' men chased them for a bit then turned back to the heath and now block the way back to the camp.'

'If I were Alfgeir I'd keep running,' Einar said. 'I'd say he's used up the last of his chances with Aethelstan now.'

Thorolf's signallers began blowing horns once more and

the vikings prepared to move. It would not be easy. They were engaged in fighting all along their lines and on the left-hand side half of Ingwar's men were between them and the woods.

Einar shouted at the attacker on the other side of his shield then unleashed a flurry of blows with his sword. He managed to strike him a couple of times on the head and right shoulder and the Welshman stumbled away.

Then they broke and ran. Each man fell out of position and charged as hard as they could for the new position. Thorolf led the way, charging back the way they had come and then towards the trees. Thorfinn the Mighty bore the raven banner behind him, so everyone knew which way to go.

Ingwar's warriors stood for a moment, taken by surprise that opponents who had fought so hard until now should all of a sudden turn and flee. Then, with the glee of hounds scenting a bleeding fox, they charged after the vikings. Einar ran as hard as he could despite the weight of his war gear. With every step he expected to feel the burning agony of a blade sliding into his back.

Thorolf arrived before the trees.

'To me! To me!' he shouted, using the others to gather around him. Einar, Egil and the rest of the vikings arrived next. Then they scrambled to reform their shield wall. The shields had just slapped together when Ingwar's men crashed against them. Einar clenched his teeth as the impact from a warrior hurling himself against his shield rippled through his shoulder and down his braced left leg.

Ingwar's men commenced a renewed assault all the way along the new viking formation. As they hacked and slashed at the line of shields, Ethils' company jogged back across the heath to join forces with them. Soon the pressure was intense but the viking line held firm. Einar and the others fell to a dogged defence, fighting just to hold the narrow strip of ground at the edge of the heath before the woods.

They alternated between crouching, head down behind the shelter of their wide, round shields and popping up to strike back, landing blows on their attackers or countering hacks and strikes with their own weapons. All the while Einar hoped that none of the enemy had a weapon similar to the mail troll slung over his back. If they did they would cut through his shield's defence like it was made of butter.

The vikings were all fit men, used to rowing long distances and veterans of many battles. Their superior war gear protected them a lot more that the lightly armed Welshmen who their weapons took a devastating toll on. Nonetheless, Einar could see there were men falling in his line and fit as they were, the vikings could not fight on forever. If something did not change then it was only a matter of time before Ingwar and Ethils' superior numbers gave them victory.

As Einar's arms began to feel heavy, Thorolf came running down the line.

'Every fifth man drop out of the shield wall and go to the standard,' he repeated at each section he passed. 'The rest of you close the gaps and shorten the line.'

Starting at the far end, men began to strike final blows against assailants then step back from the shield wall at intervals. As they did so those to their right and left slapped their shields together to stop the enemy getting in.

When it came to Einar's section he realised he was the fifth man. He lashed out at a Welshman on the other side of his shield, making him stumble away, then withdrew from the line. When he was sure the gap he left was closed and secure, he jogged over to join the others where Thorfinn the Mighty bore the raven banner.

'Lads, we can't stay here all night,' Thorolf said. 'Or day either, seeing as the sun is coming up. We need to do something.'

'Why don't they send help from the camp?' Einar said. 'They must see we are in trouble.'

'With us down here and Alfgeir taken to his heels there aren't enough of them left to be much help,' Thorolf said. 'And if they leave the camp they risk leaving it unguarded for more of Olaf's men to take it. Then Aethelstan loses the field and the battle before it even starts.'

'So what do we do?' Einar said.

'We have to sort this out ourselves,' Thorolf said. 'If we remain standing here eventually Ingwar will overcome us. He and his brother outnumber us by many. We're surrounded on three sides. If we try and run into the trees they'll cut us down before we get ten paces in that undergrowth.'

'It doesn't sound like we have too many options,' the man beside Einar said.

'We're going to attack,' Thorolf said.

Einar's eyes widened in surprise. The others nodded. Some smiled.

'When you hear the signal we break out of the shield wall,' Thorolf said. 'Stick together. Make for Ingwar first. We'll make him regret attacking us tonight.'

Einar knew they only had moments to prepare. He took deep breaths in through his nose as he swung his shield over his shoulder then grasped the mail troll in both hands. The men around him readied themselves in similar ways.

Slightly out of immediate danger and with nothing now to do but prepare for a desperate charge, Einar found the tension mounting within him unbearable. He felt no fear, just a longing to come to blows with his enemies. Standing behind the shield wall had been frustrating. Now he would have a chance to strike back and hit back hard. The sensation like all his gums were itching returned as he screwed his eyes shut, fighting to control the rush of emotions within him.

'I heard you were an úlfheðinn.'

Einar opened his eyes to see Thorolf was talking to him. He nodded.

'Well, we could do with some of Odin's fury tonight,' Thorolf said. 'They say úlfhéðnar are Odin's chosen warriors. If the old man still listens to you, ask him to bless us with it.'

Einar opened his mouth to say that he was no longer a wolf warrior. He was oathsworn to Aethelstan. But something stopped the words coming out and he made no sound.

The other warriors around him were sucking in air through their noses and striking their chests, sending the mail rings of their brynjas rattling as they wound themselves up for the fight.

'Let's go,' Thorolf said. He nodded to his signallers and they blew their horns. The men in the shield wall, recognising the signal, broke formation and opened up a gap. Thorolf let out a guttural roar and pounded forwards, an axe in one hand and a short sword in the other.

The others charged after him. Einar found himself screaming like the others. He saw the startled faces of Ingwar's warriors beyond the shield wall, their open mouths and frozen stances. Then they were crashing into them, slashing left and right, driving their spear points into them and cutting a bloody swathe through their ranks.

Ahead, in the grey light of the coming dawn, Ingwar's banner flew from its standard. Thorolf was making straight for it. Einar fell in behind him, as did the others. The column of vikings forged through the lightly armoured Welsh and Scots opponents, scything men down like hay in the meadow and trampling their bodies beneath their charging feet.

Einar felt like he was in a dream or under water. All those around him appeared to be moving very slowly while he went at normal speed. He knew what they were going to do even as they began their movements. He had all the time in the world to counter whatever attack they made and strike back, driving the blade of the mail troll into their guts or smashing their heads in with the weighted, spiked head. He knew he was screaming at the top of his lungs but somehow the sound seemed far away, as if it was someone else making the noise.

He looked up and saw they had almost reached Ingwar's banner. Looking back he also saw that their contingent of men was deep among the enemy. The rest of the vikings had closed up the shield wall. There was no going back now.

Ingwar's bodyguards closed ranks before his standard. For the first time Einar saw Ingwar. His bald head was wet in the rain and his beard was straggling. He had no helmet but wore the extra-thick mail Einar had seen him in before. He bore a shield in one hand and a great bejewelled sword in the other.

Thorolf cut one of the bodyguards down with his axe and stepped over him. Einar and the others stormed after Thorolf, knocking the other bodyguards aside with sheer momentum and the weight of their numbers. Men sprawled in every direction, friend and foe alike, knocked off balance in the churning throng.

Einar went down with the others. For a few moments he was caught in a thrashing tangle of limbs. Then he was on his feet again and pushing forwards towards the earl.

Thorolf reached Ingwar's banner. With one mighty slash of his sword he decapitated the man who bore the banner and severed the standard pole he carried. The flag dropped straight to the ground as the life blood of the man who had borne it gushed out and splattered all over it.

Another viking reached the earl. He hit him a swipe across

the shoulder but as Einar had seen before, the blade just skidded off Ingwar's thick mail. The earl drove his own sword into the viking's face, killing him outright.

Thorolf attacked next. He struck at the earl with his axe. The earl blocked the blow with his shield. The axe blade lodged in the wood and Thorolf swung his sword. He struck the earl in the side but his blade too was useless against the earl's iron-ringed protection. The earl struck at Thorolf with his sword but the big viking leader jumped back and the blow missed. Thorolf still grasped the long handle of the axe. He tugged it back, wrenching the shield from Ingwar's grasp.

Let's see what you can really do, Einar thought as he grasped the shaft of the mail troll in both hands and charged forward. The earl saw him coming and readied himself to strike. Einar did not feint or try any other tactic beyond ramming the blade of his weapon as hard as he could into Ingwar's guts, putting all the weight of his charging body behind it.

As the point struck the earl's belly, Einar felt the shaft buck and twist in his hand. Then he felt the stout, specially made feather-shaped blade split the rings of Ingwar's brynja and slide on in.

Ingwar's eyes widened in astonishment and pain. Einar gritted his teeth and shoved the blade in further, parting the heavy mail rings wider and carving deep into the flesh and guts beneath.

Now Ingwar screamed and a great gout of blood burst from his lips, spraying Einar and Thorolf with gore. He made one weak attempt to strike Einar with his sword, missed, then the weapon fell from his grasp.

'Let's make sure his men can see him, Einar,' Thorolf shouted. He grabbed the shaft of the mail troll along with Einar and between them they hoisted Earl Ingwar into the air, still impaled on the end of the spear. Thorolf planted the butt of the mail troll in the ground. Ingwar hung, suspended above them, eyes bulging, mouth agape.

The rest of Ingwar's bodyguards retreated while the other vikings gathered around Thorolf and Einar in a ring.

For a moment all fighting ceased. Einar could see the dismay and disbelief on the faces of Ingwar's men as they gazed up at their dying lord. Beyond them he could also see Earl Ethils' men looking on.

How would Ethils react to the killing of his brother? The vikings were still badly outnumbered and now they were stranded, away from the rest of Thorolf's war band over by the woods.

Then horns began blowing from the camp up the slope. Einar looked and saw in the dawn light that the perimeter of the camp was lined by many warriors. Many banners – much more than when they had left in the night – fluttered in the air above the men and the tents. The flag that flew highest, above all the rest, was the dragon of Wessex.

'The rest of the army has come,' Thorolf said. 'Not a moment too soon.'

The warriors in the camp began filing out onto the battlefield. This was enough for the remains of Ingwar's company and his brother Ethils'. They broke any semblance of formation and ran for the trees. Crossing the heath above Thorolf's vikings, Ethils' men ran into the woods and scattered. Ingwar's men fled off down the slope in the direction of Olaf's camp.

Just above Einar's head Earl Ingwar gave a deep groan then stopped breathing.

'We did it!' Einar said, breaking into a grin. 'We've seen them off.'

'Aye, we did,' Thorolf said. 'Now all we have to do is fight the main battle against the rest of Olaf's army.'

Forty-Six

They trudged back to the camp, the vikings carrying their dead and helping their wounded. The many butchered corpses of the enemy they left strewn across the heath, as they did with the enemy wounded as well, abandoning them to a lingering end. The wolves began creeping in from the woods and the clouds of ravens circling overhead began to descend.

Einar felt cold and dog-tired, as if every last drop of energy in him had been used up. His arms hung at his sides like he could no longer hold them up and his legs felt like they were made of stone. The thought that he would have to fight again, maybe soon, filled his heart with dread.

The sight that awaited Einar when they reached the camp, however, made him forget his exhaustion. Growing up in Iceland, Einar had been to the district courts and the Alþing, great gatherings of the people when it seemed the entire population of the country came to one place. He had been at Viken at the battle when Eirik Bloody Axe had defeated his brothers, Olaf and Sigrod. He had seen vast herds of people in both places but he had never seen anything like this before in all his life.

The army of all Aengland had arrived at last. The camp overflowed with men. They filled the heath from trees to the river and they were still arriving. A great snake of men wound back to the town and the Roman road. Some were already making their way onto the battlefield before the camp.

The air was filled with the clattering of war gear, the clinking of chain mail, the barking of orders and the excited chatter of men. As the vikings trudged back into the camp the Saxons parted their ranks to make way for them, shouting their congratulations at the early victory and clapping them on the back as they passed.

'It's like the whole world has gathered on this spot to fight,' Einar said to Egil who walked beside him. Thorolf was just behind them, grinning and waving to all around.

'I keep wondering about that. What if this is the Ragnarök?' Egil said. 'The last battle at the end of the world. How would we know if it was or not?'

'There have been no signs or portents,' Einar said. 'The lore of our folk tells us that before Ragnarök there will be five years of terrible winter. Evil and chaos unleashed on the world. A time of treachery and deceit, wars and cruelty.'

Egil raised an eyebrow, a half-smile on his face. Einar frowned.

There were red-cloaked warriors pushing through the throng before them. Einar knew what that meant and sure enough King Aethelstan appeared through the gap his bodyguards made for him. At the sight of the king they all stopped and bowed their heads.

'Thorolf, Egil,' Aethelstan said, smiling. 'I heard what you did and I thank you most deeply for your bravery and the victory you have won. You will have my friendship for as long as I draw breath.'

'Thank you, Lord King,' Thorolf said. 'I am honoured and grateful for both your thanks and your offer of friendship. Though I hope you appreciate that my men tend to treasure other rewards more. That is, *actual* treasure of the silver and gold kind.'

'Don't worry, Thorolf,' Aethelstan said. 'You will all be well rewarded for this, and with good silver too. I cannot argue. If you had not held the field Olaf would have taken it all and had every right to claim victory over all. I owe you all my throne, and that is worth a lot. And I'm afraid I am going to have to ask you to fight again. We'll need every man we can get when we fight Olaf today.'

'We'll be ready, lord,' Thorolf said. He threw an arm around Einar's shoulders. 'This man played his part too last night. He didn't have to go with us but he did.'

Aethelstan's face darkened. His smile disappeared.

'Einar is oathsworn to me,' he said, glaring at Einar with eyes that were filled with reproach. 'I do not have to pay him to fight for me.'

'Lord, I wasn't suggesting—' Thorolf began to say, sensing the king's annoyance.

'I've no doubt you weren't,' Aethelstan said. 'But Einar and I need to have a talk. Einar: meet me at my tent.'

He turned on his heel and walked away. His red-cloaked bodyguard went after him.

'What was that about?' Thorolf said. 'He changed his mood fast.'

'I think I've a good idea why,' Einar said with a heavy sigh. A deep sense of dread grew in his heart. Had Ulrich indeed infiltrated the camp under cover of the earls' attack? 'I'll tell you later if I get the chance.'

'I think it would be wise not to keep him waiting,' Egil said.

Einar nodded and jogged off towards the tent of the king. When he got there he found Ine guarding the entrance.

'He's not happy,' the West Saxon bodyguard said as Einar approached.

'I'm not in the mood for your taunts, Ine,' Einar said. 'Just let me in.'

Ine laid a hand on Einar's shoulder. Einar frowned, wondering if he should knock it away. Was this some sort of new goading?

'Look, I know we haven't always seen eye to eye,' Ine said. 'It's my job to keep the king safe and alive and when I see one of our enemies – a Dane – getting close to him, can you blame me for being a bit suspicious? But I heard what you and the other Danes did last night and I respect you for that. There can be no doubt now that you can be trusted.'

Einar could not have been more shocked than if the bodyguard had thrown a bucket of icy water over him. He did not know what to say.

'Now get in there,' Ine said, releasing Einar of the problem.

Taking a deep breath, Einar stepped into the tent.

The leather the tent was made of cut out the light, so lamps were lit to dispel the gloom. By their strange, orange light Einar could see Aethelstan standing beside a bed, head bowed and hands clasped in prayer.

The bed was one of the kind made of strong cloth stretched across a folding wooden frame so it can be easily carried. Lying in the bed was a man. Looking closer, Einar saw that the man in the bed was Bishop Wigred from the shrine of Saint Cuthbert. He would have thought he was asleep but for the livid open wound that was slashed across his throat and the dark pool of blood congealed under the bed.

The king looked up and saw Einar. Einar felt frozen by his glare. Aethelstan waited a long time before speaking, each moment feeling like an eternity for Einar.

'Last night, Einar,' the king said at last, 'I was supposed to sleep here. You urged me, however, to sleep in the town, where it was "safer". I thought about it and I decided it would certainly be more comfortable, so I did. Poor Bishop Wigred here, however, thought my tent wonderful. Warmer than the monastery he was used to, with furs to sleep in and a comfortable bed. He did not go to the town. He stayed here. During the night, someone crept in and murdered him.'

Einar swallowed again. He glanced at the ghastly pale face of the dead bishop, preferring to look at that than the intimidating glare of the king.

'Someone so stealthy, so quiet,' the king went on, 'that they were able to get into our camp, kill the bishop and disappear into the night again without detection. There are very few people I can think of with those sort of skills, with that level of guile and craft. In fact the only ones I can think of is Ulrich Rognisson and his band of werewolves. The company you used to belong to.'

'Lord, I—' Einar began to speak but Aethelstan held up his hand to silence him.

'You warned me not to stay here last night,' the king said. 'Was it your intuition or did you *know* something like this was going to happen?'

He looked Einar directly in the eyes. Einar felt yet again the intensity of the king's stare, the dark eyes that seemed to be looking deep inside him, examining his very heart and the secret hidden there. He knew he would not be able to lie.

'I saw Ulrich in the camp yesterday,' Einar said. 'He and Skar were beside your tent with a blind harpist. I thought they might have been trying to find out where you slept so they could murder you.'

Aethelstan's jaw dropped open a little.

'Why did you not tell me this before, Einar?' he said. He

looked both hurt and angry. 'Why did you not have Ulrich seized? You wouldn't have had to do it yourself but we could have got rid of him. You swore an oath to me, remember? *My* enemies are *your* enemies.'

'Lord, I—' Einar began again then hesitated. Why had he not, indeed? The question had plagued him most of the night. Then he realised the answer. Einar took a deep breath and straightened his back.

'Lord King,' he said, 'the oath I swore to you I once swore to Ulrich. I was never released from that by him. I am sworn to protect both of your lives. Yesterday I fulfilled that oath.'

Aethelstan took a deep breath. He shook his head and Einar felt a pang inside him, understanding what Alfgeir had meant when he said the king's disappointment was hard to bear. There was something about Aethelstan that made folk around him want to please him and when he was not pleased it was distressing.

'Now I have a dilemma,' the king said. 'You saved my life but did not say a word when an enemy – a very dangerous enemy – was right under my nose. It has cost Bishop Wigred his life. What am I to do? I had important plans for you, Einar. I wanted you to rule in the north in my name. Alfgeir has proven unworthy of the responsibility given to him. Now you do this.'

Einar felt anger spark in his heart. Why should he feel bad when he had done the right thing? He had kept his oath.

'I did it for the right reasons,' he said through clenched teeth.

'And look at you,' Aethelstan said, an expression of disdain on his face. 'Where is the red cloak I gave you? You're wearing the filthy heathen wolfskin again! You've let your beard grow too. You look more like one of Thorolf's vikings than one of my Christian warriors.'

He sighed and rubbed his forehead.

'You are an honourable man, there is no doubt about that,' Aethelstan said. 'But what I need more than all else is loyalty. An oath to me prevails over an oath to anyone else, except perhaps God. Cynewulf will tell you – *if* you listen to him – that an oath to an anointed king is the same as an oath to God. I have had enough plotters and rebels around me. Now I need to know that those I put in positions of power can be trusted to do *my* will at all times, even if it means doing something dishonourable.'

Einar looked at the floor, his heart a maelstrom of churning emotions. Anger began to boil above the others.

'So what are you saying?' he said, raising his head again to meet the king's gaze. 'That you can't trust me because I'm a man who keeps his word?'

Aethelstan started, then his brows knitted. At last a rueful smile crept onto his lips.

'As long as you keep your word to *me*, Einar,' the king said. 'That is what I demand. But right now we have a battle to win. Once that is out of the way we will talk once more about this, if we both survive the day. It will take time for the army to assemble. If I were you I'd try to grab some rest. You look terrible.'

Einar nodded. He turned and left the tent. Still in a half-daze either due to his exhaustion or the encounter with the king, he stumbled back to his own tent to snatch whatever rest he could get.

Forty-Seven

Affreca hurried to her brother's tent. She had been with the others, readying their weapons and war gear for the coming battle when Ulfr had arrived, telling her Olaf wanted to see her straight away. She had been reluctant to go. The whole army was likewise preparing and some companies already beginning to move to the battlefield so there was not a lot of time but Ulfr had said the king ordered it.

More than a little impatient when she got there, Affreca strode into Olaf's tent to see he was in the last stages of arming. A slave was tightening the straps on his magnificent brynja while he drew on a pair of heavy leather gauntlets. Another slave held Olaf's helmet and shield while a third knotted the leather garters wrapped around his britches to protect his shins.

'You wanted to see me, Olaf?' Affreca said.

'Ah yes,' the king of Dublin said. 'I need you to take up a particular position for me. I know I can't persuade you to not fight today and I think I will need your superb bow skills. So I want you to hang back behind my division. See if you can pick out and hit enemy leaders with your bow. Your aim is amazing. It should be easy for you.'

'Whenever you compliment me I get suspicious, Olaf,' Affreca said. 'You're not trying to keep me out of harm's way are you?'

'Of course not,' Olaf said. 'Just do this for me, will you?'

Affreca nodded.

'I'll go and tell the others where we need to stand now,' she said.

'No need,' Olaf said. 'I just need you. Ulrich and the rest will lead the division. They'll be in the front rank. There is no place for an archer like yourself there. Not that there is a place anywhere on a battlefield for a woman.'

'Olaf, that is not a good position to put Wolf Coats in,' Affreca said.

'Why would I not want my bravest and most fearsome warriors right in the teeth of the enemy?' Olaf said.

'Because that is not the strength of úlfhéðnar!' Affreca said. 'You know that. They hit and run. They use stealth and guile. They damage the enemy in critical ways then run away so they can do it again and again until he is beaten. They don't stand in shield walls and wait for the enemy to charge into them.'

'I need every warrior I have on the battlefield today,' Olaf said with a shrug. 'There can be no exceptions.'

'Except for me?' Affreca said. 'It seems you want to keep me out of danger and put Ulrich and the others in it. For my part, I assume this is something to do with your plan to marry me off?'

'Well, Jarl Eirik isn't likely to want to marry a woman with missing limbs, is he?' Olaf said, anger entering his voice. 'Which is highly likely to be what you get if you stand with your Wolf Coat friends in the front rank. That or dead.'

'I hope you're not punishing Ulrich for failing to kill Aethelstan last night?' Affreca said. 'It wasn't his fault Aethelstan wasn't where you expected him to be.'

'This has nothing to do with that,' Olaf said. His cheeks were flushing now.

'So you *are* trying to get rid of him!' Affreca said. 'Is this something to do with Eirik Bloody Axe too? I bet it is.'

'Enough!' Olaf shouted. 'I have a battle to win and no time for this anymore. I am your elder brother and you will do what I tell you to. You are going to stay out of this battle whether you like it or not and Ulfr here is going to make sure of it.'

He signalled to the big Irishman who grabbed Affreca by the upper arm with one meaty fist.

'Take her away,' Olaf said.

Ulfr's grasp was so strong Affreca felt like her arm was in an iron vice. She struggled and shouted but there was little she could do.

'Bye, sister,' Olaf said in a mocking tone as Ulfr dragged her out of the tent.

Once outside he trailed her along, struggling and kicking through the maze of tents pitched all around. After a little while of this Ulfr stopped, turned to her and slapped Affreca across the face hard with his free hand.

Affreca rocked sideways from the blow. She would have fallen except Ulfr still held her by the upper arm. Her ears rang and her cheek felt numb. She put the back of her hand to her mouth and when she moved it away saw there was blood on it.

'Did you like that?' Ulfr said, leaning forward to shout in her face. 'Now are you going to stop wriggling or am I going to have to hit you again? King Olaf says I can if I have to, so don't think I won't do it. He says you need to learn to do what you're told. Now are you going to behave?'

Affreca, looking sheepish, nodded.

Ulfr, seeming satisfied, straightened up.

'Good,' he said. 'Now let's go.'

Affreca kicked Ulfr in the balls, driving her foot into the big man's groin like she was trying to kick an apple into Asgard in the heavens above.

Ulfr's eyes bulged. He let go of Affreca's arm as both hands shot to clutch his injured genitals. His breath escaped in a low groan as he sank to his knees. Confusion and agony clouded his vision and stopped his breathing for a few moments.

When he recovered a little he looked up to see Affreca standing above him. She was holding a large clay pot lifted from a campfire nearby above her head with both hands. Then she brought it down, shattering it over the big man's head.

For Ulfr, everything went black.

Forty-Eight

Einar did not sleep. After his encounter with Aethelstan his mind was in too great a turmoil. Added to that was the looming thought of the ever-nearer battle and on top of both was the noise of the camp preparing for battle around his tent. All meant sleep was impossible. After a little while of futile trying, he dragged himself from his tent again and made his way out of the camp and onto the battlefield, where he intended to spend whatever time he had left sitting on his backside on the heath and resting that way.

The king had directed the army to be drawn up in three divisions. The main part would be made up of the Saxons and Angles, the army of Aengland. This formed up in the centre of the battlefield. Their purpose was to confront the army of Olaf and do the hard fighting.

Aethelstan ordered Thorolf and his vikings to split and form two contingents to protect the flanks of the main army. The Scots were famous for wild charges which if successful could cause all sorts of havoc among an army but if countered hard they could also be driven off before they did too much damage. Thorolf took his men to the west, protecting the side of the army along the woods. Egil took the rest to the east, to stop any attacks on the river side. Einar went with Egil. He did not think Aethelstan would welcome him among the ranks of his own men at this time and he realised he felt more at ease among his own folk.

When they were in position, Einar plonked his shield and his mail troll down on the ground then lay on a springy patch of heather. He rested his weary limbs as he gazed up at the sky above. Already it was filled with swirling ravens and crows. Many were picking on the dead from the earlier fight while more and more arrived to wheel and hover overhead. After a while Einar felt as though he had recovered a little and sat up. He looked around. At the other end of the battlefield a steady stream of men were lining up from Olaf's camp. It looked like the enemy were planning to form into two divisions, one towards the river and one towards the road.

A raven swooped down and landed on a clump of heather not far away.

'There's no dead here, my black-cloaked friend,' Einar said to it. 'At least not yet.'

He expected the bird to fly off; however, it stayed where it was. Surprised at how brazen the creature was, Einar looked closer at it. It was a big one, there was no doubt about that. It was probably just fancy but Einar got the impression the bird was looking at him. He could see his own reflection in the glassy, obsidian orb of its eye.

'I see you, Raven,' Einar said. 'What is it you are watching for? What do you see? Are you here to see which men are heroes and which shit their britches? Some men do both in a battle you know. But of course you know. You see us all when we're dead. When there are no poets to make up lies about how we died without fear.'

He thought again of the impaled Ingwar's crimson face hovering above him, silently screaming in agony so great he could not make a sound. Would his own death be as painful? He thought of the men who had died at his hands the night before. If his end came today would he face it with bravery or would be cry like a terrified, screaming child?

Then the bird flapped its wings and took off into the sky. Behind where it had sat, Einar saw a monk approaching. He soon realised it was Cynewulf and it was clear from the way his head bobbed back and forth that he was looking for someone.

Einar raised an arm and waved.

Cynewulf came over.

'There you are!' the monk said. 'I've been looking all over for you. I have a message from Aethelstan.'

'For me?' Einar said.

'For all of you,' Cynewulf said in a loud voice. 'The king wants this company to join the main army. With Olaf's in two divisions we should try to match them rather than divide our strength.'

His face became serious.

'And I have something for you, Einar,' he said, speaking in a much lower voice so only Einar could hear. 'You need to come with me. Now. There is something you must see.'

Einar thought he had never seen the monk look so grave. Rather than argue, he dragged himself to his feet again and picked up his weapon and shield. Telling a nearby Norsemen to relay the new deployment orders to Egil, Einar followed Cynewulf back into the camp.

'I heard what happened,' the monk said as they walked. 'You should not have let Ulrich go.'

'That's easy for you to say, Cynewulf,' Einar said.

'You don't understand how bad this is!' Cynewulf said. Einar was surprised to see glints of light in the old monk's eyes. Were they tears? 'Aethelstan had great plans for you. You were to rule in the north in his name. I was training you for that and you would have been great at it! You are a good man. The sort people need as a leader. But now you have given Aethelstan reason to doubt you.'

'I don't need you going on about this as well,' Einar said. 'I've already heard it all from the king.'

He stopped, intending to turn back to the battlefield.

'I will say no more about it,' Cynewulf said. 'But the king has received an unexpected visitor. A man you know. And I think you should see what is happening.'

Einar had to admit to himself that he was intrigued and he resumed following the monk as they made their way to the king's tent once more.

A small crowd was gathered outside Aethelstan's tent. The noblemen who Einar had helped entertain the previous evening were there, as were the king's bodyguards and a few curious warriors from the surrounding camp. All stood in a circle. In a clear patch in the middle of this stood Aethelstan, hands on hips, looking down at a man who was on his knees before him. The kneeling man had his hands in the air, which told Einar that his present position was not one of voluntary reverence for the king. Several of Aethelstan's bodyguards had spears levelled at him too. He wore plain clothes, but Einar recognised him. It was Bishop Wulfstan.

'I don't know how you have the audacity to walk directly into my camp,' Aethelstan said. 'Do you think I don't know what you have been up to? Do you think I don't know about the part you've been playing to help my enemies?'

'Lord King,' Bishop Wulfstan said. 'I only did what I thought was right in the eyes of the Lord. I was thinking about what would be best for the people. For those who will have to live on after this war.'

'When I am dead, you mean?' Aethelstan said.

If Einar had thought the king angry when he spoke to him earlier, it was nothing compared to now. Aethelstan's chest heaved. His eyes glared. His teeth were bared in a grin of anger.

'Whatever the outcome, lord,' the bishop said. 'All I was trying to do was make plans to ensure the best outcome for the ordinary people of the north. Now I beseech you to hear me out. I come with a proposal.'

'He's remarkably cool about all this,' Einar said out of the corner of his mouth to Cynewulf. 'Considering the position he's in. If I were him I'd be begging for my life.'

'He's the bishop of Jorvik,' the monk replied in a low voice. 'Second only in importance to the bishop of Canterbury. He's a very holy man. The king would never put him to death. He knows that.'

'Why should I listen to more of your lies?' Aethelstan said.

'Hear me out, lord,' the bishop said. 'With such a mighty army it seems you will be victorious.'

'And that is why you are coming grovelling back, no doubt,' the king said.

'Lord, I promise you, that is not the case,' Wulfstan said. 'I am a servant of Christ. Whoever of the worldly powers wins this conflict I must still work with them for the good of the Faithful. This war will end, but you will still have the same old problems with ruling the Danes who have settled in the north. It will be easier ruled if you put a fellow Dane on the throne of Jorvik to rule in Aethelstan's name. It worked well when you put Hakon there. The folk just want to be ruled by one of their own, even if behind it all the real power is you.'

'That may already be my plan,' Aethelstan said.

'Lord King, Eirik Haraldsson, the Jarl of Orkney, offers you his services in that respect,' the bishop said. 'I am here to relay that offer. He is willing to rule Jorvik in your name.'

'What makes Eirik Bloody Axe, a man I deposed from the throne of Norway through my foster son Hakon,' Aethelstan said, 'think I would offer *him* such a prize? Why does he think I would ever trust him?'

'Lord Eirik does not resent you for usurping his throne,'

Wulfstan said. 'He understands that it is all part of the game powerful men play. That is why he is willing to submit to you now. Eirik has experience of ruling a realm. Where will you find someone else like that? And the folk of Jorvik would willingly accept a man like him too. I know it. You would have no more issues with the rebellious north. Not only that but as a sign of good faith, Eirik has let me baptise him in the True Religion. Just think, Lord King, not only will you save the soul of Eirik Haraldsson, but all the many followers he will bring with him.'

This made the king pause. Though his cheeks were still flushed with anger, Aethelstan did not reply. Instead he glared at the ground. Einar knew, to his own dismay, that the king was thinking it through. In many ways this offer made sense. If only it was not Eirik Bloody Axe who made it. The Serpent King who had already stolen so much from Einar. Would he take this too?

'I must return to Eirik now,' the bishop said. He dropped his hands and rose to his feet. 'What shall I tell him your answer is, lord?'

Aethelstan shook his head. His angry grin widening once more.

'I will send my own messengers to Eirik,' he said. 'You're going nowhere, Wulfstan. You are still a traitor.'

For the first time the bishop's face blanched. His look of supercilious confidence evaporated.

'Surely you would not kill me?' he said, his voice cracking. 'I am a bishop. A man of God!'

'You are a prince of the Church, Wulfstan,' Aethelstan said. 'Of course I will not kill you.'

The bishop's shoulders sagged as he let out a sigh of obvious relief.

'Thank you, lord,' he said.

Aethelstan turned to Ine, his lead bodyguard.

'Blind him,' he said.

Einar felt Cynewulf tugging his sleeve.

'We must go,' the monk said.

They walked back to the battlefield as behind them the bishop's howls of protest turned to screams of terrified agony as Ine fulfilled his king's orders.

'What do you think the king will do?' Einar said. 'Will he accept Eirik's offer?'

'I don't know,' the monk said. He sounded very tired all of a sudden. 'But one thing I do know is that your best ploy now is to fight well today. Make sure when the tales are told tonight around the campfires after the battle that everyone will be speaking of the heroic deeds of Einar Unnsson.'

'Thousands of men will clash here today,' Einar said. 'How will the king know the deeds of one man among all of them?'

'You can't go into battle with an attitude like that, son,' Cynewulf said. 'I was once a warrior too, remember? When you go to the fight you must believe that there are eyes watching you. You have to think that every move you make, every brave deed, every shameful act of cowardice, will be seen and known of by all. That is what makes men brave and stops us all being cowards.'

Einar looked at him for a moment, wondering if the old monk was referring to Odin's ravens, the birds that would carry news of brave men's deeds to the one-eyed god so he would reserve a bench in his Valour Hall for them. But then who had seen the men who died, screaming in the dark the night before?

'You told me that after a few thumps to the head, warriors start forgetting folk's names,' Einar said. 'You were a warrior. Do you still remember the faces of the men you killed?'

'Every night before I fall asleep, lad,' Cynewulf said. 'Every single night. Now let's go and join the king's army.'

Forty-Nine

Einar moved with the other vikings to join the ranks of the main army. With it already nearly assembled, the only places they could find were near the front. Einar spotted Egil and fell in beside him.

'You don't think this was all a ploy just to put the Norsemen at the front, do you?' Einar said.

'Maybe,' Egil said. 'But I'd rather be here than lurking at the sides, hoping something will happen.'

'Why do you fight, Egil?' Einar said. 'For the king? Do you think Aethelstan stands for something Olaf doesn't? Something... better maybe?'

'Better?' Egil grunted. 'Einar, you and I are Icelanders. We care nothing for kings or jarls. Our fathers and grandfathers left the old countries to get away from the tyranny of such men. We *choose* who rules us. The goðar rule in Iceland because we grant them that power. A king or a jarl will tell you to do this or that. He will lead you into battle with the promise of some dream. But it's all just a kenning – a symbol – for what *he* wants.'

'Yet you will fight for Aethelstan today,' Einar said. 'And maybe die for him.'

'Make no mistake,' Egil said. 'I fight today for the only two queens who will never let you down: silver and gold. But kings and jarls do not really matter. Not to free people like us. All that really matters is folk, family and friends. They are the ones who will remember you in the end.'

'What of reputation then?' Einar said. 'What of the only thing you can be sure lives on after you die: what folk say about you. The tales they tell. The memories they have of you. A thousand years from now, will they still talk of you? Of me?'

'I don't know about you, Einar,' Egil said. 'But I intend to make sure they talk of me. I will enhance that reputation today. It's the single thing in all this chaos I have power over.'

'But that is only if someone sees the deeds you do,' Einar said. 'In the crush of battle, who knows what is going on?'

'I will see. But there is someone else who sees all,' Egil said. He pointed to the swirling cloud of black birds in the sky above. 'The slaughter, the sorrow, the cowardice, the shame, the cruelty, the bravery, the deeds of great renown. All is beheld in the eye of the raven.'

Horns began to blow. Then eight horsemen came riding out before the army. The king was first, then the Ealdormen of Sussex, Wessex, Mercia and Kent. Singrin of the Wiccii was there and Thorketil of the Five Boroughs. To Einar's surprise Cynewulf rode with them, his simple monk's habit contrasting with the shining mail and garnet-encrusted helmets of the noblemen.

They reined their mounts to a halt and stood, facing the assembled ranks before them. A hush fell on the warriors as Aethelstan cast his gaze across them all.

'At least we're in a prime position to hear what he has to say,' Egil said, then someone in the rank behind told him to hush.

Aethelstan began to speak.

'Men, I stand before you today as your king,' Aethelstan said. 'But also as a West Saxon. As I look around me today I see men of Northumbria and Mercia, as well as some of you whose parents came to this country and we still call Danes. And, of course, our new friends from Iceland and overseas.'

He nodded to Thorolf's company on the west side of the battlefield.

'But we all have one thing in common. Our forefathers came to Britain seeking a new life and led here by my God,' the king went on. 'Like His chosen people who He led through the desert to the land of Israel, he put us here for a purpose: to establish a kingdom that will be a light to the rest of the world. A shining beacon of civilisation and faith in the darkness of barbarity and sinfulness. We flourished here. We established kingdoms – great kingdoms like Kent, Northumbria, Essex, Sussex, Wessex, East Anglia and Mercia.

'Most of you probably think of yourselves as belonging to one of those. You see yourselves as East Saxons, Mercians, Northumbrian Angles. But you are also something else. You are Aenglisc folk, united by one tongue, one purpose and one king. For centuries we have fought each other but now we fight as one.'

Einar could see many of the warriors around him – the Saxon ones at least – straighten their backs.

'And now we face our first real test,' Aethelstan said. 'This land of ours, this Aengland, has only just been born but our enemies – the Scots, treacherous Welshmen, heathen Irish Danes and even some of our own folk – hating what we stand for and frightened by what we could achieve – have joined together to annihilate us. But they…'

He swivelled to point at Olaf's army.

'…the only thing that unites them is hatred of us,' he said. 'All they want is to rob and pillage. They have nothing to offer the world like we have. You are the army of the Aenglisc, the warriors of Aenglalonde, and you stand together in this battle.

The Lord God himself will judge the outcome. He will grant victory to the righteous!'

Enthusiastic cheers broke out all around. The noise was deafening and echoed to the sky, testament to how many men were there. To his surprise Einar realised that the hairs on the back of his own neck were raised.

'He's good,' Egil said. He stood, arms folded, an admiring smile on his face. 'I've never seen such statecraft. That man's words could move the stoniest of hearts.'

As the cheers subsided, Aethelstan spoke again.

'Men, I had hoped Bishop Wigred of Saint Cuthbert's shrine would have blessed us today,' he said. 'But as some of you may already know he was cruelly murdered by our enemies in the night.'

An angry murmur went through the gathered warriors.

'So I will ask Cynewulf here to bless us and lead us in prayer before we go into battle,' Aethelstan continued. 'Many of you will know him. He was a great warrior of Wessex, one of my father's personal guard. Now he is a man of God. Cynewulf?'

The monk moved his horse forward. To Einar's surprise, he was greeted by many cheers of recognition from the warriors, especially those with grey or white in their beards.

'It seems that old monk who's been following you around was once quite a hero,' Egil said.

'Men of Aengland,' Cynewulf said in a loud voice when the cheers subsided. 'Many of you know me. I am not one for speeches. When the king asked me to do this I was at a loss as to what to say, however, I believe the Lord has given us a message. I went into the blessed bishop's tent this morning and I found a book he had brought from the shrine of the saint. It is something they are working on there. Thanks to a brave band of warriors sent by the king to Francia to rescue a very rare book, the monks at the shrine of Saint Cuthbert are translating the gospels and the holy books from their ancient tongues into our own, Saxon words. We will actually be able to read the words of Christ in our own tongue. And the bishop had brought one of these books with him, which I believe he was going to read this morning. So I will instead.'

'He doesn't half like the sound of his own voice does he?' one of the warriors behind Einar said.

'Monks are all the same when they have a captive audience,' another said. 'They can't help taking the chance to preach.'

'Men of Aengland,' Cynewulf continued. 'Some of you may be struggling today with what you will have to do in this battle. One of the Lord's Commandments says we should not kill. How can you reconcile that with the deeds a warrior must do in war? Well the holy book the bishop carried here was the book of the Prophet Samuel, translated into our own tongue. We can see from it the Lord God does not tell us not to kill in all circumstances.'

The monk lifted a big, leather-bound book from his saddle bag and opened it.

'This is what the book of Samuel says: *I will punish the Amalekites for what they have done. Go now and smite them. Annihilate all traces of them. Spare none. Kill the men and women. Kill their children and babies. Kill their oxen and sheep. Kill their camels and their donkeys.* These are the words of the Lord! I tell you now, these are the Amalekites!'

Cynewulf flung his arm behind him, his finger pointing at Olaf's army.

'Heathens! Heretic Scots and apostate Picts!' he shouted. Spittle flew from his mouth. 'The Lord commands us to smite them. Now go and do the work of the Lord!'

Cheering erupted, every bit as loud as that which had greeted Aethelstan's words, except now it had a bloodthirsty edge.

'He has unleashed the beast,' Egil said. 'Men will do all sorts of murder if they think their god commands it.'

'Now let us pray,' Cynewulf said, as the cheering died away. The warriors bowed their heads. '*Fæder ure þu þe eart on heofonum...*'

At the far end of the battlefield the signallers of Olaf and Constantine's army began to sound the advance.

The battle had begun.

Fifty

The two armies advanced towards each other. They were some way apart, so charging would only result in being too tired to fight by the time the warriors clashed. Every tenth man on both sides rapped their spear shaft against their shields in time, creating a beat that kept everyone at the same steady pace. As the two front lines got closer and closer, the beat quickened and their speed picked up.

Ahead, Einar and the others could see Olaf's division advancing towards them, a veritable sea of shields, spears and banners rippling in the morning breeze.

When they reached a hundred paces apart a dark wave rose into the sky above Olaf's army as if countless crows were taking off and soaring high.

'Arrows!' The warning sounded all along the line. Aethelstan's army halted its advance. Everyone raised their shields towards the sky and crouched beneath their shelter. Einar waited in the half-dark for moments that seemed endless. Then an insane drumming began all around as the arrows rained down onto the raised shields. He heard a few men cry out and knew some of the arrows had got through to cause casualties. Then the beating of the spears began again and they started to march forwards again.

The Saxons replied with their own hail of arrows and Einar

saw men falling among the enemy. This exchange happened once again between them and then the opposing sides reached a point where they were about thirty paces apart.

Horns blasted all along both front lines. Einar felt the old familiar fire of bloodlust ignited within his heart. All he wanted to do now was hurl himself at the enemy. With a roar that shook the heavens, the armies launched throwing spears at each other then broke into a charge. They tore forwards, eager to get at each other. Einar threw his shield over his shoulder and dashed forwards with the others, his mail troll grasped in both hands. As he charged, Einar could actually feel the earth tremble with the impact of so many pounding feet.

Then came a huge crash as the armies collided. The air was filled with the deafening tumult of howled war cries, the ring of metal clashing on metal and the screams of the injured or dying. Einar stabbed, swiped and hacked with the mail troll, cutting down men left and right. There was chaos all around as men fought hand to hand in one-on-one battles. The clash of steel on steel reverberated through the air like the tolling of many bells. It mingled with the sound of men screaming. All around warriors killed and died in the swirling melee, their blood mingling with the already churned earth beneath their feet.

The air was thick with the acrid scent of sweat and fear, the metallic tang of blood, and the stench of opened guts and emptied bowels. The ground became slippy and Einar dreaded to look down to see why. Warriors all around fought with savage intensity, their faces contorted in expressions of rage and desperation as they hacked and slashed at their enemies with merciless abandon.

A Scottish warrior came screaming at Einar, slashing with his sword in an attempt to take off his head. Einar ducked just in time. There was a clang and his head rocked as the Scotsman's blade smacked off Einar's helmet. Einar crouched then sprang forward, driving the blade of the mail troll into his opponent's chest. The triangular blade, made for ripping apart iron rings, had no problem separating his enemy's ribcage. The man's scream turned to a gargling as he toppled backwards and Einar stepped over his dying body.

The slaughter continued for some time, both sides taking their toll on the other and the ground became littered with corpses and severed limbs. Despite the summer heat, the earth was mashed into mud from spilled blood and the churning feet of countless men.

Horns began to blow again, just audible over the din of battle. Einar heard them but at first their meaning did not register through the fog of rage that clouded his mind. Then he felt a tug on his shoulder. Looking round he saw Egil, his shield splattered with blood and his face a similar mask of spilled gore.

'Pull back,' Egil shouted. 'They're signalling for a shield wall.'

If they were caught on the wrong side of a shield wall they were as good as dead. Einar, Egil and those around them began stepping backwards, fighting off those who attacked them as they did their best to align with others with shields painted with the white cross.

Horns blew once more and Einar glanced over his shoulder to see that the shield wall was forming several ranks behind them. The warriors making it had left several gaps for men to retreat through and it was now or never if they wanted to get behind it.

He drove the blade of the mail troll into the belly of an enemy before him, then turned and sprinted for the line of shields. He and the others piled through the spaces left for them then the wall closed together in a tremendous clap of wood on wood. Moments later the pursuing enemy smashed into it.

The enemy warriors hit the shield wall in loose array, in ones and twos, making them easy picking for the Saxon warriors behind the shields. In moments they had cut down perhaps a hundred of them, before signal horns began blaring on Olaf's side as well and his warriors began to form their own shield wall.

Egil grabbed Einar's elbow and dragged him back through the ranks of warriors in Aethelstan's army.

'We've done our bit for the time being,' Egil shouted. 'Time to let someone else have a turn.'

A heavy weariness came over Einar and he found himself unable to resist Egil's pull. Olaf's shield wall advanced and Einar heard the mighty crash as the two formations met. The battle then descended into the grinding scrum of men shoving against men as they tried to stab each other over the top or beneath the rims of their locked shields. Einar and Egil had time to catch their breaths, though now and again they had to contribute by throwing their weight into the men in front when it felt as if Aethelstan's shield wall was losing ground.

For a long while the two formations remained locked in a deadly embrace, neither side able to gain so much as a footstep of ground. Spears thrust and swords swung, their deadly arcs halted by the unyielding wall of shields that stood between the warriors.

Slowly, inexorably, Aethelstan's shield wall began to push forward, the sheer weight of their numbers driving Olaf's men back step by agonising step. Then the Dubliners who formed most of Olaf's shield wall let out a fierce battle cry. They rallied and Aethelstan's advance halted again.

Axes swung and swords clashed, the air was thick with the sound of steel on steel as the warriors fought with a savage intensity born of desperation.

The battle raged on, the two shield walls locked in a deadly dance of death. Spears splintered, shields shattered, and blood continued to soak into the earth.

'We may be going nowhere but Thorolf is making headway,' Egil said. Einar could hear the pride in his voice as he spoke about his brother.

Looking to the left, across the battlefield, he could see a similar clash happening between Constantine's Scots and Thorolf's vikings, except they were not bound in the turgid, draining pushing match of shield walls. Men fought freely and the vikings were pushing the Scots back. The raven banner flew high in the air, leading from the front of the men.

'My brother will be with his banner,' Egil said. 'He will be carrying the fight right to the enemy; I wish I was with him now.'

Then, as Einar and Egil watched, they saw the formation of vikings ripple sideways. Something had hit them from the side. Egil took a sharp intake of breath as they caught sight of many warriors pouring from the trees, attacking Thorolf's vikings all along their unprotected flank.

'He's put his faith in the trees protecting him again,' Egil said. 'Olaf must have sent men into them. It's a trap!'

Einar saw the banner of Jarl Ethils carried among the men sweeping from the woods.

'That bastard Ethils still lives!' Egil said.

'It looks like he wants revenge for his brother,' Einar said.

As they watched, like a mighty tree at the edge of a flooding river, they saw the raven banner borne by Thorfinn first tilt, then fall into the flood of warriors beneath it. This was not good. The company supposed to be protecting Aethelstan's flanks had been outflanked themselves.

'I must help my brother,' Egil said. His eyes were intense and glaring amid the bloody mask of his face. 'Gather as many of my men as you can.'

They went along the line, grabbing vikings wherever they came upon them. When they reached the edge of Aethelstan's formation, Egil led them out onto the open heath. Beyond the clashing armies there was an open, empty space that the vikings jogged across, heading forwards and diagonally in the direction of Thorolf's company who had pushed Constantine's back beyond the front ranks of Olaf's.

By the time they reached them, Thorolf's company was falling back. There was no sign of the standard, Thorfinn the Mighty or Thorolf among the retreating vikings. Seeing Egil and his men, however, they stopped.

'Egil,' one of them shouted. 'Thorolf is dead. They were waiting for us in the woods. They took us by surprise.'

Egil drew his sword.

'I swear this blade will not sleep in my hand until it has tasted the blood of Jarl Ethils,' he shouted. 'What are you doing running away? Come with me and we shall take our bloody revenge on those bastards.'

With a primal roar, Egil surged forwards. The others, Einar among them, fell in behind him. They tore back down the slope towards the now combined forces of Ethils and Constantine. Their blades flashed in the sunlight as they hewed through the enemy ranks with merciless efficiency. With Egil in the centre and the others fanning out on either side of him, they began slicing a gory swathe into the enemy. On either side of him, his warriors fought with equal ferocity, their weapons dealing slaughter as they cleaved through their foes.

The fight was fierce and unforgiving. The air was thick with the clang of metal on metal and the anguished cries of the wounded and dying.

Egil, with Einar beside him, pressed on. Egil's gaze was fixed on the banner of Ethils. They fought their way through the crowd then, amid the swirling melee, they found themselves face to face with Jarl Ethils.

Ethils readied his sword and shield to defend himself. Egil just barrelled into him, shield first, knocking him flat on his back.

Without any further hesitation, Egil drove his sword down into Ethils' throat. The jarl opened his mouth to scream but only gushing blood came out. His chest bucked and his legs kicked as Egil worked his sword from side to side. Then his body ceased all movement as his head was severed from it.

Einar swung the mail troll like a club, stoving in the face of the man who bore Ethils' banner. Like Thorolf's before, the tall standard toppled like a felled tree to the earth.

Egil bent over and lifted the now severed head of Ethils. He held it up, blood streaming from the neck, for all to see.

Cries of dismay rose from Ethils' men. Several turned and fled for the trees once more. This was enough to spark panic in the rest and in an instant the trickle of men turned to a full-blown rout. Those within reach of the vikings' blades were cut down without mercy.

Egil hurled the jarl's head into the ranks of the Scots. In fear of a similar onslaught from Egil's vikings to the one that had just devastated Ethils' company, they began to withdraw. It began as an ordered retreat, then several men stumbled and many fell over them. Then panic spread through them like a wild fire through dry grass in summer. In moments Constantine's whole division had dissolved into a chaotic maelstrom of men fleeing for their lives.

'Egil, look where we are!' Einar said, pointing towards the two main companies fighting on the other side of the heath. They had pushed so far forwards they were now past the front line of Olaf's warriors. They were behind Olaf's shield wall.

Egil nodded, a fearsome grin spreading across his blood-soaked face.

Forming up again, the vikings bounded back across the heath, forming a svinfylking as they ran. The formation powered into the unprotected flanks of Olaf's company, dealing death and injury on all sides. The unexpected assault caused havoc among the enemy as men struggling to cope with the Saxons before them now turned to try and meet a new threat to their sides and rear.

Aethelstan's signallers began to blast their horns. The king had seen what was happening and sounded all-out attack. The whole army surged forwards into the weakened shield wall of Olaf, tearing open cracks and smashing holes in it.

Then the whole division came apart like a fox being torn apart by hounds. In the chaos that followed, King Olaf's men began to flee in panic, their terrified cries of defeat mingling with the triumphant shouts of Aethelstan's warriors.

Bloodlust still raging within, Einar, like the others, began to run after the fleeing enemy. Then he felt a hand on his shoulder. Turning he saw Egil standing beside him.

'Let them go,' he said. 'At least let the Saxons pursue them. This battle is over. Aethelstan has won. The Saxons will hound Olaf and Constantine's men down. There will be a great slaughter but what have we to gain from that? Only the possibility of an accidental death or injury when the battle is already over. Come on. It's time to look after ourselves.'

Einar stood for a moment. He was covered in the blood of his enemies. His arms and legs ached from effort. His heart pounded and his breathing was heavy. Taking deep breaths he tried to calm the fires of rage that still blazed within his heart.

Egil was right. He knew it.

And he also knew what he had to do next.

Fifty-One

Einar wandered through the deserted camp. In the distance the sound of the battle still raged on as Aethelstan's victorious warriors chased Olaf and Constantine's shattered army into the river and down the road, murdering countless numbers of them on the way.

There was no one in the camp now. Even the servants and monks left behind had gone out onto the heath to watch the battle. Einar found a horse and led it through the tents until he came to the big one with the dragon of Wessex flying above it and presumably the corpse of the dead bishop still inside. Tying the horse to a post outside, he pushed open the flap of the smaller brown tent beside the big one and went inside.

There he stopped dead. Though the camp had been deserted, the tent was not. He had half expected guards to be left behind to watch over the silver. Had he found them there he would have made some excuse about being there by mistake and left.

The eight people in the tent, however, were not Saxons. As he entered they too turned to look at him and froze also. Einar found himself face to face with the úlfhéðnar.

They were in a semicircle facing the doorway. Ulrich was in the middle with Skar, Starkad and Sigurd to his left and Kari, Surt, Wulfhelm and Affreca on the right. Everyone except Ulrich was lifting a chest of coins each.

'You!' Ulrich said. His hand went straight to the hilt of his seax and he drew it. 'What are you doing here?'

'I would ask you the same question,' Einar said. He left his mail troll slung over his shoulder by its strap. 'But it seems obvious.'

'Kill him,' Ulrich hissed through his teeth.

No one moved.

'Did you not hear me?' Ulrich said.

The others looked at Skar. Einar knew whatever happened next would depend on whatever action the big man chose to take.

'Ulrich, Einar saved your life,' Skar said. 'Saved both of our lives. I think that evens up the score. We can let it go.'

'You might,' Ulrich said. 'But I won't. He betrayed us. He betrayed *me*. He deserves to pay for that. Now do what I tell you.'

Still no one moved.

'You swore an oath to obey me,' Ulrich said. Anger was tightening his throat so the words came out like a growl.

'We also swore an oath to protect each other,' Skar said. 'To fight for each other and revenge our fallen brothers. Einar was part of that oath.'

'He's not one of us anymore,' Ulrich said. 'He lost that right when he chose to take the book back to Aethelstan.'

'We swore those oaths to each other, Ulrich,' Skar said. 'As men.'

He glanced towards Affreca,

'And women,' Skar said. 'They bind us whether we are in a company or not. Einar honoured that oath when he let us escape this camp.'

Einar could see how difficult this was for Skar, a man who for most of his adult life had followed Ulrich without question.

He felt moved and tears began to sting his eyes. He bit his lip to dispel the unwelcome sensation.

'I'll just have to do it myself,' Ulrich said.

He raised the seax and stepped forward. Einar tensed. Skar caught Ulrich's wrist, the one that held the blade.

'If you kill him, Ulrich,' Skar said. 'We must avenge his death. We swore it. If he kills you we will have to kill him for the same reason. Are you really going to put us in that position?'

Ulrich locked eyes with Skar for a long, uncomfortable moment. Then he sighed and rolled his eyes.

'Very well,' Ulrich said. 'But I don't see why the oath you swore to me should be any less important than the one you swore to each other.'

The tension that had filled the air in the tent like an approaching storm dissipated in an instant. Grins broke out all round. Skar let go of Ulrich's wrist.

'You left our company and yet you still have the nerve to wear your wolfskin,' Ulrich said in a surly voice. 'What makes you think you still have the right?'

'I earned it, Ulrich, remember?' Einar said. 'And it's probably the one thing in my life I'm actually proud of. Look: I left the company because I was chasing an ideal. A dream. I still don't know if that ideal is right or wrong but I do know that dreams and ideals are what get men killed. What I've realised is that I'm not the person I *thought* I was, or at least who I wanted to be. But I do know not that I'm still the person I always was: a Norseman and an úlfheðinn. Let me go with you now.'

'Oh no.' Ulrich wagged a finger in Einar's direction. 'Don't now be expecting me to just let you rejoin my crew. That's too much.'

'Oh come on, Ulrich,' Affreca said. 'We need Einar.'

'It's been boring without him singing to us on the voyages and when there is nothing to do,' Sigurd said.

'He's blessed by Odin with the divine rage,' Starkad said. 'I'd rather have someone like that with us than against us.'

'Let the lad back, Ulrich,' Skar said.

Ulrich let out a loud sigh and rolled his eyes again.

'All right,' he said. 'But only as a trial. If he lets me down one more time he's out. This time for ever.'

The others cheered and gathered around Einar, clapping him on the back or hugging him. Skar embraced Ulrich in a great bear hug.

'I hate this,' Ulrich said, his voice muffled in the fur of Skar's wolfskin cloak. 'We're supposed to be vikings, remember? We don't forgive like weak Christians. We're supposed to seek vengeance to the end. Look at us. This is pathetic.'

'So the crew is back together, eh?' Affreca said, grinning. She laid an elbow on Einar's shoulder.

'I'd feel better about that if you hadn't tried to kill me twice,' Einar said. 'I was lucky you missed.'

'In my defence, I was unsure it was you,' Affreca said, making a mock hurt expression. 'If I had been certain, you'd be dead for sure.'

She winked and the others laughed. Einar did not.

'Enough of this nonsense,' Ulrich said. 'The monks and guards won't leave us alone here for ever. Let's get moving. Get those chests filled.'

'So where are we going now anyway?' Einar said. 'After we've taken as much of this silver as we can carry that is.'

'We'll steal horses and head for the coast,' Ulrich said. 'Roan should have our ship waiting there. After that...'

He shrugged.

'Norway is out for us. We fought for Olaf so Hakon won't

welcome us back there,' Ulrich continued. 'Ireland is out for us if Olaf survives and makes it home. Aethelstan will rule all of Britain after this battle today so this country won't welcome us either. Eirik Bloody Axe is in Orkney. Aethelstan's lapdogs rule Francia. We've managed to piss off just about every powerful person in this part of the world now. It doesn't leave many options for us.'

'Personally I am tired of this benighted, barbaric realm of the world,' Surt said. 'The cold is creeping into my bones and I long to see my homelands once more. I ache for some civilised company too. Perhaps we should think of sailing south? The weather would be a lot better for a start.'

Ulrich looked at Skar, who nodded.

'Maybe,' the big man said.

'Right now let's concentrate on getting this silver to the ship,' Ulrich said. 'Then we'll see where the wind takes us.'

Author's Note

THE BATTLE of Brunanburh in 937 CE, the conflict that is at the centre of this novel, has achieved much significance as 'the battle that created England'. Some readers may be surprised by two aspects of my portrayal of the fight: the location, and the presence of Norse mercenaries in the army of Aethelstan.

The current elevated status of Brunanburh is relatively new. Until recently, it was quite obscure. When I first came across the battle, I was in my final year at university. A poem about Brunanburh from the *Anglo-Saxon Chronicle* was one of the pieces we had to criticise in our final exams. It's quite the piece, full of gory battle imagery and triumphant phrasing. It tells the story of Aethelstan's famous victory, the greatest 'slaughter upon this island ever yet'.

Since then, thanks to years of academic and amateur research, as well as the attention of a few historical novelists, Brunanburh has come to be seen as the event that defined the nations Britain and Ireland have been divided into ever since.

The battle no doubt deserves its current reputation; however, for such an important event it appears to have been forgotten about for many years and much of the detail remains unknown. The most glaring example is its exact location. The account in the *Anglo-Saxon Chronicle* neglects the detail of where the battle took place beyond its name. Modern scholarship, as well as some amateur archaeologists, suggests the fight happened at a spot on the Wirral. On the other hand, several medieval accounts point to a location in Northumbria.

One of those medieval accounts, *Egils saga Skalla-Grímssonar*, is an Icelandic saga that dates to around the late twelfth century. Based on that account, Stefán Björnsson and Björn Vernharðsson have put forward a convincing argument that the location of the battle was at Vincaester, or modern-day Hunwick in County Durham. It was for this reason I put Einar and the others there.

Egils saga is also the source of an account of the battle that includes Aethelstan hiring overseas fighters, including Norsemen:

En Aðalsteinn konungr safnaði herliði at sér ok gaf mála þeim mönnum öllum, er þat vildu hafa til féfangs sér, bæði útlenzkum ok innlenzkum.

King Athelstan therefore gathered him an army, and gave pay to all such as wished to enrich themselves, both foreigners and natives.

Egils saga, kalfi 50

And a surprisingly tolerant workaround was found to allow the Christian king to hire heathen foreigners, and those warriors to take the pay without having to actually revoke their own faith. This was called 'prime signing' and involved being marked with a cross in some way.

At þeir skyldi láta prímsignast, því at þat var þá mikill siðr bæði með kaupmönnum ok þeim mönnum, er á mála gengu með kristnum mönnum, því at þeir menn, er prímsignaðir váru, höfðu allt samneyti við kristna menn ok svá heiðna, en höfðu þat at átrúnaði, er þeim var skapfelldast.

For this was then a common custom both with merchants and those who took soldiers' pay in Christian armies, since those who were 'prime-signed' (as 'twas termed) could hold all intercourse with Christians and heathens alike, while retaining the faith which was most to their mind.

Egils saga, kalfi 50

Hopefully this will convince some that I have not strayed too far from medieval sources by including Einar in Aethelstan's ranks at Brunanburh.

Where next for Ulrich's Úlfhéðnar? They have worn out their welcome pretty much everywhere in the North Sea world. We shall just have to see when the next book comes out...

Thanks for reading,
Tim

About the Author

TIM HODKINSON grew up in Northern Ireland where the rugged coast and call of the Atlantic ocean led to a lifelong fascination with Vikings and a degree in Medieval English and Old Norse Literature. Tim's more recent writing heroes include Ben Kane, Giles Kristian, Bernard Cornwell, George R.R. Martin and Lee Child. After several years in the USA, Tim returned to Northern Ireland, where he lives with his wife and children.

Follow Tim on @TimHodkinson
and www.timhodkinson.blogspot.com